The Search

A Novel by Gordon W. Fredrickson

BEAVER'S POND
PRESS

This is a work of fiction. Names, characters, places, and incidents are either the products of the author's imagination or are used in a fictitious manner, and any resemblance to actual persons, living or dead, businesses, events, or locales is purely coincidental.

Edited by Kellie M. Hultgren
Front cover artwork: *Farmhouse*, acrylic on canvas by Judy Malz, 2025

ISBN 13: 978-1-64343-500-8
Library of Congress Catalog Number: 2025916748
Printed in the United States of America
First Printing: 2025 29 28 27 26 25 5 4 3 2 1

Book design and typesetting by Dan Pitts

BEAVER'S POND
PRESS

Beaver's Pond Press
526 Seventh Street West Saint Paul, MN 55102
(952) 829-8818
www.BeaversPondPress.com

Contact Gordon W. Fredrickson at www.gordonfredrickson.com for more information about the author.

Youth: I need to find myself.

Wisdom: Search with an open mind.

Youth: What if I don't like what I find?

Wisdom: Then it's not the real you.

Youth: What should I do?

Wisdom: Search inside yourself.

CONTENTS

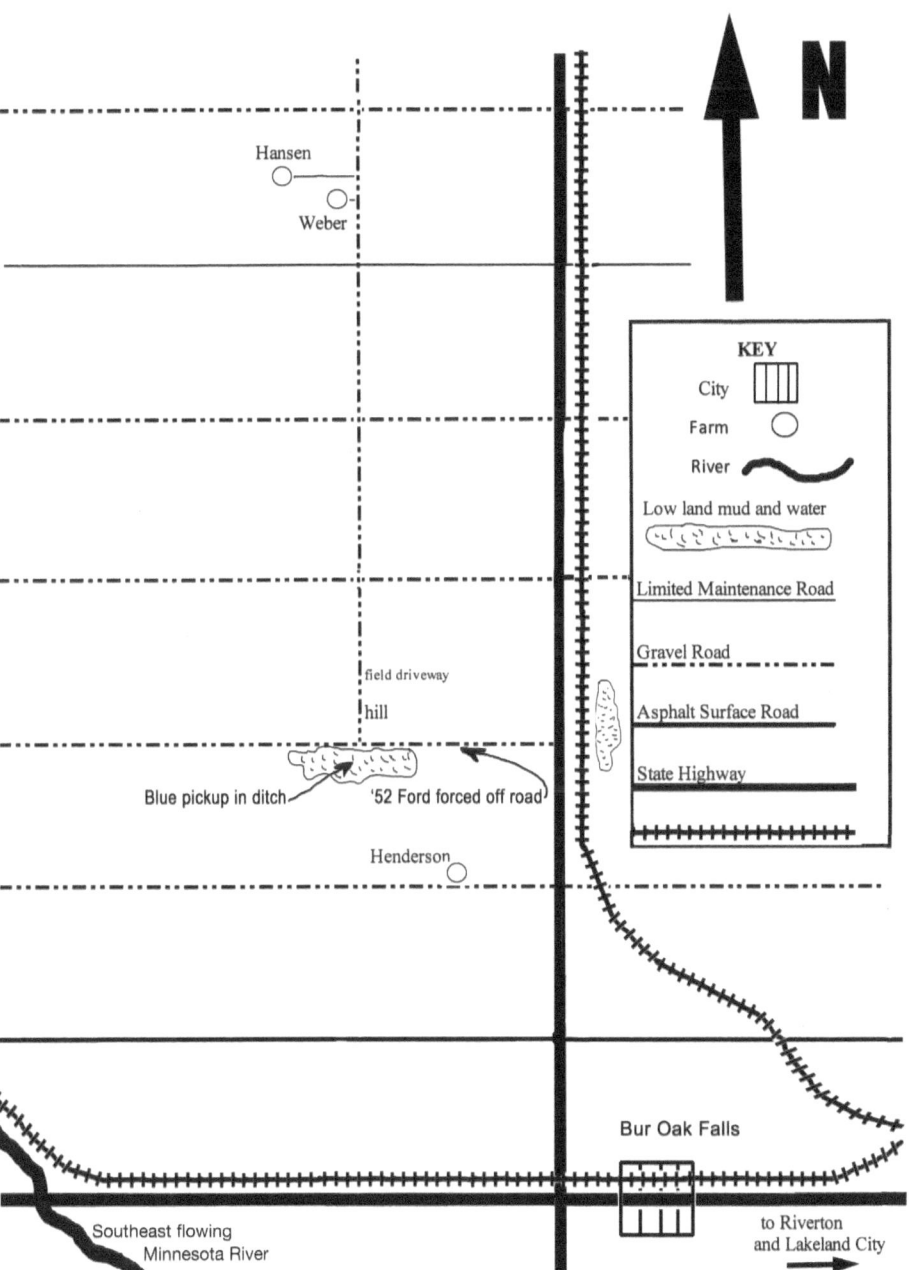

Seating Chart for the Neighborhood Country School, 1955–1956.

To enhance readers' understanding of the familiar relationships among the students from the country school, displayed below is a seating chart for the neighborhood country school for the last years in session, 1955–1956. During a birthday party in *The Dance*, Joey began to organize a ballgame for the country school students. In the third book of the series, *The Search*, the kids play the game during the summer. The next school year would see them bused to town where their farm neighborhood identity would be scattered among the masses of students in a larger school.

KEY

| NAME. |
| GRADE IN 1955–1956 |
| DATE OF BIRTH |
| (AGE during summer 1956) |

LIBRARY

Mrs. Anfin

TEACHER'S DESK

STOVE

Blackboard

TABLE FOR CLASSES

P I A N O

Seating

Katherine O'Keran — Grade 8 — April 27, 1942 (14)
Robert Schoen — Grade 8 — Nov. 14, 1942 (13)
James Schoen — Grade 8 — Sept. 25, 1942 (13)
Margaret Shaurel — Grade 8 — Oct. 5, 1942 (13)

Elizabeth Brummer — Grade 7 — June 28, 1943 (12)
Mary Ryan — Grade 7 — January 28, 1943 (13)
Mary Shaurel — Grade 8 — Oct. 5, 1942 (13)

Joey Carlson — Grade 6 — Dec. 27, 1944 (11)
Caroline Shaurel — Grade 6 — May 30, 1944 (12)
Ronald Schoen — Grade 6 — March 15, 1944 (12)

Patrick Fischer — Grade 3 — Dec. 15, 1947 (8)
Barbara Schoen — Grade 3 — Jan. 25, 1947 (9)
Ed Fischer — Grade 4 — Oct. 3, 1946 (9)
Paul Haber — Grade 5 — May 10, 1945 (11)
Janet Fischer — Grade 5 — March 5, 1945 (11)

John Haber — Grade 1 — Nov. 10, 1949 (6)
Bonnie Schoen — Grade 1 — August 8, 1949 (6)
Ruth Haber — Grade 2 — Sept. 23, 1948 (7)
Betty Schoen — Grade 2 — July 8, 1948 (7)

CHAPTER 1

THE NESTLING

Suppertime, Monday, June 11, 1956

"Aunt Dory, you promised you'd mail the letter today!" Mary exclaimed. "I came down here to get my supper, and the letter is still on the kitchen counter!"

"I changed my mind," Dory said bluntly as she picked up the letter from the countertop. "I'm worried someone might see it."

"You said you'd take it into town today and mail it at the post office instead of putting it in your mailbox. I followed your instructions—I didn't put a return address on it."

"I know, I know, and I read it over before I sealed it so I made sure you left no clues as to where you are. But I thought it over last night. Fact is, I worried all night and didn't get much sleep. I decided it's too soon." As she opened a small drawer in a cabinet, Dory added, "I'll keep it in this drawer for a while yet."

"It's been nearly four months since I ran away and left my friends. I just want to let them know I'm safe."

"The deal is, Mary, we need to *keep* you safe. And to do that, we need to keep the fact that you are staying in my attic a secret. Look, you escaped this Jack Drude fellow once, but you admitted that you were lucky. Well, you may not be so lucky next time. You stole his car, and I'll bet he'd like it back. If the cops found you, they could arrest you for car theft, and maybe me too as an accessory. We could end up in jail. Well, maybe not you, because you're only sixteen, but the fact that you are a minor means you're under the guardianship of your married brothers. And I know you don't want that to happen."

"But you promised!"

"Let the letter sit a month or so."

"But you promised!" Mary whined her repeated plea, hoping to guilt her aunt into action.

"Look, Mary," Dory said, appealing to her with a smooth tone and low volume, "you know I have your welfare at heart. Right? Let's just wait a while yet. Any day they might put up a poster on runaways in the post office, and if your photo is on there, we will need to be extra careful. Let's wait another month before we send the letter."

"Okay, I guess," Mary said.

"For now, get back up to the attic. I'll bring your supper up to you."

"Can't I at least eat down here?"

"No, we can't risk someone coming over and seeing two plates on the table. Remember how Rusty surprised us when she came over? Granted, that turned out okay, and I know we can trust Rusty. At thirteen, she looks up to you. And the fact that the Webers' house is less than a hundred yards away means she can sneak over and visit you and give you some relief from your loneliness. But we can't risk more people finding out you're here. I have to treat you like my little nestling. Although you have your feathers and you can fly, I have to keep you in the nest like a baby bird who cannot yet leave home."

"But I've already left my home and all my friends. I understand I must stay hidden, but I can't bear the thought that they don't know if I'm safe. I want to at least let my friends know I'm safe."

"Give it some more time, child. Let's wait until after the Fourth of July. We need to be sure you're safe. Now, take a glass of milk with you, and I'll bring the rest of your supper up in a few minutes."

After supper, when Dory left the attic bedroom to take the dishes to the kitchen, Mary escaped to her rooftop refuge to watch the June sun linger in the west. Dressed in red pajamas with white stripes, her blond hair hanging loose down to her neck, Mary sat on the south-facing slanted rooftop, west of the dormer window of her attic bedroom, listening to the frantic screeches of baby barn swallows as their mother brought them food. The nest was tucked under the peak of the eaves of the dormer and shaded by rows of evergreen trees that stretched fifty feet into the sky west of the house. *I'm stuck in this attic room all day. I feel as penned up as the nestlings, but I'll bet they'll get a chance to fly before I will. Dory can be so stubborn!*

One mouthful of insects fed to her babies, the momma barn swallow swooped down from the nest and away into the evening sky, searching for more mosquitoes. Mary took advantage of the bird's absence to scoot back into her room. The short return trip was not without risks—her path from window to roof was in plain sight, but during the return trip, Mary had to grab the overhang and blindly feel with her toes to balance briefly on the short piece of slanted roof before stepping through the open window.

Going back is riskier than leaving. Maybe that's true for a runaway like me who misses her home too.

As she crawled into her bed, Mary longed for the comfort of a clear path. She had found some comfort in escaping from her home, where painful paths had been forced upon her since she was a child. But now, miles away from her childhood friends, she had no idea what path lay ahead for her, nor did she know where to search for one, and as she lay in bed, her heart ached with loneliness.

I feel safe with Aunt Dory, but I can't even imagine what will happen to me in the future. And my friends are so far away! Yet, I'm happy that Jack Drude is far away too. His threats are in the past. My brothers and my stepfather are in the past too.

With that thought she closed her eyes, and as she tried to block horrible memories from her thoughts, she hoped the night would be free of the dreams that made her relive past traumas. *I'll think of Maggie and Jimmy. Nice memories. I need to tell them I'm safe. Okay, I won't say a word to Dory about the letter until after the Fourth of July, but on the fifth, Dory will be hearing from me. I'll make sure she sends that letter then.*

CHAPTER 2

THE LETTER

Thursday evening, July 12, 1956

"So, what's so important to talk about?" Jimmy asked Maggie as she hurried into the upstairs bedroom he shared with his younger brother. "You've been antsy to talk about something all afternoon. I'm surprised you waited until everyone was in bed."

Handing him an envelope, Maggie urgently whispered, "Came in the mail today. Guess who it's from."

Without a clue as to what the envelope might contain, Jimmy grabbed it, glanced at the front, and remarked, "No return address. But, wait just a minute—that address looks like Mary's handwriting!"

"Not so loud, dummy!" Maggie shushed her brother. "It may be early, but the folks are in bed."

As Jimmy hurriedly opened the letter, his eleven-year-old brother, Joey, got up from his bed to look over Jimmy's shoulder alongside Maggie while Jimmy read the letter to himself.

Sunday morning, June 10, 1956

Dear Maggie,

I know I said I was not going to write, but I miss you guys so much! I think about you and Jimmy all the time. My aunt is great, but I have to stay hidden so no one sees me. I am a runaway wanted for car theft, so I won't give you my return address. My aunt is so worried about mailing the letter, but she says her friend at the post office will make sure the cancellation ink is smeared and unreadable. The less you know, the better. I don't want you to get into trouble as an accessory to my crimes. My aunt (I'll call her D) thinks the statute of limitations might be three years, but I might stay hidden for five years, until I'm twenty-one. She is so concerned about my safety that she wouldn't let me write to you until now. I want to tell you everything that happened, but I will spare you the worry. So, I won't talk about that anymore. OK?

I am healthy and happy, but lonely. I admit that sometimes I feel like a prisoner locked in a cell, but D is a wonderful person. Sometimes we play euchre late at night. She has a sewing machine in her bedroom that she lets me use. I just started using it a few days ago. I hadn't sewn anything since Mom died over a year ago, and it took me a while to start again. The machine is similar to the treadle sewing machine Mom had at home, but years ago, the salesman who came to D's farm to sell sewing machines mounted an electric motor on her machine! Wow, I love it, and I've made a couple blouses for myself already. There's a good fabric store in town and D says she will buy more fabric, but I can't go with her to help pick it out. D is so good to me, though, and said she has some money saved up and will use it to buy a new sewing machine for me for my birthday in October! There's no store in town that sells them, but she can order it from one of the catalog stores in town. I've been looking through D's Sears and Ward's catalogs ever since. She calls them wish books. If I get a new sewing machine, I will have plenty to keep me busy this winter. D says I need to stay busy and forget about all the people I knew in the past, including my friends. That makes me sad, but she is probably right.

Please say hi to Jimmy and Joey, and I'll leave it up to you how much you want to tell your folks and Rosinceks. I think you should just tell them that I am safe and happy. And I love them. Pass that on to Jimmy, Joey, your folks, and Rosinceks.

I love you all.

Your friend always,

Mary

PS: Do not try to find me.

Jimmy looked up and said, "This was written a month ago. Why did she wait so long to mail it?"

"Maybe her aunt had second thoughts and waited," Maggie offered.

"She said she felt like a prisoner," Jimmy muttered. "That's must be terrible for her."

"Yeah, cooped up in the house. But the house is on a farm. You'd think she could go outside sometimes."

"Sounds like D keeps a pretty short leash on her," Jimmy suggested, trying to distract his mind from other statements in the letter. *She said she thinks of us all the time. I think of her all the time too. I try not to, but I can't shake her out of my head.* "I'll bet D read the letter to make sure nothing was in it to give us a hint as to where the farm is." Then, to mask his thoughts, he turned to his brother and asked, "What do you think, Joey? You've said nothing so far."

Joey crossed his arms at his elbows and rested them on his chest, which gave him a self-important look. "I'd have to read the letter again, but what sticks out is that she said, 'Do not try to find me.' I don't know why. Maybe because she said it last."

"Yeah," Maggie said. "Why would she think we would try to find her?"

"Well," Jimmy said seriously, "she still owes me a date."

"You've got to be kidding," Maggie said pushing his shoulder in jest. "You still want to date her?"

"And why not?" he responded, adding defensively, "She said she'd go to the movies with me. She owes me that."

"Well, I guess she owes me an explanation too," Maggie said.

"She must know that I'd like to see her again," Jimmy admitted as he turned his face away, "for all sorts of reasons." He felt a lump in his throat. *Don't be a wimp, dummy.*

Maggie reached over to touch Jimmy's arm as she said, "I'm sure Mary wants to see you too, Jimmy."

"Do you really think so?" he asked, and without waiting for an answer, he looked up and said, "You know what, Mags? You know what? I'll bet you're right. For all the concern about secrecy, there seemed to be a lot of clues about the town."

"You're right about that," Maggie whispered as she grabbed the letter from her brother. "The town has catalog stores, a fabric store, no sewing machine stores, and a post office. This is a good-sized town, not some rinky-dink wayside store and tavern."

Jimmy asserted, "But we don't know which direction the farm is from here."

"Actually, I do know the direction," Maggie confessed. "You see, when Mary told me her plan to steal Jack's car and drive away in the dark night to her friend's place, I told her I was worried she would get lost."

"But she went anyway," Jimmy said. "She's so stubborn."

"Sure, she is, but she reassured me the place would be easy to find. She said all she had to do was drive west, cross the river, go through one big town, and turn north onto a big highway. She said her aunt had sketched a map from the highway to the farm."

Jimmy thought a moment before he said, "She mentioned crossing the river just once, eh? Well, if she only crossed the Minnesota River once, that means the farm is somewhere north of the sixty-mile piece of highway between river crossings."

"Right," Maggie said. "And there is probably only one big highway going north between the two river crossings."

"But she said she doesn't want you to find her," Joey reminded them.

His statement stifled their momentum for a few moments before Jimmy said, "What if she said that just to fool D? I mean, she probably knew D would read it."

"Possibly," Maggie agreed. "And we know she really wants to see us. She said so. She said she misses all of us."

"I know I miss her," Jimmy confessed. "And if she misses me half as much, I think she would like it if we dropped by for a visit. What do you think, Mags?"

"I don't know." Mags seemed to have second thoughts. "What if we're wrong? Her plea sticks in my head. What if we put her in danger by finding her? I mean, we don't want to risk her safety just so we can see her. Sounds kind of selfish."

"There are so many things I want to say to her. And ask her too. I deserve some answers. Don't I?"

"Now you're sounding selfish, Jimmy. Are you willing to put her life in danger just so you can ask her questions? Too risky."

"She's taken risks before," Jimmy countered. "So have we. I think it's worth the risk, don't you?"

"But she took risks for the safety of us all," Maggie argued. "You can't claim you're taking risks for all our benefits if you go searching for her. You just want to find out stuff for your own personal reasons."

"Maybe so, but you're just as curious as I am."

"Sure, I'm curious," Maggie said thoughtfully. "But I'm afraid too. Afraid for her and for us. I can still see the fear in her face when she talked about Jack Drude."

"I got pretty darn close to sharing that fear with her myself, if you remember what happened the night she ran away. No one got closer to Jack than I did that night."

"I can't deny that," Maggie admitted. She noticed that her younger brother was reading the letter again. "What do you think, Joey?"

He looked up and said, "She says she is lonely and really misses you guys."

"There," Jimmy jumped in. "Even Joey agrees we should go look for her."

"But when? Dad won't let us take the car on our own. You only have a permit."

"You could call Robert tomorrow from Droesers' phone. He might be willing to drive. Or if he isn't willing, I can drive and use him as the licensed driver accompanying me to make it legal."

"Does the licensed person have to be twenty-one?"

"Don't know. And neither does Dad."

Joey spoke up. "You guys are nuts. The trip will take you all day. Dad and Mom will never let you take the car all day long."

"He's right. We shouldn't go." Maggie took the letter from Joey and said, "I'll put this in the box on the bookcase in the hall where any of us can read it again if we want."

"Wait a second, Mags!" Jimmy blurted. Then he whispered, "The folks don't have to know, and this Saturday is the perfect time. The folks are riding with Uncle John to go get Rose. Dad said they'll be gone all day."

"All day?" Mags asked. "Are you sure?"

"Absolutely. Dad cut some second-crop alfalfa on Tuesday because he wanted to be sure we could put it up before Saturday because they're going with Uncle John to go get Rose. He said Uncle John would pick them up at nine in the morning and they would be gone all day and would depend on us to do chores. John will be driving his new Chevy. Dad said that I could use the car. I don't have to tell him how far we're driving."

"What if he checks the mileage?"

"He won't. He trusts me."

"We'll see how long that lasts," Maggie said wryly.

"Come on, Mags. He won't find out."

"I don't know," Maggie said. "Mom and Dad usually find out the truth, right, Joey?"

Joey smiled. "Yeah. By the way, this Saturday is my ball game at the country school. You know, the one I planned with the Schoen boys the day of your birthday party."

"Yeah, we know," Jimmy said. "You've been talking about it for days."

"Well, I'm really looking forward to it! So, if you guys are searching for Mary, you won't have me tagging along. But you didn't want me with anyway."

"Not so, little brother!" Jimmy exclaimed in a whisper. "We always like to have you along. Every teenager likes to have a mascot on a road trip."

"Funny," Joey said without smiling. "Anyway, I'm staying home."

"Right," Jimmy said. "And Dad seemed okay with Joey going on his own."

"Yeah," Maggie said, "but I'm sure they expect us to stay close to home."

"Well, we just won't tell them we're out searching for Mary. Joey will be fine."

"Yeah, I'm not some little kid," Joey said. "I don't need you guys around for protection. I hate it when they treat me like a little kid."

"I know. I know," Jimmy said. "And you'll be with neighbors at the schoolyard. I mean, what could go wrong?"

"I hate to think about it," Maggie said with some doubt.

"It'll be fine," Jimmy reassured her. "As long as we get an early start and get home by six to do chores on time, it'll be fine."

"I need to think this over," Maggie said. "But right now, I'm thinking we shouldn't go."

"Come on," Jimmy pleaded. "Think how great it would be to see Mary."

"I'm thinking of Mary's safety."

"So am I!" Jimmy insisted.

Maggie paused before she sighed and said, "I don't think you are, Jimmy. But I'm too tired to argue about it now. Let's talk about it tomorrow morning. If we decide to go, I can walk over to Droesers' before noon to call Robert to see if he's free on Saturday. But now, I'm going to bed. Goodnight."

"Wait," Jimmy whispered to her before she left. "Think of this—we'll have a whole day to drive around searching for Mary. Just you and me and Robert. What an adventure that will be!"

"But can we make it back on time?"

"I'm sure we can search for Mary and be home by six in plenty time to do chores. Hey, wait until I climb into bed before you pull the chain on the light on your way out, will you, Mags?"

"Sure." And she walked down the hall with the light in her room guiding her path.

Tired, Maggie crawled into her bed quickly, but her mind filled with thoughts of Mary—the fear in her face when Jack Drude had trapped them in Schroedlers' house and the terror she and Mary both felt as they scrambled out of the cellar and ran out the kitchen door. And she thought of Mary's courage when she had planned her escape in February.

How can I be part of a plan to find her when I know it can put her in danger? I don't think Jimmy is thinking straight. He seems so set on finding her. Why? Does he want to be some kind of hero to her? Would he go if I refused to go with? One thing's for sure, he's made up his mind to go, and if he goes searching, I'd better go with him to be sure Mary stays safe. I'd better call Robert tomorrow.

And with those thoughts, she fell asleep.

CHAPTER 3

DEPARTURES

Early Saturday morning, July 14, 1956

"If you and Robert use the car," Dad instructed as he and Jimmy finished prebreakfast chores, "don't use all the gas and then park it. Fill it up before you come home, okay?"

Jimmy nodded, and his dad continued, "But before you go anywhere, clean off the concrete slab in front of the barn."

"Jeez, Dad. The reason I stacked the bales in the barn after milking last night was so I would be done with work when Robert got here this morning. Cleaning the slab will take me over an hour."

"It's going to rain later today," Dad said. "The muck is deep but fairly dry now. A heavy rain will turn the dry muck into wet muck and make it heavier. You know I'm right, Jimmy."

"Okay, okay, but tell Mom I won't be in for breakfast, because I don't want to clean up for breakfast and then get all stinky again cleaning the slab."

"That's why we cleaned the barn before breakfast," Dad explained. "Mom and Maggie are washing the milking utensils and Joey is doing the chicken chores. Mom had figured we'd all have a late breakfast together before John picks up your mother and me at nine to get Rose. We won't be back until after milking this evening, and we're depending on you kids to handle the chores. We figured you could have the whole rest of the day off, but then I thought of cleaning the slab. Sorry, Jimmy, but it needs to be done."

As soon his dad left for breakfast, Jimmy grabbed a scoop shovel, set it in the wheelbarrow, and wheeled the rig into the far corner of the concrete slab bordering the south entries of the barn. Before he began pitching, Jimmy surveyed the job ahead of him. He and Maggie had dubbed the forty-by-thirty-foot patch of concrete "the cow porch" because it served the same purpose for cows as a porch did for humans. Of course, they had never intended to train the cows to wipe their feet before they entered the barn, but as the cows walked on thirty feet of clean concrete before going through the barn door, a lot of the mud and dirt fell off their hooves, keeping the aisles inside the barn a bit cleaner.

As a measure of his determination, Jimmy inhaled and exhaled deeply before he began rapidly scooping the mixture of wet and dry cow dung and dirt off the concrete and piling it into the wheelbarrow. When the muck was heaped high above the wheelbarrow's sides, he grabbed the handles, lifted, and pushed hard, trying to gain speed and momentum to go up the steep twelve-foot-long incline of a ten-inch-wide plank hooked temporarily to the top of one side of the manure spreader. At the top, he stopped abruptly and, using the forward momentum to help lift, tipped the wheelbarrow forward, letting gravity empty the contents into the spreader while he held back with all his strength to avoid falling into the bed of the manure spreader along with the muck. Once he'd successfully dumped the first of many loads, he tipped the wheelbarrow to a horizontal position, rotated himself around to face the other way, and pulled the wheelbarrow behind him to set up for another load.

Proud of his skill with this task, he mused about when he was younger and the many times the momentum had taken him over the edge, landing him knee-deep in the muck. Dad would just laugh and say, "Put a brick in your back pocket to give yourself some weight until you get bigger." Once in a while Dad had helped him get the wheelbarrow out of the spreader, but usually he'd say, "You gotta get yourself out of your own messes."

After dumping many loads of muck, his sister's voice interrupted his thoughts.

"Hey, Jimmy," she yelled from the other side of the cow-yard fence, "it's nine o'clock! I'm cleaned up and ready to go, and I've packed some sandwiches."

"Good. I'll need the kitchen to myself so I can clean up in a hurry. Have the folks gone yet?"

"They just drove out of the driveway."

"Good, I'm glad they left before Robert got here. I'm nearly done. Then I just have to take the load out to the field. I should get to the house in less than half an hour."

At half past nine, Jimmy hurried from the barn and met Maggie, Robert, and Joey on the concrete steps that led to the enclosed porch of the house. Wearing a white T-shirt tucked into his jeans, which hung low on his hips, and his long hair combed back into a ducktail, Robert sat on the edge of the landing, dangling his feet over the side, his pointy black dress shoes and white socks reflecting the bright sunlight. Dressed in a green blouse and jeans, Maggie sat on the top step with her feet on the step below it. Joey, wearing jeans, a short-sleeved shirt, and his everyday work shoes, stood nearby.

"Glad you're early, Robert," Jimmy greeted his friend with enthusiasm.

"I'd have been here earlier, but Mom made me straighten and clean the garage before she'd let me use the car!" As Jimmy approached, Robert gave an exaggerated whiff and exclaimed, "You've got some cleaning up to do, Bandit!"

"Won't take me long, but I'll need a good scrubbing," Jimmy said before he teased, "I hope you don't mind spending time with my little sister while I'm gone, Planet?"

Robert grinned. "You ain't left yet?"

"Joey, keep an eye on them," Jimmy said as he hurried into the house.

"Oh, shut up, Jimmy," Maggie said.

"Take your time, Bandit," Robert yelled after him. "I'm sitting in the morning sunshine with a beautiful girl."

Maggie suddenly felt a little self-conscious as Robert grinned at her. *I need to say something. I just can't sit here and blush.* "Here's something I've been wondering about," she said in earnest. "I know you call Jimmy Bandit because he ties his red handkerchief over his nose and mouth in the winter when he runs home after detention, but why does he call you Planet?"

"I thought I told you this once, but I love telling the story. I'll bet Joey will like hearing it too. Here goes. My folks had just moved to Rock City. I was new in school when I started the ninth grade."

"The ninth grade was Jimmy's first year being bused to the high school too," Maggie interrupted, "but he knew a few kids from the country school."

"Anyway," Robert continued, "Mrs. Simm assigned our seats next to each other in ninth-grade general science. She was a kind teacher, young, and kind of good-looking too. One day she was explaining that planets were surrounded by gases, creating their own particular atmosphere. I faked holding back a snicker to get attention from everyone. When the teacher and everyone in the class turned to look at me, I said, 'Yeah, that's like my uncle Albert, who's always surrounded by his own gas.'"

"Wow!" Joey exclaimed. "You said that in class?"

"Yeah! Jimmy was sitting across the aisle from me, and he stifled a laugh and made this bark-snort noise, which made me break out laughing. We couldn't stop, and everyone but Mrs. Simm started laughing. She didn't know what to do, so she gave each of us an hour's detention. But by that time, we were laughing so hard that tears were streaming down our cheeks. Mrs. Simm's complexion turned from white to rosy red, and her voice squeaked higher and higher when she yelled, 'Stop laughing! Stop laughing!' Then she sent us to the office.

"At the office we sat on a bench giggling until Mrs. Leon, the principal, came and grabbed each of us by the back of our shirt collars before demanding to know why Mrs. Simm had sent us to the office. That was the first time either of us had met Mrs. Leon, or Mrs. L., as most students called her. She was a big woman. About five feet, ten inches tall, and she had wide shoulders that matched the breadth of her backside. And her sturdy arms and legs gave her credibility. She could've slapped up two ninth graders like nothing. Ironically, she had a kind heart and actually loved kids, plus, unlike most faculty members, she enjoyed finding the humor in everything. When Mrs. L released her hold on us, I sensed my chance to explain.

"I said we were sorry, and I apologized and threw in special words of praise for Mrs. Simm. I explained that none of it was her fault and that I liked her as a teacher and that I was learning a lot about science. Jimmy agreed and promised that this was not our usual behavior. Then Mrs. L said,

'I checked your grades as you came in.' And reading from a piece of paper, she continued, 'Let's see, Robert Joseph Plathe, you have an A in the class so far, and, Martin James Carlson, aka Jimmy, you have a B+, so I know you both do well in the class.' After a short pause, she added, 'I should probably call your parents.' Then Jimmy blurted out, 'Oh, you can't do that, Mrs. L.' And she looked kind of upset and said, 'And why not, young man?' I thought we were in more trouble for a moment until Jimmy said in a fake innocent voice, 'We don't have a phone,' and he quickly added in his best hick dialect, 'But you kin send a note home with me, Mrs. L, cuz both Ma n Pa kin read.'"

"Sounds like something Jimmy would say," Maggie said as she laughed.

"Then Mrs. L snorted as she stifled a laugh, and I jumped in and said, 'I couldn't help but make the comment about Uncle Albert, because we were talking about planets and Uncle Albert's last name is Pluto!'

"Mrs. Leon snorted another laugh, and that set off me and Jimmy to giggling again. Finally, she said, 'I don't want to hear any more, boys, and when you serve your detention, I suggest you don't sit anywhere near each other. Also, tomorrow, I expect Mrs. Simm to tell me how you politely apologized to her. Now, sit here until the bell rings and stop the giggling.'

"From then on, Jimmy often called me Planet. And we've been friends ever since."

Joey laughed at the story before he said with a grin, "But Jimmy says the real reason you want to be his friend is because you like Maggie."

Robert repeated a line he used often: "What other reason could there be?"

Although the attention made Maggie more uncomfortable, she just grinned. *Robert is so fun. I like how he's so good with Joey. I kind of wish Joey were coming along today.*

"So, Joey, you're sure you don't want to come with us?" she asked.

"What's this? Joey's not coming?" Robert asked.

"He's planned a ball game at the country school," Maggie explained.

"You guys don't really want me tagging along anyway."

Maggie assured him, "You may be our little brother, but you know we *really do* want you to come with us."

"I know you don't want me around. I can tell it's a teenager thing. I'm not one for another year and a half."

"Look, Joey, I see that fake pout," Maggie kidded him, "and I know you're just having fun playing the neglected little brother. You can't fool me. But tell me, who's all coming to the ball game today?"

"Last year's eighth graders and below."

"Who did you talk to?"

"Liz Brummer first. Then she told the Shaurel kids, so Caroline, Mary, and Margaret will be there. Not the older ones, like Jane or Jo Anne, or Ann. Well, Ann might come. All the younger Schoen and O'Keran and Ryan kids should make it, and the Fischers and Habers too. Some said they'd bring cookies and Kool-Aid. Liz lives close, so she said she'd bring lots of water from the well."

"You're quite the organizer!" Robert said as he tapped Joey on the arm. "I'll miss you. I like all the weird things you come up with."

The three shared a laugh before Robert asked Maggie, "By the way, where are we going exactly? You were pretty vague on the phone."

"I had to be. It's a party line, and I called from Droesers' phone, so Frank always hears some of it and gives me crap."

"About what?"

"About her boyfriend," Joey joyfully explained.

"Gotta like this Frank guy," Robert said. "But where are we going?"

Maggie took a letter out of her small purse. "We got a letter from Mary Schroedler, and she accidentally or intentionally put in some clues to where she's living. Jimmy decided to search for her. And I decided to come along to make sure he didn't do anything stupid. Here, read the letter yourself."

Joey and Maggie stayed silent as Robert read the letter. When finished, he exclaimed, "Wow! She actually wrote to you. I remember you told me she had said she wouldn't. She sounds lonesome."

"That's why Jimmy wants to search for her," Maggie said.

"But she told you not to," Robert emphasized.

"Jimmy has this strange idea that he needs to save her or something. He wants to be her hero. I think she really would like to see us, but I also think she doesn't want us to search for her. She wants to stay hidden."

"Right!" Robert exclaimed. "The PS says 'Do not try to find me'!"

"Well," Jimmy asserted as he returned, "I decided to look for her anyway." Dressed much like Robert, with a white T-shirt tucked into low-hanging jeans, he continued to comb his ducktail hairstyle as he declared, "Mags may not be too keen on the idea, but Joey kind of agrees with me."

"Oh, well, if Joey agreed, it must be the right thing to do," Robert said with some sarcasm.

"I have my doubts," Maggie said. "but Jimmy is set on going, and I'm not going to let him go alone."

As he shoved his comb in his back pocket, Jimmy admitted, "It's not like I don't have some doubts too. Maybe the trip is more for me than for Mary, but Mags and I agree that she wants to see us. Look, I understand if you don't want to go, Robert."

"Hold on, Bandit," Robert said. "I've never been one to avoid adventure just because it was stupid."

"That's what I thought, Planet," Jimmy said.

"Count me in!" Robert exclaimed.

"Great!" Jimmy exclaimed. "The search for Mary is on! Now let's get started."

"Wait a minute," Robert said. He looked at his friends and confessed sadly, "I've got bad news. Mom told me not to drive all over the country-side with the car today. Dad wrote down the odometer mileage and warned, 'There'd better not be more than twenty miles added to that when you get back here. And be home by six!'"

"Jeez," Jimmy said. "What happened? They're usually so willing to have you drive the car all over."

"I have my hunches about what has made them grumpy, but I'll tell you later. No use ruining the day with my problems. Right now, though, we stay here unless you can drive."

"Not a big deal. Dad told me this morning I can use the car all day as long as a licensed driver is with me. That's you, although I'm not sure if the licensed driver needs to be over eighteen or even over twenty-one. But I wasn't going to tell him that. Anyway, one good thing is I doubt he knows the odometer reading. Dad keeps the keys in the car. Let's get going!"

But before either boy stepped toward the car, each took a moment to retrieve a comb from his back pocket and comb his hair with his right hand as he used his left hand to ensure the strands of hair fell into place. Although their hairstyles and costumes were similar, the contrast in the two boys' appearance was stark: Robert's big mop of hair balanced atop his thin body made him look top-heavy, while Jimmy's powerful build easily managed to make his hairstyle a good fit for his torso.

Turning to Joey, Jimmy instructed, "Be careful, but have fun, Joey." And the three teens eagerly piled into the front seat of the blue Ford and drove down the driveway. After Jimmy turned the car west onto the road, he cranked down the window and waved to Joey, who stood by the front steps waving at them.

Sitting in the front seat between the two boys, Maggie reached over and squeezed Robert's hand. "Thanks for coming along."

"Glad to be with!" Robert exclaimed. "And today, the special benefit is I get to sit close to you for the whole trip. Maybe later we can sit in the back seat together."

"In your dreams," Maggie said as she slugged him gently in the arm. The three teens laughed.

Robert looked up as if to picture the moment. "But a guy has to dream." He paused a little before he added, "I'm a lucky guy—out here on an adventure with two of my best friends. One is a pretty girl and the other is a nice guy but a danger to all mankind. Should be great fun. What could possibly go wrong?"

As Jimmy concentrated on the road, Maggie cranked the dial on the radio to find songs she liked.

"I get mostly static," Maggie complained. "The clear stations aren't the ones I want to listen to."

"Dad never uses it," Jimmy said. "He says it distracts from his driving. I kind of agree, but I wouldn't mind if we got some good tunes on it with no static."

"This isn't bad," Maggie said as she turned up the volume. "It's called 'See You Later, Alligator.' I think it's by Bill Haley. He sings 'Rock Around the Clock' too."

With the radio blaring, Jimmy's mind turned to imagining what he would do when he met Mary again. For months he had longed to see her and to feel her touch. Her kiss had lingered on his mind and even controlled his thoughts sometimes. Of course, he kept these thoughts to himself, but as he piloted the car toward a possible rendezvous with her, he needed a plan.

I'll slowly take her hand. I won't expect a kiss or even a hug. Holding her hand and seeing her smile at me like she used to—that's all I need at first.

These thoughts filled his mind until after he passed through the town of Lakeland City.

Jimmy glanced briefly over at Robert, who was in a world of his own with his hand stuck far out of the window, playing with the wind, changing the slant of his hands to let the wind force his arm up and down. As Jimmy turned his eyes back to the road, he smiled at his friend's antics. *Good old Robert. Glad he came along—*

His thoughts were interrupted by his friend's frantic cry.

"Pull over, Jimmy!"

Without hesitation, Jimmy braked and steered the car onto the gravel shoulder. "Jeez, we've been on the road about an hour. Got to pee already?"

Robert jumped out of the car and pointed back down the road behind them. "The tree in the pasture has a kid in it! And it looks like a big cow is not letting him down. The animal is huge! Is that a bull?"

Maggie and Jimmy climbed out of the car and hurried around to see what Robert was pointing at.

"Hell, yes, it's a bull," Jimmy said in awe. "He's mad, too. See him butting his head against the tree? That tree isn't very big. We've got to save that kid, and we need to hurry!"

"There you go again," Maggie whined. "Trying to be the hero."

Astonished at her response, Jimmy asked, "You think we should just leave?"

"Of course not," Maggie replied. "But don't do anything stupid."

Jimmy took a moment to turn toward Mags and grin wide before he said, "Now, why would you think I'd ever do something stupid?"

"Been known to happen, Bandit," Robert said as he grinned at his friends.

CHAPTER 4

ROAD TO ROSE

10:45 a.m., Saturday, July 14, 1956

Even after nearly two hours of riding alone in the back seat of her brother-in-law's new 1956 Chevrolet Bel Air, Mary Carlson was not bored. Never having traveled more than seventy-five miles from where she grew up in her thirty-odd years, she enjoyed watching the scenery pass by, and she looked forward to seeing what the countryside was like as they got further north. Although John had insisted there was plenty room for all three of them to sit in the front seat, she had replied, "No, if I sit in the back, you two won't have to talk around me like you would if I was sitting between you." Secretly, though, she preferred to be alone in the back with her own thoughts. Let John and her husband talk their farm talk—cutting hay and baling hay, the yield per acre, how second crop was coming along nicely already because of the moisture from the rains before they'd cut first crop. *Important stuff! But jeez! Just a month ago, tension between Rose and her son was so high that Billy was ready to leave home, and then Rose left instead.*

A woman of average height, she had plenty of foot room in the back, but she was glad she'd remembered to wear the dark-blue sweater that buttoned in the front over her blue sleeveless summer dress. John had warned her the air-conditioning in the new car would feel cold, even as both men removed their suit coats before they got in the car. Martin, a strong, broad man who was a bit above medium height, had commented, "The suitcoat always binds me when I sit in a car."

Although the car offered plenty of headroom, John had removed his fedora and placed it on the seat next to him. Ten years older than Martin, John usually wore a hat, but headgear had disappeared from men's formal wardrobe during Martin's generation. Mary mused, *Farm men have no casual apparel. They either wear a faded bib overall for work, a new-looking bib overall for town, or their church clothes—a matching pair of pants and jacket, a white shirt, and a choice of two or three ties.* Due to Mary's strong preference for blue, all of Martin's ties were predominantly blue. Today he wore the blue tie with dark gold squares, one of her favorites. John wore a light-gray suit, a white shirt, and a red tie with dark-blue designs on it. Red was Rose's favorite color.

Neither Martin nor John was especially talkative, so Mary was not surprised by the lack of chatter after they had covered their standard farm talk about the weather and crops. There was one question she was eager to ask John.

"How are you getting along with my brother Roman?" she asked, fearing the answer.

"Great! He moved in with his button accordion, his fiddle, and his harmonica. He didn't have many clothes, so he didn't change them often, which would have been a problem for Rose if she'd have been home long. When Roman first came to our place, he insisted on sleeping in the barn, but after Rose left home, I told him to move into an upstairs bedroom. Then, I took him to town and bought him a couple new overalls and shirts and lots of underwear. Billy and I liked how he played his button box in the evenings before he went upstairs to bed. I'm really glad he was with us the last few weeks. We needed his help haying and doing chores, and he's a better cook than Billy and I are."

"I was afraid you might get tired of him. He can be pretty annoying."

"Not at all. He sings Czech songs during milking. Billy and I enjoy his music. He started doing our laundry regularly too. He's quite the handyman."

Relieved, Mary sat back to enjoy the ride in silence, but she was surprised when John continued to speak.

"Rose insisted on getting air-conditioning when we ordered the new car. I didn't want it, but you know how convincing your sister can be, Martin." He looked at Martin until he nodded in agreement.

"You're right," Martin said, "but you've been married to her longer than we lived with our folks. You know her better than I do."

"And Monday is our twenty-fourth wedding anniversary," John said. "And I'm pretty excited to be getting Rose back today so we can plan how to celebrate. I called her yesterday to confirm they were expecting us, and she seems to be doing better."

"That's good to hear," Mary said. "I was going to write to her, but I thought I'd wait until I heard from you. Then when you told us about today's trip, I thought maybe I'd just wait."

"Right," John said. "I brought the letter from her I told you about. Got it a week ago. I want you to read it because I think it shows how much she's improved. She kind of explained things and lifted my spirits." He moved his right hand from the wheel and fished into his shirt pocket to pull out an envelope. "Here," he said, handing it to Martin. "Read it. Tell me what you think."

Martin handed the envelope off to Mary. "You read it to us aloud. Is that okay with you, John?"

After John nodded, Mary reluctantly reached for the letter, opened the envelope, and prepared to read.

"Thursday, July 5, 1956

"Dear John, I am enjoying my stay with Betty and her husband. Pastor Terquist is such a decent man and a really effective pastor. More like him would surely result in fewer leaving the flock. And Betty's friendship is exactly what I needed to help me through my pain. Not that the pain will ever totally go away, but the two of them have allowed me to immerse myself in helping others, as they both do routinely.

"Even though Billy is still living on God's earth. I feel like I have lost him just as decisively as I lost John Jr. when he was killed in Korea. As you witnessed, I've been unable to deal with things at home, and after we had that last argument, I knew it was best for all of us if I left. I had devoted myself to our family, but maybe in a more selfish way than I care to admit. Pastor Terquist and Betty helped me see that I pulled my boys toward me without regard for you. Because I made my life only about them and not you and the farm, the place seems less like home than it used to.

"Betty and Pastor Mark, as many call him, have included me in their work. In the short time I've been here, I've worked on music programs for services and have been embraced by the Luther League group as someone they can lean on. I've been practicing my piano skills to help rehearse a group of youth singers. I know you and I have had good friends at home, Mary and Martin especially, but I've always felt like I couldn't quite be myself without being a pain in the neck to everyone else.

"I look forward to seeing you on Saturday. Pastor Mark and Betty expect you in the early afternoon to eat with us, and we should all have a nice, long visit. A youth group meets at five thirty, but you will be leaving before that time anyway.

"Until then, goodbye. Love, Rose."

Mary looked up but said nothing, reluctant to express her reaction to what she had read—*Rose said 'you will be leaving,' not 'we will be leaving.'*

"I'm glad she wrote to you," Mary managed to say, hoping to steer the conversation in a positive direction. "She seemed to be wanting to put things right."

She handed the letter up to Martin, who handed the letter to John and said, "She indicated we will have time for a long visit."

Mary held her tongue. *If she were riding back with us, we could visit in the car.*

"I've heard a lot about Pastor Terquist," Martin said. "I'm looking forward to seeing him again. Been a long time."

"Oh, you won't be disappointed," John said enthusiastically as he stuffed the letter into his shirt pocket. "He's a good guy and has a wide variety of interests. He's pretty entertaining. I'll be happy to see him and Betty again, but I'll be mostly happy when I bring my Rose home to me. I think the letter shows she wants us to do better together."

"We're happy for you!" Mary said trying to match his mood. *I've never seen him this cheerful! And he looks unusually dapper today. He's made an effort to look good for Rose.* Sensing that John wanted to talk, Mary stayed silent, and in a moment he spoke again.

"After John Jr. died in Korea, Rose still had Billy. But even after she succeeded in preventing Billy from marrying Anna, she became more and more hysterical each time she tried and failed at running his life. No one could settle her down until I called my sister. After Betty's letters and phone calls, she seemed better, but when Billy told her he was leaving, she broke down and there was nothing I could do. She decided to visit Betty for a couple of weeks. I think that she made the right decision. Like I said, she sure sounded good on the phone yesterday.

"My sister and Rose were close friends for years in school. They shared interests in subjects and were both true followers in their Lutheran religion. Our parents brought up Betty and me with strict Lutheran teachings, which steered Betty's social life toward church activities and school activities. But me, well, I had almost no social life, which was fine with me at the time. When my father became ill, survival of the family and the farm rested in my hands, so I quit school to take care of the farm and Mom while Betty helped out in the house. I didn't mind quitting school—in those days half the farm kids wanted to quit, and I loved to farm. Quitting school to farm was my dream. Mom died before Betty graduated, but I insisted she finish high school. Because I was farming, they didn't draft me for World War II, and I could dedicate my life to farming the land and improving my herd of dairy cattle. But you guys probably know most of this already."

"Not really," Mary said. "Rose has told us some about after you two met. How you two hit it off as soon as Betty introduced you to Rose."

"I remember that too," Martin said. "I was just a teenager then, but I remember Rose had been disappointed with the men she dated until you came along. I didn't really understand her. We were sister and brother, but Rose and I were really different from each other."

"And," John added, "I think Rose expected me to be more like my sister, but Betty and I were about as different from each other as a sister and brother can be. I was quiet, and although I didn't hate people or anything, I was uncomfortable around them. Betty always liked to be around people. Pastor Terquist was a perfect match for her. Now he leads a congregation where he does youth outreach and works with residents in homes for the elderly. He's constantly helping others. I think Rose thought I would be more of a people person like him when she married me."

"I don't know where she would've got that idea," Martin said. "You never pretended to be anything other than a farmer. And you're one of the best."

"After we married," John continued, "I started to enjoy being with people more. Rose opened me up some. Then later, when you guys married and we started to hang around with you two, our social life stretched quite a bit despite the fact that Rose and Emma had the big religion rift. Then, because Mary and Emma were sisters, Rose seemed to carry a grudge against you,

Mary, but I've got to hand it to you because you didn't let that last. In 1950 you invited Emma and Joe and their five girls over for Thanksgiving dinner along with Rose and me and Billy, and we all had a good visit. I really enjoyed visiting with Emma and her husband, especially when he played old-time music and sang in Czech. Martin, remember how we tried to sing along with Joe and Emma and Mary? So much fun. You and I, Martin, were raised by Lutheran parents, but it seems our sisters hung on to the teachings more than we did."

"True, but we all seemed to get along," Martin said. "Until the last six months Billy and Anna were going out."

"Yeah, Rose was convinced Emma's daughter was stealing our Billy away from the faith."

Mary commented, "But I really don't think she expected you to be more like Pastor Terquist, John, any more than Betty expects Pastor Terquist to be more like you."

"Not at first, no, but I think Rose's disappointment in me grew as the boys got older."

Mary wanted to say more, but she held her tongue. *He loves Rose so. But he needs support too. Being alone was not good for him. I hope the time Rose spent with Pastor Terquist and Betty helped, and I hope Rose is ready to come home. John needs her.*

John's calm voice interrupted Mary's thoughts. "Mary, do you have the road map unfolded on the back seat?"

"Sure do."

Looking at his wristwatch, John said, "It's eleven o'clock. We should be getting close to the turn where the highway goes either north or east. I don't want to end up in Wisconsin." He laughed lightly at the prospect.

"About a couple of miles," Mary said. "Then, according to what I can tell from the map, you cross the bridge and go straight. Wisconsin is a right turn."

Martin asked, "Was this the route you took to your brother's farm?"

"No, that was easier to get to. We didn't have to cross the Mississippi River on a busy narrow bridge like we do today. In fact, we never had to cross it at all. We drove west, not east, and then crossed the Minnesota River and then drove north. Traffic was slim, and it was a nice drive through the countryside. We didn't go there often, though. Hardly at all."

Mary was glad that Martin stayed silent. Maybe he sensed it too—that John was ready to talk about his family, a topic he seldom mentioned. *I need to give Martin more credit for being sensitive.*

Sure enough, John started again, but slowly. "My brother is a sad story. He got married too young. I think he was eighteen. I was ten at the time, and Betty was only six or so. When I look back at it now, my parents were so different for each of us. Not that they meant to be. I mean, they didn't favor some of us over the others. Well, maybe a little. Betty always got what she wanted.

"When he was young, Dad was pretty strict, especially with Fred. I saw him use a switch on him more than once. He never did on me or Betty. He wasn't as religious as Mom was. Mom prayed a lot. We'd see her praying in the dark living room sometimes when we came up from chores. Dad mellowed on his strictness, but Mom increased her praying, especially when Fred was having problems."

John refocused on his driving and said nothing for a while. Deciding to encourage his purge, Mary asked, "Fred was quite a bit older than you. Did you know him well?"

"Not really. No one did. He kept to himself. I don't think he was close to anyone, and the distance between him and our parents grew daily. Fred never seemed to get along with our folks like Betty and I did. He rejected the strict Lutheran line. I went along with it, but Betty absorbed it all. I think that's why Fred got married so young. He and Ida were seventeen when they met, and they clung to each other because they both seemed like outsiders to the world. I remember it so well because Dad set him up with a farm after he got married, and he really didn't want much to do with our parents after that. Dad reached out to him, and Mom prayed for him all the time.

"Fred was never quite good enough for the family, according to our folks. He tried and failed at so many things—he lost money on hogs, brucellosis wiped out his herd of Holsteins in the early fifties. I don't know when he started drinking or even if he always drank, but alcohol and bad decisions ruined him. His wife stuck with him as best as she could. Neither of them deserved such bad luck, and of course, alcohol can ruin anyone if they can't control it. Last I saw them was on New Year's Day when they had Rose and me and Betty and her husband over to visit. They'd been able to patch their lives together and rebuild a small but successful herd of dairy cows. They seemed happier than I'd ever seen them. Betty told Rose and me later that she was so happy Fred had found God again. In January, the two of them were coming back from grocery shopping in the middle of the day and a truck went through a stop sign, hitting them on the driver's side of the car and killing them both. They had no kids and not many friends, so the funeral was small. Betty explained that God took them at a good time because it seemed they had come back into the fold. Kind of a harsh thing to say, I thought, but we agreed that it was too bad our folks had never seen them that happy or successful."

Silence followed as they approached the bridge, leaving Mary wondering why John had told them the details about his brother. Burning to ask a follow-up question, she decided to take her cue from Martin, who seemed to have patience to let his fellow farmer say as much or as little as he wanted. Martin seemed to know John in a deeper way than she did, and in that moment, Mary was proud of her husband's understanding of people. *He pretends he is so dense, but he senses that John wants to talk. He's never talked like this before. Maybe the driving gives him freedom. He can talk about personal things without making eye contact with anyone. He can keep his eyes on the road. Martin often talks a lot when he's driving too. Sometimes he talks about things he wouldn't mention otherwise. Maybe it's like confessing when no one can hear, even though they know someone's listening.*

After they crossed the Mississippi River, the road turned north and John began again. "Anyway, what I was getting at is that after John Jr. was killed, Rose used that same explanation to comfort herself. She'd said that his last letters indicated that he was growing closer to God, so it was a good time for God to take him into His arms, or something like that. It didn't work for me, but then death is something I never question. I never try to assign a reason for it. Rose seems to need to."

"I noticed that when we were kids," Martin inserted. "Rose surpassed everyone in the family with her devotion. I always figured it had something to do with her hanging around your sister for all those years. They went to catechism and got confirmed together. And Rose and Betty went to a lot of youth groups too."

"That's how Betty met Pastor Terquist, although he hadn't been ordained yet. He was five years older than Betty. I met Rose shortly after that, but we got married before they did. When I think about it now, it's kind of funny that Rose and I hit it off. She's so much more devout than I am. I often wonder if I haven't spent a lifetime disappointing her."

Mary felt the need to console him. *This is the second time he's brought that up. Must be bugging him.* "Come on, John. You've had a good life together. Raised two wonderful boys. And Martin and I have always enjoyed your visits. You had a happy family."

"Yeah, but with Rose and me, it was always about the boys. I was kind of just *there*. You know, she never seemed part of the farm. She was a good homemaker and all, but she was not interested in the farm."

"Lots of women aren't," Martin offered. "In our neighborhood I can think of several women who don't do fieldwork or milk cows."

"Actually, there are two or three," Mary said, "out of—let's see—out of ten or so, if you count me. But Mrs. Drude helped before she had the kids, and so did Mrs. Shaurel until her girls took over. Only Mrs. Ryan never did any fieldwork. I don't hold it against anyone, though. It's a matter of preference."

"I guess you're right, Mary. As usual," Martin admitted. "I like it when you're out there working with me and the kids. I like how it brings the whole family together for a common purpose. I'd miss that if you weren't there. Not to mention, of course, that you're better at it than most men I can hire."

Mary smiled at his comment. "Of course."

John was quick to jump in. "Yes, and, you see, we never had that as a family. After the kids were born, it was Rose and the kids or me and the kids. The four of us seldom felt like a unit, except at church."

Mary marveled, *He just keeps spilling his guts as he keeps his eyes on the road. I suppose John has no one else to talk to about it. Is that why he asked us along to go get Rose? Sure, it's a long drive, and it's nice to have company, but maybe he had another reason. He seems to believe that he and Rose have drifted apart and sees this as an opportunity to change things for the better. But the letter leaves me with too many questions. I wonder how the meeting with Rose will go?*

CHAPTER 5

THE BULL

10:45 a.m., Saturday, July 14, 1956

The three teens stared in awe at the massive Holstein bull, which was predominately white with many small patches of black on his back and his feet. He shook his huge head and neck back and forth and up and down before pushing against the small tree trunk again.

"His forehead is a couple feet wide!" Jimmy exclaimed, exaggerating only slightly. "Good thing he has been dehorned. With a neck that thick and powerful, he could lift up the side of the car and roll it on its side." He turned to his companions to add, "Don't get too cocky standing behind the fence for protection, kids. He could bust through it without a grunt."

Robert and Maggie took an involuntary step back, even as Maggie exclaimed, "He's beautiful!" She giggled a little and added, "His four legs are black from his hooves to below his knees. Like he's wearing knee-highs."

"What can we do?" Robert asked. "The boy's only fifty yards from the fence, but he can't outrun the bull, can he?"

"No, we've got to help him," Maggie offered. "But how?"

"I have no intention of leaving the kid there, but he's fairly safe in the tree for now, so we don't want to rush into things. We have to have a plan. Get back in the car, and I'll back up and pull in that driveway next to the fence. That way, if the bull gets too interested in us, we can get in the car. Then I'll try to talk to the kid. I think he'll be able to hear me."

Once the car was parked in the field driveway with the hood a few feet from the fence, Jimmy got out and walked up to the wires.

"Hey, can you hear me? I'm Jimmy," he called, no louder than he needed to.

"Yeah. I don't know what got into our bull. He's usually real peaceful!"

Maggie said to Robert, "Dad says to never trust a bull or think it's tame."

"Are you doing okay in the tree?" Jimmy shouted.

"I got a good spot, but this tree isn't very big. I hope he doesn't break it off or push it over."

"Well, stay still. We don't want him to decide to attack the tree with all his force."

"I just set out to get some apples, but I never made it to the apple tree. The bull started following me and then ran toward me."

"What's your name, and how old are you?"

"Tony Keller. I'm ten."

"Look, I could drive to your place to get your folks."

"They're not home. They won't be home till suppertime."

"Okay then, we will try to get the bull away from you, and if we do, I'll signal you to climb down. Whatever you do, stay in the tree unless I tell you to come down. Then walk fast—don't run!—to the fence and don't look back. Only run if I tell you to."

"Okay," the boy shouted back to them.

"From here, he looks big for ten," Jimmy said to Maggie.

"They left him home alone all day and he's only ten," Maggie said pronouncing judgment before she remembered and muttered, "Oh jeez, we left Joey home alone and he's only eleven."

"And I'm starting to regret that already," Jimmy said. Then he yelled to the boy, "Do you have the bull in the pasture all the time?"

"No, only when there is a cow in heat."

Jimmy looked at Maggie. "I wonder what distracted the bull from servicing the cow?"

"Maybe she isn't in heat anymore. The herd isn't that far away. It's a big herd!" Maggie exclaimed.

"That bull is nearly twice the size of some of the cows. He's almost too big to be serviceable. Wonder why they keep him."

"My guess," Maggie said, "is that he's normally very calm and friendly, and the family is fond of him. It's hard to get rid of an animal that you've had for years. Remember, Jimmy, how we hated to sell our bull—the one we named Thor?"

"We sold him before he got that big, though. They must have a steel bull pen in the barn to keep him in. Jeez, he could walk through this fence like an elephant."

"What can we do?" Maggie asked. "Don't rush into doing something stupid, Jimmy."

At that moment, they heard Tony holler, "Get back!" and they turned to see the bull butting his massive head against the tree.

"Just hold on, Tony!" Jimmy yelled before he turned to his friends. "That tree isn't very sturdy. It could give out any second. You two get in the car. Robert, you get behind the wheel. The keys are in the ignition. If he goes for the car, just drive away."

"Wait a minute, Jimmy!" Maggie yelled. "I said don't do something stupid!"

"Too late for that. This whole trip was stupid, and anything I do with this bull is stupid to the nth degree."

"Leave it to Bandit to do an algebra joke as he is about to risk his life," Robert said.

"Give me a break, buddy. You know I'm fast and a lot smarter than Mr. Knee-Highs."

Maggie yelled, "Don't let your pride get in the way of good sense, Jimmy! Do you always have to be the tough guy? The big hero?"

"Just get in the car! I know what I'm doing."

"Let's go, Maggie," Robert said, gently tugging her hand.

As Jimmy hopped over the fence, Maggie screamed, "Damn it, Jimmy! What happened to not rushing into things and having a plan? What happened to that?"

"This is my plan, Mags," he muttered to himself. *Let's see, Dad said to be bold and direct when dealing with a bull. Let the animal know you intend to be the boss.* "Look here, Knee-Highs, don't be bothering the boy. Get back to the herd and earn your feed." His voice was loud and commanding as he walked briskly toward the bull.

The bull, a mere fifty yards away, turned his head to face Jimmy. *Got his attention.* Jimmy saw Tony begin to climb down. "No, you stay in the tree till I tell you otherwise." Tony climbed back to his safe spot.

Jimmy's brisk walk had taken him half the distance to the bull, and his plan was to go no closer. The bull stepped around to face Jimmy directly. *Good. His attention is off the boy. Now, it's a matter of facing him down.*

Jimmy yelled, "Hee-ahh! Hee-ahh!" and the bull shook his great head up and down and trotted toward him.

As Jimmy turned back toward the fence, he muttered, "I'm stupid, but I'm no darn fool." And he burst into his fastest sprint. Within seconds he'd cleared the fence, landing in the grass with a roll that took him to his feet, which propelled him through the back door of the car. Hearing that Robert had started the engine, he exclaimed, "Don't back out. Leave the car here. It may discourage him from going through the fence. Maybe his tamer nature will prevail."

"I wouldn't count on that," Robert said wryly.

"Me either. Leave the engine running."

The bull slowed his trot to a stop and butted a wide split-oak fence post before raking the massive forehead up and down.

"He's not put his weight and strength into it yet."

"What do you suppose he's thinking?" Robert asked.

"Don't know. It's all about anger and power and dominance with him. I don't think he does much actual thinking."

"Just like someone else I know!" Maggie shouted at her bother. "You lunatic! You could have been hurt or even killed! You gave no thought to yourself or to us either!"

"Sorry, Mags. But I did have a plan. I knew if I only met him halfway, I could easily run twenty-five yards back here before he could run fifty yards toward the fence. And I knew I could easily clear the fence without losing a second. My only concern was if he would stop at the fence."

"Looks like he did," Robert said with relief.

"You could've tripped and fell down. What would have happened then? He'd be rolling your body around the pasture, and we couldn't have done a thing about it."

"Come on, Mags. Not likely that I would trip."

"Or what if you couldn't clear the fence?"

"I've jumped fences a little higher than that without any trouble."

"Not with a bull chasing you, you haven't."

"Old Knee-Highs was my motivation."

"You're impossible!" she yelled. "Now do you see, Robert, why I was not about to let him go on this search alone? You could've at least told us what you were going to do, Jimmy."

"Yeah, I should've. Maybe I was afraid you'd talk me out of it."

"And I would've, too."

"Nice to know you care so much," Jimmy said, grinning at her.

Mags gave her usual response to end their discussions: "Shut up, Jimmy."

Robert broke in to say, "Hey, guys, he's still out there watching us. Do you have a backup plan?"

"As a matter of fact, I do. And the fact that we still have his attention will help make it work."

"It better be better than your first plan," Maggie said angrily.

"Here's my idea," Jimmy offered. "I'll drive east down to where the herd is and call them until they come up to the fence. Then I'll keep calling them as I drive near the fence where the bull is. When the whole herd comes over by the bull, maybe he'll lose interest in Tony and us. I mean, it's a big herd, as you've said. Chances are good there may be another one in heat this time of the year, three months after March calving."

"What makes you think the cows will come when you call?" Robert asked.

"Oh, they'll come," Jimmy said. "I'm better at calling cows than even Mom or Dad. They'll come, all right."

As Jimmy and Robert switched places, Jimmy took a moment to yell at Tony, "Stay put. We'll have you safe in no time at all." He waited until Tony waved and shouted, "Okay!"

Knee-Highs remained by the fence as Jimmy drove the car toward the herd and pulled over to the side of the road. He moved about ten yards along the fence line away from the car and put his hands to either side of his mouth to form a megaphone before he called, in a voice that varied in pitch, volume, and rhythm, "Come, boss! Come, boss! Come, boss! Come, boss!" He repeated the call several times.

After less than a minute, Maggie exclaimed, "I see some heads perking up!"

"Yeah, they're starting to come," Robert said. "I learn something new every day with you guys."

But the moment of satisfaction was brief, as the bull turned his humongous head and trotted toward them, turning their hope to fear. With his head high, he pranced toward Jimmy.

Jimmy turned back to the car, saying in an even voice, "Walk, don't run. Get in the car slowly, kids." He was in the car with them in less than half a minute as the bull postured, jumping in the air, coming down on his front legs, and kicking his back legs toward the sky. He stopped at the fence where Jimmy had been and stared at the car, standing motionless for a moment.

Inside the car, the three teens stared at the bull as Maggie said, "He must weigh a ton."

Jimmy nodded. "I'm no bull expert," he said slowly, "but that kick in the air is different from the snorting-and-pawing-the-earth-with-his-front-feet kind of thing I would expect from an angry bull."

"More like what the cows do when they are let out on pasture in the spring after being locked up all winter," Maggie said.

"Maybe he wants to play with us," Robert joked.

"Yeah," Jimmy said. "He'd like to roll our dead bodies around in the grass and dirt."

"Bulls do that?" Robert asked.

Maggie answered slowly. "A neighbor, Axel Rexen, was leading his so-called tame bull to another barn when it turned on him, killed him, and rolled his body around in the cow yard for over an hour. He wouldn't leave the body alone. Neighbors came to surround the bull with their cars and tractors until someone could get a good shot at it with a high-powered rifle."

In an anxious voice, Robert said, "What do you think is going through his big wide head? What's he planning?"

"I don't know if he plans or thinks or just acts, but the cows are coming fast now. Maybe they see the car and are curious. I'll drive the car farther away from the tree, and maybe they will follow if I get out and call. Maybe the bull will follow too."

After stopping the car about fifty yards further east, Jimmy said, "Stay in the car," as he jumped out and called again, "Come, boss! Come, boss!"

The bull had followed them along the fence, and now the herd moved around Knee-Highs.

"My plan is working!" Jimmy exclaimed as he got into the car. "We'll give them some time together. He'll calm down around the cows. Cows are really pretty sweet, but if you try to mess with their calves, they can be as mean as a bull. Billy told me he worked with a guy who raised beef cattle, and they let the calves out with them all summer until they weaned them in the fall, like the ranchers out west. Those cows are like wild animals compared to dairy cows that are used to having humans milking them every day."

"How come I've not seen a bull at your farm?" Robert asked. "I mean, you have to have one, don't you?" He laughed nervously, realizing that maybe this wasn't the conversation he wanted to have in front of his girlfriend.

"No," Maggie said in a matter-of-fact manner. "We use artificial insemination. We got rid of our bull last year, and I am so glad."

Robert was silent, but Maggie noticed an inquisitive look on his face. "If you want to know more about artificial insemination, ask Jimmy," she added.

"Enough said," Robert responded with a chuckle.

"I think there are more than one hundred animals in this herd to keep Knee-Highs company," Jimmy said. "The herd keeps moving farther away from the tree, and I think he's lost interest. It's time to have Tony make a run for it."

Jimmy drove back to the field driveway and parked next to the fence before he got out of the car. Standing next to the fence, he shouted to Tony, "When I signal with a wave that it's time, climb down and then walk, not run, to the fence by us. I'll lift the wire so you can roll under it, okay?"

"Okay."

"I repeat: Walk fast, don't run unless I tell you to, and don't look back. We'll watch the bull. Got it, Tony?"

"Got it!"

Double-checking that the bull and the herd had drifted east over a hundred yards, Jimmy motioned to Tony, who climbed down the tree, walked to the fence, and rolled under it with ease as Jimmy lifted the bottom wire.

Sensing the boy was still scared, Jimmy patted him on the back and offered his hand. "Nice job, Tony. You did good. The best thing was to stay in the tree until we had that bull away from you. You couldn't outrun him, and he could've gone through this fence like nothing. You did good."

"Thanks. Thanks for helping me. No one else did. Lots of people saw me in the tree and just waved."

"Well," Jimmy said, "you're a big kid. They probably thought you didn't need help. Jump in the back seat, Tony, and we will run you home. By the way, this is my sister, Maggie, and her friend, Robert. It was Robert who saw you in the tree."

"Thanks, Robert."

"Glad we could help out," Robert said as he climbed in the back seat with Tony.

As they drove Tony home, Robert asked, "Don't people usually plant apple trees in their yard? Why did you plant an apple tree in the pasture?"

"We didn't. The tree grew there on its own. There's at least four of them out there. The pasture is about eighty-five acres."

"We have two in our pasture," Maggie said.

"How does it happen?"

"Don't know the exact facts," Jimmy said, "but we can guess a bird dropped the seed or a cow ate an apple and the seed even had fertilizer when it came out. I know one thing for sure, and that is getting an apple tree that produces good apples from a seed is rare as heck."

"Wait a minute," Robert said. "How do we get certain kinds of apples if we can't get them from seeds?"

"Grafting," Jimmy said. "They graft a branch of the kind of tree they want onto the root of another tree."

"Oh, yeah. I guess I knew about grafting from biology class," Robert said. "But I didn't know seeds from an apple did not produce the same apple. That's strange."

"Kind of blows up the whole Johnny Appleseed story, doesn't it?" Maggie asked.

"They should've called him Johnny Applegrafter," Robert offered.

The three teens laughed.

"Just doesn't have the same ring to it," Jimmy said.

"Don't the cows eat the apple tree when it's little?"

"I looked this up once to find out why they maybe don't," Jimmy said. "The apple tree is part of the rose family, and the twigs are thornlike. Most of the wild apple trees have really sharp twigs, sharp enough to discourage a cow from nibbling on them."

From her post riding shotgun, Maggie turned to face Tony in the back seat. "We're so glad you're safe."

Robert said, "You must be a strong kid, Tony, to lift yourself up the trunk of that tree. It looked like that lowest branch was quite a way off the ground."

Tony paused a little, reluctant to say what was on his mind, before he blurted out, "I am strong, but Dad says I'm too fat."

Stunned, Jimmy turned to look at Maggie, who was about to speak, but Robert spoke before she could get a word out.

"You look like you have lots of muscle! My dad says I'm too skinny. Sometimes, I think dads are hard to please." As Robert held up his left arm to make a fist, and to flex his bicep, he used the fingers of his right hand to push up the flesh to swell the bicep into a massive lump before he bragged, "But see, look at the size of my muscles!"

Maggie laughed at the sight of Tony's face as he reacted to what he believed was Robert's bicep. Then, as Robert broke into a laugh, he turned his arm to let Tony see how he had enhanced his muscle.

"Hey, you can do that too," Robert encouraged Tony.

Tony grinned as he used his left hand to push up his right bicep. "How's that!" he exclaimed.

"Pretty scary!" Robert exclaimed. "Show that to your dad and tell him how you can climb trees . . . but you maybe don't want to tell him about the one in the pasture. Your secret is safe with us, right, kids?"

Jimmy and Maggie nodded and proclaimed loudly, "You bet, Tony."

After they dropped Tony off at his yard, Robert climbed into the front seat next to Maggie, and as Jimmy turned west out of the driveway, Maggie remarked, "I'm proud of you, Robert, for making that kid feel good. That was a good deed."

"Are you proud of your big brother too?" Jimmy asked, honestly searching for approval.

"No!" Maggie exclaimed. "I'm still mad at you for risking your safety and our safety too!"

"A good deed never goes unpunished," Jimmy said ruefully.

"That's a cynical attitude," Robert proclaimed. "But I agree."

"I'm a cynical guy."

"Anyway," Maggie continued, "what you did was not a good deed. It was a dangerous stunt, and you did it for pride and to show off."

"Ouch," Jimmy said. "Maybe Robert did his good deed for the same reason."

"No! Robert did it out of kindness," Maggie said. "I admire kindness, not heroics." Then, turning to Robert, she added, "After I saw the look on Tony's face when he said his father tells him he's too fat, I felt bad for him, but I didn't know what to say. But you just jumped in to say the right thing. You made Tony feel good about himself."

"Yeah, I am kind of an expert on how not to please a father," Robert said seriously before he smiled and remarked in his usual smart-ass manner, "Well, that's enough excitement for a while."

"I thought you liked adventure?" Jimmy teased.

"Can we get some with less danger involved? That bull scared the hell out of me! And I'll tell you this, Bandit, you scared me even more when you jumped in the pasture with him."

"Don't worry, Planet. That's probably the last of the danger for today. Besides, I need to concentrate on driving to make better time."

Five minutes later, they reached the crest above the Minnesota River, and Jimmy had to brake the car lightly for nearly a mile as the road angled down the face of the clifflike hill before it leveled off to the riverbank, leading Robert to exclaim, "Wow! That was almost like driving down a mountain. A small mountain, but still high. They even had a runaway ramp for trucks near the bottom."

"I saw that," Maggie said, "but I didn't know what it was."

"You see," Robert explained, "if the brakes get too hot after braking so long and the trucker loses control of his speed, he can pull into the runaway ramp and the loose gravel and steep incline will slow him down to a stop. He'll have to get a wrecker to pull him out, but he will live to drive another day. They have lots of them in the mountains where my folks used to take us on vacation."

"This is the reverse of a mountain," Jimmy said. "Once we cross the Minnesota River and get through Riverton, we have to climb back up before we hit the wide prairie."

"Wait a minute!" Robert exclaimed. "You said that was the Minnesota River. I figured it was the Mississippi."

"No, we won't be crossing the Mississippi River today, stranger," Jimmy teased.

"Learn something every day, I do," Robert remarked with just a bit of sarcasm.

"That's what I like about you, Planet. You are a curious lad."

"I've got to ask, though, why are you driving so slow? We spent an hour helping Tony. I figure you would want to make good time. The road is flat.

There's river swamp on both sides. You said the town was on the other side of the river, and we haven't crossed the bridge yet. So, why the pokey thirty-miles-per-hour speed?"

"It's the speed limit. There was a sign back there at the start of the river bottom. And the speed limit lasts from there all the way through town. Dad says it's kind of a speed trap. Drivers forget about the speed limit because the road is straight with no intersections, and they don't slow down after they come barreling down the steep grade. But there's a dead-end driveway ahead where a cop parks, ready to nail you for speeding."

"There he is!" Maggie exclaimed. "The way the big willows hang over the driveway, drivers can't see him till they're nearly on top of him. How did you know about it?"

"A couple of years ago I rode with Dad out this way to look at some hay for sale during a drought. Even Emil Rosincek was short of hay that year."

"Is the cop there all the time?"

"No," Jimmy joked, "just when the town is short on funds. I don't know what the fine is, but you can pay it and stay out of court."

"Boy, that's just what we do not need—to be stopped for speeding. Good going, Bandit. I mean, we're already delayed because I had to clean the garage."

"And I had to clean muck off the concrete cow porch before we left."

"Come to think of it, Hercules had to clean the Augean stables."

"How do you know about that?" Maggie asked.

"Well, Maggie, I confess: I read mythology. I find it fascinating. And by the way, Hercules had to capture a bull too. I mean, we didn't exactly capture it, but we—well, you, Jimmy—had to deal with it somehow, right?"

"You are a wonder, Planet."

After another few minutes, they were through town and at the base of the hill. Jimmy sped up to fifty before the road's steep incline slowed the car, forcing him to shift into second gear. "And now," he announced, "we have a steep hill to climb."

"Story of my life," Robert lamented with a smile.

CHAPTER 6

ON THE ROAD

Noon, Saturday, July 14, 1956

After the Ford climbed the steep hill west of the river bottom, the land opened up to prairie and sky. With both hands guiding the steering wheel, Jimmy managed to poke his left elbow out of the window, which was a pose he had seen his father take many times. Also like his father, Jimmy drove at moderate speeds. He preferred to enjoy the trip rather than rushing to get somewhere. Driving in the countryside with his sister and friend, he felt a kind of freedom he'd not felt before. At the moment, he answered to no one. The open road was in front of them, and although they had a mission, the course of action was up to them. The goal was to find Mary.

How good it will be to see her again. I was so lucky we were sweethearts in school all those years. I miss her now, and school seems so empty without her. Good thing I have Robert as a friend. Glancing over, Jimmy smiled at the sight of Robert holding his arm out the window while he played with the wind. "Are you glad you came along, Planet?"

"Heck yes," Robert answered.

Jimmy glanced over at Maggie, who was struggling to unfold a Minnesota road map as it flapped in the breeze. She looked irritated, so he asked her gently, "Too much air, Mags? Want me to close the side vent window a little? You seem a little frustrated."

"Yeah, close the vent window," she said as she tried again to straighten the map. "I thought I'd show Robert where we're headed."

"Don't care," Robert said. "I'm having fun just being here." His entire right arm stuck out the window, and he let the wind take it up or down, depending on how he slanted his hand. Looking at the watch on his left wrist, he said, "It's only noon, and I feel like I'm being chauffeured into an adventure that will last all day. And with the breeze blowing in my face while I bask in the presence of two friends, I feel lucky."

Jimmy laughed. "I like how you can just roll with things. No urge to be in control."

"Being in control is just an illusion," Robert offered in his mellow imitation of a philosopher's voice. "Besides, Maggie is always in control. I'll just follow along. But okay, I'll bite. Where are we headed, and why do you think Mary is at the end of the trail? I know there weren't enough clues in the letter for me to find her."

"Mary wouldn't say much about where she was running away to," Maggie explained, "but when I told her I was worried about her taking a wrong turn in the dark of the night, I remember her saying how easy the place would be to find. 'Not a lot of turns,' she said. 'I drive west from Lakeland City, cross the river, and keep going until I get to a town and turn right.'"

"Isn't there a lot of prairie to get lost in out there?" Robert asked. "Lots of wrong turns to make?"

"But she used the phrase *cross the river* just once," Maggie said.

"Why is that important?" Robert asked, honestly curious.

"Well, the river she meant was, of course, the Minnesota River, which we crossed at Riverton, but if we stayed on this road another sixty miles or so, we'd cross it again."

Robert said, "I don't get it."

Jimmy explained, "See, the Minnesota River flows southeast from the north, under this highway, and southeast another fifty miles or so until it makes a kind of sharp turn to flow northeast. It flows under this road at Riverton and then north toward the Cities, where it flows into the Mississippi River around Fort Snelling. Show him on the map, Mags."

"Here's where we are now," Maggie said, pointing to a spot on the map. "Here is where we crossed the river at Riverton, and here is where we would cross it again if we stayed on this road. But since Mary only mentioned one river crossing, she must be somewhere north of the stretch of this highway between the two bridges."

"Okay, I get that, but there's still a lot of prairie out there."

Maggie eagerly continued, "But she accidentally gave us other important clues in the letter: The letter said there was a good fabric store in town. I know good fabric stores are rare. It also said there were no stores in town that sold sewing machines, but the town had both a Sears and a Ward's catalog store. I figure we'll drive west to check out Bur Oak Falls to see if it has those stores. If it does, we know we're close."

"But isn't she hiding on a farm?" Robert asked. "How are we going to find the farm, Sherlock?"

"Hey," Jimmy interjected with a big grin on his face, "that's when we'll have to rely on some of my good luck."

"Since when are you lucky, Bandit?"

"Starting now, it looks like." Jimmy slowed the car as he looked into the rearview mirror. "Is that a convertible full of girls following us and waving?"

Robert and Maggie both turned around to look. "There's three of them," Robert said. "They look like teenagers. It's a 'fifty-six Plymouth Belvedere convertible. Beautiful! Someone's got Daddy's car for the day. I love the turquoise-and-white two-tone. They're waving to us."

"Yeah," Maggie countered, "probably because they haven't seen you guys up close yet."

"Don't worry, Maggie," Robert proclaimed in his overly gallant voice, "I wouldn't trade my spot next to you for a seat in that convertible."

"Sweet of you to say, but I'm not worried."

"They're passing!" Jimmy exclaimed. "We'll all get a good look now."

The highway was straight, allowing them to see that passing was safe for a mile or more. The Plymouth passed slowly, giving the girls ample time to wave and flirt with strangers from the safety of the faster vehicle. For at least thirty seconds, the driver held the convertible alongside the Ford. All three girls wore white T-shirts. The driver and the girl in the middle had short dark hair, but the girl riding shotgun had long light-brown hair tied up in a ponytail. All passengers got a good look at each other before Jimmy slowed down.

"I'm not keen on driving games. Call me a coward if you want."

The Plymouth sped away with the girls motioning them to follow. Jimmy kept pace but slowed when they reached seventy miles per hour. "Call me chicken, go ahead."

Neither Maggie nor Robert spoke. All eyes followed the Plymouth as it became smaller in the distance. Then, suddenly, it grew larger again—they'd stopped.

When they caught up to the Plymouth, Jimmy slowed and paced it several car lengths behind. "They're only going thirty," he said.

"They're really pretty girls," Maggie said suddenly. "Haven't seen those short haircuts look so good on anyone like they do on those two. Maybe I'll try having mine in a short style. What do you think, Robert?"

Robert took a moment before answering, "You look great now, but you'll look good in short hair too."

"Good answer," Jimmy said.

They watched in awe as two of the girls climbed into the back seat and stood on the seat cushion. When they began dancing, motioning for Jimmy to turn on the radio, Maggie turned the dial to search for a clear station and stopped when she heard Dean Martin singing "Detour."

"I'll bet they're on the same station," Maggie said. "I can tell by the way they move."

"Holy shit!" Robert exclaimed. "What are they doing now?"

And in that moment, the two girls lifted their T-shirts and shed their bras as they faced the car behind them.

Without even thinking about it, Jimmy shifted the car into second and sped up until they followed only a car length behind.

"Want a closer look, eh, Jimmy?" Maggie teased.

"Why not? It's long-distance second base."

The girls pulled their shirts down, threw kisses to the trio behind them, and lifted their shirts again in a routine that entertained even Maggie. When the song finished, the car sped away with everyone waving their goodbyes.

Jimmy sped up to about fifty before he said, "I'd like to talk to those girls."

"With their shirts off, of course," Maggie said.

"Well," Jimmy answered slowly, "I won't deny I enjoyed the show, but I know they're just teasing us. Note that they didn't pull over to stop and chat. And, Robert, you probably should say nothing. Anything you say will be used against you in a court of Maggie."

Robert laughed and nodded.

"The question is," Maggie teased, "how would you boys have acted if I had not been along?"

"An interesting question," Robert said. "I like to believe Jimmy and I would've resisted the temptation of those teenage sirens, just like we did with you along."

Maggie laughed. "And they had the faster car."

"Exactly," Robert said, smiling.

"But what's a siren?" Maggie asked.

Robert was eager to answer. "In the eighth grade, before I moved here, we had a teacher who loved Greek mythology. She got us into it, and I started reading on my own. I found the stories fun and more interesting than science fiction or Westerns, which was what most of the other kids were reading."

"Yeah, we know you're weird, but answer her question."

"Okay, okay. A siren is a female creature that lures sailors to sail their ships into rocks. They sing or move or gesture to sucker the sailors in with their sex appeal."

"So, they are women who live out on the rocks?" Maggie asked.

"It's a Greek myth. The women are half fish or half bird."

"And sailors find that alluring?"

"It's their song or their dance that they find alluring. In Homer's *Odyssey*, the hero is tempted by sirens. Somehow his own sailors save him even though he wants to give in to the sirens' charms. I can't really remember how it goes."

"Just like my being along saved you guys. If I hadn't been along, the siren episode would've put you in the ditch?"

"Or worse," Jimmy said. "But, you know, I'd like to talk to them. They might know something about Mary. The sign back there said Bur Oak Falls was only five miles. I'll bet that's where they're headed, and that's where we're headed too. We need to stop at a drugstore or café."

"Right," Maggie agreed. "Let's cruise through town to see what we can see. If we do see the girls, I'm pretty sure they'll have their bras back on."

"A guy can hope they don't," the boys said simultaneously.

A loud *bang!* startled the three searchers. Jimmy struggled to steer straight ahead as the car pulled to the right. He let off the accelerator before it coasted to a sudden stop.

"Flat tire," Jimmy said. "Maybe we've used up all of our luck."

"And maybe not," Maggie said cheerfully. "I'm sure Dad got a tire fixed in town last week."

"You're right, but he didn't replace the spare with it. So, the blowout is on the spare, not a good tire. Hope I'm right. Won't take long to change a tire."

With a special key on the key ring, he opened the trunk. "Yep, that's the good tire in here. I should've changed it before we left. At least the tire is just loose in the trunk, so we don't have to go through the ordeal of unscrewing the mounting." Jimmy fished around until he found two bricks. "Here, Robert, put these in front and back of the front tire. There's a small slant on the road, and we don't want to lose the car after we jack it up."

"Right-o, Bandit."

Jimmy removed the tire from the trunk before he knelt by the flat. "The lug nuts should come off easily. They were screwed off and on only last week." Jimmy popped the hubcap off and set it upside down alongside him. After loosening each lug nut half a turn or so, he inserted the jack under the bumper and jacked up the car until the tire nearly came off the ground. Then he removed the lug nuts one at a time and placed them in the hubcap to keep them clean and secure. After jacking up the car a few more notches, he removed the tire, mounted the good one, and screwed on the lug nuts, making sure they fitted tightly to the rim's beveled holes.

As he let down the jack, he hollered, "Can you bring me the bricks?"

"Sure thing," Robert answered.

Jimmy tossed the bricks and the flat tire into the trunk, slammed it shut, and said, "We're off."

"With no spare tire," Maggie warned.

"Maybe we can get it fixed in town. That would be the smart thing to do."

They came upon the town in less than a minute, and Jimmy slowed. The main street was long, and businesses of all kinds had shops on both sides of the street.

"Be on the lookout for the stores Mary said were in her town," Maggie said, just before she exclaimed, "Hey, that small storefront is a Sears catalog store!"

Turning his eyes away from the street ahead of him for a moment, Jimmy said, "And there's the Ward's catalog store on the other side of the street."

"And there's the fabric store!" Maggie exclaimed. "It's part of that three-story department store. All three clues. That was almost too easy."

Robert tried to be objective. "Maybe every town has those stores."

"No," Maggie stated, "a department store with a fabric shop is fairly rare, and the Sears and Ward's catalog stores are limited too."

As they headed west to the other end of town, Maggie yelled, "Hey, there's a Dairy Queen next to the bus stop."

"I don't remember that in the letter," Jimmy said seriously.

"No, stupid brother, but I'd sure like something cold to drink with those sandwiches I packed. We can get the tire fixed later."

"Yeah, I'm hungry too," Robert said. "It's close to one o'clock. Tell you what, I'm buying DQ cones and a soda for everyone. A treat for you for taking me on this adventure."

"You are a generous sport," Jimmy said. "But we call it pop in Minnesota, not soda. You need to learn the lingo if you want to fit in, Planet."

"Never cared much for fitting in," Robert said. "But you probably know that already."

"We do," Jimmy said. "And that's one of the reasons we like you—but buying us ice cream and pop is a bigger reason, of course."

"Of course, it would be," Robert agreed in his fake-serious voice.

"Thanks for the treat, Robert," Maggie said, squeezing his hand slightly. "That's really sweet of you."

Jimmy pulled over, and they piled out of the car and crossed the street toward the DQ.

Standing in line at the outdoor window, Jimmy said, "Looks like there's just a guy and a girl at the picnic table around back. Should be room for us."

Carrying treats and the bags of sandwiches, the trio walked toward the tables but stopped when they heard the voice of the young man grow louder.

The girl was sitting on the bench connected to the picnic table with her back to them as they approached, and Jimmy noticed she looked to be about seventeen and had her brown hair tied back into a ponytail. The guy, sitting on top of the table next to her with his feet on the bench, looked several years older.

Leaning down toward her, he asked, "And you tell me this now? Now, when I'm in a hurry to get back to Fort Leonard Wood?"

She tilted her head up to him and said, "I didn't want to tell you over the phone, so I called to tell you to meet me here on your way back."

"I've got to pick up two of my Army buddies in fifteen minutes!"

A few yards away, the three searchers traded embarrassed looks, as they had no choice but to hear the squabble. The man glanced at Jimmy, stood up, and said gently, "Where's my manners? Here, you guys sit at this table. Or I'll just stand. I see you guys need to set down your sandwiches and drinks so you can work on those ice cream cones."

"Thanks," Jimmy said as he led the others to sit. *Seems like a nice guy.* Although his large muscular frame was a little intimidating, the stranger's big smile was welcoming. He wore a blue short-sleeved shirt rolled up at the sleeves, and his jeans hung on his hips. His black hair was cut in a short crew cut style. Although he was clearly upset, he seemed to mellow before he spoke to the three searchers.

"I'm Jerry Weber. You're not from here, right? Welcome to our town, strangers."

Picking up on Jerry's friendly tone, Jimmy answered, "I'm Jimmy, and this is my sister, Maggie, and my friend Robert."

"Pardon the soap opera, here, but Diane has just dumped me! After a year of dating and making promises and then writing to me when I was in basic training, now she calls this going-away meeting and says we should break up. So much for love, eh?" Jerry forced a loud laugh as he sat down at the table and then took a big drink of pop.

Jimmy saw the sadness in Jerry's face and knew the humor was a mask to hide his pain and assert his pride. Taking a drink was a distraction.

When Diane turned toward them, though, the searchers' mouths dropped open. Diane's face went blank.

Robert muttered to Maggie, "The convertible dancer." The words came out louder than he intended, and tension grabbed the scene. Jerry was big, and he seemed angry.

Jerry said, "You recognize Diane?"

"Not with her shirt on," Jimmy said quickly, seldom able to suppress a smart remark.

"What!" Jerry gave a forced chuckle and tilted his head, waiting for an explanation. "Well, you sure have a lotta balls." He sucked a long drink of cola from his straw.

"No, just the standard two," Jimmy quipped, hoping he had accurately read Jerry's good humor.

Cola sprayed from Jerry's mouth and nose onto the table, followed by a series of coughs and snorts as he struggled to control his laughter. For a moment Jimmy thought he'd gone too far (the image of pounding on Jack Drude's Model A came to his mind), but as Jerry's coughing subsided he said, "Well, then they're big ones, I'll bet." And he laughed as he caught his breath. He turned to Diane. "So, that's how my girlfriend spent the last hours of my two-week leave after basic training. I have to admit, I was hoping for a romantic drive in the countryside or maybe a serious kiss at the DQ. Or even a few tears. But you were out flashing these three travelers. What a dummy I am!"

Diane said nothing.

"Yeah," Jerry said, "You don't have to say anything. I'm mad as hell, but I'm glad you told me now instead of sending me a Dear John letter."

At last Diane spoke. "I'm nearly seventeen, Jerry, and I'm not sitting home waiting for you. I don't want to just write letters and wait for life to happen. I want to live now."

"And so you should, Diane. You're only young once, and you want to see what else is out there. I get it, but I'm sad to find out our time together meant so little to you. I'm glad you were *finally* honest with me, even after a year of being dishonest."

Diane's ponytail bobbed as she stood up and declared, "I wasn't ever really dishonest! I really liked you, Jerry. But I changed a lot over the last year or so."

"As we all do. And we all will continue to change. You'll find out, just as I did, that being sixteen is nothing compared to the next year and the next. I'm less than three years older than you are, but I've learned that life gets sweeter every year, if you don't screw it up." He turned to Jimmy, who had settled just beyond the wet cola-burst area. "Don't you think, Jimmy?"

"I sure hope you're right," Jimmy said. "There's nothing more depressing than some older person telling me that being sixteen is as good as it gets. But the piece you added about 'if you don't screw it up' is the real kicker. It's all too damn easy to screw up!" His thoughts went to Mary. *Did I screw that up? Somehow, I need to make it right.* His heart ached for a moment as he understood Jerry's pain.

Jerry sat back and smiled. "Sounds like you're talking from experience." But he didn't wait for Jimmy to elaborate. "Say, I've got to leave soon. I got lucky for a draftee. When I volunteered for the draft, I knew that Uncle Sam could send me anywhere after basic training, but the DI—the drill instructor—told me that he wanted me to stay at Leonard Wood and train recruits with him. He said that he wanted someone with my ability to replace the soldier leaving. He got my orders cut before I left, and I even know which barracks I'll be in."

"What will you be doing?"

"While the DI tells the troops what to do, I demonstrate and keep pushing them to do more and make it look easy. I'm really looking forward to it."

"Sounds like a lot of hard work."

"It will be, but Fort Leonard Wood is within driving range of a three-day pass, and I thought it'd be easy to come home and see my girl. Ha! Things can turn on a dime."

Jerry waited as the three searchers nodded.

"But enough about that. I'm curious. What brought you here? You're farm kids, right? But not from around here."

Jimmy looked at Maggie and, after catching her nod, said, "We're looking for a girl. Name is Mary Schroedler. She is a close friend and ran away for fear of harm from a boy who had threatened her and her friends. She ran away to keep us all safe."

Maggie had taken a photo out of her purse before she walked over to Jerry. "Here's her eighth-grade photo from a couple of years ago. She's sixteen now, so she looks older than the photo. She's even prettier now, too."

"Ooo-eee," Jerry squealed. "She is a cutie." He held the photo up for a better view. "She has a face I'd remember. I haven't seen her, but you know what? I suggest you go to my folks' farm to ask Dad. It's not far. He knows people in town who might know if a new person moved in somewhere. And he's got a neighbor named Dory who is aways up on the latest." He took a pen out of his pocket and grabbed a napkin off the table. "I'll map it out for you. It's only a few turns. You can't miss it."

Eager for a clue, Maggie and Jimmy watched him sketch the map. Jimmy said, "Looks like your folks' place is on this side of the river. Good. Crossing the Minnesota River again would take time."

Smiling, Robert said, "Yes, we don't want to have to cross it again."

Jimmy and Maggie shared knowing smiles at Robert's newfound knowledge.

Robert commented, "I hate to admit it now, but I thought it was the Mississippi when we first crossed it until you mentioned it was the Minnesota."

"Where did you find your friend here?" Jerry joked. "Obviously, not from around here."

"He's from the East Coast. We hired him as our navigator," Jimmy quipped.

"From the East Coast, eh? Well, that would explain his ducktail hairstyle. But you're a farm kid, so how do you explain yours?" Jerry added sarcastically, "Has he been a bad influence on you?"

"Yeah, you know how we farm boys are," Jimmy joked, "always ready to jump on the latest fashion."

"I had a ducktail too before I joined in April. Started when I was a senior in high school. Want to hear a good one?" Jerry asked rhetorically. "When I signed up to join the Army, the recruiting sergeant told me to cut my hair shorter before I went in. He said the Army barbers are eager to hack off long hair, and some of them even like to draw a little blood."

"And you didn't believe him?" Jimmy asked.

"Oh, I believed him, all right. But I figured once I'm in the service, I belong to Uncle Sam. Why would they hurt me too bad?"

Jerry laughed at his own foolishness, and after he finished drawing the map, he wrote his folks' phone number on the napkin before handing the artwork to Jimmy. He grinned wide as he admitted, "I have to warn you, though. When I left, Dad had finished baling about six hundred bales. Usually, we pull the wagon behind the baler and load as we bale, but he dropped them on the field because he wanted to get it baled fast before the storm this afternoon. But I'm not there to help. Uncle Sam waits for no man, so I have to get on the road now to report to my barracks by Sunday evening. Of course, I have to change into my uniform before I sign in."

Jimmy volunteered, "Hey, we can help him haul hay! We have experience. Even Robert has experience, and he's a proud town kid."

"Yeah, I helped Jimmy's folks hay a couple days last week."

"Trying to impress his sister, right?"

"What other reason could there be?" Robert remarked.

"It's not the money, that's for sure," Jimmy added.

"Well, I can't promise you Dad will pay you much, if at all, but Mom will feed you well and you'll meet my younger sister and brother. Mom's due to have another in a few days, but she's getting around okay. I hate to miss the occasion."

Jerry shook Jimmy's hand and then shook hands with Robert and Maggie before he headed across the street to his car. He turned to say, "Bye, Diane. I'll send you a letter once I get my new address. Just to let you know how I'm doing. Write back only if you want to. I'll understand either way. You've given me no choice." He looked down, turned abruptly toward his car, and in a few long steps reached the door. The searchers' eyes followed him as he drove away.

"That was sad," Maggie said softly, but loud enough for Diane to hear.

"Happy endings, unhappy endings, or new beginnings," Robert said in his philosophical voice.

Diane sucked on her straw, making a bubbling noise that indicted the drink was empty. She stayed seated as if she had something she wanted to say to them. Jimmy looked over at her, hinting he was ready to listen.

"I suppose you all think I'm a terrible person," she said.

Jimmy knew she was fishing for acceptance, but he decided to joke. "No. I think you're a good dancer, though."

"You might want to be careful picking the boys you flash, but to us, you're tops!" Robert added.

Diane smiled. "I mean, you must think I'm terrible for dumping a nice guy like Jerry before he leaves for service. I really did like him. I was over to his place for meals on Sunday a few times. His family is great. You'll like them."

"You have to do what you have to do," Jimmy said. "I think you're brave to do it."

"Mom always says that telling the truth causes less pain in the long run," Maggie inserted, even as she recalled the lies she had told to help Mary escape.

"Well, we've got to go help a guy with hay. It was nice seeing you," Jimmy said; then he looked down, embarrassed, and added quickly, "I mean, meeting you."

She laughed and teased, "Well, I hope it was both, Jimmy."

And the three searchers left to cross the street to where the '52 Ford awaited them.

CHAPTER 7

VISIT AT THE PARSONAGE

Noon, Saturday, July 14, 1956

Fascinated by the changes in the countryside, Mary had been enthusiastical-ly peering out the window from the comfortable back seat of John's Bel Air. They had stopped only once to refuel and to stretch their legs, but no one brought up any concerns about what lay ahead. At the filling station, they took turns at the single-stool toilet, drank a cup of coffee from the thermos Mary had brought, and ate a couple of the cookies she had packed. Every-one seemed eager to get back on the road. And Mary was glad to get back into the car to watch the countryside pass by, which distracted her from concerns about Rose and John. Traveling was a unique experience for her. So much to see.

She chuckled to herself. *The farthest north I've been is the Minnesota State Fair on the northern edge of the Twin Cities. Getting there was a night-mare of stop-and-go lights and traffic, unlike today's scenic trip through the countryside.*

Compared to where Mary lived, the north had many more conifers in natural clusters in forests. She was only familiar with the area south and southwest of Minneapolis and St. Paul, where spruce and pine were seldom seen, except for the river bottom bluffs or in yards where they had been planted by someone. Up north, the fields were small and hilly, much like where they lived, but not as vast and level as the land south and west of where they lived. Their trip definitely took them away from the edge of the prairie and onto a different terrain.

Gazing out the window at a large field of hay that had been raked into rows, she smiled. *Lots of work ahead for that farmer.*

"Lots of work ahead for that farmer," Martin said with a chuckle.

"I was just thinking the same thing."

John spoke for the first time in many miles. "I hope he has a baler."

"No, no, he doesn't!" Mary exclaimed. "See them coming into view at the bottom of the hill? He's pulling a hayrack with a hay loader behind it."

"Looks like the wind is giving him some trouble, too," Martin said. "I don't take any pleasure in seeing them struggle to put up loose hay. Not one bit."

"Me either," Mary said. "We've all been there. It's hard work, and it takes so long to get much hay in the barn."

"Look over to the left after we make the next curve," John inserted quickly. "It's been a while since Rose and I made the trip, but I think you can see the south side of Pastor Terquist's church."

After they stared out the car's windows but failed to see a church, John said, "Well, I said it's been a while." He chuckled at his own error before he added, "Maybe it's the next turn." And as they rounded the turn to the left, John hollered, "There it is! You'll only see the top of it. The steeple. I think the trees have grown quite a bit since we were here last. Those big trees don't seem like they grow, but they do."

Mary and Martin both agreed that they'd spotted the church, which seemed to gratify John as he perked up to say, "We'll be there soon."

He seemed to expect a reconciliation, but Mary feared a confrontation. *What must be going through his mind?*

A few minutes later, John drove west past the church and turned up the fifty-yard driveway to the home of Pastor and Betty Terquist. Mary was struck by its Victorian style and idyllic setting. The large, white two-and-a-half-story parsonage stood among tall red pines, and a grove of oak trees on the west and north extended another fifty yards east to shelter the church, a simple white wooden structure with an addition in the back. A worn footpath—not a concrete sidewalk—leading from the parsonage to the church added to the charm.

As soon as John parked the car by the entryway, Pastor Terquist, Betty, and Rose stepped out of the house to greet them. Rose and John embraced while the pastor exclaimed, "Welcome! Welcome!" with a voice and body language that were both honest and meant to impress.

Pastor Mark Terquist may have been as much as average height, but he seemed larger. His sheer exuberance—as reflected in his confident voice, his wide smile, and his zealous handshake—filled the yard with energy, dispelling any lingering doubts Mary might have had about visiting his home. Although everyone already knew each other, Rose seemed determined to reintroduce her host to Mary and Martin. When she introduced him as Pastor Terquist, he said, "I prefer my friends call me Mark. Or, if you prefer, Pastor Mark."

Mary said, "Pleased to see you again, Pastor Mark." *Seems happy to see us.*

Martin took the pastor at his word. "Really glad to see you again, Mark. This is a beautiful place you have here."

"Believe me, it looks grander than it is, but we love it. The parsonage is owned and maintained by the congregation, and they even modernized it a few years ago, but the place is so big and kind of a maintenance nightmare that keeps skilled tradesmen in the church busy working on it all the time."

Pastor Mark and Martin paired up to talk as Betty and Mary struck up a conversation, everyone allowing Rose and John a few intimate moments alone.

Still, Mary eyed Rose and John as she let Betty lead the chit-chat. Neither of them had ever been comfortable hugging or kissing in public, but they seemed more open with their affection now than usual. *I hope my interpretation of the letter was wrong. I would love to be wrong.*

Eventually Rose broke up the paired discussions. "It's way past noon. Let's go in and eat dinner. Betty has prepared a feast for our special guests. She has roast beef and mashed potatoes and her special cranberry sauce. We have some vegetables from the garden, which is early for here, and several kinds of pie for dessert."

"Rose is too humble to tell you that she baked the pies," Betty said. "She's been such a help these past weeks. But she's right. Let's go in for dinner. It's ready and on the table. You folks must be hungry."

"I admit that I am," Mary said. "And if I am, you know the men are." She followed Betty into the house.

"We'll give you a tour after we eat," Pastor Mark said. "The place is an interesting structure."

"Will you be available to take them through the church too?" Rose asked. Then, turning to Mary, she said, "The church is really magnificent.

All the bright, varnished wood and ornate windows. You'll love it! You'll like it too, Martin. It'll remind you of the Norwegian church where we were confirmed, though it isn't as old."

Mary glanced at Martin to see how well he feigned enthusiasm. *No, he really seems to want to see the church. Why do I always underestimate him?*

The square dining room had a large table that would seat twelve, but places were set so that one end remained empty and Pastor Mark sat on the side across from his wife. Mary and Martin sat to his left, with John across from Martin and Rose across from Mary. Pastor Mark led with a prayer that thanked the Lord for the bounteous meal and all blessings, especially the safe arrival of their guests John, Rose, Mary, and Martin, and he prayed for their safe arrival home. *Another good sign?*

Pastor Mark began passing the food around as Betty poured coffee, and soon the room filled with the soft clatter of silverware against plates and the mild chatter of people curious about how events might unfold.

Rose praised the commitment of the pastor and Betty to the members of the congregation. "I've only been here a few weeks, and I see that every minute of their days is dedicated to fostering love and kindness. They visit the sick and give food to the needy, and minister to the youth and the aged along with the Sunday sermons. On Saturday Pastor Mark teaches catechism to two different ages groups in the living room of the parsonage while Betty cleans and washes the place. It's the constant kindness—the way they treat everyone—that impresses me."

Mary noticed Pastor Mark shift in his chair. *The praise makes him uncomfortable. I don't doubt that he deserves it, though.*

"Well," Pastor Mark inserted, "the people here are so very kind and understanding to Betty and me. They take such good care of us. And as for me, sure, my job is to minister to my congregation, but being kind to people is a main part of my job, really. No one wants a mean pastor." He laughed softly before he added, "In my opinion, being kind and understanding to all of humanity is a clergy's number one job, really."

Martin smiled as he added, "And it would be a better world if all people, including all clergy, followed your lead on that, Pastor Mark."

"Hear, hear!" Pastor Mark exclaimed with sincerity. "Rose, you told me your brother was a straight shooter and a straight talker, but you didn't mention he was a strong humanitarian."

"Must've slipped my mind," Rose said wryly.

Martin laughed. "If you call me a humanitarian, I'd have to say I'm not a perfect one."

"None of us are," Pastor Mark said.

"I've been married to Martin for over sixteen years," Mary remarked, "and he still surprises me sometimes. And usually in a good way." *He seems to enjoy Pastor Mark's company. I guess we all do. John isn't saying much, though. But he never did talk much, except after he had a few beers. Then we all become motormouths. His chatter on the drive up was a real exception.* "Anyway," Mary added with a wide smile, "the kids and I keep him humble."

"You see," Martin joked, "with a witty wife, two teenagers, and an eleven-year-old at home, I'm not used to any praise."

"We understand that. Don't we, Betty?" Pastor Mark said. "We had two teenagers in the house too, but now they're both on their own, sort of. Linda and Laura are both working in Minneapolis and engaged to marry some great fellows."

"Congratulations! I'm sure you miss them," Mary offered.

"Of course," Betty said. "But the way of the world is to go forth and multiply, not stay home with Dad and Mom."

Mary looked over at Rose. *She seems somber. This talk about kids is probably not helping her. I need to change the subject.* "I'm looking forward to tasting one of Rose's pies."

"Right!" Rose said, and she got up to fetch the pies. As she set them on the table, she asked each guest their preference—apple or banana cream or a slice of each. Betty refilled the coffee cups as the guests raved about the food. They remained at the table as Betty offered them more coffee. On one side, Martin, Mary, and Pastor Mark discussed his work at the church, and although Mary found some difficulty in following the conversation across the wide dining room table, she understood they were discussing how helpful Rose had been during her stay.

Suddenly, Betty rose and remarked, "After we clear the table, I'll stack the dishes and do them later. Let us give you a tour of this old mansion we live in."

This tour, no surprise, was marked by too many people scrambling through doorways meant for one in an effort to see the same things at the same time. Predictably, the three women shifted into one group and the three men in another. While the women talked of furnishings, the men talked of the building's architecture, but both groups marveled at the size and the number of the rooms. When Betty opened the door to Rose's room, Mary noticed that her clothes were in the closet, not packed in a suitcase.

"Looks like a very comfy room," Mary remarked as she caught Betty giving a knowing look at Rose. "I suppose you have lots of room for guests."

"Especially if they are working guests, as Rose has been," Betty quipped. "Neither Mark nor I has time to care for a boarder."

After seeing countless bedrooms on the second floor and the large finished rooms in the attic, the group came back downstairs to see the three reception rooms and the utility room, which was part of a new addition. "With all the laundry I do for the church, the board was kind enough to build a first-floor laundry room. I love it."

"That way, they could leave the basement unfinished," Pastor Mark added. "There is so much venting from the furnace and pipes from bathroom plumbing that finishing it was unpractical. The addition added two more bathrooms, for a total of four, which is really handy with all the entertaining we do for the church."

"Why don't they do that in the church?" Martin asked.

"Good question," Pastor Mark said. "The church has limited space, but before we do any additions, we are examining how to preserve its architecture while adding a kitchen and a reception room for funerals and weddings. If we decide to do it in the basement, we will have to jack up the church and redo the whole foundation. If we do a first-floor add-on, we have to deal with architecture. It's a tough choice."

"And money factors into every decision," Betty said.

"The congregation is quite generous, and some are well off and willing to lead," Pastor Mark said. "But everyone on the board and in the congregation agrees that we want a new addition that is at least as grand as the church itself. The grand look doesn't come cheap."

Next, as they walked the path to the church, Martin commented on the natural beauty of the area. "Here you are among the trees, but you seem to be up high enough to have a view of distant hills."

"Yes," Betty said, "and in the fall the colors are spectacular—lots of white birch and aspen, some maple and oaks, all interspersed with greens of red pines and spruce!"

After entering the church through a side door, they toured the altar and the side rooms where little kids could be taken during the service. Mary especially liked the balcony, which presented an overview of the pews and stained-glass windows.

The walk back to the parsonage was filled with small talk about the drive up, and Betty explained the many trips Pastor Mark made around the area to fulfill his obligations. "He's gone so often. I was glad to have Rose's company and assistance with my work."

They stepped into the parsonage, and Betty ushered them back through the dining room.

"I think Rose wants us all to go to the living room to talk. It's after three o'clock already, and we have so much to tell you about her stay with us."

Mary heard her statement with a mixture of skepticism and fear. *Rose could tell us about her stay on the way back.*

Betty led them to the smaller of the two living rooms, where Rose was already seated on a red cushioned armchair and Betty indicated she and John would sit on a sofa on the left and Mary and Martin should sit on a similar sofa on the right. A tray of clean coffee cups and saucers was placed in the center of a small coffee table located between the sofas. Pastor Mark said from the doorway, "I'll be in the vegetable garden pulling some weeds."

Rose replied, "Please stay. I know you think it's family business, but I would really like you to stay."

Reluctantly, Pastor Mark closed the double doors behind him before he stepped over to sit in a red armchair located across from where Rose sat, completing the intimate, oblong-shaped seating arrangement for the six participants.

Five of them turned their attention to Rose, as if she were about to chair a meeting. Mary feared her hunch was right, but she remained silent, hoping for the best. She readied herself to listen as Rose cleared her throat and began.

"Thanks for this time with you. I hope you know that I love you all. Before I sent the letter to you, John, I had Betty read it. And I'm sure you shared it with Mary and Martin, right?"

Mary nodded along with the others but said nothing. *She seems to be struggling with this.*

"I wasn't sure what I wanted to do then, and I'm still not, so I need to talk with all of you. The real question for me now is, Where do I belong? I don't know where I'm wanted or if I'm wanted anywhere at all."

Mary glanced at John, whose astonished face and tense body reflected fear.

John answered, softly but emphatically, "I want you at home with me. You must know that!"

Rose shifted in her chair as her eyes teared. "Are you sure? I'm not the same person I was when you married me. I don't even know who I am anymore."

As Rose began to cry softly, John started to rise from the sofa to go to her, but Betty did not let go of her brother's hand. "Please, John," she said gently. "She wants you to stay by me."

Mary turned toward Martin, and as they exchanged shocked expressions, Mary caught Martin's whisper, "Never seen her so unsure of herself."

Pastor Mark got up from his chair. "I think we need to give Rose a few minutes. Cups and saucers are on the coffee table. Grab yourself one while I go get the pot of coffee."

CHAPTER 8

THE LAST RECESS

12:30 p.m., Saturday, July 14, 1956

Joey had spent the morning preparing for the day. First, he had made sandwiches with homemade bread sliced thick, just as he liked it, with lots of butter, and with minced ham or summer sausage sliced thick too. Instead of packing it in his Superman lunch bucket, he used the big black lunch pail his father used when he plowed late into the night in the fall. He filled the thermos with a mixture of lemon and lime Kool-Aid sweetened with a little sugar. Then he practiced batting. With his old bat—Maggie called it Hazel, a proper name for an old bat—he hit rocks against the barn, pretending he was batting at a real game. The game at the schoolyard was important to him. He'd show them he could not only dance but play ball, too. He had organized the gathering, and it was up to him to make it a success.

He had considered pulling the wagon to haul his gear, but it seemed too clumsy, and it made him look like a little kid. He discovered he could carry a couple of softballs and both his new and old gloves in the pillowcase that he'd used for trick-or-treating. He tied the pillowcase around the handle of his new bat so it wouldn't slide around, and he slung the bat over his shoulder and held the wide end. He carried the lunch pail in the other hand. Nothing was very heavy. He grabbed his favorite cap before he left for the schoolyard at 12:30. He felt like Huck Finn.

In ten minutes, the road took him past the end of Brummers' driveway. Wearing jeans, a flowered green blouse, and the kind of striped railroad cap that many farm kids wore, Liz Brummer came out to meet him, pulling a red wagon full of water jugs and big picnic baskets. Secretly, he had hoped she would be waiting for him. He liked her. She was never mysterious. She always blurted out what she felt.

"I knew you'd be the first to go by," she said as they set off, "so I filled my water jugs and waited for you. Mom made dozens of meat sandwiches too. It's going to be a fun day! Like a last recess for the country school. They're closing it, and next year we will all get bused to Rock River. Grades seven through twelve will be in the high school and grades one through six will be in little schools parked outside the big school. Most of the neighborhood kids in grades one through six will go to the Catholic school."

And there it was. In thirty seconds or less, Liz had said everything. This is why Joey liked her, even though she was a whole year and a half older than he was. "Yeah," he added, "they won't let us wear jeans or carry pocket-knives. Instead of recess, we'll dress in short pants for a physical education class and have a teacher pick our games. I won't like it much."

"Oh, we'll get used to it. We'll get to have a lot of different teachers. One for each subject."

"I got enough trouble getting used to one teacher. Now I'll have to deal with several."

"Oh, you'll do just fine. You're smart like your brother and sister."

How could a guy not like a person like Liz?

They pulled the wagon up the steep road bank onto the schoolyard and then toward the small ball field north of the school. The grass had grown tall during the last six weeks when no kids played there. But they knew that the grass and weeds would level off after an hour of foot traffic. It always did.

Soon, the Schoen, Fischer, and Haber kids came from the west. Robert and James Schoen were cousins and a year older than Joey, but Ronnie was in Joey's grade and his best friend. Robert said his three little sisters didn't want to come. Jerome and Ralph Schoen came too, even though they had complet-ed eighth grade in the country school a year ago. All of the Schoen boys wore jeans and short-sleeved shirts, with high-top everyday shoes on their feet and striped or solid blue caps on their heads. Hand-me-down shirts were easy to spot—either the shirt was clearly too big for the boy or the boy was getting too big for the shirt. This spring's fifth grader, Paul Haber, and the Fischer kids were dressed similar to the Schoens. Patrick Fischer had finished the third grade this spring, Ed the fourth, and Janet the fifth. Paul said his younger brother and sister weren't coming, but with so many older kids showing up, Joey was excited to think maybe they'd have enough for two teams.

Tom Ryan came driving his family's WD Allis-Chalmers, pulling a wagonload of kids, a few picnic baskets of food, and another bat. He took the key out of the tractor and gave it to his sister Peggy, who acted pretty cocky because she'd driven his car, a light-green 1951 Dodge.

"Drive the tractor home when the game is over," Tom said. "I probably won't be back." Then he got in his car and left. Mary Ryan, Katherine O'Keran, and four Shaurel girls—Ann, Mary, Margaret, and Caroline—all wore jeans and short-sleeved blouses, but only the Shaurel girls wore work shoes and caps. Mary Ryan and Katherine O'Keran wore black-and-white tennis shoes and went hatless, with their hair tied back. As the girls eagerly jumped off the wagon, Joey grew even more excited about all the people showing up for the ball game.

All of the kids came dressed to play ball except for Ann Shaurel and Peggy Ryan, who each wore tan dress slacks, white tennis shoes, and a solid-colored blouse—red for Ann and green for Peggy.

"I just came to watch," Ann explained to Joey. "I know I'm the oldest one here."

"Me too," Peggy Ryan said. "I just want to watch. Joey made it clear the game was only for this year's eighth grade and younger. But Ralph and Jerome are going into the tenth grade. Maybe they shouldn't be allowed to play either."

"If we were on opposing teams," Ralph said, "that would make it fair. We'd like to play. What do you think, Joey? It's your game."

Proud of his role in the decision, Joey said, "Without Ann and Peggy, we have sixteen, enough for two teams of eight if Jerome and Ralph play. As long as they're not on the same team, it would be fair."

"Make them team captains!" Ann exclaimed.

"Perfect!" Peggy shouted.

"Good idea!" Joey exclaimed. He climbed on the hayrack to announce, "Thanks for coming, everyone! I didn't expect this many people. I thought we just might have enough kids to play workup or something, but we have enough for two teams. Since this is like the last recess, we need to have the oldest one here set it up. That's Ann."

"Okay, Joey, but it's your idea and I'm not playing, so you need to approve of my ideas before we go ahead with them."

Joey expected a little flak from the older boys, but Ralph and Jerome nodded in agreement.

Ann began. "If Ralph and Jerome agree to be captains, they should flip a coin to see who chooses first."

"I agree," Joey said. After the two boys agreed, he asked, "Who has a coin?"

"No one brings money to the country school," Peggy Ryan groaned.

Everyone laughed as several kids muttered, "Yeah, there's nothing for sale out here."

"Okay," Ann said, "whoever rolls the ball closest to home plate from the pitcher's mound without going past it gets to decide who chooses first. Ralph, you roll first."

The rolls were both close, but Ralph won, and the selection began.

Ralph: "I choose Robert Schoen."

Jerome: "James Schoen."

Ralph: "Joey."

Jerome: "Ronnie."

Ralph: "Margaret Shaurel."

Jerome: "Katherine O'Keran."

Ralph: "Mary Shaurel."

Jerome: "Mary Ryan."

Ralph: "Liz Brummer."

Jerome: "Paul Haber."

Ralph: "Caroline Shaurel."

Jerome: "Janet Fischer."

Ralph: "Ed Fischer."

Jerome: "Patrick Fischer."

Ann stood on the hay rack and announced, "First, I just want to say to those of you who were chosen last, there is no shame in it. Every single one of us here has been through the experience of being chosen last." Groans from the players indicated they agreed.

Ann continued, "The players bat in the order selected. There are no called strikes or balls. To get on base, a runner has to hit the ball or be hit by the ball to earn a walk. To strike out, the batter must swing and miss three times. Close calls on a tag go to the runner, and we must all try to be fair on recognizing when we are out. In the field, the team captain always pitches. Catchers can be replaced by the pitcher or any fielder on a throw to home plate." She looked at Joey. "Did I cover everything?"

"Perfect," Joey said. "I'll just add that we play to seven innings and we do no extra innings if we tie. But, Ann, how about if you be our umpire from behind the pitcher? You wouldn't call balls and strikes, but just call safe or out on the bases. We will all get too excited to be fair about that."

"Jeez, Joey. I don't know. I hate to make a bunch of enemies."

"What does everyone else think?"

Calls from the group supported Ann as umpire. Both captains agreed. Joey added, "Ann, we trust you. Please."

"Wait a minute," Peggy protested. "Ann gets to be part of the game and I don't!"

"Come on, Peggy," Mary Ryan said. "You're too dressed up to play! And you're too old to be a crybaby."

"Yeah," chimed in Mary Shaurel, "you haven't changed a bit."

As others laughed and chanted, "Peggy's still a crybaby," Joey sensed some bad old feelings between kids surfacing. But what could he do about it? *Can't let our last recess turn into a big argument! I got an idea.*

"What if we made her everlasting pitcher?" Joey suggested. "I mean, the whole goal is to let the batter hit the ball, since no balls or strikes are called. She could throw nice pitches to both sides and field the ball for both sides fairly. She's a good fielder. I trust her."

"But maybe you don't want to get your good clothes dirty," Ann said to Peggy. "We'd all understand that."

"Not a big deal," Peggy said immediately.

"So, I'd trust her to be fair too," Ann said in support. "Anyone disagree?"

After no one protested, Ann said, "With Peggy pitching, we have enough players for all the field positions! Okay, Ralph's team chose first, so Jerome's team bats first. Take the field!"

Ralph assigned the positions. "Ed, catcher; Robert, first base; Liz, second; I'll be shortstop; Margaret Shaurel, third base; Mary Shaurel, left field; Joey, center field; Caroline, right field. All of you, be sure to call it if you are close so you don't run into each other. I still have a bump from our last game in May. Does everyone have a glove? Okay, gang, let's get them out."

After they were in position, Ann announced, "Play ball." And the fun began.

Jerome Schoen led off with a home run, hitting the ball over the woven-wire fence and into the alfalfa field beyond center field. His cousins James and Ronnie each hit the ball to center field, but James hit the ball to deep center, making Joey run and jump to catch it, preventing another home run. Next up, Ronnie hit the ball to short center, where Joey had to run toward the infield to catch the ball before it dropped in for a hit. With two out, the first inning was not looking good for Jerome's team, but the next three hitters got on base, and then Janet Fischer hit a drive right over the head of shortstop Ralph, who vowed he would never play her up close again. Then Pat, Jerome, and James got on, and Ronnie hit a home run, making the score 9 to 0. Katherine O'Keran hit a hard bouncer to short, which Ralph fielded and threw to Robert at first to retire the side.

With his team now up to bat, Ralph shouted praises to all his teammates. To Joey he said, "Way to cover short center field and deep center field, Joey. You're fast. That's why I put you out there." Then he shouted to his team, "Now we need to get lots of runs! We can do it!"

Like his cousin Jerome, Ralph led off with a home run. Then Robert hit a double and Joey hit a home run. With no outs and three runs scored, Ralph's team had hopes of catching their rivals. Margaret and Mary Shaurel each hit hard drives back at the pitcher, but Peggy fielded them like a pro and threw both girls out at first base. The three batters at the bottom of the lineup got on base, and Ralph brought them in with a home run, taking his team up to seven runs. Robert and Joey got on base, and Margaret Shaurel brought them home with a short fly to center that dropped in for a hit. Mary Shaurel got on base with a hit, and Liz Brummer hit a drive over the first base that brought both of the Shaurel twins home. Caroline got on base with a short fly over second base, but Katherine O'Keran caught Ed Fischer's low fly to left to leave both Liz and Caroline on base and end the first inning with Ralph's team leading 11 to 9.

Before his team took the field, Ralph asked Jerome, "Want to play two more innings before we eat lunch?"

"Good idea," Jerome responded as team members from both sides cheered the decision.

After the fielders were in place, the second inning began, and the next two innings featured lots of hits and mostly good fielding from both teams. By the end of the third inning, Ralph's team led 25 to 24 and everyone agreed it was time to eat lunch. Joey and Liz shared their sandwiches, and Shaurels shared a huge bag of popcorn and two two-gallon jugs of Kool-Aid that Ann had made. Ryans and O'Kerans had brought enough cupcakes for everyone. Schoens brought cookies, and Fischers brought two jars of homemade strawberry jam and two loaves of store-bought bread. Paul Haber brought a pan of brownies.

The kids hungrily dug into the food as they kidded each other about errors in the game—missed fly balls, overthrows at first, or ground balls that swiftly passed between an infielder's legs. The younger children were spared the razzing, but the older players made fun of their own follies as well the errors of others their age. But praise was dished out too.

Ann proclaimed, "I've not seen any pitchers handle the balls hit right back to her any better than Peggy did. Wow! Quick thinking. As ump all I can do is get out of the way."

Everyone agreed Peggy fielded the balls fairly, and Joey added, "Ann is calling the bases right too."

"It's a pretty high-scoring game so far," James said.

"And not having the real little kids play with us makes it a lot more fun," Joey remarked. "We don't have to all slow down while the pitcher rolls them a grounder."

"Yeah," James said, "that really slows down a game while we have to stand around watching some little kid hit a grounder."

"Makes the scoring unfair too," Joey added.

"Hey," Ralph said, "don't be so cocky, you two. We were all there in first grade once, and we were lucky the teacher made us all play together."

"Heck, yes!" Peggy claimed. "And Joey, how does it make the scoring unfair if each side always had the same number of little kids who were pitched grounders? It doesn't."

"Well, sometimes it can," Joey countered, "if a little kid is getting grounders when a team has kids on base and they don't score."

"No different than when a big kid who is a poor hitter is up to bat when kids are on base," Peggy argued.

"Give up while you still have some pride," Ann said as she chuckled. "You know you can't win an argument with Peggy."

Feeling the pressure of his peers to be quiet, Joey tried to change the subject. "Well, with just the big kids, we get lots more action and scores. More fun, I think."

"You mean big kids like you, young fella," Peggy teased.

"I mean the kids in the older grades," Joey muttered in an attempt to save face.

"Come on, Peggy," Ann said, "give the kid a break. After all, the whole game today was his idea."

"Okay, okay," Peggy agreed. "I just like picking on Joey. I'd sooner pick on Jimmy, but he isn't here. I need to add one thing for sure that's true: As the dedicated pitcher, I'm giving good pitches to every batter, which makes it a hitters' game and causes more action than a game where the pitcher takes time to try to strike out batters with poor pitches or close strikes. Also, a hitters' game gives the fielders a chance to handle the ball. So, I agree with Joey. Today's more fun than recess."

Jerome said, "Katherine, I can't believe how fast you got under that low fly ball to left field. That was a great catch."

Katherine smiled, but added in a burst of honest humility, "Colleen was the fast one in the family. I could never catch up to her."

"She was the fastest runner in school ever since she got to the seventh grade or so," Ann said with authority. "Your brother was almost as fast, Joey, but he was two years younger than Colleen."

"Jimmy used to brag about how fast John Ryan was," Joey said, "but according to him the best all-around player was Al Rosincek. He finished the eighth grade before I started school."

"Yeah," Ann reminisced, "and Al didn't let the big kids pick on the rest of us, either. Even Jack Drude didn't mess with Al."

Hearing Jack's name put a damper on spirited conversation, as if each one of the children was privately reliving their own Jack Drude nightmare.

Finally, Joey said, "Not all the memories from the country school were good ones, but I wish I were going to school here through the eighth grade instead of getting bused to town."

"Oh, it's not so bad," Ralph asserted. "Even me and Jerome made it through the ninth grade. So I think anyone can."

Everyone chuckled as he added, "The bus ride is a big waste of time, though."

Heads nodded, and Ronnie Schoen said, "Not everything was so sweet in the country school, either. Some bad memories, all right. Not many as bad as our first day of school, Joey. Worse for you than me. Remember what happened?"

Joey looked down and smiled, "Are you kidding? I'll never forget it."

"I remember it too," Ann said. "It was a bad day for you, but it turned out bad for the teacher in the long run."

Sensing that the group was looking to him for the story, and realizing that the younger kids might not have heard it yet, Joey sat on the edge of the hayrack, letting his feet dangle over the side, and began his tale. "You probably won't believe it when you see me now, but I was kind of an ornery kid."

Laughs from most of the older kids reinforced Joey's confidence.

"Oh, we believe it all right!" shouted Ralph.

"Come on, Joey, you had a short temper, but I liked you right away," Ronnie claimed. "And we had just met that day for the first time. That's why it all started. I was just trying to be friendly."

"Okay, okay," Joey said. "Anyway, I was five years old and excited about starting school. On visitors' day in May, Maggie and Jimmy had taken me in to meet the teacher, Mrs. Lynstad, and we got along just fine. She thought I would be okay to start in the fall, although I could've waited a year because I wouldn't be six until December twenty-seventh. Well, guess what? When I started that fall, Mrs. Lynstad wasn't there. She'd been replaced by a new teacher, Miss McHone.

"So, she assigns seats and I'm in the front and Ronnie's behind me, and he kind of tickles my neck with his finger a couple of times. So, I turn around and yell, 'Stop that!' and Miss McHone is over there faster than a bullet, saying something like, 'No one yells in my classroom,' and she said something about making an example of me. In a second, she picks me up by my shirt collar with one hand and the seat of my bib overall with the other and carries me down the aisle to the cloakroom, where she holds me by the seat of my pants with one hand, opens the door handle with the other, and then grabs me with both hands again as she kicks the door open and tosses me as far as she can, like you might throw out a pan of wash water. I landed hard on that piece of grassless clay a couple of yards from the door."

"You were only five?" Janet Fischer asked. "How can you remember all that?"

"You don't forget something like that," Joey said. "My arm got all scratched up from the sharp little rocks on the hard ground."

"Did it hurt, Joey?" Janet Fischer asked.

"Heck, yes! I cried like the dickens, but mostly because I was so darn ashamed. As she was carrying me down the aisle, all I could see were the faces of kids laughing. I was so ashamed that I crawled into the woodshed behind a bunch of desks so no one could find me. I hid there the rest of the day."

"I have to add a couple of things, Joey," Ann said. "Everyone here that is older than you remembers how much we liked Mrs. Lynstad. She was tough, but fair, and she did a pretty good job of keeping the bad apples in line, like Jack Drude. She'd been around a long time. The new teacher had never taught anywhere before. It was her first day of school too. She was probably scared as heck when she saw all those big, rough-looking boys who were to be her students."

"But, jeez," Liz broke in, "Joey was five. You'd think she could have handled it better."

"I agree," Ann added quickly. "I'm not making excuses for her, but she was green. I was in the sixth grade then, and I remember it like yesterday because I was sitting in the front row by the teacher's desk. Mary Schroedler sat one row over to my right, and Jimmy sat behind her. Maggie sat in front, two rows over to my right. I could see Jimmy and Maggie get so mad that I thought they were going to jump out of their desks. Jimmy told Maggie to stay in her desk, and he headed toward the door to find Joey, but Miss McHone met him in the aisle and pushed him back to his seat. By this time the kids were all over the room. Some were looking out of the windows to see Joey. Most of them had quit laughing and were concerned about Joey. Finally, Jimmy just ignored the teacher and went to find him when she was trying to settle the others down. In a few minutes, Jimmy came back and told everyone that Joey was in the woodshed behind the desks and wouldn't come out. The teacher tried to go on with issuing books and stuff, but from that day on, the kids were all against her. She only lasted a couple weeks before they replaced her with an experienced teacher, Mrs. Anfin. She was old, but everyone liked her."

"Yeah, the kids never seemed to forgive Miss McHone for mistreating one of us," Peggy Ryan said.

"Right," Ann added. "We didn't really plan on sticking together, but I guess we all did. Our goal was to get rid of Miss McHone."

Ralph confessed softly, "I like how we all stuck together. Even Jack Drude stuck up for Joey."

"Sure, but those older boys used to put new kids through some pretty rough initiations," Ann declared.

"They sure did," Peggy said. "My brother John said that when he and Jack Drude started first grade, a couple of seventh and eighth graders tossed them into Brummers' culvert and chased the pigs over them."

"Dad got really mad when he heard about that," Liz said. "He said that the culvert gives the pigs a safe way to get to the hog lot on other side of the road. Chasing them over the kids could injure the hogs and the kids. We kidded him about being more concerned about the hogs than the kids."

As the players all laughed at this, Ann suggested, "Maybe kids aren't as mean as they used to be."

The kids smiled at the thought. At that moment, a black '52 Chevy turned into the driveway of the school. It sped past the schoolhouse toward the kids, who jumped out of the way. The driver stopped the car with the front bumper just a few feet from the side of the hayrack, which was still laden with food and drink.

Joey looked to Ann. "Who are they?"

"Troublemakers," Ann whispered.

CHAPTER 9

HELPING OUT

1:00 p.m., Saturday, July 14, 1956

"I've followed Jerry's napkin map," Jimmy said as he paused the car at the end of a driveway, "and I'd say that the name *Weber* painted on the mailbox in white letters erases any doubt about the place being the correct destination." He steered the blue Ford west into the short driveway, which brought them to the yard in seconds. As he stopped the car, a barking black-and-white dog of mixed breeds warily ran toward the car from the barn area. "Stay in the car until he calms down little and we get our bearings."

The three searchers eyed the place from the safety of the car. The light-yellow two-story house was bordered by a thick stand of trees on the north and west, but the steady *clackety-clack* of the power-take-off shaft of a WD Allis-Chalmers drew their attention to an elevator on the other side of the yard. There, on a flatbed loaded with hay bales, a woman and a teenage girl, both wearing blue long-sleeved shirts and bib overalls and caps on their heads, were busy lugging hay bales to the apron at the base of the elevator, which carried them to the hayloft about twenty-five feet above. Although they seemed to have noticed the car in the yard, the two women kept working.

Maggie said the obvious: "Looks like they're hauling bales, all right."

Jimmy pulled on the leather strap attached to his pocket watch. "It's a little after one o'clock now," he said brightly. "I figure we can make it home in a little over an hour and a half. So, we got time to help them haul bales, and if we do, maybe they'll be more likely to tell us if they know anything about Mary. We'll easily get home by six."

"We'd better," Maggie said.

"Don't worry, we will," Jimmy assured her before he turned to look out the window. "The dog looks fairly calm, but we need to wait till they're done unloading." While everyone settled in to wait, Jimmy commented, "Nice barn, and I can't get over how level the land is out here. South of the barn, I can see a piece of the cow yard and a lane that probably leads to a pasture where the land is too low to farm. Nice land. Nice barn. Nice house."

"Don't be breaking a commandment by coveting thy neighbor's farm," Maggie said as she elbowed his ribs.

"Not coveting, not coveting! But I am imagining how I would love farming a grand place like this one."

"Good for you," Robert said. "A guy has to dream big."

Maggie added, "Yeah, Dad always discouraged us from farming for a living, but I've heard him tell Jimmy many times"—she lowered her voice to imitate her father—"'Jimmy, if you got to farm, get a good farm, not some hilly rockpile like the one we have.' I think this one would qualify."

"How did your folks end up with the farm they have?"

"That's a long story," Jimmy said. "Another time."

Robert mused, "Maybe when God was handing out farms, they thought he said *charms*, so they asked for a . . . sorry, I've got nothing. No, wait, wait. Maybe when God was handing out hills, they thought he said *thrills*, so they asked for a lot of big ones."

"That doesn't explain the rocks," Maggie said.

"The dog is standing by my door, ready to ambush me," Jimmy said. "He's big, but he's wagging his tail. You guys stay here. I'll step out of the car."

"That's my brother," Maggie said sarcastically, "always willing to do something stupid to be the hero."

Jimmy stepped out, crooning, "Good doggie. Nice puppy. Did we disturb your nap?" The dog moved in to sniff Jimmy, who stood still and continued his soothing talk.

The flatbed was now clear of bales, and the older woman jumped off to disengage the power to the elevator before she shut off the tractor. She removed her gloves as she strutted toward the newcomers.

Jimmy saw blond hair tucked under her cap, and an image of Mary Schroedler popped into his head to briefly hold him speechless. This lady was in her thirties and taller than Mary, with a wiry build and long, confident stride. Although her voice was friendly, she made it clear she was in charge of the moment. Jimmy decided he liked her even before she spoke.

"Hello, I'm Dory. I see you've already made friends with Cookie. He's not much of a watchdog, but he's sweet." She stopped a few yards away and continued, "If I can help you with directions or something, let me know. We're in kind of a pinch. We've still got almost five hundred bales on the ground out there, and we don't have a lot of time to get them in." She pointed to dark clouds that hung low on the western sky.

"Well . . ." Jimmy stalled a little as a man and a boy exited the barn door and walked toward them. "I'm Jimmy Carlson, and this is my sister, Maggie, and our friend Robert. I think we're at the right place. You see, we met a young man at the DQ—name was Jerry Weber. He said he was off to the Army and that he hated to leave his family when they had bales on the ground. He asked us to come and help. In turn, he said you might know where a friend of ours is that we're looking for."

"You met Jerry at the DQ?" Dory asked with some doubt in her voice.

Jimmy shook his head and was about to answer when the man reached them. "I'm Tom Weber. Dory is our hardworking neighbor, and that's my son John. He's twelve. That's my daughter, Jean. She's thirteen, and she likes to be called Rusty because of her hair. Same color as her momma's hair. She's not helping because she's due to have a baby soon. Anytime, really."

"That's what Jerry told us. Anyway, loan us some gloves and put us to work. Caps too, if you have them, to keep the sun and my hair out of my eyes."

Tom smiled. "I don't think I've ever had my prayers answered so fast. John, get these kids some gloves and find some caps that fit them. Dory, can we use your Jubilee Ford?"

"Of course, I'll run through the windbreak to get it. Be back in a jiff."

"That way we can leave the WD on the elevator and leave the Oliver hitched to the baler. Saves time. Hitch your Jubilee to the other flatbed," Tom yelled after Dory as she ran off. "Rusty, you drive the Farmall H that's hitched to this wagon, and Maggie, you'll drive the Jubilee. Dory and John will stack bales in the hayloft, and Robert will help the driver unload. We'll run two wagons and make a hell of a dent in the job before it rains. Let's go load!" As he hoisted himself up to sit on the edge of the empty flatbed, he added, "Oh, yeah, and Jimmy, you and I will load and stack the wagon from the ground. We'll see if those muscles of yours are just for show or if your daddy taught you how to work."

Loving the challenge, Jimmy remarked, "Yeah, he did, and my momma did too." He hustled to claim a spot beside Tom on the wagon before Rusty started the tractor and headed for the other end of the field.

Earlier that day, Mary had spotted activity in the hayfield west of Webers' farmyard, which was directly south of her attic room in Dory's house and only thirty yards beyond the two white stones. With her binoculars, she watched Tom bale hay as she listened to the baler's plunger hammer the hay into perfectly shaped bales. When she tired of the predictable scene, she tried to go back to reading Dickens's Victorian novel *Oliver Twist*, but for the moment, her mind was numb to the struggles of the child protagonist because images of the two round white gravestones displaced that historic prose. *Why does Dory have the stones where she and I can see them daily? Her bedroom is below mine. I need to ask her some time.*

Dory had warned her there would be such times, when guilt and sadness about her miscarriage would seek control of her heart and her mind. Dory understood because the first of the two stones was for her own baby, a secret she had shared with Mary on the night of her arrival last February. A week or so later Dory had loaned her a book of poetry by Robert Frost, and Mary recalled her aunt's words: "Not a perfect man by any measure, but wisdom seldom comes from those who are perfect." Mary had not read much poetry, and what she had read hadn't encouraged her to read more, but Dory's description of Frost intrigued her: "He had tried to farm, but he wasn't very good at it."

Then Dory had opened the book to the poem "Home Burial" and given her a note, which Mary kept to mark the page. Although she had read the note many times, Mary picked up the book and silently read the note again.

Dear Mary,

Read this poem when you start thinking about our babies and you feel alone and like no one understands you. Lots of people feel that way, so you are not alone. Robert Frost has lost his wife and four of their six children, one just three days after the child was born. So, he understands loss, and he understands the pain and guilt that come after losing a child. The poem isn't so much about him as it is about anger between a husband and wife who don't understand each other. I want you to know that I understand you, and I think you understand me too. Together, we are never alone.

Love,

Aunt Dorothea

Mary had read "Home Burial" several times over the past months, and she hesitated before she began reading it again. *The poem is long, but I don't have to finish it.* But she read until she felt the pain and frustration of the man and wife in the poem, and somehow, her own pain decreased.

Suddenly she realized that she no longer heard the baler's rhythmic strokes. Mary returned to the south window, and when she saw her neighbors in the field loading bales, she wished she could help them. She longed to work outside with others, but staying hidden was her duty to herself and to her aunt. Only Rusty knew she lived with Dory, and it needed to stay that way for a while.

She easily recognized Dory and the three Webers on the first load. Keeping a safe distance from the window so none of them could see her, she kneeled on a pillow out of the light, focusing her binoculars on each of their faces in turn as they worked.

When the Webers returned for another load, Dory was no longer with them. Instead, a man sat on the wagon alongside Tom, and as Rusty sped down the field, Mary focused her binoculars to try to identify the stranger. Suddenly she gasped and exclaimed too loudly, "My God, it's Jimmy!"

I hope no one heard me. No, they're too far away.

As Rusty turned the rig around to drive east, Tom said to Jimmy, "Thanks for coming to help. Normally, we pull the flatbed behind the baler and load as we bale. But with the storm coming, I thought I'd better get it all baled fast and just drop them on the ground. Makes more work, but the hay is safer in the bale if it rains only a day or so. Those storm clouds are probably two or three hours away at most."

"You can see storms coming a long way off around here," Jimmy offered. "Where we're from, about twenty miles south of the Cities, you don't see the storm until it's nearly on top of you."

As they drove past the windbreak, Tom pointed to a large white house north of the field. "That's Dory's house. Can't see it from our place, though."

Jimmy nodded as he looked over the close treetops to view the house. "Not very far away."

"No, our property line is only a little more than one hundred feet from her house. The few trees you see are on our land, not hers. She's such a great neighbor. We're lucky she lives so close."

Jimmy nodded.

"We'll start loading from the far end of the field so she ends up near the barn with the full load. That saves travel time."

When they reached the west end of the field, Rusty turned the tractor east to face home and the men began loading. "Try not to stop, Rusty," Tom hollered. "We'll keep up to you. Jerry wouldn't have sent this kid out here if he were a slacker." And he laughed.

Jimmy enjoyed the fast pace and the challenge of stacking the heavy bales tightly on the flatbed so as to withstand the bouncing ride across the field. Tom was a little taller than Jimmy, giving him an advantage when stacking from the ground, but he was not a match for Jimmy's speed, strength, or stamina. Tom was in his forties and fit, but when either of them loaded a bale that needed adjusting to be neatly stacked, only Jimmy could hop onto the flatbed, stack the bale, and jump down in time to load his next one from the ground.

Mary followed Jimmy's movements from her window, drawing pleasure from watching him work. *He moves so fast! But he never loses his usual swagger. Anyone can spot him a mile away.* She giggled a little and adjusted her binoculars for a better view. But as Rusty drove the flatbed east, the Webers' windbreak soon cut off her view. *I can sit here and wait for the next load.*

She didn't have to wait long before Dory's Jubilee came speeding to the west end of the field with Tom and Jimmy riding along. She focused her binoculars on the driver. "It's Maggie! What a sight for my sore, lonely eyes!"

Mary wanted to jump up and down, but she controlled herself as she focused on Jimmy again. *How he makes the work look so easy. He looks like he's talking to Tom as he works. What if I just went to the edge of the field and stood behind one of those trees? No, I can probably see better from here without being seen myself. So, what if they did see me? I could explain to Maggie and Jimmy. They wouldn't tell anyone. But Tom doesn't know about me. Damn!*

Although Mary took great pleasure in watching her two friends, her frustration grew, and she had to step away from the window. She tried to write about the moment in her journal, but after beginning the entry twice, she ripped out the page and threw it across the room before throwing herself face down on the bed. *Jimmy and Maggie are right outside my window! And all I can do is stay here.* Still, she allowed herself to smile as she rolled onto her back and recalled the days when she would sit on Maggie's bed and talk and plan with her. *They must want to see me. They drove all this way. What would Dory want me to do? Stay hidden, that's for sure.* She closed her eyes tightly. *Does Jimmy remember our kiss? I do. I can feel it!*

Suddenly, she jumped up, admonishing herself in a whisper, "Mary Schroedler, you are pathetic. Not worthy of their friendship or love. What if Jack Drude finds me because of them or hurts them to try to find me? Or what if I went to jail? How would that make Dory feel, or Jimmy or Maggie? They'd probably feel guilty about it."

Despite her frustration, she returned to the window, drawn by her need to see her friends. But when she focused her binoculars to see them return for another load, she exclaimed, "Where's Tom? Jimmy is loading alone, and the guy on the wagon is Robert!"

Although curious as to what happened to Tom, she lost herself in watching Jimmy run from one side of the wagon to the other, throwing on bales without asking for the driver to stop. *They look like they're having fun. I think they're laughing!*

She moved closer to the window and into the light. Suddenly, her eyes caught Rusty's arm returning to the steering wheel from what must have been a wave and Jimmy looking in her direction. She slid back from the window, brushing the curtain as she pulled away from the binoculars. *Did Jimmy see her wave at me? Did Jimmy catch sight of me in the window? Jeez, Rusty!*

As Rusty dropped her hand back to the steering wheel of the Farmall, Jimmy's eyes followed her gaze toward the north, where the curtain in an attic dormer window swayed slightly. *A ghost in the attic? I must tell Mags. She'll love to hear of my conversion.*

Then the next bale was within reach, and he shifted back to loading as fast as he could. He shouted to Robert, "The storm clouds are coming fast!"

"How many loads are left?" Robert asked.

"After this load, we'll probably load Maggie's rig one more time. Then, when Rusty returns and we load her flatbed, that will clear the field."

"Losing Tom slows us down some," Jimmy said.

"Yeah," Robert said, "but a baby waits for no one. He was pretty happy when you told him we would stay while he took his wife to the hospital."

"Yeah, they left in a hurry, but if John helps each driver put the bales in the elevator, Dory can stack them in the barn alone, like she said. And if she gets behind, we'll stack the piles later. She's quite the worker. Reminds me of my mom."

"She seemed to think I couldn't stack from the ground like Tom and you do," Robert said, feigning hurt feelings.

"Want to try it?" Jimmy asked seriously.

"Hell, no!" Robert said. "I've got nothing to prove."

The two boys laughed. "We make a great crew!" Jimmy crowed. "And look how good Rusty is at handling that Farmall!"

The compliment was just a casual comment, but Jimmy noticed when Rusty looked down, smiled, and almost giggled. *Cute kid. Too bad she's only thirteen.*

Then he checked the sky and turned back to loading bales. It was now a frantic race as the dark clouds moved in from the west with increasing speed.

Maggie and John had their flatbed ready to leave as Rusty pulled her load up to the elevator. As Jimmy and Robert hastily took their places on the flatbed, Jimmy hollered, "The storm is a-coming! Give it more gas, Mags. We'll hang on tight!"

When they reached the field, Robert yelled to Jimmy, "Let's both load this one. One of us can jump on the rack to stack as needed."

"I'm so proud of you, Planet!"

They loaded in record time. Rusty and John worked faster too, and they had their flatbed ready to leave as Maggie arrived at the elevator.

"Let's go, Rusty!" Jimmy shouted as he and Robert jumped onto the flatbed to repeat their run. "Double time on this one, Robert, and drive a little faster, Rusty. We've got to load this in record time."

Rusty pulled the loaded rig up to the elevator just as a strong wind blew dust and leaves toward them, announcing the storm's arrival.

At a sharp flash of lightning, Jimmy shouted, "Everyone, get in the hayloft! Stay clear of the elevator. I'll be sending these bales up as fast as I can pitch them in."

"I'll stay to help, Jimmy," Rusty volunteered.

"No, get in the barn. The lightning likes to strike elevators."

But Jimmy didn't argue when she stayed to help, and the two of them unloaded the wagon at top speed. When only half a dozen bales remained on the flatbed, Jimmy ordered, "Get in the barn, Rusty. I'll wait here to stop the tractor when the last bale drops."

The wall of rain missed Rusty just as she closed the barn door behind her, but Jimmy's clothes and body were soaked in the few minutes he took to finish up. Crawling up to the hayloft with the others, he boasted, "I love it! The water is so cool! I'm soaked and it feels good!"

For ten minutes, the workers sat on the bales, enjoying the fresh, damp air blowing into the barn through the large haymow door where the elevator poked through. The dense rainfall cut visibility to nearly zero as they stared out the door, each worker proud of their part in completing the task.

Dory spoke first. "Thanks to you guys, we saved Webers' hay. What a day!"

"A fun time," Jimmy said. "If we didn't live so far away, we'd love to do it again."

"Speak for yourself," Robert said and laughed. "No, I agree. I had fun."

John stayed quiet but smiled when Rusty whispered something to Maggie that made them both giggle.

Dory said, "I know Katy was preparing a big supper before she left, even though she was moving pretty slow. She had a hamburger hot dish in the oven and some vegetables cooked and ready to warm up. Rusty baked a two-layer chocolate cake this morning too. It's awful early to eat supper, but we may as well eat it now. I'm sure we're all hungry.

"This rain will probably continue for a long time. I say we all walk to the house and let the soft water rinse off the hay dust. We all need to wash up before we eat anyway."

The six workers scrambled out of the hayloft, bursting out of the barn door and into the rain. Removing their caps and gloves, they giggled and screamed as they scrubbed themselves with the cool rainwater. Maggie was the first to run for the house, with Rusty close behind. Dory stripped down to her bra and bibs and the boys took off their shirts to enjoy the moment.

Once in the house, they took turns washing up and drying off in the bathroom before Dory and Rusty laid the table. The six hungry workers chowed down, consuming many glasses of lemonade and milk and plates of food.

At the offer of a second piece of cake, Jimmy proclaimed, "Heck, yes! I'd be glad to drive up here anytime for another piece of Rusty's cake."

Maggie elbowed Rusty in the ribs as they both giggled.

As they finished eating dessert, the hard rain diminished to a drizzle. Maggie produced the eighth-grade photograph of Mary and passed it to Dory.

"Here's the girl we're looking for. She was in the eighth grade in the picture, but she'll be seventeen in October. The picture was taken nearly three years ago."

Dory examined the photograph closely before saying, "Pretty girl! I haven't seen anyone like her in town. Have you, Rusty?"

Rusty scrutinized the photo carefully before somberly shaking her head and proclaiming, "She's really pretty." After she passed the photo to her brother, she asked, "Is she your girlfriend, Jimmy?"

Jimmy smiled. Unsure how to answer without lying, he hesitated before saying, "Well, not anymore, I guess." He thought Rusty seemed to like that answer.

Maggie stepped in to explain, "They were childhood sweethearts ever since they were in the first grade. And she was my best friend ever since I started school. We both miss her."

Sensing some uneasiness among his hosts, Jimmy said, "It's after four o'clock, and we need to get home by six. We'd better get going. We have a long drive ahead of us and chores to do when we get home."

John announced that the rain had stopped, and as Dory and the Weber kids walked the guests to the car, the sun produced a rainbow.

"Maybe that means good luck on the way home," Dory suggested.

"Then it hasn't started yet," Robert said. "The back tire is flat on the car, Jimmy."

"Jeez," Jimmy said. "That's the one we just replaced on the way to town. We don't have a spare."

"Look," Dory said, "you take off the tire while I walk to my place to get my pickup. Then I'll run you and your tires into town to get both of them fixed right away. You don't want to head home without a spare. I know the guys at the station, and they'll do it while we wait if I ask them to." She stepped off toward her place, saying, "See you in a bit."

When the rain had begun to pound hard on the attic roof, Mary had gone downstairs to get a snack, thinking, *They're probably in the house eating now, but I can't go over there. Too many people other than just Jimmy and Maggie. Too risky.* After the rain stopped, Mary remained at the kitchen table, although she knew she should return to her attic refuge.

Suddenly, Dory thrust open the kitchen door and blurted, "I'm sure you were watching our visitors when they loaded hay. Be careful they don't see you. They have to leave now, but their car has a flat and their spare is flat. I'm taking the boy to town to get the tires fixed. I figure Lugwrench will do it for me right away, and they need to get on the road. Oh, and Rusty is riding along. She has kind of a crush on the on the boy named Jimmy."

Dory kissed Mary on the forehead and rushed out the door to the pickup.

Mary thought, impatiently, *Just have to wait till Dory gets home. Maybe I'll get my chance to drop in on my friends yet.* She ran to her room and peered out the east window in time to catch a glimpse of Dory's pickup exiting Webers' driveway and turning south. *Might as well blindfold myself. Half the time I can only see half of what's going on. Wait a minute. Maybe this is my chance to get a closer peek at Maggie. Just John and Robert are in the house with her now!*

Upset that they were not going to get home by six, Maggie consoled herself with the chance to spend some time with Robert alone, or at least without Jimmy present. Not that she didn't enjoy the banter between the two friends, but if Jimmy was in the room, the focus was always on Jimmy, not her.

As John filled the dishpan with water from the faucet, Maggie commented, "Hot and cold running water in the house. Nice."

"You don't have that?" John asked.

"No, but Dad says we might get it put in next year."

"What do you do for water?"

"We have hot and cold running water in the milk house because we have to have it if we want to ship Grade A milk. We haul cold water from the milk house to the kitchen in an eight-gallon can. For hot water, we dip some out and heat the water in a kettle or a pan on the cookstove. I don't mind that so much, but I hate that when we drain the water from the sink, it goes into a five-gallon pail underneath the sink that always seemed to need to be emptied. When we get indoor plumbing next year, Dad said they will put in a drain there too. The Carlsons are coming up in the world."

John shook his head to indicate he understood, but Maggie didn't think he got the joke. Taking charge, Maggie said, "You probably know where stuff goes in the cupboards, John. So, if I wash and you and Robert wipe, the two of you would easily keep up with wiping, and you can put the dishes away too. Okay?"

"Okay."

"Maggie likes to be in charge," Robert teased, "but I don't mind. Truth is, I kind of like it."

"Is she your girlfriend?" John asked innocently.

"Oh, yeah," Robert bragged. "She may not always admit it, though. She likes to play hard to get."

Maggie smiled more than she wanted to and exclaimed, "Shut up, Robert!" as she threw the dish towel at him. "Get busy."

Maggie worked fast, forcing Robert and John to hustle to keep up with her.

"Look at how fast she works!" Robert exclaimed. "She washes dishes, handles bales, and drives tractors. Yet, through all that she remains a perfect beauty!"

"You really are full of it, aren't you?" Maggie said, even as she enjoyed the foolish praise.

John had held back from the banter so far, but now he said, "You handled the Jubilee really good. Like you had driven one before."

"I learned to drive on a Ford 8N. Very similar, though smaller. Now we have a Ford 860. Very similar, but much bigger. But I can drive any of your other tractors too because when our neighbors come over to help thresh grain, I sometimes drive their tractors. Dad encourages all of us to learn as much as we can about everything on the farm. I used to kind of not want to, but I decided I might as well learn what I can."

"We got a combine a few years ago. I really don't remember too much about threshing except what Dad and Mom tell me."

"I don't know the difference between threshing or combining," Robert said.

Maggie explained, "They're just two different methods of doing the same thing—separating the grain from the straw. Combining is the modern way, and threshing is the old way. Come over this summer when we thresh and learn all about it."

"I'd really like to," Robert replied. "Knowledge is knowledge. I've learned more about farming in the last few weeks than I ever thought I'd care to. As a city kid, I thought farming was about as uncool as you can get. But now I've seen the light." He laughed to punctuate his thought.

"Or maybe you're just doing it to impress your girlfriend," John inserted.

"What?" Robert teased. "You catch on fast. And oh, yeah, what other reason could there be?"

Maggie loved being the center of attention, especially Robert's attention. *Mom won't let me date yet, but if I get to know him really well and the folks do too, maybe I won't have to wait until I'm sixteen. He helped us with haying last week. I know Dad and Mom liked him. He's probably the best friend Jimmy ever had, and I know that has nothing to do with me, although Robert will say otherwise just to kid Jimmy. I'd really miss him if he weren't around.*

Finished with the dishes, Maggie was wiping her hands when the phone rang. John grabbed the phone off the hook, said hello, and listened for a moment before he turned to ask, "Do I want to accept a collect call from the hospital?"

Maggie blurted, "Yes, yes, it's probably your dad."

John accepted and listened.

"The hospital isn't that far away," Robert said, puzzled. "Why is that a long-distance call?"

"Strange as it seems, dear boy, it's not the distance that makes a call long-distance. The hospital probably has a different exchange than Webers do. The operator has to hook it up through the switchboard or something like that. So it costs quite a bit. Maybe even a dollar for three minutes. I'll bet Tom just called collect instead of putting money in a pay phone."

"Once again, I've learned something from my pretty farm girl, who is not just a pretty face."

"It's a boy," John said without emotion. "Mom said it would be a boy. Seven pounds and ten ounces. They'd talked about names and said James, if a boy, and Judy, if a girl, but Dad said to tell the boy who helped us hay that they were naming the baby after him."

"That'll swell Jimmy's head," Maggie said. "Until I tell him the truth, of course."

"You're such a cruel sister to my best friend," Robert said. "But I would've preferred it if they'd named the boy Bob."

"We're done with the dishes," Maggie said. "Let's play three-handed euchre."

"I thought you had to have an even number to play euchre," Robert remarked, and John nodded.

"You don't need an even number. I can teach you," Maggie said.

"As long as there's no money involved," Robert said.

"You don't trust me?" Maggie feigned feeling hurt.

"As I said, as long as no money is involved."

As they played, Maggie peeked at Robert and marveled at how he brought out John's personality by treating him like an equal, even teasing him with respect. *He's done that for Jimmy and me too. We both benefit so much from his friendship. And he's so smart. He knows things I never thought of, and yet he is so eager to learn the mundane farm things that I know and he doesn't.*

"What are you looking at? Do I have a hair out of place?" Robert joked.

Startled, Maggie managed, "No, but I was wondering how you keep it in place."

"Training," he said. He took out his comb and ran it through his hair to shape his ducktail. "Training."

As he dealt the cards, Maggie thought, *He's so cute in his own way, not in the tall-dark-and-handsome way. And he's so fun. Maybe Mom would let me go to a movie with him on a Sunday afternoon. He asked once, but I had to tell him I couldn't go. He didn't give up on me, though. I'll work on Mom. First, I'll see if he's still interested.*

Mary tucked her hair under a brown cap and donned a dull green coat before she exited out the back door and followed the trees east along the property line until she was just north of Webers' house. Binoculars in hand, she stayed low as she crept from tree to tree in the windbreak to kneel behind a bush, where she pointed the binoculars at the dining room window and spotted them at the table.

There, they're playing cards! She watched the three of them for several minutes, enjoying their smiles and imagining herself sharing in the fun. *We could be playing four-handed euchre if I were there. What if I just walked around and knocked on the door? Maggie would be so happy to see me. To know I'm safe and happy. But what would I tell John? Dory would be mad at me for taking the risk. For putting both of us in danger of being arrested.*

Her thoughts were interrupted by a cheerful *Yip, yip!* of recognition from Cookie, who came running to the bushes, wagging his tail. Staying low behind the bush, Mary whispered, "Get lost, Cookie!" But to her dismay, the dog stayed where he was. *What if John checks to see what he is barking at?* "Well, at least don't follow me, then." Cookie remained where he was as Mary crawled far enough away to stand up and run, behind the cover of the trees, back to the safety of the house.

"That's not Cookie's angry bark," John said as he got up to look out the north window. "Sounds like he's chasing a squirrel in the windbreak. Yeah, I see him wagging his tail near a tree. Maybe it's a rabbit or something behind the bush."

A memory of how Jack Drude charmed dogs nudged Maggie but faded quickly as she gathered the cards to prepare for her deal.

"I'd better go out to check," John said as he headed for the back door.

CHAPTER 10

MEETING AT THE PARSONAGE

3:30 p.m., Saturday, July 14, 1956

When Pastor Mark returned with the coffee, Mary dutifully rose to bring each empty cup to his end of the table. After he filled each one, she set it on the table near a guest. No one spoke, and the moments were filled with the dull noise of cups against saucers, of Mary's footsteps, and of Rose's sniffles. Mary felt she didn't belong in the room. *This is between John and Rose. Why did she want all of us here?*

After a sip of hot coffee, Rose said, "You probably wonder why I didn't just work this out with John. You wonder why all of you have to witness my blubbering like some teenager about not knowing who I am. The honest truth is that I do not know how I want this to go . . . how I want the talk to proceed . . . or how I want it to end. Strange, for me. I mean, you all know me as someone who never held back on speaking my mind. I always knew what I wanted to say, and I said it regardless of whether anyone liked it or not!" Rose smiled, which seemed to give everyone permission to chuckle at her own critical description of herself.

To Mary's embarrassment, Martin whispered too loudly, "Never heard Rose joke about herself like that before."

"That's right, Martin," Rose responded with a wide smile. "You see what I mean when I say that I don't know who I am anymore?"

Nervous chuckles rolled through the room as everyone welcomed some relief from the tension.

"What I know for sure is that I cannot just get in the car and go back to the farm without airing my feelings to my husband, my brother, and my closest friends."

Pastor Mark, cleared his throat before he spoke. "Ahem. I think we want to hear about those feelings, Rose. I know I do."

"Yes," Mary added softly, "Martin and I want to hear them too." She saw John's jaw clench as his brow furrowed in sadness and disappointment.

John said evenly, "If you have gripes about me and our marriage, might as well say them now. I never claimed to be perfect."

"And none of us claim to be, either," Pastor Mark interjected.

"That's why I want everyone here, John, because it isn't just about you or about you and me. It's about me and where I fit in, or if I fit in anywhere at all now that my boys are gone. Because if I fit in anywhere, the people in this room will know. And maybe they can help me figure it out."

Everyone in the room understood the uniqueness of the moment, especially Mary. Asking for help was not something Rose normally did. *She's a different Rose. She seems lost and unsure of herself. More compassionate, maybe. But does she really not have a plan for where this is going? I don't believe her. That's not like Rose.*

"Why don't you feel your place is with me?" John asked. "Do our years together mean nothing to you?"

"All those years with you were wonderful for the time they lasted. I was an important part of the family with you and the boys, but I never became part of the *farm family* with you and the boys and the farm. John Jr. is gone forever, and I'm pretty sure I've lost Billy."

"But I need you, Rose. You and I are the family now."

Rose shifted in her chair as she appeared to struggle for the right words. "When we first married, you and I were connected. As the boys grew and matured, it seemed my only connection to you was through the boys. They filled the space that connected us. Now, John Jr. is gone, and the gap separating Billy and me seems too wide to bridge. With the boys gone, there's a space between us too, John. More like a huge gap. I feel alone and disconnected from everyone."

John stood up and exclaimed, "So, what are you saying, Rose!? We have no connection? But we're married!"

Rose put up the palm of her hand in an attempt to ease his rage. As he sat down, she continued, "I know you will say I have a place with you. You are a kind and generous man who wants to comfort and care for his wife. I mean that sincerely, John. But I have been a cold wife ever since our first son died. You have been patient with me. Much more than I deserved. But I am not capable of being comforted or cared for on that farm and in that house. And it hurts me to say this, and I know it hurts you even more to hear it, but the house is empty without the boys, and I cannot go back to living with you there."

"So that's what we drove up here to find out?" John shouted. Then, toning his voice down, he continued, "You had me drive all the way up here so you could put me in front of my sister and friends just to announce that you're leaving me!" John's shoulders sagged as he folded his hands on his lap and looked down. Betty moved closer to him and took his hands tightly between hers.

Betty seems more interested in restraining him than in comforting him, Mary observed. *As if she knows where this is going. Rose knows too. She lied when she said she didn't know how she wanted this to end. Have the two of them planned this?*

Pastor Mark broke the silence. "I don't know if it is my place to say this, but I think it is the duty of any clergy to say that marriage is a gift of God through which you can create lives and make your lives happier. As a pastor, I always advise couples to try to work out their issues and stay together."

Mary was shocked to hear Martin ask, "But as a man who is Rose's friend, what do you advise her to do?"

"Yeah," Betty asked quietly, "what happens when the marriage is no longer making them both happy? Because if one isn't happy, the other will soon be unhappy too."

John scowled at his sister. "Whose side are you on, Betty?"

Pastor Mark responded without hesitation, "I couldn't advise two people to live together if living together made them unhappy."

"Do I make you unhappy, Rose?"

Rose looked down.

"Do I?" John asked, his voice getting louder. "Because if I do—" He hesitated a moment to regain control. "If I do, well, the last thing I want to do is make you unhappy."

"I have found a calling with Betty and the pastor. I feel needed by many people, old and young. That makes me happy."

Mary saw John's demeanor change. His jaw clenched and his neck stiffened as he stared at his wife.

"Well, well," John said angrily. "So, the truth comes out. Guess what? You haven't exactly been brightening up the house for the last few years, either. More concerned about Billy and Anna than about me and you. Living with you has been no picnic from the start, but these last few years there's been times I'd sooner stayed in the barn than come into the house after chores. Billy felt the same way. You drove him away."

Rose once again raised her hand to stop him. "So, you admit you're tired of living with me?"

"I'm tired of trying to get along when you seem to have given up."

Rose took a few deep breaths. "Maybe I have given up. My discussions with Betty and the pastor have made me realize what I need to do to become better. I need to serve people, and I can do it if I stay here. If I go back to the farm, I will wither from lack of use. Our own church has no place for me like this one does."

John shot up off the couch, with Betty still holding onto one of his hands. He looked at her sternly, pulled his hand free, and remarked, "So that's the deal! My sister and my wife have schemed against me, brought me here under the pretense that Rose was coming home with me, but the real purpose was to put me in front of a rigged court and accuse me of making my wife unhappy. But Rose, no one has had a bigger hand in your unhappiness than you. Yes, you! Because you aren't happy unless you are controlling everyone around you. And you failed to control Billy, even though you were willing to ruin his life trying."

"I just want those around me to be happy!"

"But it's always your version of happiness, not theirs. Whether it was John Jr. or Billy, you never gave them any freedom."

"And what happened to Billy when we gave him his freedom to go to the dance?" Rose demanded. "He said that he wasn't going to return home!"

"If you hadn't interfered, he'd have been the groom at the wedding! And he would've been happy." Giving Betty a stern look that made her give him more room, John sat down hard on the sofa.

After a short pause, John turned to Pastor Mark and said, "I apologize for the outburst, especially since it is in your home. Seems to me everyone has backed me into a corner, here. Like an ambush."

"I feel a little bit that way myself," Pastor Mark said with humility. "I've been aware that Betty and Rose were working well together with the youth groups and the choir, but I had no hint of any plan to keep Rose here. I do not want to be a party to encouraging a married couple to separate."

Seeing John's color fade to white and his head drop as he looked at the floor, Mary wanted to move to sit by him, but Betty stayed put.

Rose begged, "Please don't blame Betty or Pastor Mark for talking me into anything. I've been searching for something to hold onto for years, and think I've found it here. I haven't yet asked them if I could stay, but if I can't stay at the parsonage, I'd still like to work with your congregation, Pastor Mark. I could stay in town somewhere."

Eyes turned to the Terquists. Betty answered, as she met Pastor Mark's eyes, "We've talked about the value of the work you've done in just the short time here."

"And," Pastor Mark added, "we've discussed how great it would be to have you help if you lived closer, but we never expected you were thinking of leaving John. At least I didn't. I don't want to be the cause of you two splitting up."

"I think my wife made it pretty clear you ain't the cause," John retorted, "although you may have given her the way out and even planted the seed. She made it clear that I'm the cause, I suppose, but I don't understand what I did wrong. And maybe I don't need to understand that. What I do understand is that my wife no longer wants to live in the place that was our home for nearly twenty-four years."

"Circumstances," Mary emphasized, "in which you had no control, John. Don't say it's your fault. There are lots of circumstances. Look, Martin and I are your friends, but we had no idea Rose was unhappy."

"Thanks for that, Mary, but it seems I've been accused of neglecting my wife, and if that's how she feels, that's how she feels, even if I don't think it's true. Rose was always hard to please. From the very beginning."

"But we're Rose's friends too," Martin interjected. "Sure, she was always hard to please, and I remember she always got her way when we grew up at home. But she's just telling the truth as she sees it, here."

Mary turned to glare at her husband. *Doesn't he see John's side?*

"I think I better understand that I was difficult now—now that I'm beginning to realize what I need in life. My boys are gone, and I need to be needed. I've found gratification working here, if they'll let me stay."

Betty glanced at Pastor Mark and said, "I'd love to have Rose stay, but it isn't up to me."

"Nor is it totally up to me," Pastor Mark explained. "I'll have to get approval from the board, and if you live here, they may want you to pay rent, but I'll advocate for approval and to pay you a salary—providing one thing."

"What's that?" Rose asked. "What must I do?"

"John must agree to it. Although I believe it's totally your decision whether to stay with John or leave him, if Betty and I are to be instruments in the separation of her brother and his wife, you must have John's blessing in the matter."

All eyes turned to John as Rose said bluntly, "John, I can't go back to the farm and live in the house we once enjoyed together. I can't. Don't blame yourself. Blame me! Even hate me for a while if you need to, but give me the freedom to leave."

John stood up, but his tall, erect frame bent at the waist and sagged at the knees. His anger was apparent, but he controlled his rage. "You're already gone, Rose! You left me years ago. I was just too stupid to see it." He inhaled deeply and exhaled as he let his body slide back down to the sofa. "You've always done what you wanted. I couldn't change that if I tried. I wish you luck. Somehow, my needing you doesn't matter to you. I just can't swallow that fact easily, but I will say this—if that's the message here, and I think it is, I'll swallow it now, and there will be no turning back. Our separation will be permanent. I expect you to divorce me. I want no tie to remain if it isn't real."

Everyone was silent. Mary knew that this very moment offered the last opportunity for any reconciliation. Rose looked at her hands as she folded them on her lap. Mary glanced at Martin, who was staring at his sister and then at John in disbelief. John glared at his wife, waiting to see if she accepted his challenge.

Rose had nothing to add, apparently, and John asserted, "That's that, then."

A cloud of silence hung in the air. No one knew what to expect next. Rose sat perfectly still. Betty and Pastor Mark looked from Rose to John. Martin shifted in his seat next to Mary. *Is he planning to get up to leave?* Mary expected him to rise, but Betty's voice brought all eyes to herself.

"You have another topic to cover, don't you, Rose?"

Rose took a deep breath before blurting, "I'll need money, John."

John shot up from his seat. "So, it all comes down to money! Sure, I'll send you money. How much do you think you want a month? How much of my milk check? You've never done a sliver of work outside the house, and now you won't be doing anything in the home anymore. So, what do you suppose you're owed for the past . . . for your past contributions to our . . . our happiness? Ha! What a joke!"

"John," Mary pleaded, "don't say any more. You're too angry. You might say something you'll regret later."

"Monday will be our twenty-fourth anniversary," John said. "For twenty-four years you've been holed up in your house like it was some fort or something. Wouldn't even bring me lunch in the field like every other farm wife does."

"Really?" Mary said, unable to stop herself. "Rose never even brought out lunch?" Mary glared at Rose.

"But John," Martin said, "Rose told me that you two talked about that before you got married. She said you agreed that she would have nothing to do with any outside work."

"Sure, I agreed. I was a lovesick bachelor who thought he'd found love. I'd have agreed to anything at the time. But who would imagine the woman you love would never soften to the beauty of the place. Or to the lure of calves and kittens and puppies outside. I had no idea she would stay so . . . cold."

Rose said nothing. Mary, shocked at Martin's defense of Rose, restrained herself from speaking. *It's as if Rose wants him to muster up every complaint he's ever had against her. She wants him to open a wound that's too big to heal. And Martin isn't helping.*

Rose leaned back in her chair, took a deep breath, and leaned forward again before she spoke. "I think most divorce lawyers would agree that I deserve half of your worth."

"Holy cow! Divorce lawyers! You've been leading up to this all along, haven't you? You and Betty scheming to get half my farm. My inheritance that I've worked on ever since I was just a kid when Dad got sick. And Mom and me sent you to high school, Betty. So, you got your education and your freedom from responsibilities of the farm, and now you want your friend to get a piece of my work too. Do I get a piece of your education? It's too late for the freedom of my youth!"

John relaxed a little before adding, "But you're right, Mary. I should shut up. I've said too much already." He plopped himself back down on the couch, glaring at Betty, who inched further away from her brother. Suddenly, John stood up once more and took a step toward the exit. "I need to spend some time in the fresh air. Pastor Mark, how about if you and I go pull some weeds in the garden? Like you said you wanted to do before the meeting started."

"Probably a good idea," Pastor Mark said. "I'll lead the way."

Mary watched them exit. *What now? What can I say? Probably best to shut up.* She glanced at Rose and then at Betty. Both women looked down at their hands, which were folded on their laps. Mary turned to look at Martin, who met her eyes. *Is he wondering the same thing I am? How long should we endure this silence before we get up to leave?*

CHAPTER 11

THE INTERLOPERS

3:30 p.m., Saturday, July 14, 1956

Joey shot Ann a surprised look. "You say these guys are troublemakers?! You know them?"

"I'm not proud to say this, but I know all these guys in the car," Ann explained in a low tone. "Gary Snider is riding shotgun. He's in my grade. The other three are a year older. Graduated this year. The driver is George Tabrine. Bob Swinner and Jesse Tosberg are in the back. Tom Ryan knows them pretty well. He was on the football team with them all through high school."

"Friends of his?"

"No, not exactly. Jimmy knows who they are too. Gary is the one who tried to cut Robert's hair and Jimmy stopped him."

"What are they doing here?"

"Probably up to no good, as usual," Ann replied.

The front door of the passenger side flew open, and Gary Snider jumped out. He staggered a bit as he took a swig out of a can of beer before he hollered, "Ann, why didn't you invite us to your picnic? I'm your classmate! And, Peggy, your brother and I are friends. Why didn't you invite us?"

Joey felt obligated to answer seriously. "Well, this is just a little get-together for the country-school kids. The country school will be closed next year, and we thought we'd have one last ball game for just the younger group."

Bob and Jesse exited the back seat slowly, each carrying a can of beer. Both were above average height, and they were husky. George slid out of the driver's seat. Medium height, with a body like a brick, he strode toward Ann and, placing a menacing hand on the edge of the hayrack on either side of her, leaned forward, forcing her against the edge of the hayrack. "I got a better idea," he crooned. "How about if Ann and Peggy come with us for a ride and the rest of you boys and girls go play your little ball game?"

"We aren't going anywhere with you, creep!" Peggy exclaimed.

Joey saw Ann's face stiffen as Peggy continued, "And I got a better idea. You guys get back into your ugly car and drive away and don't come back."

Peggy's stern words hung in the air, and as the younger kids backed away from the hayrack, Joey and the five Schoen boys moved closer to Ann and Peggy. Mary and Margaret causally walked over to the two bats left near home plate, a few yards away.

Fearing the mounting tension, Joey tried some humor and kindness. "We're done eating, so if you guys are hungry, go ahead and help yourself to what's left while we finish our game. I mean, last time I had some beer, it made me hungry."

"Last time you had some beer!" Gary exclaimed. "Who are you kidding, you little twerp! Who's this little man, here? Offering us leftovers!"

"Just a kid who wants to get back to playing ball," Joey said evenly as his mind raced for a plan. *What would Jimmy do? He'd have a plan. He'd size things up. But what defense can we have against these big kids?* He took stock of his surroundings. *Bob and Jesse don't seem too interested.* Now he had a plan.

"Now, I got a better idea," George said. "We'll play ball with you. Us four against all you kids. We bat first." But as he staggered toward the bats, Mary picked up one and Margaret the other, and they ran in different directions.

"Stupid little shits! I suppose you think I can't catch you!" He stepped off after one of the twins and promptly tripped, tumbling to the ground.

Although Joey was wary of how the older boys would react, he couldn't help but join his friends as they laughed at the fall. Bob and Jesse laughed even louder, and Bob teased, "Hey, buddy, you always did have trouble catching girls!"

The comment made everyone laugh harder, except Gary, who yelled, "You punks think that's funny? I'll show you what's funny!" And he lunged at Joey.

Prepared, Joey ducked under the rack, crawled underneath the wagon, and stood up on the other side with a mocking "Over here, Gary."

Bob and Jesse laughed even more loudly, but Joey's companions had quit laughing. Joey's throat was dry and his knees weak. *What did I get myself into? I'm not Jimmy. What now? I'd better try to stick with my plan."*

Remembering Billy's warning about drunk guys—*they're bold but slow*—he planned to use Gary's boldness and slowness against him. *But I can't hesitate. Don't give him time to think.*

He ran a few steps to the edge of the road bank and hollered, "Come get me, Gary. My brother, Jimmy Carlson, says you're a pushover!"

Gary's faced flashed anger. "You're Jimmy's little brother! I got a score to settle with him!" He charged.

Joey thought, *He won't slug a little kid. He'll just push me down. I'll see if Jimmy's moves work on this guy. He's big. Too late to change my mind.* Joey grabbed the larger boy's arms and torso and let his momentum carry them both over the sharp edge of the five-foot road bank and into the ditch. They rolled over together several times and stopped with Gary on top. Gary trapped Joey's arms under his knees and raised a hand.

Slap! Slap! The sound of the impacts echoed in Joey's head as he struggled against the larger boy.

"You little shit! I ought to slap you till you bleed!" Gary yelled as he raised his arm to strike again.

But before he could swing, Ralph and Jerome Schoen arrived, each grabbing one of Gary's arms and dragging him off Joey. Bob, Jesse, and George just watched. In the next moment, kids poured over the road bank, crowding the ditch with so many bodies that Gary had to struggle to stand. Ann and Peggy pushed the others aside to help Joey sit up, but Gary broke free and took a swing at Ralph, who easily avoided his reach.

"Hold on, Gary," Bob said, finally hurrying toward him. " Jesse and I didn't ride along to watch you beat up little kids. We knew George was too drunk to catch the kids, and we never wanted to hurt anyone. I admit we kind of enjoyed watching the kid take you down the bank with him, but you've gone too far."

"Yeah," Jesse added, "we didn't even want to drive into the schoolyard. You know we ain't the type to pick on little kids, Ann."

"Yeah, I believe you and Bob had no bad intentions," Ann admitted.

Peggy yelled up at George, "Anything to add, Georgie?"

Shocked to sobriety by Bob's and Jesse's statements, George said, "Yeah, you're right, Jesse. It was Gary's idea to stop here. Let's get out of here, guys." He got into the driver's seat as Bob and Jesse jumped into the back seat.

Gary climbed up the bank after them as fast as he could as Ralph said, "Stay away from our neighborhood, okay?"

"Sure thing," Gary said before he got into George's car.

After the car sped away, Joey said, "Thanks, you guys. I guess I ran out of moves."

"That's one way to put it," Ralph said, laughing. And as kids scrambled up the road bank, he continued, "I don't think anyone wants to play ball anymore today. Jerome and I have agreed to call the game a tie and just eat some more before we go home, if that's okay with you guys."

"I'm too dizzy to play ball," Joey admitted as he rubbed his face. "I could eat some, all right. The excitement made me hungry again."

Soon they were all sitting around the wagon, listening to various versions of the day's events. A few kids even called Joey a hero, but he agreed with Ann when she said that everyone was a hero in their own way.

And Ralph repeated what he had said earlier: "I like how we all stuck together."

"Me too," Joey said. He enjoyed being part of the group, but why did they treat him like an outsider sometimes? Why did the girls pick on him when they walked home from school? *Jimmy was right: People do act different in different situations. But we're one big club now.*

Then Joey looked at his pocket watch and exclaimed, "I've got to go. I told Maggie I'd take care of the chicken chores." *I can't wait to tell Jimmy and Maggie when they get home. They'll probably be home before I will. I hate that the day is over.*

"Yeah, it's getting to be chore time," Peggy agreed. "We have to get home. If you're headed my way, get on the wagon and I'll drop everyone off at their doorsteps."

As the Schoens and Fischers and Paul Haber headed home to the west, Joey helped load Liz's wagon into Ryans' hayrack, and the other children climbed aboard before Peggy started the tractor to drive east.

Enjoying a hero's status, Joey sat on a bale of straw next to Mary Ryan, with Katherine O'Keran and Caroline Shaurel and her twin sisters sitting on the floor nearby.

"We were really worried about you when we saw you go over the bank, Joey," Mary Shaurel said, speaking for herself and her twin.

"Yeah," Mary Ryan added, "I thought you were hurt."

"I was afraid you might have hit your head really hard," Caroline said. "And then when Gary started slapping you, I was worried you might never get well."

Joey recognized his chance to rid himself of some smoldering concerns. "I didn't think any of you kids would've cared what happened to a heathen like me."

"What?" Mary Ryan and Caroline said at once.

"Well, when we walked home from school, you girls always picked on me. You call me a heathen all the time."

"Silly boy, we tease you because we *like* you," explained Katherine, the oldest of the small group. "There are five of us girls, and you're the only boy in the group when we walk home. How else is any one of us going to get your attention?"

The girls giggled. Joey felt foolish, but he decided he liked the feeling.

CHAPTER 12

FINDING OUT

4:30 p.m., Saturday, July 14, 1956

Jimmy rode shotgun and Rusty sat in the middle as Dory drove to town. The two tires sat in the pickup's bed atop a wet and faded tan tarp that sheltered some tools from the weather. The dull green '49 Ford pickup had four speeds on the floor, making the seating cozy for three.

Dory said, "You could've stayed home and helped with the dishes, Rusty, but I admit that I like to have you along with me."

"John said he didn't care if I went with, and Maggie and Robert said they'd help with the dishes and that I should go if I wanted."

Jimmy smiled at her. "Everyone likes a trip to town after a good rain."

When they arrived at Bur Oak Falls, Dory parked in front of the closed garage door at the double-stall filling station. Jimmy and Rusty followed her through the open garage door, where a tall thin young man in dark green coveralls worked on a tractor tire.

"Hi, there, Lugwrench. I see you're busy as heck, like usual."

"I am, but always glad to see you, Dorothea. And that cute little neighbor of yours."

Rusty smiled and turned to Jimmy, who grinned back at her.

"Jimmy, here"—Dory nodded at him—"was helping us with the bales, but when he was going to leave, he had a flat tire, which was his second one today. Can you fix both of them while we wait? I know you're busy and there is a line of tires for you to fix, but he really needs to get on the road."

"Sure, I can. But it should be worth one of those lemon soda pops from the machine. Even a working stiff like me likes a treat once in a while."

"Absolutely. Now or later?"

"Later, when you pay for the work."

Lugwrench carried the tires to his work area, where he placed the first one flat on the floor. He removed the valve core to deflate the tire before he used a tire iron and a crowbar to force the seam to the outside of the rim. He pulled out the tube, commenting, "I could patch this, but I see it's been patched twice already and the rubber isn't the best anymore. A new tube doesn't cost much. The tire looks good."

"I'll take a new tube," Jimmy said.

"Good. It's safer." Lugwrench grabbed a box, removed the new tube, screwed the valve core into the valve stem, and used the compressor to add some air before he expertly shoved the floppy rubber donut into the tire, carefully poking the valve stem through the steel rim.

Jimmy watched the whole process, marveling at Lugwrench's skill and speed. *Are his hands that big normally, or does all the rough work with his hands make them bigger? He handled that tire like a toy!*

As Lugwrench used a crowbar and tire iron to force the outer ring of the tire to the inside of the rim, Jimmy commented, "That would've taken me half a day."

As he used the air compressor to inflate the tire to the right pressure, Lugwrench responded, "Yeah, I know what you mean. I've been doing this for nearly ten years. Either I got good at it or got another job. And believe it or not, I like this job. I get to talk to lots of good people, like Dory here. And her young neighbor. And now you." He checked the tire pressure with a gauge twice before he announced, "All done. The tire had been repaired recently. That made popping it off the rim easier. Now for the next one."

Lugwrench repeated the process and suggested a new tube for the second tire too. Jimmy looked at Dory.

"Don't worry," she said. "If you don't have enough money with you, I can loan you some, and you can send me the money when you get home."

Work complete, Lugwrench announced, "Let's go settle up and you can buy me that lemon pop, Dory."

Jimmy reached for his wallet, but Dory said, "We'll settle up later, Jimmy. I'll pay him now."

Jimmy nodded, uncertain of why she insisted on paying the bill.

"Haven't seen you before," Lugwrench said to Jimmy. "What brings you this way?"

Jimmy turned to Dory. "Too bad we didn't bring the picture."

"Just describe her," Dory said.

"Okay." Jimmy thought for a moment. "We're looking for a pretty blond girl. Petite. Nearly seventeen years old."

"Who isn't?" Lugwrench asked rhetorically. "I've been looking for a girl like that since I was seventeen. Though now I'd want her to be a little older. But no, I can't say that I've seen anyone new around here like that. I'll keep an eye out for her, and if I see her and she won't marry me, I'll let Dory know."

On the drive back, Dory explained how much she liked the town of Bur Oak Falls. "It's just the right size. We have movies and even a community theater and a band. We've got stores of all kinds and sizes and several filling stations, grocery stores, hardware stores, a lumberyard, and two small motels. There's a creamery that buys and sells eggs and chicken feed, and there are two banks and, of course, a post office. Restaurants and taverns. Nothing fancy, unless you count the Edgewood Supper Club, which is kind of special."

"I see you have a couple of catalog stores to order from too," Jimmy asked nonchalantly. "Do you use them much?"

Dory paused before she answered, cautiously, "Sometimes. But Bur Oak Falls has most of what I need in town. And I know most people in town and they know me. I like that."

"Yes, that's what I like about Newburg, although it's not nearly as big as your town. People know me, my folks, my grandparents, and more. I suppose it's the same for you here."

Dory shifted her weight in the seat and glanced out the window to her left as if she were about to say something, but Rusty exclaimed, "Dory came over on the orphan train with her younger brother!"

"So, you have a younger brother?" Jimmy asked quickly.

"He's been dead for years," Dory replied.

"Sorry," Jimmy said with reverence, and he waited for Dory's follow-up explanation. But instead Dory changed the subject.

"Hey, I know Tom would want me to pay you something for today."

"Not necessary. And if I don't have enough money for the tire fix, I'll mail it to you when I get home."

"Let's see. Hauling bales around here pays about seventy-five cents an hour. Three hours for each of you. That's three times three times seventy-five."

"That's six dollars and seventy-five cents," Rusty said before the others had done the math.

"A math whiz, eh?" Jimmy said. "Gotta like a math whiz."

"Let's round it up to nine bucks so you each get three dollars."

"How much was the bill for the work on the tire?"

"He does free labor for me sometimes. He just charged me for the new tubes. I can deduct that from your wages."

"Okay, but free labor? I know he seems kind of sweet on you, but free labor?"

"Hold on," Dory said as she laughed at the thought. "I'm almost thirty-eight, and he's about twenty-eight. I used to take care of him when he was a young teenager. He had rough going. Webers and I hired him for farmwork, and when he turned eighteen and tried to get a job in town, Tom and I knew his honesty and work ethic and talked to the owner of the filling station where we do all of our farm business. Asked him to just give the kid a chance. Well, a chance was all he needed."

"I've seen the way he looks at you." Jimmy teased. "He's a good-looking guy, Dory."

Dory laughed. "Larry—that's his real name—loves me like a mother. Just mount your tire, Jimmy." She turned into Webers' driveway. As she dropped Jimmy and Rusty off at the car, she remarked to Rusty, "I'll take the truck home and walk back here. Then we'll start chores, okay?"

"Okay," Rusty said. "I'll help Jimmy with the tire."

Then Maggie came running out of the house, calling, "It's a boy! Mrs. Weber already had the baby and it's a boy! They called a while ago. Tom said everyone is doing great."

"Good news all around," Dory said as she left to return the truck.

Jimmy mounted the tire, and Rusty handed him the nuts for the tire bolts one at a time. When Dory returned, she paid Jimmy and the others for their labor less the cost of the two tubes.

"Good deal for me and Dad: two new tubes plus some cash for us kids. Thanks, Dory."

Goodbyes were said as Dory and the Webers headed for the barn to do chores.

After Jimmy steered the blue Ford south out of the driveway, he asked Robert for the time.

"It's after five o'clock," Robert said. "I hope you're not going to try to make it back by six! That would be crazy."

"No, I'm not going to do anything crazy," Jimmy said. "I'll be careful."

"Not do anything crazy, eh?" Maggie said sarcastically. "That would be a first."

CHAPTER 13

JOEY'S JOURNEY

4:30 p.m., Saturday, July 14, 1956

Joey hopped off the hay rack at the end if his driveway and shouted, "Thanks for the ride, Peggy!" And then, as he waved goodbye, he yelled back to everyone, "Thanks for coming. I had fun. I hope you all had fun!"

"Thanks, Joey!"

"We had fun! Thanks for planning the day, Joey!"

"You are so brave! Glad you didn't get hurt, Joey."

"You're our hero, Joey."

Surprised, he laughed out loud, and as he walked toward the house, he wondered what the kids really thought of him. *Doesn't really matter, but I'll probably never feel this good again. Might as well enjoy it.* Jimmy had warned him that friends could be fickle and feelings could change. *Maybe Jimmy was too doubtful. What was Maggie's word? Skeptical. Maggie said Jimmy was too skeptical about people.*

He was disappointed to see the parking spot for the '52 Ford vacant and Robert's car still in the yard. He expected his folks would be really late, but he urgently wanted to tell Jimmy and Maggie about the day's events. Once in the house, he wasted no time before running upstairs to change into his chore clothes. He wasn't hungry at all, so he would feed and water the chickens and pick eggs right away.

The house had a different sound to it when he was home alone, and as he hurried downstairs, his footfalls echoed. For a moment, he was lonely. And for another moment, he envisioned no one coming home. *What would*

I do if no one came home? Well, Jimmy said they'd be home by six. That's an hour away. Plenty time. But he wanted to have the chicken chores done before then.

Thunder in the distance encouraged him to hurry, but the rain never exceeded a light drizzle. He looked at the dark clouds in the northwest. *Too bad most of the rain will miss us. Dad said we needed a good rain.* He made two trips to the chicken coop—one to carry feed and the other to carry water. He took his time picking eggs, talking to the chickens and even stopping to pick up one that Maggie always talked to. He put his head close to hers as she emitted what Maggie called a chicken purr. He used to kid his sister about petting a chicken, but now he enjoyed stroking her smooth white feathers and listening to her sing.

He carried the eggs to the house and placed the pail on the porch. He looked at the kitchen clock. *Half past five. We'd be going out to get the cows soon if the folks were home. They're on good pasture, so they won't be in the yard. I'll have to go get them. May as well start out and bring them home since Jimmy and Maggie will be home soon. I'll close the gate to lock them in the yard—that's what Jimmy would do—until Jimmy and Maggie are ready to milk. But they'll probably be home by the time I get the cows to the yard anyway.*

He went through the barn to check if Jimmy had scattered a few bales of hay in the manger to get the cows interested in going into their stalls. He had. Sure, there was plenty grass in the pasture so they wouldn't be hungry, but the grass was high-moisture, and the hay was dry, which gave them a tasty variety. He left the barn door closed. Dad always said the cows seemed to know when the barn was unattended and they'd rush around inside like bunch of kids. *Besides, Jimmy and Maggie will be home by the time I bring the cows from the pasture. The sky is clearing up a little. Looks like the rain is over already.*

Striding uphill through the wet grass, he reached the summit of the big hill south of the barn and saw the cattle lying down in the far corner of the pasture, less than half a mile away. The light rain had not brought them to the barnyard like a storm would have. He covered the next quarter mile in record time by taking long strides, and he trotted another two hundred yards before he stopped. Putting his hands on either side of his mouth for a megaphone effect, he used a high pitch to call, "Come, boss! Come, boss!

Come, boss!" He repeated the call often as he approached the herd of about seventy cattle, including heifers, dry cows, and thirty cows currently milking, or wet cows. He smiled to himself as he recalled how Jimmy had taught him the cattle call when he was little.

By the time he circled behind the herd, most of the cows had clumsily gotten to their feet, farted, crapped, and started to move toward the barnyard. To get them moving faster, Joey clapped his hands and yelled, "Hey! Hey!" or called them fond names. "Come on, you lazy bags of bones! Get going, you floozies! There's some hay waiting in the barn. Besides, I know you all want to get milked. Don't you? Get going, you money-makers!"

He didn't want to chase them too fast. The recently freshened cows would leak milk if they broke into a trot and set their enlarged udders swinging from side to side like pendulums, the momentum forcing milk to flow from the teats. That was like throwing money on the dirt, according to his father.

He had a clear view of the house as he descended the high hill to chase the cows into the cow yard. *No car in the yard yet.* And as he closed the temporary two-wire gate to lock them all in the yard, he decided to open the barn doors and get ready to milk, figuring, *They'll be home soon.*

He flung the doors open and stepped aside, careful to stay out of the way of the half-ton animals as they rushed by him. As usual, most of the cows went into the right stalls, but two went in the wrong stalls and another walked into the manger. *Too many heifers came in with the cows. No use closing the doors until I get them out.* He used Jimmy's tactics and yelled angry threats to encourage the cows to go into their correct stalls. "Suzie, get the hell out if the manger or I'll kick you between the eyes. And Popcorn, haven't you learned your place yet?"

He was always amused how they seemed to take the threats seriously. Suzie speedily backed out of the manger to go to her stall, but Popcorn, who had had her first calf a few weeks ago, backed out and then bolted for the door. *Damn!* Without thinking, Joey yelled and gave chase, frightening the young animal. *My first mistake was to not close the door when I had them all in the barn. Jimmy always closes the doors before he yells at them.*

Popcorn reached the two-wire gate long before Joey could stop her, and the wires failed to slow her down. She ran through the wires without regard for their sharp barbs, pulling them off the posts and dragging them along several feet before they released her hide. She headed up the hill toward the back pasture. *I forgot all of Dad's warnings: Frightened cows can go through closed doors or fences or run over people. Never be cocky about being in control, because you are only in control if they let you. Their size and strength make them the boss.* He stopped for a moment and yelled at the sky.

I messed up bad. Now what do I do? Run back to close the doors and lock up the cows while Popcorn runs to the back pasture? Or chase Popcorn? He had some decisions to make.

Deciding he couldn't catch Popcorn, he turned back and closed the doors before going to close each individual stanchion. To lock a cow's stanchion, he had to carefully but aggressively force his small body between two cows, whose balloonlike stomachs extended to within inches of each other. Squeezing between their hot hides as they jerked about in their stalls and stretched to reach hay in the manger, Joey recalled the wisdom learned from his older brother. *Be especially careful a cow doesn't stand on one of my feet. Jimmy says that when they're reaching for hay, they'll plop their foot down anywhere.* Joey smiled. He's right: "They're worse than kids at the supper table."

Joey opened the doors and chased out a few heifers and dry cows who wanted to gobble the dry hay. After closing the doors, he grabbed a pliers before he rushed ahead of the animals to close the gate. *Maybe if I keep them in the yard, Popcorn will get lonesome and return on her own.* Glad that the gate could be easily fixed with just the pliers, he worried that Popcorn might have caught her udder on the wire. *Her teat just healed a few weeks ago. If she hurt it again, I'll get hell for that.*

To calm the animals in the yard, he dragged a few bales of hay out, broke them open, and spread the contents around on a grassy area. He placed a chunk of good hay on the other side of the fence. *Maybe that will tempt Popcorn to want to hang around.*

Back in the barn, he scraped the muck brought in by the cows off aisles with a scoop shovel, hoping desperately that he could get Popcorn in the barn before anyone came home. All he could do now was wait. He'd have to put Popcorn in before he set any milking equipment in the aisles. Doing nothing when there was so much to do was the hardest.

After ten minutes, he looked out the top half of the barn door to see Popcorn eating the hay he'd put on the other side of the gate. He opened the door and slowly walked toward her, murmuring calming apologies. "Sorry,

Popcorn. I know you meant no harm. My fault. I frightened you." Repeating the same words in the same tone, he stepped through the two-wire gate, unwrapped the wires from the corner post, and pulled them to the side. She kept eating. *Kindness usually works best. And don't blame the cow when you do something stupid. That's what Jimmy always says.*

He worked his way behind her and softly urged her toward the barn, thrilled when she seemed to be ready to go inside. *I don't even care if a few heifers go into the barn too.* Once she was in the barn, Joey closed the door behind him. *I am one lucky kid. If she hadn't gone in now, I could've been monkeying around with her all night.*

Joey's sigh of relief when the young animal went directly into her stall was barely audible, but he continued to praise Popcorn in a calm deep voice. "Atta girl. Good bossy," he said as he squeezed between her and the next cow to lock her stanchion. *Click!* She was locked in. He touched her thigh to let her know he was going to touch her udder. *No scratches! No cuts! I'm a lucky kid!*

Relieved and humbled, he opened the barn doors and chased out the three heifers that had come in, saying kindly, "I understand you girls just wanted a little snack. No harm done." He clapped his hands to get them to shuffle out. Then he scraped the muck off the aisle for the second time that evening. *Not much muck on the aisles. I'm glad Jimmy cleaned the cow porch.*

Figuring his siblings would be home any minute, he brought the pails and the three milking units down from the milk house. Returning to the milk house again, he was glad to see the valve was closed on the bulk tank, and he struggled to secure the pad in the strainer as Jimmy had taught him before he removed the cover on one of the ports where he parked the strainer. He popped his head out the door. *Still no car in the yard.*

He checked his watch. *Six-fifteen. Might as well wash the udders and put some belts on the cows and get ready to milk.* In the milk house, he measured a large spoon of disinfectant soap into a pail before he filled it with hot water from the faucet. *Wish we had hot and cold running water in the house. Dad said maybe next year. We might get a telephone next year too.*

He carried the pail of soapy hot water to the east aisle to begin washing. *Let's see, Jimmy says that before you step next to the cow and place the pail near her udder, touch her upper thigh to let her know you're coming. If she doesn't know you are there, she might jump her big body around for no reason at all and knock your little body to the floor. Oh, she won't do it on purpose, but it's up to you to let her know your intentions. Say something to nice to her.*

"Easy, sweetheart," Joey said as he patted the cow's thigh. "I have some nice, warm water to wash your udder with." With a small washcloth, he carefully scrubbed each of the four quarters, making sure no dirt clung to the tender skin on her teats, nor the short hairs of the udder. After washing the nine cows on the east row, he carried the pail of water to the west aisle, which had two uneven rows of cows for a total of twenty-one. He decided to wash them all right away.

After he'd washed all of the udders, something happened. His thinking changed. He no longer thought of himself as an eleven-year-old waiting for help. He became *the herdsman.* But he was a humbled herdsman, one who understood that his puny presence was only tolerated by these calm giants. With adequate regard for the danger posed when a child works with animals that weigh over a thousand pounds, he decided to begin milking. *I know a cow could accidentally knock me down or step on me and leave me wounded and alone. I'll be careful.* He knew what he was doing. Jimmy had trained him, and he would follow his brother's instructions every step. Although he expected Mags and Jimmy would be home any minute, he quit obsessing about their arrival. He checked his watch. *Let's see how long it takes me to do chores.* He strode over to the wall to the switch for the milking machine, grabbed it in his small hand, and pushed it up. The loud thudding of the vacuum pump began. *No turning back now.*

Joey had watched his father, his mother, Jimmy, and once or twice even Maggie use the buckets. His father had encouraged all the kids to learn the procedure. Joey followed the steps closely now: After he placed the belt around the cow's large stomach, he hooked the chain to the right height. Then, with the heavy bucket in one hand, he firmly stroked the cow's right thigh near the top, letting her know what was about to happen as he addressed her in a calm, steady voice. "Easy girl. Easy." After he squeezed between the two cows, he reached above the cow's stanchion to slip the air hose onto the petcock of the vacuum pipeline, which carried the suction of the vacuum pump to the pulsator attached to the bucket, which enabled the rubber cups to inflate and deflate, squeezing out milk when encompassing a cow's teat. He kneeled down to hang the bucket on the belt hooks under the cow's belly. Then, one by one, he took a little milk from each teat to wet it before he eased the teat cup or inflation onto the teat. Usually, this was a signal to the cow to release her milk. His dad had told him, "Nature would provide the natural instinct for a calf to butt its head hard against its mother's udder, and a mother cow would tolerate that treatment from her offspring. But a dairy farmer knows that he has better success getting the animal to release her milk by gently stroking her udder." Once the cups were on the cow's teats, Joey stood up slowly and adjusted the cow's belt to the proper height. "Good girl," he said as he carefully stepped over the gutter to the aisle. He installed the next two buckets and then pushed the hay forward in the manger so the animals didn't reach for it and jiggle more than necessary as he tried to mount a bucket on them.

Removing each bucket was more challenging. Although behavioral differences between cows were important to note when mounting a bucket on them, the differences became even more important when removing the bucket. Each teat cup needed to be removed individually to ensure the teat had no more milk. If too much milk remained in the udder, a bacterial infection could ruin the milk for weeks or possibly damage the cow forever. Joey understood the responsibility he had taken on. *This is how we make a living. If I mess up, I could damage our ability to pay bills.*

Joey removed the first bucket with confidence after he checked each teat. He reached over to close the valve and pull the hose off the petcock. He bent down to grab the bucket's handle and struggled to lift the bucket, straightening up before stepping over the gutter to pour the milk into the tall, straight-sided shotgun pail. *About two gallons, and even that was a struggle. A couple cows give nearly four and quite a few give three. Well, I'll just have to lift harder. With the bucket, four gallons will weigh about forty pounds, and it's awkward, lifting with one hand from under the cow's big gut. But I have to do it.*

Joey had to move fast to ensure milking units were not left on cows too long. Between removing and mounting buckets, he hurried to move belts to cows not yet milked and carry pails of milk up the stairway to dump into the strainer mounted on a bulk tank portal. The cows' body heat increased the temperature in the barn, and after half an hour, Joey was wet with perspiration. Squeezing between the animals was like entering a steam room. Leaving each cow out after he finished milking her might lower the temperature in the barn, but he just did not have time. *When I finish milking all the cows in the east row, I'll let them all out at once. They'll go out the east door and not bother my pails that I have sitting in the west aisle.*

Occasionally, Joey glanced toward the stairway, hoping to see Jimmy and Maggie, but he had little time to worry. He rejoiced briefly when he finished the single row of cows on the east side and had moved all the three buckets to cows in the two rows of stanchions of the west aisle. *Won't have to be running from the east aisle to the west aisle anymore, and the trip to the bulk tanks will be so much shorter.* With all three buckets mounted on cows, belts changed, and pails emptied into the bulk tank, Joey decided he could take a moment to let the east row of cows out. When he heard some racket in the manger, he exclaimed, "Darn it! Cows fighting over the shared drinking cup." *I'll bet the tank is empty. I forgot to start the water pump.* After flicking the switch to start the pump, he ran up the stairs to check if the tank was empty. "No, plenty water. Maybe they're just scratching their heads on it." He ran back down the stairs and to the manger, only to discover water gushing from a pipe joint.

"You dumb fools!" he cried. He opened the stanchions one at a time to release the nine cows in the east row. *I should've done that right away after I milked each one, but I just didn't have time. Now, I've got water leaking out of a broken joint in pipe above the drinking cup. I'm going to have to shut the valve off to the whole line of drinking cups for the east side, but first, I'm going to take the time to chase those cows off the cow porch and then shut the east door so they don't come wandering back in. Jeez, what else can go wrong?*

Joey shut the door and returned, but before he could deal with the leak, he had to remove a bucket from a cow, dump the milk into the pail, and set the bucket down in the aisle. *I'll shut the valve off quick before I put the machine on another cow.* He returned to the broken pipe and found he could not reach the valve, so he had to get a bale of straw to stand on. Standing on the bale and eyeballing the valve, he exclaimed, "Jeez! It's one of those real old valves! But I've seen Dad do this. He leaves this old heavy hammer on top of the stanchions just to use for closing the valve. This may take a while. I'd better remove the other two buckets and set them in the aisle."

As water leaked from the broken pipe and ran toward the gutter, Joey rushed to the west aisle and, with heroic effort, lifted each bucket from under the cows and emptied the milk into pails. *I'd better carry the milk up to the bulk tank before I try to shut off the valve. I hope I can do it in two trips by taking two pails at a time.*

Returning from the second trip, he checked the water tank. *Nearly full. I'll shut off the pump, but if I don't close that valve, gravity will empty the whole tank through that leaky pipe.*

Standing on the bale, Joey eyed the valve, making sure he understood the task ahead of him. The valve consisted of a long steel peg that was hammered tightly into a beveled hole in the junction of the pipe. The peg had a hole running perpendicular through it, which allowed water to pass through. To close the valve, Joey would have to hammer the steel peg from the other side of the junction until it was loose, turn the steel peg so the hole was perpendicular to the water flow, and then hammer the peg back into the beveled hole until it was wedged tight, closing off water to the pipe below the junction.

I've seen Dad do this a couple of times, and I think he has to hold the valve in so that when he hits it with the hammer, the peg doesn't fly out the other side. He said there was a spring missing or something that was supposed to hold the valve in place.

Joey grasped the heavy hammer with his right hand and held the other side of the peg with his left, but the hammer was too heavy for him to swing at this awkward angle. Instead, he grabbed the hammer with both hands and swung hard, hitting the peg dead-center. He swung again and again until the peg shot out the other side, hitting the concrete east wall about ten feet away. Water gushed from the open valve, immediately drenching Joey and the bale of straw on which he stood. "Holy cow!" Joey yelled. "Where did that peg go?" Water poured from the open valve, drenching the nearby cows and filling the gutter behind them, and as he scrambled to look for the peg, he muttered, "I sure could use some help. Why isn't anyone home yet? I wonder what the heck everyone is doing?"

CHAPTER 14

WEEDING

4:30 p.m., Saturday, July 14, 1956

After John and Pastor Mark left the meeting at the parsonage, the awkward silence lasted less than a minute before Betty spoke. "I confess, Rose and I did talk about how great it would be if she stayed, and we did talk about how to maybe convince John that it was the best thing for them both. But we didn't mean for it to come off like some kind of conspiracy."

Martin bristled. "*Conspiracy*. That's a big word, Betty. Good thing John quit school so you could get that education of yours. Family members sacrificed so you and Rose could do what you do now. Help teach those young people. But I guess the old saying is true, 'A good deed never goes unpunished.' I never went to high school either. Everything in the family was done for Rose. But there was nothing left of the farm for me to inherit. Now, you're both just too good for either one of us."

"Is that the way you feel too, Mary?" Rose asked.

"I'm sad that John had to feel that we were all piling on him, as if he were some evil person. He's not. And Rose, I think it might be good if you learned to appreciate what you have instead of always trying to hammer it into something else. You're always preaching to count your blessings. Well, maybe you missed that chance. Martin and I wish you the very, very best. And I hope staying up here with Betty works out well. Right now, though, Martin and I are going to go pull some weeds in the garden."

Rose got up too, saying, "I'm going to the kitchen to do the dishes alone." Betty offered to help, but Rose said, "No, Betty. I want to be alone."

"Well, I'm not leaving you alone at this time," Betty declared as she followed her into the kitchen.

Mary felt Martin's hand grab hers as they hustled out the door to the back yard. *He grabbed my hand. He never does that.* Once outside, Mary felt his arm around her shoulders as they met Pastor Mark and John in the garden. Pastor Mark was on his knees, pulling weeds. John stood nearby, back to the garden, staring at the trees north of the parsonage.

"I must've missed these tiny weeds the first time," Pastor Mark said as he stood back up. "Weeding the garden helps clear my mind."

"What do you do in the wintertime?" Martin teased.

"I make a snowman. Sometimes Betty helps."

"You're an unusual pastor, if you don't mind my saying so."

"I don't mind, regardless of how you mean it, but I want you to know that I had no idea the discussion was going to go in that direction. Rose wouldn't tell me exactly what she was going to say, and now I understand why. Some things are just for the close family."

"Rose delivered a tough message in there," Mary admitted. "Tough for her, but especially tough for John. He had no idea what was going to happen."

With his arm still around Mary, Martin said, "Although she claimed otherwise, Rose seemed to know where she wanted the discussion to go. Her mind was made up to stay here if she could."

"Maybe Betty and I praised her work here too much. Maybe I should've reached out to her pastor to help her find a place to help at her own church."

"I don't think that would've helped," Martin said abruptly. "He's not like you."

Mary clarified, "When Martin said you were an unusual pastor, that was high praise. He's not belittling the efforts or the accomplishments of another clergy. He's saying that you are one of the few who could've drawn Rose out of her funk to serve others and enjoy life again."

"If that's what I did, good, but I am not totally sure our embrace of Rose and her work didn't do some damage."

Martin spoke slowly, measuring his words with care. "It turned out to be a tough day for John, but I think you and Betty showed Rose the love she needed. Surely, you would agree that love is always a good thing."

Pastor Mark sighed. "Thank you, Martin." He paused a moment and said, "I just wish they hadn't come to the conclusion that divorce was the only solution."

"What would you have us do?" John asked. "She doesn't want to be with me anymore."

"What would you advise, Pastor Mark?" Mary asked.

"As a person in the clergy, I usually advise against divorce. The church only accepts divorce as a path if there is adultery involved. But withholding companionship from a spouse does not make for a Christian marriage. Betty and I have agreed to take her in temporarily. For her to live here long-term is a decision for the church council. They'll probably approve, but she will have to pay them rent. If she gets divorced, I don't know what their reaction will be. I'll argue to keep her, though. She does great work with the kids and old folks. She's good on the piano, and everyone likes her. Betty and I like her too. Several of the more reticent young girls really came out of their shells when Rose helped with the youth groups. You should see her when she's with the kids. She's like another person! Positive and funny, not sarcastic, and never critical. She needs those kids as much or more than they need her. She has a place here. And I think she needs this place."

"And it doesn't sound like there is any chance for reconciliation," Mary said.

"No," Pastor Mark said, "and that's mostly because of two opposing feelings Rose seems to have: First, she likes to blame everyone else for everything. And second, she blames herself for everything. She won't forgive herself for what she sees as her shortcomings and bad behavior during the past several years. She mentioned her faults again and again, and it bothers her even more than she lets on. I think Betty and I can help her with that. And I agree with her. I don't think John can help. You're a good man, John, and Rose knows it, but for whatever reason, what the two of you once had is now lost."

With a hint of sarcasm, John said, "I'll leave the philosophy to you wise folks, but I need to add one thing. Not a warning but a caution. Rose likes working with your young people, Pastor Mark, and she's good at it, so you say. Maybe they like her putting some direction in their lives. Good. But at what point will they want her to let go? And will she?"

"I never considered that could become a problem," Pastor Mark said.

"And I hope it never does," John answered. Then he added with a broad smile, "I'm just speaking from my limited experience of living with Rose for nearly twenty-four years."

John took a few steps away from the others before he stopped. Trying to keep his head raised high, he said, "Let's say our goodbyes. I'd like to just go now rather than later. Thanks for the tour of the church and the parsonage, Pastor. Maybe I'll see you another time."

"And in better circumstances," Pastor Mark added.

"Want me to drive, John?" Martin asked.

"Maybe later. Look, Pastor, I want to thank you for being there for her. I guess I'm not what she needs. Maybe you and Betty are." He offered his hand.

Pastor Mark shook hands with John and then Martin and Mary, but before they left for the car, Mary asked him, "May I use your bathroom before we go?"

"Of course. You know where it is."

Mary entered through the back door, passing the kitchen where Rose and Betty stood by the sink, doing dishes. *Oops! Don't really want to face either of them for a while. What would I say to them, anyway? What would Rose say to me?* She hurried into the bathroom, eager to leave the place and get on the road home.

But the moment she exited the bathroom, Mary no longer had to guess what Rose would say.

"I suppose you think I'm a rotten person? Leaving a nice man like John."

Mary's mind flooded with smart-ass remarks. *Not any more than usual, dearie.* But it was not the time to be insincere. Rose's remark was not a question. She was looking for support. Mary stepped toward her, trying to gauge her facial expression. Rose's red, puffy eyes contrasted with her natural stern demeanor.

Mary tried to sound sympathetic. "Look, I'm not much used to telling others what to do and—"

"And I suppose I am," Rose snapped.

Mary paused, reluctant to argue with the woman who had routinely brought controversy to the family, but forged ahead. "Rose, that's not what I meant! Think about it. I'm saying I have no right to tell you what to do. But if you don't want to be judged as a 'rotten person,' as you put it, you might want to try to not treat others as if they were."

"You're talking about my treatment of Anna."

"No, Rose!" Mary exclaimed, even as she realized Rose's bringing up Anna enraged her more than it should.

"Then you must be referring to the friction between you and me when you married Martin. I thought you were over that."

"Quit dragging everything else into this moment! You're the one who never gets over anything, it seems. What I'm referring to is your reaction to me right now. Why, when you could use some empathy from others and you even kind of asked for it, do you have to push me away before giving me a chance to give you that support?"

"Rose is just under a lot of stress," Betty said. "You'll have to forgive her."

"I have to forgive her! Of course, I do, and I'm good at it because I've spent my entire married life having to forgive Rose for something she said or did or didn't do—and meanwhile, she never apologizes, so forgiveness is more like pretending it never happened."

"Let's stick to one topic!" Rose exclaimed. "Answer me this. Why didn't Anna forbid Billy to come to her wedding? Why did the family seem to try to hang onto him even after the two broke up?"

Mary picked her words to cut deep. "One topic, eh? Perhaps, the 'red-haired demon,' as you called her, was not capable of hating your son. And neither was her family."

Rose's face broke into an angry sob. As she regained her composure, she said, "I shouldn't have called her that, and I know it hurt Billy when I did. I'm so sorry. I have to live with what I did to my poor boy. The punishment is inadequate for my sins, but it may be more than I can bear."

"Oh, you'll bear it, all right. Rose, I don't think you're a rotten person, but I'll repeat myself. Sometimes you treat people as if they were rotten—me, Martin, Emma, Anna, Billy, and today, John!"

"Really, Mary," Betty said. "I can't just stand by and have you say those things about Rose. She's never treated me that way."

"That's because she doesn't feel *superior* to you like she feels toward the rest of us. Lucky you!"

When Betty did not respond, Mary continued. "Look, Rose, Martin and I know your recent behavior was driven by loss, loneliness, and anger. I only wish we could've been more helpful. But when you and John are hammering out this divorce, remember that he is a good person and you have a last chance to become one too."

"But Mary," Betty said earnestly, "we never thought the discussion would end with a divorce."

"Well, I don't believe you!" Something inside Mary clicked, shifting her anger into high gear. "You really didn't think John would go that far?"

"I didn't," Betty said.

Mary took a deep breath and tried to stay calm. "So, you're saying you just wanted to take his wife away from him so you can have the benefit of her work and her talent and her company for yourself, and leave John home alone on the farm to continue to make a living for his wife. And you would be just fine with that as long as they stayed married so you wouldn't feel like you broke them up, because you'd just repeat that your church's stance on divorce is to discourage it and work through problems. You think that doing that to John is an example of working things out? I'd call it scheming to allow you and Rose to feel guilt-free! And you'd be free to pursue being do-gooders and continue to feel superior to the rest of us! Wow! You guys are something!"

Rose and Betty said nothing.

"Now, I'd better go before I have to use the toilet again. Thanks for having us over, Betty, and, Rose, you make great pies. Goodbye."

Mary's rage stayed with her as she left the kitchen, but regret filtered into her mind as the outside door closed behind her. All those years she had kept her rage inside as she listened to Rose's rude comments about others, but now, after spilling her anger, she regretted losing her composure. *I've held this anger in for years; I could've just as well shut up for a few more hours.*

As she walked around the house toward the car, she saw the two men she would be spending the next few hours with, the brothers of the two women she had raged against. *I'll probably have to confess about my rant before they hear it from Rose and Betty. Truly, Rose has been insensitive and mean ever since I've known her, and Betty has always acted superior. The two of them together are almost unbearable. Smug and righteous. I didn't say anything they didn't deserve to hear, but I wish I had just walked away today. I hope Martin and John will understand why I didn't.*

Once John drove the car onto the roadway, Mary said, "I saw a clean filling station at the crossroad when we came. Please stop there, John. I have to pee again."

Martin added, "I do too, but I didn't want to break the rhythm of leaving after goodbyes were all said."

John agreed. "Good call. We need gas anyway."

In a few miles, John swung the car into the station, where they took turns visiting the toilet. After John paid for the gas, he handed Martin the keys. "Drive us home. I'd like to close my eyes for a while. Get rid of this nightmare."

"I'll sit in front," Mary said, "so you can stretch out in the back seat."

Two hours later, John opened his eyes and remarked, "Boy, was I tired. I hadn't slept much at night since I got Rose's letter." He stretched his arms and rotated his neck to relieve stiffness. "I was so excited about going to get Rose. I have to confess, I was shocked to hear her say she couldn't come home. That she didn't want to come home. I'm still weak in the knees."

"You did good, John. You did good. Better than I could've done if Mary left me."

"Yeah, but Mary hasn't been giving you hints for the last four years or so. Have you, Mary?"

Mary responded, "No, no." *Quite the opposite, in fact.* "Since when did you think Rose was giving you hints?"

"I only figured out the hints as I was falling asleep back here. I remember once a few months ago she told me that maybe we weren't meant for each other. That hurt at the time. I'm glad she didn't dwell on that today. Not sure I could've stomached it. She'd always said you and Martin weren't meant for each other but that she and I were meant for each other. Quite a turnaround, I'd say, wouldn't you?"

Rose was still playing the same old tune, trying explain the past, the present, and the future with her meant-to-be theories. The kitchen confrontation still fresh in mind, Mary changed the subject. "We're only about fifteen minutes from home now. You can come in for coffee and sandwiches, if you want."

"I didn't realize we were so close to home," John said as he glanced out the window. "Hey, we're coming up to the truck stop, the Coffee Cup Café. Billy and I eat lunch here at least once a week. It's easier to drive here than to bug Rose to make lunch at home. Stop here, and I'll buy you guys supper. Then we can talk about the day. I've got a few things to get off my chest. It's after seven thirty. Your kids got the chores, right?"

"Yes, but that doesn't mean I don't worry," Mary said. "The kids are probably done milking or just finishing up. Either way, if we go home now, it would put my mind at rest, and you can talk to us over coffee and sandwiches at our place."

John said, "Well, what do you think, Martin? The turn is coming up fast. We go home now to check on the kids, or I buy you guys supper?"

CHAPTER 15

DITCHES

5:30 p.m., Saturday, July 14, 1956

Resigning herself to waiting impatiently for Dory's return from town, Mary went to her bedroom and sat on a pillow near the east attic window to keep watch while she continued to read *Oliver Twist*. After a short time, she leaned back against the wall and fell asleep.

All eyes were on her, accusing her of terrible things, of things no one uttered—Dory, Maggie, Jimmy, all pointing a finger at her. And then the threatening gestures by Jack Drude, her stepfather, and her brothers, each leering down at her as she lay helplessly struggling to move to safety.

She awoke in a sweat from the bad dream. Even though she knew immediately where she was and that she was now safe, she trembled. Setting the book aside, she gathered her legs beneath her to stand, rubbed her eyes, and focused out the window in time to see Dory parking the truck in its spot next to the shed. Mary pulled back from the window to remain out of sight, but when she realized Dory was alone and running toward the kitchen door, Mary hurried downstairs to meet her.

Mary reached the kitchen as Dory barged in to exclaim, "I think they may be on to us. Rusty spilled the fact that my brother and I came over on the orphan train and that he is dead. I'd figured out they were your Maggie and Jimmy early on, but I didn't think they had a clue as to who I am until now. You had told your friends about your father and me, right?"

"Right."

"Well, they're mounting the tire now, so they'll be gone soon. Maybe we're still safe. By the way, Tom called. It's a boy and everyone is doing fine, but he won't be back for hours, so I'd better go help milk. See you later."

Mary's eyes followed Dory, who hurried out the door toward Webers' farmyard. *I'll be alone another two whole hours.*

With hope for a last sighting of the blue Ford, Mary ran to the attic. Her persistence was rewarded when she spotted the blue Ford exiting Webers' driveway and turning south. "They're leaving!" she shouted. And then she added sadly, "I've missed my chance." *I'm so alone. But maybe I can see them without Dory knowing!*

Mary raced downstairs. *It'll be just the three of them now. Maybe I can catch up to them! Jimmy never drives fast.* Hoping Dory had left the keys above the visor, Mary ran outside without a plan for what she would do if she caught up to her friends. As she started the pickup, she said to herself, "I'll worry about that when I catch them." And she hoped none of the Webers were looking east as she sped by their farmyard.

As Jimmy drove south after leaving Webers' farm, he felt good about the new tubes in the tires. Sure, it cost a few bucks, but he felt safer than if he'd had the old tubes patched. Although his mind filled with questions about Dory's past, Maggie and Robert wanted to talk about other things.

"It'd be hard to get lost in this country. There's either a road or something marked as a low-maintenance road every mile."

"Until there is a swamp and the road stops, like it does up ahead," Jimmy said.

"So, maybe we didn't find Mary," Maggie said, "but I think you have a new girlfriend, Jimmy. Rusty absolutely worships you."

"She's too young," Jimmy asserted. *But she is smart. Rusty spilled some things about Dory and her brother. Dory didn't want to talk about it.* He tried to remember what Mags had said about Mary's dad and aunt, but Mags kept talking. And as he turned left onto a larger road with a loose gravel surface soaked with rain and the shoulders soft and squishy, he tried to concentrate more on his driving.

Maggie continued, "John was a nice kid. Quiet, but fun. We did the dishes and played some three-handed euchre while you were at town. What did you guys talk about on your trip?"

Jimmy didn't answer, staring out the windshield as he exclaimed instead, "What the heck?"

All eyes looked forward to see a pickup truck speeding toward them in their lane as it passed the Plymouth convertible the dancing girls had been driving earlier that day. With only a few car lengths left to avoid a collision, Jimmy steered into the ditch and braked while trying to stay parallel with the road. The pickup breezed by, missing the blue Ford by less than a foot as it skidded to a halt on the wet grass and gravel.

The three searchers remained in their seats, relieved that the pickup had missed them.

After a moment, Jimmy asked, "Are you guys okay?"

"I might have to check my underwear," Robert said.

"Me too," Jimmy said. "I didn't know what else to do, so I took the ditch. Lucky there was a slanted bank before it drops off to shallow water. Not a very wide place, but better balancing on this bank than in the water upside down."

"You made the right move," Robert said seriously. "You probably saved our lives."

Mags spoke haltingly in a low tone, as if she was out of breath. "Jeez, Jimmy. The whole thing happened so fast. I was talking to you and . . . all of a sudden, we're in the ditch."

"Those SOBs could've killed us!" Jimmy exclaimed, his anger growing. Then, assessing their situation, he added, "The angle isn't too steep. Maybe we can push the car onto the road." He opened the door and briefly struggled to climb out uphill. "We got tire chains in the trunk, but the ground is really soft. The wheels will just spin with the chains on and dig us deeper into the mud. The rear end is nearly on the road, though, so maybe if I try to back up, you two could push on the lower side fender and the hood."

Mary enjoyed speeding down the gravel road in fourth gear, although she was still a little unfamiliar with Dory's four-speed transmission. Upon reaching the crest of the small hill that descended to the dead end, she spotted the blue Ford in the ditch and slammed on her brakes, skidding on the soft gravel. *Better be careful. Wouldn't do to run in the ditch.* She made a U-turn and accelerated north from where she had come, stopping just beyond the crest of the hill, where she hoped she was out of sight. *Did they see me? What does it matter? I came to see them.* Confused about her mission, she walked to the back of the truck, leaned on the fender, and used her binoculars to discover Jimmy emerging from the car. *Doesn't look like he's hurt. That's good. Should I go to help?* And as she considered what she should do, a Plymouth convertible skidded to a halt at the edge of the road near her friends.

Jimmy recognized the Plymouth and its occupants immediately when the convertible stopped next to him.

"Are you kids okay?" Diane asked as she and the driver jumped out.

"Yes," Jimmy said. "Thanks for coming back."

"Yeah, I'm Jane, the driver. Those crazy guys chased us all over and we tried to get away, and then from nowhere they showed up to pass. I pulled over as far as I could, but . . ."

Jimmy looked at her hard. "When did they start following you?"

"Okay," Diane admitted. "Barbara and I were standing up in the back seat doing our dance, but instead of just having fun with it, they tried to make us pull over. They pulled alongside us and called us names, like *bitches* and *whores*. We got scared and lost them."

"Then out of nowhere, they showed up again and tried to pass," Jane said. "I saw you guys coming, but I didn't know what to do. We had a ditch full of water on our side. I'm so sorry. I wish I could've done something to stop them."

By this time the third girl had scrambled out of the Plymouth. "I'm Barbara, the one in the middle. I just about threw up. I was screaming so hard."

Jimmy glanced at Maggie and Robert in a silent communication. *A fun joke gone bad, but it could have gone much worse.* "Look," Jimmy said, "if you girls are willing to push, maybe we can get out of this quickly. Push on the lower side of the hood and on the right fender to help me back up. If it starts skidding, just get out of the way."

Jimmy got in the car. He slipped the clutch a little as he yelled, "Push!" The upper wheel just spun. "Try rocking it. Push. Then let it go back. Push. Then let it go back. I'll give it gas only when you push. Got it? You know how to do this, right, Mags?"

Jimmy waited for her nod, and they began. Push. Release. Push. Release.

After several repeats, he felt the car move and floored the accelerator, spraying dirt toward the front as the five kids pushed. In a glorious moment, the tires took hold and the car shot backward onto the gravel road.

"Thanks, everyone. We couldn't have done it without you. But we don't have time to visit. We're supposed to be home by six, and it's nearly that already. We have an hour-and-a-half drive to get home."

"Wait," Diane said as she handed him a small piece of paper. "Here's my number. If you're in the area again, give me a call."

"Unlikely," Jimmy said, but he took the paper and put it in his wallet.

"You never know." She shot him a wide smile and tilted her head. "Stranger things have happened. Goodbye to all of you. Glad you are safe."

Everyone declared their goodbyes, and the girls sped off. As Jimmy turned to get into the car, he noticed in the distance a dull-green pickup parked near the top of a small hill on the road they had come down before turning onto the road where they met the blue pickup. He squinted his eyes and placed his hand above his eyebrows to regulate the light. *Looks like Dory's pickup. Naw, why would she drive out here? Besides, she should be milking. Could be someone else. Probably a million trucks with that ugly dull-green color. But why does someone by the truck seem to be looking at us? Maybe with binoculars?* Determined to discover the spy, Jimmy got in the car as he made a plan of action.

"What the hell are you doing!?" Maggie yelled after Jimmy made quick U-turn to head west.

"Someone in a green pickup was spying on us with binoculars. I want to see who it is."

"We're already too late to be getting sidetracked again. We've got to get home!"

"I don't see any pickup," Robert said as Jimmy turned north.

"That pickup must've taken off when they saw me turning around below the hill!" Jimmy exclaimed as he sped up the hill.

When Mary saw Jimmy turning his car around, she rushed to board Dory's pickup and drove fast to get distance from the blue Ford. Luckily, she spotted a field driveway after the land flattened out at the top of the hill and drove the pickup onto the field of recently cut alfalfa for about fifty yards before she parked the truck behind a small grove of trees bordering the field.

She sighed as Jimmy's blue Ford drove past the field driveway. *What am I doing? Why did I run? I want to see them, don't I?* She watched Jimmy's car continue north and then turn around to head south. *He had to turn around and drive past here to go home. Should I stay hidden? I'm going to feel pretty stupid if they find me hiding behind the trees. I remember the last time I spied on Jimmy from behind some trees.* Smiling at the memory, she saw Jimmy's car slow down as he approached the field driveway. *Darn it! Is he going to turn in?*

"Come on, Jimmy," Maggie barked. "Why are you slowing down? I don't see any green pickup. I think you're seeing things."

"Maybe." Jimmy eyed the grove of trees on the border of the field. *Nothing can disappear that fast. Dull green fits right in with the undergrowth, but I can't spot anything.* But in that moment, sunlight reflected off something in the trees, and Jimmy knew he was right. *Glass from the pickup. It's Dory's. Why would she spy on us?* He braked abruptly and turned the car into the driveway to park. "Stay here, you guys. I'll be right back." He jumped out of the car and raced toward the trees.

CHAPTER 16

CONFRONTATION

5:50 p.m., Saturday, July 14, 1956

"Where the heck is Jimmy going?" Maggie asked Robert as her brother ran toward the small grove of trees.

"Maybe he had to pee all of a sudden."

"Why not do that by the car? After all, I've seen him pee before."

"You've actually watched your brother pee?"

"No!" Maggie slugged Robert in the arm. "I didn't say that. I mean when we were driving somewhere, the boys peed alongside the car when me and Mom were in the car. They didn't go running to a bunch of trees far away."

"That's a relief to hear. Maybe it's number two, then."

"Maybe. It's probably best if we wait in the car."

"Good alone time for us, Maggie."

"So, what's your plan?"

"Well, I could tell you how much I like you and how I'll miss you over the summer."

Maggie couldn't resist teasing him. "Are you telling me that or just saying you could tell me that?"

"Both."

She sensed he was serious. "Hey, I'll miss seeing you every day at school too, but you can come over, you know. We don't have to be putting up hay for you to be welcome."

Maggie liked that he laughed in his usual way, but he seemed to want to say more. *He's never been hesitant to speak. Not like him.* "You got something on your mind?"

"Let's get out of the car and walk toward the trees," he said.

"Okay," Maggie agreed. "But let's walk slowly."

As they got out of the car, Robert said, "I hear shouting."

Without another word, the two of them hurried toward the trees.

Jimmy had reached the trees in less than a minute and opened the pickup's door to find the cab empty. Glancing in the truck's bed, he exclaimed, "That's the tarp Dory had in the back! I'm sure this is her truck!" A small movement under the tarp momentarily silenced his voice before he choked out, "Who's under there?"

With shocked anticipation, Jimmy stared at the tarp as if were itself a living thing. Then, in a swift movement, the tarp flew aside, and Jimmy exclaimed with joy and confusion, "Mary!"

Mary sat up to exclaim, "I'm sorry, Jimmy! I feel so stupid hiding under the tarp, but when I saw you running toward the truck, I didn't know what to do! Yeah, I was spying on you, and when you spotted me, I panicked. I wanted to see you, but I knew I shouldn't."

Her eyes wide and her face unsmiling, she kneeled and set her hand on the edge of the truck's bed. Jimmy saw his opportunity. His heartbeat increased with the anticipation of a tender moment. Placing his hand gently on top of hers, he said, "Don't worry, Mary. It's okay. We're all safe."

"Safe!" she exclaimed with a blank stare.

Jimmy's heart began to pound in his chest as he watched for some positive reaction. Finding none, he worked his fingers under her palm to hold her hand gently in his. A lump in his throat made speaking difficult. "I missed you so much. So good to see you." No reaction. He squeezed her hand tightly and repeated, "You're safe. You're safe!"

But his words of comfort had no positive effect. Instead, a look of terror overtook her face as she remained stiff and still, gazing blankly ahead and groaning, "Safe. Safe. Safe."

This wasn't the reunion Jimmy had imagined. His foolish heart had hoped they might pick up where they left off. If not with a kiss, at least with a hug. *What is she thinking? Did that parting kiss mean nothing to her? Does she even hear me?*

Looking down at their clasped hands, Mary suddenly pulled hers roughly away from his grasp. She stood up and declared, "You have to leave,

Jimmy! I told you not to come. I know Maggie and Robert are with you too. I don't want them to see me! Don't tell them you saw me!"

Jimmy's mouth dropped open in silence. How could she not feel the tender moment of their hands touching? After months of separation, had she not longed for this moment like he had? He struggled to say, "Mary, I came here to see you. To see that you were safe and—"

"I told you in the letter that I was safe!" Mary shouted. "And I told you not to try to find me! Why did you come? Are you trying to be some big hero?"

"I love you, Mary!" Jimmy exclaimed. "And I thought you loved me!" he added, watching her face closely for any sign of compassion. He found none, for her features hardened as she expressed harsh words that cut into his heart.

"We were just kids. Foolish kids with foolish crushes. Go away! It's dangerous for us to meet! You could get me arrested if anyone else learns I'm here. Your finding me is a stupid kid stunt." At the top of her voice she shouted, "Grow up, for God's sake!"

Jimmy rubbed his face with his hands and looked at her in disbelief. *She's like a wild animal, cornered and dangerous! But how can she be so hard? So cold?* After taking a deep breath, he said, "Okay, Mary. Okay. I guess this was a bad idea—our coming here was a bad idea." He waited, trying to give her a chance to soften her response. When she remained icy, he said, "Sorry, Mary. I won't bother you again, ever. I promise."

Seeing nothing but terror and anger in her face, he turned away, wondering if he could actually stay true to his word. When he lifted his eyes to the path ahead, he discovered Maggie and Robert watching them through the trees only a short distance from the pickup. *How much did they hear? Did Mary see them?*

Running toward them, Jimmy said, "She doesn't want to see us." When they didn't move, he growled, "Come on, let's go!"

"I want to see if she's okay," Maggie said.

Jimmy grabbed her hand and pulled her toward the car. "Let's go! She doesn't want to see us, Mags."

Maggie shouted, "Mary was yelling at you! What did you say to make her mad? You must've done something. I clearly heard her yell 'Grow up, for God's sake!'"

Jimmy stopped for a moment to stare at his sister. "And you just assume the worst about me? Look, she's mad at me mostly, but she's mad at us all for coming to look for her. It's not just me. She's mad at all of us for putting her in danger."

"She's my best friend! You must've said something to make her mad at us!"

Feeling weak, Jimmy kneeled down in the field, bowed his head, and gripped a fistful of new-growth alfalfa with each hand. The sweet odor of the young plants filled his nostrils as tears gathered in his eyes. *I told her I loved her, but I can't tell Mags that. I can't tell anyone I said that to Mary. And I'll never say it to anyone again!*

Maggie demanded again, "What did you say to her?! What did you do?!"

"Nothing," he muttered. "All that anger came from her. Now, get in the car. We've got to get home."

He stood up and began walking back to the car, the pain of Mary's rejection increasing with each step. His legs still felt weak, but he resisted the temptation to kneel again. He wiped away tears before they got too far down his cheeks. By the time they got in the car, his self-defense had kicked in enough to force an attempt at humor. "So, I've had fun today—how about you guys?"

Robert smiled briefly, but Maggie slugged him in the arm. "How can you joke about this? My best friend—your girlfriend—hates us!"

Maggie's response surprised and hurt him as much as Mary's had, but his face remained stoic. He methodically put the keys in the ignition. As self-doubt and disappointment grew inside him, his own ego spawned a rational self-defense that grew into anger. *What the hell did I do to deserve Mary's rage? She went nuts! Why couldn't we just talk? Damn. And now Mags keeps yelling at me too!*

"You must've done something!" Maggie shouted. "I'll bet you tried to be her hero! Tried to brag about finding her. Did you pretend we were here to rescue her? Did you try to kiss her? What did you do to get her so mad that she told you to grow up?"

"Why blame me?" he yelled back at her, and he slammed the accelerator as he backed out of the driveway. He shifted the car to low, and the engine roared as the car bolted south, the back wheels spinning and spewing gravel behind them.

In the bed of Dory's pickup, Mary stood stunned and alone. Jimmy was gone, though she could hear Maggie shouting in the distance. She tried to recall her feelings when Jimmy had demanded who was under the canvas. She had been overwhelmed with embarrassment, shame, and then fear—fear of Dory's reaction, fear of Jack Drude and his threats against Jimmy and Maggie, and fear for herself and the possibility of jail time. Only now did she recall the touch of Jimmy's hand on hers and the word *safe*, and how her mind had journeyed to moments of her brothers holding her down, of her father's visits to her bedroom, and of Jack Drude's threats. *What did I say to Jimmy? Why was I so cruel?* She flung herself face down on the tarp and sobbed. *What am I afraid of?*

For a moment she thought about getting in the truck and racing after them, but she controlled herself, recalling fond thoughts of Jimmy and the memories of good times with Maggie. She comforted herself with the idea that they were both concerned for her safety. Then a realization came to her. *Maybe our past is too painful? Or is it just a dream I don't want to spoil? But the past is over. Don't drag it up again.* With a heavy heart, she decided to drive back to the safety of Dory's farm.

With the rear tires spinning on the wet gravel, Jimmy recklessly accelerated the Ford, trying to ignore Mags yelling into his right ear, "You do stuff without thinking! Then you don't want to take any responsibility! What did you do to Mary?"

Enraged, Jimmy exclaimed, "You don't know what the heck you're talking about!" He glanced in the rearview mirror and announced, "Ha! There's that damn blue pickup that tried to run us off the road!"

The pickup pulled up close behind them. Jimmy sped up, but the pickup stayed menacingly close to his bumper. With anger already on edge, Jimmy's rage grew quickly, and his boldness grew too.

"Hang on, kids. I'm going to see how smart these guys are." He shifted into second to pull away. They followed closely. He slowed and sped up, slowed and sped up several times until he was sure of their response. "I am now driving their truck just as surely as if I was behind the steering wheel," Jimmy declared, and he shifted to high and sped down the small hill toward the dead end where they would turn east.

"Don't do anything stupid!" Maggie shouted.

Just before the turn, fully aware of how the car would handle on the loose wet gravel, he shifted to second, floored the accelerator, and turned hard to the left, setting the car tires spinning as they turned north and he shifted to low gear.

Unprepared, the blue pickup drove at high speed straight into the ditch. It came to a stop about ten yards off the road in six inches of water and mud.

His rage peaking, Jimmy parked, jumped out of the car, slammed the door, and ran to the edge of the ditch. "What do you think of that, you hot-shot assholes! Driving like maniacs. Endangering us and those three girls in the convertible. You could've killed us all! And for what! For fun? Deranged assholes, that's what you are!"

"Jeez, Jimmy," Maggie warned from the car. "Don't be stupid. There are three of them!" The boys were already climbing out of the truck.

"Robert, get the tire chains and the lug wrench. Bring them over here. I don't care if there are ten of them. Let them come two at a time."

Taking the tire iron Robert handed her, Maggie asked, "What do you want me to do?"

"If one of them sets foot on shore, you hit him on the head," Jimmy yelled. "And Robert, swing that chain around and around to knock one down." He turned to yell toward the pickup, "But I'll dare any one of you to come to shore just to meet me. Just me!"

Jimmy pulled off his T-shirt and threw it on the gravel. "Any two of you, even. I'll rearrange the gravel on the road with your ugly face!"

Robert menacingly swung the tire chains above his head and said, "I'd stay in the truck if I were you guys. Jimmy here is known for breaking bones. 'Bone-breaker,' they call him. Or 'bone-buster,' to some. Yeah, 'Jimmy the bone-buster.' And these tire chains are my favorite weapon!"

Seemingly undeterred, the two larger boys sloshed through the water, the taller and heavier one leading the charge. As the first one stepped out of the water, Jimmy kicked his shin hard. As the boy felt to his knees, Jimmy used the heel of his hand to smash the boy's nose, sending him back into the water.

"I think you broke my nose!" the big kid honked in surprise.

Undeterred, the second boy charged toward Maggie, but Jimmy easily beat him to the shoreline to deliver a kick to his face, which rolled him into the muddy water.

"Just trying to improve your looks. No charge," Jimmy yelled. He ran at the first boy, beating his chest like a gorilla, and took a couple of steps to get some speed before doing a forward flip and landing on his feet. He beat his chest again before dodging left into another flip. He landed on his feet again, but slipped at the next step and fell onto his side. *I've got to be careful not to hurt myself. Calm down a little. Get up fast while the boys are still recovering from their backward fall into the mud.*

Jimmy jumped up, inhaled deeply, and exhaled slowly to calm himself. "Look, I think even shit-for-brains guys like you can see that I can keep this up all day. All I ask of you now is to go sit in the bed of the pickup while we discuss the next step."

"Damn you!" the larger boy exclaimed.

"Shut up and get going!" Jimmy waited until the three boys had climbed onto the pickup bed before he spoke with authority. "Okay, I've calmed down a bit, but I can ramp myself up to a kick-your-ass mentality in a second. And my two able-bodied lieutenants are standing by. So, stay seated. I would hope you guys learned something about safety, but if you didn't, just ask yourselves, how many people have to die before you swallow some wisdom? Who was driving, anyway?"

The two attackers pointed at the younger boy.

"No, I know that's a lie."

"The big guy was driving," Robert said. "I saw the young one in the middle and the other one has a tan shirt. I saw his arm sticking out the shotgun window."

"They'll try to pin this on me!" the younger one exclaimed. "I don't even have a license, but Dad sent me to town to pick these guys up to help haul hay today. Then they made me let them drive, and we never did get to help with haying."

"You're the one who didn't attack me. I'll be glad to drive you to your dad's place. He'll probably be willing to pull you out since it's his truck. What's his name?"

"Jacob Henderson. He'll kill me when I get home."

"Just the same, young Mr. Henderson, you'd better get home soon. Slosh out to shore here. Be sure to bring the keys to the pickup with you. And you two, stay put till we leave."

The pair remained in the pickup's bed as the young man hurried to shore to climb into the back seat of the Ford.

"Those two assholes will be gone as soon as we clear the area," Jimmy said.

CHAPTER 17

GOING HOME

6:15 p.m., Saturday, July 14, 1956

After dropping off the Henderson boy, Jimmy sped off to seek the road home, his mind replaying the scene in the pickup with Mary. But Maggie gave him no peace.

"I'm still mad at you, Jimmy! No, not mad, but furious!" she exclaimed.

He turned his head to briefly glare at her before focusing again on the road ahead. "I've got nothing to say to you, Mags. And I'd welcome silence from you both for the rest of the way home. It's after six o'clock, so we're late already and I need to make good time."

As he approached the turn toward home, he found himself unable to explain Mary's actions or his own. He wanted answers. *Why did she send me away? Why was she so cold? If she didn't want to see us, why follow us? Damn, we came here to find her. And we found her. But—* Suddenly, he remembered the movement in the attic window at Dory's. *Rusty waved at someone. Maybe Mary lives in Dory's attic. She was driving Dory's pickup. Why did she hide?*

For a brief moment he entertained the idea of turning in the other direction, going back to see Mary. But, reluctantly, he tried to embrace the answer he feared. *She no longer cares for me. Maybe her love for me was just my own foolish imagination. I'd better just go home.* Decision made, he turned toward home and accelerated way beyond his usual speed.

I feel like a dumbass after what Mary said to me. She didn't even want to touch me. Did she ever really like me at all? And five months ago, I thought we were about to start dating. How could I be so stupid? Maggie accused me of trying to be a hero. I think Mary did too, but I don't remember for sure. Is it so bad—to try to be a hero for someone? Her words made me feel worthless and stupid. And angry! I was so angry I wanted to strangle someone—not Mary, of course. I'd never hurt Mary. But those boys. I was stupid to challenge them, but I was angry enough to kill them. His anger had taken him to a dark place, and he realized now it was a place to which he never wanted to return. Still, his mind gave him reasons for his actions. *They could've killed us! Mags, Robert, me! And the three girls too!*

"You're going too fast!" Maggie exclaimed. "We're late, but don't speed!"

Her voice brought Jimmy back to the present. Glancing down at the speedometer, he slowed down before he said, "Right."

"So, it's okay for us to talk now?" Mags's words were sharp. "A mile or so back you told us to be quiet for the rest of the trip home."

"I'm sorry I said that. What I need is a change of subject. A distraction."

"Can't do that," Maggie asserted. "I have too many questions about what happened back there."

"Okay, ask away, but no more questions about Mary for a while."

"Try this, then. Back there with the boys in the ditch, you had me scared! I mean, you were a totally different person. One I'd never seen before. And one I don't want to see again. And how can I ever forgive you for making Mary so mad at us?"

"You scared the hell out of me with that gorilla act!" Robert exclaimed. "When did you learn to do that?"

Jimmy ignored Maggie's question about Mary. "I've been practicing the flip in the hayloft for a year, but this is the first time I did it where I didn't have soft hay to land on."

"That was stupid!" Maggie exclaimed. "You could've hurt yourself, and then what would we have done? It was just another stunt to prove you're brave."

"But we had to defend ourselves! We had to show them we were ready to do whatever it took to keep ourselves safe. Every fight is a fight for survival. What do you say, Robert?"

Robert hesitated, and Jimmy saw him shifting in his seat as if trying to work out a safe answer that would please his friend and his girlfriend. "You don't have to answer now. Think on it a while."

"I've been thinking of nothing else ever since we left! First, I've got to say that I was glad you were on my side, Jimmy. Crazy as you were. You were on my side, and I was ready to swing that chain at any one who got near the bank."

"But I wasn't ready to conk someone with the tire wrench!" Maggie inserted. "I was so glad that you came over to kick the guy before he got to me. I was scared. If I would've hit him, my God, what if I'd killed somebody? I'd be going to jail."

Robert exclaimed, "You were still like some fierce Amazon warrior. Wow!"

"I know! But that's not me!"

Jimmy kept his eyes on the road and his face neutral. "Maybe we become who we need to become at the moment. Maybe the real us comes out when needed."

"If that's the real me, I don't much like me," Maggie protested.

"I don't much like that side of me either," Jimmy said. "But what do you do when you're trying to figure out who you are, and after you figure it out, you don't like the answer? I can't erase what I did back there, but I am going to try to control myself more."

Jimmy kept his focus on the road. "Look, I was crazy mad after Mary told me to leave, but I'm not the kind of guy who loves violence or doing violence to others. So, I got to kind of work myself up to it. Beat the drum. Sound the bugle to charge or do a war dance, you know? I think it worked up you two as well."

"Are you saying you were totally in control?" Maggie asked. "I don't believe it."

"No, once I started, my anger fed on itself and I lost control. I'm not proud of that. When I think that maybe I could've really hurt those boys, I cringe at the thought of how much I could be regretting the whole thing now."

"Two of those boys, as you call them, were bigger than you," Robert reminded him. "And their crazy driving could've got us killed. I don't regret what you did back there. Not at all."

Maybe it was the realization of their brush with death that kept the three of them silent for a while. Maggie spoke first. "But now we know why the boys were chasing the girls. They were doing their topless dance. Not an excuse for the boys to try to pull in front of them or run us in the ditch, but they didn't just pick on them out of the blue."

"Yeah, we can understand that," Robert added. "But you're not going to claim Jimmy and I would've acted that way if you hadn't been along, are you?"

"You tell me."

"Jimmy wouldn't endanger lives needlessly like that."

"Well, Jimmy drove pretty recklessly too—like that skidding turn he did that put the guys in the ditch."

"I think it's called a power turn," Robert said. "And where did you learn how to do that, Jimmy? Or even more of a puzzle to me is *when* did you learn how to do that? You don't even have your license yet!"

"Yeah, I have to admit that I had never done turns like that before with a car. I was hoping the car would handle a little bit like a tractor when the ground is wet and you spin the wheels on purpose by gunning the engine. When the cow yard was slippery after a rain, I used to skid around and do power turns with the Ford 8N tractor when I was only about ten. I'd cut out after supper pretending to be eager to get the cows, and Dad would let me drive the tractor to the pasture to get them."

"Wow!" Robert exclaimed. "And I thought you were such a good kid."

"I was . . . and I am, but I like a little adventure."

"But it was dangerous!" Maggie exclaimed. "You could've rolled the tractor! And today, you could've rolled the car!"

"I won't say the practice wasn't risky, but the wheels on the tractor were set wide for cultivating corn when I used to do it. Hard to roll a tractor with the wheels set wide, and the 8N is low to the ground."

"Did Dad ever see you sliding around?"

"Once. He didn't get as mad as I thought he might. He explained that he had seen my tracks from sliding around once before and wanted to catch me at it to talk. He told me it was best to experiment when the tractor was wide, but he said I'd better never try it when the tractor's wheels were set to the normal distance apart."

"And did you?" Maggie demanded to know.

"No, he had that look on his face when he told me not to. You know the look?"

"I do. He doesn't use that look often."

"Anyway," Robert said. "I'm glad you did what you did. Sure, you drove a little crazy, but you needed to."

"I plead self-defense," Jimmy argued. "But I'd never drive alongside anyone and call them names. I'd never drive alongside those girls and call them bitches or whores. That's mean and rude and just plain uncalled for."

Maggie boldly added, "I'll just say this: If they don't want to be called bitches, they shouldn't act like bitches."

"Ooo-eee!" Robert exclaimed as he laughed and gently elbowed Maggie in the ribs. "So, you might say the girls *bare* some responsibility for the whole mess, eh?"

"Okay, okay, I get your joke. But seriously, they sure do. Actions have consequences!"

"I don't disagree," Jimmy said, "but seriously, if a guy had been with those girls, I'll bet their behavior would be stifled, just like you claim ours is when you're along."

Maggie moaned. "Okay. I agree. Mixed company changes the agenda and the behavior. That's how I'd put it."

"My girlfriend has such a way with words," Robert said as a true compliment.

Conversation paused at that, and Jimmy turned the encounter with Mary over and over in his mind as he struggled to mask the pain in his heart. He welcomed Maggie's interruption of his thoughts—until he heard the topic.

"I'm not letting you off the hook for what you said to Mary," Maggie said. "I didn't hear it, but you were a different person when you came back from talking with her. You were angry and kind of crazy. Did you yell at her?"

"So, you didn't hear it all, but you know it's all my fault, eh? Wow! What's the use of my saying anything if you are just going to blame me? Hey, I'm the guy who saved you at the pond, remember?"

Maggie snapped, "You're the guy who got us into the mess, remember? And it started with your meeting with Mary. What the hell happened to make her hate us?"

"I don't know. But let me tell you what I've put together. First, I thought it was kind of strange that Dory insisted that Rusty went along, as if she wanted to keep an eye on her, you know? Sometimes when Rusty spoke, Dory seemed to want to change the subject, and one time Rusty blurted out some interesting facts about Dory before she could stop her."

"What did she say?"

"After Dory raved about how she liked Bur Oak Falls, I talked about how in small towns people know your parents and grandparents, and I asked Dory if it was the same in her experience at Bur Oak Falls. She didn't answer right away, and Rusty jumped in to fill the gap. She said that Dory and her brother came over on the orphan train."

Maggie let out a gasp. "Did she say if the brother was younger than Dory?"

"Yes, he was, but he is dead. Dory is definitely Mary's aunt."

"The world really is that small," Robert muttered.

"All of it fits in with what I remember from the letters Mary had from her aunt. I wish I could remember her aunt's name. It was an old-fashioned, pretty name. Not Dorothy . . ."

"*Dorothea*," Jimmy said. "I heard Lugwrench call her Dorothea. And I'm pretty sure Mary lives in the attic of Dory's house."

"How do you know that?"

"I saw Rusty waving to someone in the attic window. She lives in Dory's attic. I'm sure of it."

The three searchers seemed to breathe in and out as one in silence.

At last Jimmy said, "We set out to find Mary and, by golly, we found Mary. But really, she found us."

Maggie asked, "So why did she run? Why not wait for us and have a grand reunion? You must've said something to upset her, Jimmy."

"I hate to have to remind you guys," Robert said, "but she told you not to try to find her."

"You know what this means, don't you?" Jimmy asked. "She doesn't want to see us. She made the effort to follow us, but when it came right down to it, she decided she was better off without us."

"Hold on, Jimmy. Remember why she left? For our safety and her safety, not because she didn't want to be with us."

"And that's why," Robert yelled, "she told you not to try to find her!"

Jimmy exclaimed, "I'm so stupid! And so selfish! I must learn to listen—when a girl tells me to forget her, she probably wants me to forget her. When a girl tells me to not try to find her, she doesn't mean I should drive across the countryside to try to discover she is living with her aunt on some farm. It means she wants me to stay home and let her be!"

"You know, Jimmy," Robert explained, "you're looking for Mary, but the Mary Schroedler you knew doesn't exist anymore. And neither does the same Jimmy or Maggie or even the invincible Jack Drude."

"Oh, he exists all right. Somewhere in jail. And I know I was lucky when we fought. Both times! Don't think I don't worry about him getting out of jail and showing up on my doorstep some time."

"But he's not the same guy! You beat him once. Broke his bones. Did permanent damage."

"I tricked him and lucked out the first time, and Billy saved me the second time."

"Anyway, back to Mary," Robert prodded. "Remember her? You found her or she found you. But nobody is the same."

"You're some philosopher."

"I agree," Maggie said.

"That Robert is a philosopher?" Jimmy joked.

"No, that we've all changed," Maggie said without smiling.

As they descended the hill toward Riverton, Jimmy was careful not to build up too much speed. At the bottom, he drove slowly through town and across the flat river bottom until he reached the base of the next hill. Then he shifted to second gear to gain speed, saying, "Now we have a steep hill to climb."

They rode a few miles in silence before Maggie said, "Hey, Robert, you said you had some news or something that had made your folks grumpy. You said you'd tell us later. Well, we'll be home in less than an hour, and we're late, so when we get home, we're going to have to go right to work milking cows. May as well spill the news now."

Jimmy's eyes were on the road, but he felt the change in mood. He briefly turned his eyes to Robert. Sadness gripped his friend's face.

Robert turned to them and said, "We're moving again."

"Damn it!" Jimmy yelled. "I got one friend, one good buddy, and he's leaving?"

"And you have to start all over again in a new school," Maggie said with compassion.

Robert lamented, "And I've never had friends as good as you two anywhere. A good buddy like you, Jimmy, and a beautiful girlfriend like you, Maggie, if you don't mind my saying so."

"I don't mind you calling me beautiful," she said, and then added, "And I don't mind you calling me your girlfriend. I like it." She kissed him lightly on his cheek.

Maggie waited a bit before she asked, "What's the big problem for your folks?"

"Mom likes it here. I like it here. And Dad likes it here too, but the money is so much better if we move. Another big promotion and a chance to do some research or something. Mom wants to stay, and there was some talk of them splitting up and if I would go with Dad or Mom."

"Your mom has a nice car," Jimmy joked. When no one laughed, he said, "Sorry."

"No, that's okay. It's almost funny. Trying to pick a parent. Can you imagine doing it?"

"No!" Maggie and Jimmy answered in unison.

"There was a lot of arguing, but this morning they put the house up for sale, which is why I had to clean the garage, and they're going to sell Mom's car so they don't have to drive two cars when we move. That's why they were so particular about the mileage. I want to stay, but I don't want them to split up, either."

Maggie asked, "When are you leaving?"

"Don't know for sure. But maybe July twenty-fifth."

"So soon, huh?"

"Yeah."

"So, this is kind of a goodbye adventure," Jimmy said, choking on the words.

"It's been a hell of a goodbye adventure! Like living a detective story. And I'll probably never see two topless dancers again without paying for the privilege." He grunted as Maggie playfully slapped his arm. "The best part, though, was I got a kiss on the cheek from Maggie."

"You'd better write," Maggie said.

"I will. I'll put a note in the envelope for Bandit too."

"We've said our goodbyes," Maggie said. "We'll be home soon. Let's just talk about the good times, and when we get to the yard and Jimmy stops the car, just get out and drive away. I don't look so good when I cry."

"Yeah, I need to get home right away, anyway. It's nearly eight o'clock, which makes me nearly two hours late too, so I'll be getting hell, that's for sure. I'll be able to visit you before we move."

"You'd better," Maggie said.

"We should get home in about ten minutes," Jimmy said. "I hope the folks aren't home yet."

CHAPTER 18

THE DIVIDE

7:00 p.m., Saturday, July 14, 1956

"You deserve a break, Mary. I'm not worried about the kids. They probably did chores early and are in the house watching television. Let's let John buy us supper."

Mary nodded in agreement, and Martin drove into the parking lot of the truck stop.

John picked a private booth in the back of the narrow café, where there were no seats near them and the hallway led to the rear exit. Mary sat next to Martin, and John sat across from them. Mary hoped for an opportunity to confess her rant against Betty and Rose. *But maybe I should just keep it to myself for now*, she thought. *Better not to rub salt into old and new wounds.*

John grabbed the menus from the napkin holder. Passing them to Martin and Mary, he said, "Order what you want. I'm having two hamburgers with everything, coffee, and apple pie."

"I'll have the same," Martin said.

"I'll have the same, but just one burger for me," Mary said, replacing the menus in the holder.

A tall, middle-aged, chubby waitress dressed in a tan uniform and a white apron appeared by the booth. With a pleasant smile on her face and a cheerful voice, she asked, "What can I get you and your friends tonight, John?"

John gave her the order, adding "Put it on my check, please, Roxie."

"Sure thing," she said. "The kitchen's pretty busy this time of the evening, so it may be a while. I apologize, but I'll bring your coffee right away."

"We're in no hurry," John assured her as she left with a swirl.

"Roxie's here every day," John explained. "She and her husband own the place."

Roxie returned with the coffee. John thanked her and waited a moment after she left before rubbing his face with his hands and exclaiming in a whisper, "Damn! I nearly fell over when Rose asked me for half my worth! I mean, jeez, is that the going rate for a wife walking out after twenty-four years of marriage? The last few years weren't all that happy, either. Every day I bent over backward to please her. Every damn day! It was like trying to run uphill in mud! Now she wants half my farm! How the hell can I do that and still stay in business?"

"Absolutely not fair," Mary said evenly. "That farm is yours."

"And Billy's inheritance!" John exclaimed. "I couldn't have done it without him these past years."

"Maybe it's not my place to say this, John," Mary ventured her opinion carefully, "but Rose left you. You didn't leave her." She caught Martin's glare, but continued to talk. "Of course, the money issue is your business, but half seems out of line to me, especially when you take into account that Billy deserves so much credit for your farm's success."

"And Rose did nothing but sit in the damn house like it was her castle or something. She seemed to treat Billy and me as if we didn't belong there sometimes. Like we belonged in the barn! Or in the field! Like the house was hers! She seemed to make no connection that it was the work we did that financed her house!"

John's anger moved Mary to feel his pain and justify her own frustrations with his wife. *Rose never supported John like she should have.* "You gave her your love and your hard work, John," Mary offered. And as she reinforced his words with her own, his anger became more righteous.

"And she'd rant against me or Billy or anything that was the least contrary to what she wanted to happen. How the hell did I put up with her all these years? She gave me less and less every year until she decided I had nothing more to give her. Now she wants half my farm, for Christ's sake! Half my farm!"

"It's too much!" Mary exclaimed, her voice and rage topping John's whispers as she glanced at Martin to see his fingers fidgeting with his coffee cup. *He seems to be holding back something. What does he want to say?*

The pause was brief, but Martin inserted a short expression of reason. "Now hold on, you two. Maybe I have no right to tell you both to shut up, but listen to yourselves bitching about Rose. I can't just sit here and listen to the two of you trying to out-bitch each other about a woman we all know deserves a little more credit than what you're giving her."

John said nothing, but Mary, feeling unfairly rebuked, exclaimed, "You think she deserves half of what John has worked for all these years?"

"I don't know. But neither do you, Mary. What isn't useful is the two of you piling on, making her out to be some kind of villain without any good qualities. Look, I can come up with just as many gripes about my older sister as either you can. But no amount of bitching will help John come to any reasonable decision about this upcoming divorce suit. If anything, all the complaining will make any kind of compromise harder. And one thing I do know is this—if this goes to court, Rose will have the advantage. She can act and so can Betty, and sorry to say this, John, but Betty is probably behind this whole thing. She's smart and she's motivated, and the scariest thing is that they probably both think God is on their side."

Hurt by her husband's rebuke, Mary stewed silently. *He's taking Rose's side. I can't believe it!*

The next minute seemed like an hour as the three of them said nothing. Finally, John spoke. "I suppose you ain't totally wrong, Martin."

Mary winced. *Now I'm the bad guy! Maybe I should tell them what Rose and Betty said in the kitchen.*

But before Mary gathered her thoughts, John simply asked, "What would you have me do, Martin?"

"Hell, I don't know. But working up self-righteous hatred isn't doing any good."

"But that's what Rose is doing!" Mary exclaimed.

"How do you know that?" Martin asked.

"I talked to her in the kitchen before I left. I didn't want to, but she and Betty stopped me. She was ready to rant about Anna and Emma even after I tried to offer some sympathy. She just wouldn't have it. And as long as Betty has her full attention, she won't be listening to much reason."

"You may be right," Martin said, "but that puts even more pressure on John to be reasonable."

"You must be kidding!" Mary exclaimed. "John will lose everything if he's the only reasonable one."

"Look, Mary. You aren't helping things by making the case against Rose. Let John figure out his own reasons to do what he decides to do. It's his farm, his family, and his wife!"

Mary hurt inside. For the first time, Martin had taken his sister's side instead of his wife's. Her heart ached. She felt even more hurt when John said nothing in her defense. *A good deed never goes unpunished.*

Roxie brought the food, explaining as she set it on the table, "Ralph always amazes me how fast he can cook when we're busy. Enjoy your food. Always good to see you in here, John."

"I know you're busy, but I just want you to meet my two best friends, Mary and Martin Carlson. They farm nearby."

"Never too busy to meet friends of yours, John." Then, to Mary, she said, "Haven't seen you in here before, have I?"

"No," Mary replied with a smile. "We don't get out much, but nice meeting you."

"Same here. Don't be strangers." And she hurried off to serve others.

"She's quite the worker," Mary said. "I'll bet it's a hard job."

As they ate in silence, Mary began to feel isolated from the men. *John called us his best friends, but I suddenly feel so alone.*

Afterward, as John drove to Carlsons' farm, Martin thanked him for the meal while Mary stewed in the back seat with her feelings of neglect. *Be glad when we get home. I suppose the kids are done milking, but I wouldn't mind sitting next to Valentine and milking her if they aren't done. Valentine will listen to my troubles.*

CHAPTER 19

JOEY'S CHALLENGE

7:00 p.m., Saturday, July 14, 1956

Joey searched frantically for the two-inch steel peg, hoping it hadn't bounced into the muck-stained water that was fast filling the gutter. He was relieved to discover it lying in the aisle just inches from the deep gutter. With the peg in his hand, he climbed back onto the bale. Water gushed from both sides of the opening, and when he tried to force the peg into place with both hands, water squirted into his face and his clothing, drenching him from the waist up and making it difficult to see what he was doing. As he reached for the hammer, the peg slipped loose from his other hand and fell to the floor again. He started to curse, but his open mouth caught some of the rusty water and he choked for a moment. *That'll teach me not to cuss. Just get the peg and try again.* Torn between hoping Jimmy would suddenly appear to help him out of the jam and hoping he could fix it on his own, Joey jumped off the bale to retrieve the peg.

On the second try, he carefully shoved the peg in with room for the water to flow through, giving less resistance and making it easier to hold in place with one hand. He turned the peg so the hole was perpendicular to the water flow and tapped it twice with the hammer too hold it in place before using both hands on the hammer to whack it as hard as he could. The peg stayed in place. He pulled his head away, relieved that the water had stopped. He turned to see the cows facing him, their big brown eyes watching him work.

"Did you enjoy the show?" Joey asked playfully, laughing at himself in his drenched clothing. "Don't tell me you weren't laughing at me, you overgrown buggers."

Sitting down on the bale to rest, Joey sighed and then jumped up to exclaim, "No use getting my undershorts wet too." Too wet to be happy but too tired to be angry, he rubbed water from his eyes before he took a deep breath. "Can't just stand around. I've got work to do. Why did that water line have to break tonight? I've helped milk hundreds of times and that didn't happen, but it's a good thing it happened often enough so I remembered how Dad closed the valve." He glanced at the gutter by the east aisle. *Full of water. I'll scoop it out after I finish milking.*

Wet and tired, Joey went back to installing and removing the buckets, changing belts on cows, carrying up milk, and releasing cows after they were milked. The air in the barn remained hot and sticky. After another hour, milking units had been mounted on the last three cows—Sandy, Popcorn, and Valentine. *I won't release you girls until I'm done with all three of you. Jimmy says it's not good to leave only one cow in the barn. She might get antsy to leave. Cows like company.*

After he removed the bucket from Popcorn, he poured the milk into the pail. *Nearly three gallons. That was heavy, but she's a thin cow, and I was able to get close to the bucket before I lifted it. Valentine has a big gut, and she usually has about three gallons.*

Joey took the bucket up to the milk house to be cleaned and returned to the barn to carry up a pail of milk. When he returned, he removed the bucket from Sandy and poured it into a pail. *Less than two gallons. I'll have plenty time to take this bucket to the milk house before Valentine is done. Some cows take twice as long to milk as others, but Valentine is the worst. She takes nearly twenty minutes while most of them take less than five. That's why Mom usually milks her by hand. I'll save some of her milk to feed the calves.*

Joey placed his hand on the top of Valentine's hip to let her know he was going to step next to her and then bent down by the milker. He removed the teat cups one at a time and with his thumb and forefinger tried to strip some milk from each teat. "Not even a dribble. Good girl." He moved close behind her stomach to plant his left foot as close as he could to get leverage to lift the full bucket out from under her.

He squatted close to her, braced his elbow on his knee, and lifted the bucket off the belt hook. *Jimmy said this gives me more leverage, but he said to keep my left foot away from her hoof so she doesn't step on it.* "Maybe it's not so heavy," he said as he began to straighten up and felt the bucket come with him. He shifted his left foot to keep his balance, and as he hefted the bucket and prepared to step over the gutter onto the aisle, Valentine's hoof came down on the toes of his left foot.

She stood there, grinding her foot hard as she pushed against the stanchion to reach the hay in the manger. "Damn!" Joey squealed under his breath. "I should have pushed the hay up to her in the manger before I took off the bucket. Now I'm stuck until she decides to move!" Valentine weighed about twelve hundred pounds, and more than a quarter of her weight was on her back leg as she stretched to reach the hay. Although the pain was excruciating, Joey focused on holding the heavy bucket of milk upright while sandwiched between cows.

His one-buckle overshoe and the leather shoe underneath kept his skin safe from tearing, but nothing protected his toes or the top of his foot from bruising or the bones from cracking. *Jimmy said not to get mad at the cow or yell. He said to try pushing on the cow to rock her back and forth to get her to move her foot for balance.* But he couldn't lean with the heavy bucket in the way, and although he tried to push the bucket into her side, his small size rendered his effort futile. *Jimmy said I could pound gently on her back, but I'd have to hold the bucket with one hand. Can't do that.*

He stood there, hoping Jimmy or Mags or Dad or Mom would come down the stairs to his rescue, and in that moment, he realized the dangers of milking cows alone. Sweat trickled down his already soaked back, and his foot throbbed. *I don't know how much longer I can do this!*

Joey took a deep breath. *I'm on my own. I chose to start this, and now I've got to have a plan. Jimmy would make a plan. I'll push on her and try to rock her. But what am I going to do if she moves her foot? I need to plan exactly.* His left foot was trapped and his back was to the aisle. If she did release his foot, he would have to step back with his left foot, turn to face toward the aisle, bring his right foot around while he held the heavy bucket of milk, and then lead with his right foot to jump over the gutter. He wouldn't have time to turn off the petcock or to pull the hose off it. *The hose is long, and I can pull it off when I get to the aisle. I'll turn the petcock off later.*

With new resolve, he took another deep breath and began pushing the bucket hard against Valentine's thigh and then letting her weight bring her back toward him, creating a rocking motion. Push! Release. Push! Release. Push! Release. Push! Release. *Don't know how long I can keep this up.* Push! Release. *I think she's moving a little when I push.* Push! Release. Push! And for a second, he felt her weight lift from his foot as she moved her hoof for balance. Following his plan, he stepped back with his freed left foot and rotated his body as he struggled to maintain control of the awkward bucket of milk. With his right foot in the lead and his body facing the aisle, he leaped clear of Valentine's stall and onto the aisle. But the sloshing liquid had more control of his landing than he did, and the weight of the bucket carried him forward and down until the bottom rim of the bucket slammed against the concrete aisle. *Crash!* Joey landed safely with his stomach on the handle of the bucket where his hands still gripped the metal. A fraction of a second later, the end of the rubber vacuum hose slammed against the back of his head.

As he lay still for a moment, assessing the damage to himself and the bucket, he listened to the hissing of the open petcock, and he resolved to tell no one of the dangerous encounter with Valentine. But before he could scramble to his feet, he heard the pounding of footsteps in the entryway. *I hope it's not Mom and Dad!*

CHAPTER 20

WEAVING THE WEB

8:15 p.m., Saturday, July 14, 1956

"Joey, are you down there?" Maggie shouted as she ran down the stairs with Jimmy behind her.

Joey rolled to the side, shouting, "Where the hell have you guys been?"

"Are you okay?" Maggie asked as she kneeled by his side. "Why are you on the floor?"

"I just tripped and fell."

"Don't get up," Jimmy said. "Let me check you out first. Can you move your legs and arms?"

"Yeah, yeah. If you guys really give a darn, you would've been home a long time ago."

"I'm sorry we're so late, buddy. It's all my fault. Don't be mad at Mags."

"I don't see any cuts," Maggie said. "And don't pretend you want to protect me, Jimmy."

"Did you do all the milking, Joey? Why didn't you wait for us?" Jimmy asked as he helped him to his feet.

"Right," Maggie said. "You could've been hurt and no one was here to help you!"

"I didn't come down here today with the plan to milk alone," Joey said defensively. "I thought you'd be home soon, so I figured I'd just put in the cows. But you guys didn't show up." His voice started to crack a little as he continued. "Then I saw that the cows were eating all the hay and crapping up the barn. Well, I couldn't leave them out again, could I? So, I decided to start milking, and once I started, I couldn't just quit without finishing! Where were you? I depended on you guys coming home soon, and you didn't!"

Maggie pulled Joey into a hug, and Jimmy put his hand on Joey's shoulder. "Hey, brother, we let you down today. We both did, but especially me. I'm the big brother here, and I acted like a kid. Of the three of us, you did the most grown-up thing. You took care of chores on time. I'm amazed you knew how to do everything."

"Hey, I just did what I've watched Mom and Dad and you guys do for years. Mom and Dad will be proud of me, don't you think? You guys are proud of me, right?"

"Look here, Joey," Jimmy said gently as he put a hand on each of Joey's shoulders. "I'm proud as heck for what you did, but I'm even more relieved that you aren't hurt."

Joey smiled. "We have to take this milk up and feed the calves yet. This should prove that I'm not just a kid."

"Darn it, Joey, I need to convince you that pulling a stunt like this proves you are thinking like a kid. Sure, you can do the work of a grown-up, but to do all this when you're home alone is too dangerous. You needed to wait for us. These cows are too big for you to be handling so many of them alone. What if one of them knocked you down? What if you slipped tying to unhook the bucket of milk from the belt under the cow and carry it to the pail? So many things could've gone wrong."

Joey's smile faded, and his lips pursed as he took a defensive tone. "But won't Mom and Dad be proud that I milked all alone?"

"But I don't know if the folks will see it that way," Maggie said.

Joey looked up with a frown on his face. "What do you mean?"

"Let me explain what happened when Mags and I started milking the cows when the folks were late from town one time. You were only about four or so; Maggie was eight, and I was nine."

"But I'm eleven," Joey protested. "Eleven is a lot older than nine."

"I know, I know, but let me explain what happened. It was just a weeknight in the summer, and we didn't want to go with Mom and Dad to town. You went with them, but we were playing catch with some of the Ryan kids, I think. Anyway, they weren't home at six, and Maggie and I had the big idea we could start milking."

"Right," Maggie said. "We got the cows, put them in the barn, scraped the aisle, dragged the buckets from the milk house. We didn't have the bulk tank then, so we lined up a couple of eight-gallon cans in the aisle."

"And they were way too heavy for us even when they were empty!" Jimmy exclaimed. "I don't know what we were thinking, really. We could've never done the milking like you did all alone."

"Lucky for us," Maggie said, "the folks came home about that time, and when they came down the stairway and saw us struggling with the cans, they began yelling at us like you wouldn't believe. I've never seen them so mad."

"I think you were sleeping in the car through the whole thing, Joey," Jimmy said.

"What did they say?" Joey asked.

"Well, you know that neither Dad nor Mom hardly ever cuss, especially around us," Jimmy said. "But Dad swore about the danger we put ourselves in and the risk to the cattle if we had let things get out of hand with them running around the barn loose. I remember one thing he yelled at me: 'What would you have done if they'd busted a damn drinking cup and water would have been squirting all over the manger?'"

Joey started to speak, but Maggie interrupted. "And I remember Mom yelling about how terrible it would have been to find her two children lying in the gutter bleeding after a cow had run over them or stepped on them. Honestly, they scared the hell out of us."

"Yeah," Jimmy said. "When they get home tonight, they will be mostly mad at me, and rightfully so, but they'll be mad at all of us. I'm sure of that."

In the short moment of silence that followed, the three siblings looked at each other and then down, as if ashamed. Then, in a soft, humble voice, Joey said, "Maybe they wouldn't have to know I milked alone."

Maggie and Jimmy both stared at Joey for a moment before Maggie spoke. "We wouldn't really have to lie. We could just finish up here and go to the house. When they come home, we could tell them the chores were done."

"Which is true, right, Joey? And maybe in a year or so we could tell them the truth and they would realize what a gutsy young man you are. So, eventually, you'd get credit for it and maybe we'd all avoid their anger."

"And punishment! Extra chores, maybe!" Maggie exclaimed. "So, what are we waiting for? They could be home any minute. Let's get going!"

"Okay," Jimmy said. "We need to get our barn clothes before they get home, so here's what we'll do. Maggie, I know you're still mad at me about what happened earlier today, but we need to work together on this. You're the most dressed up, so run up to the house, change into your barn clothes, and bring me my barn boots and shirt and cap. The boots will fit over my good shoes. Joey and I will finish up by feeding the calves and taking up the milk. While Joey scrapes the aisle, I'll take the equipment to the milk house and wash the pails and strainer. Meet me there, Mags. It's after eight o'clock! They could be home any minute. Hurry!"

"It's a plan, but it'll only work if I get changed and back to the milk house with your clothes before they get home!" Maggie exclaimed before she rushed up the stairs.

As Joey began scraping the aisle with the scoop shovel, Jimmy noticed that he limped and asked, "Did you hurt your foot?"

Joey kept scraping in a rhythm and said nothing.

"Don't pretend you didn't hear me, Joey! Are you hurt?"

Joey looked up at his big brother and sniffled. "I'm okay."

"Don't lie to me, Joey. Please! This is serious stuff. If you're hurt, we have to tell the folks everything right away."

"Valentine stood on my foot and I couldn't get her off. I tried to lean into her like you told me to do and rock her back and forth, but she was too big. And she was pushing on it to lean forward to get at some hay in the manger and it really hurt, but I was finally able to rock her and get my foot out, and then I fell when I jumped over the gutter. That's when you and Maggie came."

"We'll have to tell Mom. She'll want you take your shoe off to look at it."

"But can't we tell her it happened when we were all down here milking? I could tell her it happened when I was putting a belt on Valentine. I could say you came over to help me rock her to get my foot out. We don't have to tell her I was down here alone, do we?"

Jimmy considered the risk of adding another layer of lies. He looked at his little brother's earnest face. *Jeez, he's such a good kid, and milking all alone was a pretty big deal for him. A big accomplishment, really.* "Okay, buddy, but we'll have to let Mags in on it too so she knows what's going on. Mom will want to soak your foot in Lysol and hot water, you know. Right now, though, I'd better get upstairs. The folks could be home any minute."

Joey nodded, smiled, and resumed scraping the aisle.

When he got to the milk house, Maggie scolded, "Where have you been? I'd have looked pretty stupid standing in here with your shirt and boots if Mom had walked in."

"I'll explain later," Jimmy said as he grabbed his clothing. "Now shut the door. I saw them turning into the driveway as I came here from the barn. Pull the door shut. I don't want them to see me pulling my boots on."

A moment later, Maggie said, "Jeez, I heard the car door slam."

"They must've seen the lights on in the milk house window and decided to stop here before going into the house." Then, as they watched the handle of the milk house door turn, he whispered, "Don't worry, Mags. We're ready," A second later, Mom stood in the doorway.

"Hi, kids. We had a hell of a day! I hope yours was better."

Jimmy had to clear his throat before he spoke. "Ahem. We're a little late, but the chores are all done." *Why does she seem angry? How could she know about . . . anything we did?*

"The chickens too," Maggie added quickly.

"Where's Joey?"

"Giving the aisle another scraping," Jimmy said. "He likes a clean aisle."

"Well, I hope your day went better than ours. What a disaster we went through! I'll tell you when you come up to the house. I'll make some supper. We ate at a truck stop, but you kids are probably hungry."

"Yes, I could eat something," Maggie said.

Moments after the door closed, they breathed a collective sigh of relief even as Jimmy said, "To make things worse, Mom is mad about something."

"Not at us, though," Maggie offered. Then, mocking her brother, she whispered, "'He likes a clean aisle.' What ever happened to saying as little as possible?"

"Lying to the folks makes me nervous."

"Me too. No, it makes me scared. We probably should've just told them the truth. If Mom is mad at something else, she may take it easy on us."

"Wishful thinking. Anyway, it's too late now. Besides, there's Joey's problem too. Being down in the barn alone with all those big cows is not something I want Mom and Dad to picture. Oh, and he hurt his foot when Valentine stepped on it. It seems to be okay. Mom will want to soak it, and we decided to tell her I helped rock her to get off. Tell them you weren't there if they ask."

"We get the blame for that too."

"That's on me," Jimmy said. "And I can handle that. Problems with this lie just keep adding up. Maybe it's not too late to come clean. Should we—"

The door opened suddenly, interrupting their scheme. Dad and Joey stood outside in silence.

"Joey's hurt his foot," Dad said. "A cow stood on it and he couldn't get it off. Said that you helped him get it off, and Maggie was in the milk house."

"Right," Jimmy and Maggie answered at the same time.

"Why is he still working with it? You should've sent him up to the house."

"Come on, Dad," Joey whined. "I told you it was nothing."

"We depend on you kids to take care of each other when we're gone. Joey, go up to the house right away. Your mother will know what to do. Tell her we'll all be right up."

"I'll go down and shut the lights off and check the barn doors," Jimmy offered.

Dad headed for the house, and as Maggie lingered, he said, "Come on, Maggie. We trust Jimmy to close up."

Jimmy understood the weak smile she gave him before she turned to go. Apparently, she felt as trapped as he did, but Dad's words, *We can trust Jimmy to close up*, put a knot in his stomach that stayed with him as he hurried down the steps to shut off the lights and returned upstairs to pull the chain on the entryway light before he braced the door closed. *If I could just talk to Mags and Joey before we get in any deeper.*

In the house, Joey sat soaking his foot in a pan while Maggie set the table for a quick supper. Mom was frying potatoes and scrambling eggs. Jimmy left his dress shoes in his boots, and with the help of Maggie distracting the folks, he managed to sneak through the kitchen and run upstairs to get his everyday shoes and jeans. He'd worry about getting his dress shoes out of his boots tomorrow when he got up early to do his training in the hayloft. His mind was set on finding a way to talk to Joey and Mags to get them to agree to telling the truth, but when he got downstairs, everyone was at the table eating, and he realized the conversation was about John and Rose. *Too late to come clean.*

"You heard me right, Maggie," Mom said. "When we left, John and Rose were both dead set on getting a divorce."

"A divorce!" Jimmy exclaimed without realizing he'd spoken. As he washed up at the kitchen sink, he listened to Mom explain.

"Quite a fight between the two of them, but Betty got into it with John too. The way the two of them went at John was just plain mean, I think."

"I agree," Dad said as he opened a bottle of beer and set it down by his wife's place at the table. He opened another for himself. "But if Rose feels that she doesn't want to come home to live with John, it's best if she doesn't. I think even John agrees with that."

Jimmy took his seat, and for a few minutes everyone focused on serving food. Then Mom asked, "How's your foot, Joey?"

"Doesn't hurt hardly at all."

"Hurts to picture you with Valentine standing on your foot. You're only a fraction of the size of one of her flanks."

"I didn't want to yell for help and scare her, so I just rocked her back and forth like I've seen you guys do until she finally lifted her foot. Jimmy helped me."

Jimmy was relieved when Maggie asked, "Please tell us more about the Terquists and Thorsons."

"Yeah," Joey said. "I want to hear about the divorce."

"Uncle John must be heartbroken," Maggie added.

"Any chance they'll get back together?" Jimmy asked hopefully.

"Not after all the crap they threw at each other," Dad said.

"Like what?" Jimmy asked, thankful to help turn the discussion away from Joey and chores. *If we don't dig ourselves in too deep, maybe we can still confess.*

"I think Dad and I would agree," Mom said, "that we can spare you kids most of the details. The short version is that Rose said she wouldn't go back to the farm. Said she felt useless. And she said she had found that she felt useful and fulfilled working with Betty and the young people in the church."

"She's teaching them piano and helping with the choir," Dad said. "And she works with the Luther League too. She and Betty were members of the Luther League at our church when they were in high school."

"Sounds like she fits in," Maggie said. "But to just leave her husband to do that—isn't that against her religion or her vows?"

"You'd think so," Mom said. "But people break rules all the time if it suits them, regardless of how religious they claim to be."

"Yeah," Martin said with some sarcasm, "they don't mind breaking the rules themselves. What they're against is other people breaking the rules."

Jimmy laughed at this, but stopped when he discovered he was the only one laughing.

"Anyway," Dad said, "they agreed to get a divorce."

"Is it simple?" Jimmy asked. "To get a divorce, I mean."

"Don't know," Dad said. "But I think it can be if you agree on the settlement without bringing in too many lawyers."

"But that isn't going to happen," Mom said. "Rose got greedy and demanded half the farm."

"She said she wanted half of John's worth," Dad said. "Which is more than just half the farm. I mean, there are cattle and machinery too."

"And I don't think she deserves half," Mom stated flatly. "The farm was John's inheritance. Betty got paid off when she got married, and John got the farm because he ran it since he was a boy. Sacrificed his young years. Had no social life because he dedicated himself to supporting everyone." Mom sounded more and more angry. "Rose never did a darn thing on the farm, so she doesn't deserve a darn thing either. My only question is why it took her twenty-four years before she felt useless. She was useless from the start, if you ask me. Isn't that right, Martin?"

Jimmy watched Dad's face. His mouth seemed to be struggling to say something but unwilling to begin. He took a deep breath and then spoke slowly.

"Well, Mary, she deserves *something*. I mean, they had two kids together, and she made the place a home for the family. She was a good homemaker."

"Until she went bonkers!" Mary exclaimed. "Then she became a home-breaker instead of a homemaker."

Shocked at the amount of anger his mother expressed, Jimmy saw his dad struggle with what to say. Even though Mom had reasons to be critical of Rose, she had never shown such blatant rage at Dad's sister in front of the family.

"Look," Dad said in a reasoning tone, "some people have breakdowns, or go bonkers, as you put it. Maybe they can't be totally blamed for that. But should that wipe out what they've done in the past? She made the farm a home and raised the kids along with John."

"And then she drove away Billy and screwed up the happy marriage she had with John. Are you telling me you sympathize with her on this? My God, what she has done to John! You've told me many times how Rose got away with stuff at home when you were kids and how she didn't contribute much work to the family."

"I always said she did her share of the housework and laundry and all of the cooking when we grew up. She did her share at home."

"But not on the home farm?"

"Right, and that's why it's not exactly her fault that she never liked the farm. My folks taught her that it was men's work. And it's not only that. As the eldest kid, she was probably more affected by Pa's drinking than I was. When things started to go to hell financially on the farm and Pa started drinking, he would leave sometimes and go on a bender for a couple days. I was about ten and she was sixteen. It was hard on me because I was just a kid, but it was worse for Rose. You see, I got out of the house to work with Pa's brother, Uncle Art, who would come over to help when Pa was on a bender, but Rose was stuck in the house with Ma's raging anger and resentment. So, Pa's drinking was harder on her than it was on me. And then, when Pa got back, he was the good father again and I got to work with him. He was a terrific father when he wasn't drinking, and Rose never saw that part of him. All she got to hear was Ma's harsh words against him. He deserved that, of course, but he was more than that too. Sure, she got out of a lot of work, but I wouldn't have wanted to trade places with her."

"But she didn't deserve half the farm as an inheritance like Rose is asking of John."

"No, but neither of us got an inheritance. If people would've paid what they owed Pa for things he had sold to them or fixed for them, he would have been okay, but no one had money in those days. And when he got a little, he drank it up. Anyway, this is different. They were husband and wife. They shared their worth. Like we share ours."

"Don't go comparing me to Rose! How would you get along if I didn't work outside?"

"Hell, no, I'm not comparing you to Rose! And if you didn't work outside the house, we'd be in a mess, especially when we first married and we had no milking machines. I needed you then and I need you now, but if you hadn't been interested in milking and fieldwork, we would've never got into farming in the first place. Our marriage was never like John's and Rose's."

"But you're saying that if I'd made the deal that I wouldn't do farm work, I'd still deserve half the farm?"

"You're not listening, Mary. I said that if you hadn't wanted to work with the cows and in the field, I would never have farmed! Pa never had many cows. He depended on crops and his hardware and repair business. I learned how to do fieldwork with the horses from Pa, and he taught me about growing crops and a little about machinery, but we only had a couple cows for our own milk. You brought the knowledge of dairy cattle to our farm, and that's where we make most of our income now. The cows and your chickens. And I knew nothing about chickens until we got married."

"You can't butter me up with flattery!" Mom shouted. "In the restaurant, you took Rose's side against John, and that will make it harder for them to settle the divorce. I'm afraid it's going to get nasty."

"If it gets nasty," Martin shouted, "it's because you were feeding John all the crap about how Rose didn't deserve anything! I was trying to convince him he should find a way to give her enough to settle without lawyers."

"You said he should give her half."

"Well, maybe I did, but you gotta start bargaining somewhere!"

Mary looked down and began to clear the table. "Time for bed, kids. While I make up my bed on the couch, finish clearing the table. Leave the dishes till after breakfast tomorrow."

Jimmy was not surprised when Maggie went straight to bed. *We really need to talk things over, but I suppose she's still mad at me.* But Joey came over to his bed and sat next to him.

"Makes me scared when Mom and Dad argue," Joey whispered.

"Me too, a little," Jimmy said, but he quickly added, "but don't worry, Joey, they'll be milking cows together tomorrow morning and all will be okay."

"I hate lying to them."

"Me too. I think I'm going to try to tell them the truth tomorrow before we come in for breakfast. Is that okay with you?"

"Yes, but Maggie will want to know. Wonder why she isn't in here to talk like she usually is."

"She's mad at me. I'll tell you why later, but she isn't mad at you. You can go in and tell her my plan and ask her to come in here."

Joey hesitated before he left for Maggie's room. He returned in a couple of minutes.

"First, she said she didn't trust you. That you've done so many crazy things today already. She was worried you might lie and make yourself out to be some big hero."

"What did you say?"

"I told her I trusted you. Then she said that I was probably on your side anyway because I'm a boy."

"I'm sorry that I dragged you into it."

"Mom and Dad are crabbing at each other and you two are crabbing at each other and I don't know what's going on except that we lied to Mom and Dad."

"And none of us is any good at it, either," Jimmy added. "I'll work on an approach to coming clean to the folks before I go to sleep. Go tell Mags that she can trust me. Okay?"

Joey left and returned in a minute. "She says okay, but says she will tell the whole truth too."

"Now let's get to bed. Tomorrow could be a really bad day."

Once in bed, Jimmy searched for an approach to the truth. *Wonder what Maggie's version of the whole truth will be?*

He fell asleep without a plan.

CHAPTER 21

THE NESTLING VENTURES OUT

8:15 p.m., Saturday, July 14, 1956

Looking out her east attic window, Mary realized she had not parked the green pickup parallel to the shed after returning from her frantic pursuit. *Dory will know I moved it. Too late to park it better now. She's due back from milking at Webers any minute.* And at that moment, she heard the front door slam two floors below her.

"I'm back from milking early. Are you hungry?" Dory's low voice rumbled up the stairs at a pitch that was meant to stay in the house.

"No, I'm not."

"I need to talk to you. I'm coming up."

"I watched you all hauling hay today," Mary said as Dory reached the top of the stairs.

"It's a good thing we had the surprise helpers, especially since Tom had to leave with Katy right after they came. They got directions from Tom and Katy's oldest boy, Jerry, in town at the DQ as he was talking to his girlfriend before he left to drive back to the Army. You've not met Jerry, of course, but maybe when he comes home, you can meet the whole family.

"Anyway, they told him they were looking for a girl named Mary and he told them Webers might know. He also told them that a neighbor named Dory would know if anyone new was around town."

Mary looked down at the floor. "I wrote them one letter, and they came looking for me. I thought I was being careful."

"As I told you before, I figured they were the Maggie and Jimmy you wrote to. They must miss you very, very much."

Mary and Dory sat on the bed, and Mary admitted, "I'm so confused. I don't know what to do! I watched them in the field today and I thought, *Why not just go out there and have a joyful reunion?* But then I remembered why I ran, and things haven't changed."

"You don't know that, but you're right. We have to keep you hidden for a few years yet. Too much is at stake."

"I have to confess," Mary added contritely. "After the rain . . . after I realized they'd left, I panicked at letting them go, and I drove the truck after them."

"I wondered why the truck was parked crooked." Dory was stern. "I was going to ask you about it."

"You don't know how close I came to driving up to them." Then, Mary decided to tell the truth and recounted the whole chase, the spying, the hiding, the short conversation with Jimmy, and arriving home as her shaking hands gripped the steering wheel.

Dory listened and paused only briefly before she said, "That was risky. It could end up exposing you to the law."

Mary looked down and began to cry. "I'm so sorry."

Dory put her arm around her niece and whispered in a low, comforting tone, "You're too hard on yourself. I know nothing for sure, but I think you made the right decision. And these people, these friends of yours, will love you anyway. They've proved that already. So, am I right in guessing that Jimmy and you are or were more than friends?"

"Childhood sweethearts for ten years, but I ran away on the day we were to have our first date. I lied to him, but I did get to confess to him before I left."

"I'm sure he understands. They seem like great kids."

Hugging Dory always made Mary better, and suddenly she admitted, "I'm tired. I think I'll go to bed early."

"Before I go, I want to show you another poem in the book I gave you." Dory picked up the book and opened it to the poem "The Road Not Taken." "I hear he wrote this as kind of a joke, but read it through your own experience, dear. Poems come alive only through a reader. Don't worry about what the author intended. Just read it for yourself. One more thing. I hope you don't mind if I ask you a very personal question."

"Ask away," Mary said, giving her aunt a weak smile.

"Well, you met Jimmy face-to-face. Your secret had been discovered already. So, why didn't you spend some time visiting with him?"

"I don't know. It all seemed so unreal. Like part of my past that no longer was real. Does that make sense?"

"Maybe, but can *you* make sense of it?"

"Jimmy touched my hand, and he said I was safe. But I didn't feel safe. I felt exposed. I had memories of . . . of things . . . of things that happened. With my brothers and with my father. And the image of Jack Drude in my mind was so real! So very real that it scared me. I got angry, and I took it out on Jimmy."

"My dear Mary," Dory said as she hugged her niece again. "Sometimes we have little or no control over how we react to things. That must've been terrible for you—to relive those moments. Don't worry. He will understand. If he doesn't now, he will one day. And I think you need to work on moving on, even if it means forgetting people or things you once cared for. It's never easy, but doing only easy things doesn't get many results."

They sat together in silence for a short while before Dory asked, "Are you going to be all right?"

"I think so."

"I'll stay, if you want."

"No, I'm better now—now that we've talked."

"Then I'll leave you alone. You must be tired. Good night, Mary."

The sound of her aunt's footsteps on the stairs triggered a short wave of loneliness in Mary. She got up from her bed and moved to the south window. *There's just enough light for me to crawl outside.*

As she climbed out the window, a screeching baby barn swallow fell from the nest and plopped down on the slanted roof by the window. Without regard for her own safety, Mary stepped out onto the slippery surface, scooped up the nestling with one hand, and, while grabbing the edge of the eave with the other, stretched high to place the tiny bird gently in the nest. After moving away several feet to her regular sitting area, she murmured, "Hope your momma takes you back. I'll bet the wind gave you quite a ride, or did you just fall out of the nest on your own?" Unable to see the nest from her perch, Mary watched to see if the adult swallow would return soon. In a moment, her patience was rewarded when the swallow swooped in to land, apparently not bothered by the fact that her baby had been returned. *Well, at least one thing turned out well.*

Although Mary heard the sounds around her—the screeching nestlings, the wind against the eaves—she felt the silence of the moment. *Jeez,* she reflected, *less than two weeks after I send a letter off to Maggie, she turns up with Jimmy and Robert to help my neighbor bale hay. I know I need to stay hidden for the safety of us all, but when Jimmy asked who was under that tarp, what could I do but answer?*

"I could've ruined everything!" she admonished herself. *I don't really remember it clearly, but I think Maggie and Robert must've heard me screaming at the end. I saw them behind the trees. And I heard Maggie yelling at Jimmy. They all know I'm here now. I hope they can keep my secret. I hope they don't hate me for being so . . . I don't know. Sometimes, I don't know what I want—to go back to my old friends or start out completely new. I know Dory wants me to start anew. And maybe after today I'm ready to.*

Mary smiled as she adjusted her seat on the slippery roof. *Just like the nestling that I rescued, I've crawled back to the safety of my nest too. But I want to be ready to fly to new places pretty darn soon.* Seeing the momma barn swallow swoop away into the shadows, she took the opportunity to carefully scoot back inside before the darkness engulfed the house.

Sitting on her bed, she returned to the poem Dory had suggested. After reading "The Road Not Taken" several times, Mary began to understand. *How many roads have I not taken just today? How many times in the past did I get forced down a road without being given a choice?* She read the poem over and over, enjoying the fact that it was short and even fun. She didn't care if the poem made her feel something other than the poet intended. *But why did Dory not point out this fun poem before she had me read "Home Burial," which makes me sad and even angry? Sometimes Dory is harder to figure out than a poem.*

CHAPTER 22

THE WEB UNRAVELS

Early Sunday morning, July 15, 1956

After their rough Saturday, Jimmy hadn't set his alarm, but he awoke at his regular Sunday-morning exercise time anyway and decided to get up. *Lots to think about. I need to work on a way to break the truth to Mom and Dad.*

Careful not to wake Joey, he pulled on his jeans, grabbed his shirt, and picked up his shoes and socks before he hurried downstairs to finish dressing. Upon opening the door from the stairs into the living room, he felt sad to see his mother still sleeping on the couch.

This has never happened before. I thought she'd get up and go to bed during the night. They hardly ever go to bed angry. What are chores going to be like if Mom and Dad are fighting? He walked silently to the enclosed porch to find his overshoes and remove his dress shoes from them. He carried the shoes to the stairway and placed them on the bottom step. *The plan may be to confess, but . . . you never know.* He left his thought unfinished as he dressed before he slipped out to the barn.

Once in the hayloft, Jimmy delighted in the strong odor of fresh hay and the dim morning light, which barely illuminated the area he used to exercise on the east end of the barn. He had stacked the bales of hay put up last week neatly to the side, leaving his exercise area open, but as more bales were put in the barn during haying season, his space would shrink. *I'll find room to do my rope exercises. The floor support is weak on the east end. Dad never lets us stack the bales way to the top. There will be room for my rope to hang.* But now, he grabbed the rope that hung from the rail in the peak, ran to one end of the barn, and then rode the rope back and forth like the weight on a pendulum. Using only his hands, he climbed to the top and then dropped down, summersaulting as he fell. Then he repeated the moves, enjoying the freedom and strength of his youth and letting his mind be free of the burdens he carried.

He felt the presence of another person in the hayloft before he heard his father say, "Quite the acrobat, my son is. Do I have to worry about you running off to join the circus?"

Jimmy saw his father sitting alone in the dim morning light on a bale of hay. "No, Dad. I'd sooner milk cows. I mean it. But what are you doing up already?"

"Couldn't sleep. I'm worried about Mom. I've never seen her so angry and so unwilling to let it go. I don't know what to do. I said I was sorry, but she just said, 'Actions speak louder than words.' I just hope that when we work together during the day, she will get over being mad."

"I hope so." Jimmy thought of Mary and Mags and their anger at him, and he was about to confess about Joey milking alone when his dad spoke.

"What did you kids do yesterday?"

There it was—an innocent question. Was this an opportunity to construct a thorough lie or spill the truth? *We haven't lied about the trip yet. It never came up until now. I could start by telling him the truth about the trip and apologizing for it. I could kind of ease into the whole tangled web.* Jimmy sat on the hayloft floor in front of his dad, took a deep beath, and began.

"Dad, I drove the car nearly two hundred miles yesterday. We went searching for Mary Schroedler. I am sorry I didn't ask you first." Jimmy scrutinized his father's reaction, fearing the anger and disappointment that were sure to show on the face of the man he loved most in the world, but his father's expression remained unchanged. A long minute passed without a sound from his dad, but Jimmy heard every squeak in the rafters as the wind blew and every chirp of the sparrows nearby announcing dawn.

Dad took a deep breath before he said, "I'm disappointed you didn't clear that with me first, son. Your mom and I would have probably agreed to let you go. Robert was with you, right?"

Jimmy nodded.

"And Joey and Mags, of course?" Dad asked. "Or did Joey go play ball?"

And there it was again. Another innocent question. *Half-truths or half-*

lies. I can't do it. "Joey played ball. He had arranged with the country-school kids to have a ball game at the country school. They'd been planning it since Mags and I had our birthday party."

"Jeez, Jimmy. Some things can stay between you and me, but when it involves Joey and Mags, we have to tell your mom. Leaving Joey home alone is a problem. There'll be consequences."

"I know, Dad." *He hasn't even raised his voice yet. Maybe now is the time to tell it all. How to begin? Let's see. I'll say we got home late and Joey had the cows milked already and then you guys came home and . . .*

"I thought something was fishy when we got home last night. For one thing, you had your four-buckle overshoes on. You never wear them for milking in the summer. Too hot. So, I looked at them last night before I went to bed. I saw them on the porch when I put my empty beer bottle in the case. They were sitting there, and I picked one up just out of curiosity. You know what I found? Of course, you do. Your dress shoes were in them. Now, why in the hell would you be wearing your dress shoes and your four-buckles to milking? I think it's time to tell me the whole story, don't you?"

Jimmy's mind raced. *Dad seems unwilling to get angry or raise his voice. Must be the fight with Mom is on his mind.* Jimmy took another deep breath. "Right, Dad. Look, we got home pretty late—about fifteen minutes before you did. I told Mags to go change clothes and bring my shirt and boots so I could cover up and look like we had all been milking." He saw the astonishment on his dad's face but pushed on. "Joey was feeding calves when we got home. He was done milking already."

Dad stood up in a flash and exclaimed, "Joey milked alone? While you and Mags and Robert were out driving around, your little brother milked the cows? Shit, Jimmy, how could you let him do that? Are you begging for an accident? I can't believe you could be so irresponsible!"

"We didn't tell him to start milking if we were late. We expected he'd wait for us."

"Damn it, Jimmy! You know your little brother. He'll decide to tackle anything on his own. He's even worse than you were at his age. Hell, last year he was ready to help Ruby start calving during my twenty-minute afternoon nap!"

Jimmy just hung his head and said nothing. *How can this get any worse?*

Dad continued. "Look at me, Jimmy. Is there anything else you need to tell me?"

"Probably, but I can't think straight right now."

"But you were there when Joey got his foot stepped on by . . . Valentine, was it?"

"Yeah, it was Valentine, but no, we weren't there. That happened before we got home."

"My God. My eleven-year-old son's foot is under a twelve-hundred-pound cow's hoof, and he's in the damn barn alone. I don't know if I can ever trust you again! Or any of you kids! Joey lied to me too. And don't tell me—I'll bet it was his idea."

Jimmy stayed silent. *Sure, it was Joey's idea, but I'll never admit that. I'm the big brother.* "Look, Dad. It's all my fault. I'm the big brother here. I should know better. The long trip, the late return, the cover-up, the lies—it's all on me. They were just going along with it."

"Nice try, Jimmy. But you get no points for trying to be a hero, especially when I know you're lying about it!"

Jimmy winced. *No points for trying to be a hero. He's right about that.* Jimmy wanted to say something, but his dad continued to speak.

"Say no more! You wait here. Your mother is probably up by now anyway, so I'm going to the house to get Maggie and Joey, and before we milk cows this morning, you are all going to tell us what happened yesterday. I'll fill Mom in on what you told me so far."

Dad left the hayloft. Worried and restless, Jimmy got up from the floor and went downstairs. *Might as well put on the lights in the barn and check it out. I was too rushed last night to do it.* With all the stanchions empty, the barn gave an echo to his footsteps on the concrete aisle. He walked to the end, pulling the chain on the two light fixtures that hung from the joists. He turned and went past the manger and then into the aisle on the east side, where he switched on another light.

"Holy cow!" he exclaimed when he saw the gutter full of water. *What happened here? Does Joey know about this?*

Suspecting a drinking cup leak, he rushed to the manger. *The water line is broken, but the valve is off. Joey must've turned it off. I'll be that was a struggle. Damn, I wish I would've seen this last night. For Dad to discover more problems after we've already confessed is big trouble.* Thinking he could avoid stoking his folks' anger further, he rushed to get the scoop shovel, opened the barn door, and began frantically scooping water into the gutter outside the door, which would drain to the east away from the barn.

Working as fast as he could, Jimmy was deaf to everything around him until he heard his father yell, "What the hell is this? The gutter's full of water. Why didn't you tell me about this? What happened? And no more lying!"

Speechless, Jimmy's jaw dropped open. *Denial means blaming Joey for not telling. Better to say nothing yet.*

Maggie exclaimed from behind Dad, "Hey, I didn't know about this! Did you, Jimmy?"

Jimmy stayed silent.

Walking to the manger, Dad said, "Here's where it came from. The pipe above the drinking cup broke open. My hammer has been moved. Someone used it to shut the valve. Did you do that, Jimmy?"

Jimmy hesitated.

"I did it," Joey confessed as he and Mom came walking to the manger from the west side of the barn. "And I forgot to tell Jimmy about it last night. I'm really sorry. I just forgot."

"When are you kids going to quit lying to me!" Dad exclaimed. "How did you even expect to keep a broken water line a secret?"

"Hold on, Martin," Mom said. "I don't think they did. It wouldn't make sense to try to. I think Joey just forgot. There's been a lot of surprises already this morning. But what I don't like is that this means Jimmy didn't check the barn out after he came home. He just hurried into trying to figure out how to lie about it to his parents."

Jimmy looked down and said, "I'm sorry, Mom and Dad." He looked up at his parents and added, "I got caught up in trying to smooth things over with lies. I'm sorry."

"But you've never lied like that before!" Mom exclaimed. "Why now?"

"Not telling you that I milked alone was my idea," Joey said. "Mags and Jimmy said you got really mad at them when they started milking alone once."

"And one lie led to another," Maggie said.

"What a tangled web we weave when first we practice to deceive," Dad uttered—the obvious adage. "Well, forget or lie or blame it on each other or share the blame—I blame you all, but especially you, Jimmy. I just don't know how I'm going to ever trust you again with anything, let alone the car! Now, Jimmy, you shovel the water out of the gutter while Maggie and Joey tell us their version of what happened yesterday."

At Mom's request, Joey began first. "I had fun at the ball game," he said brightly, but Jimmy noticed no one smiled at the good news. "I didn't mean to milk alone, but I figured they'd be home soon. And I just kept on doing chores one step at a time, and then the drinking cup broke and . . . well, gee, water was pouring out and when I tried to close the valve, the valve flew out when I hit it hard and then I couldn't find it. The water started coming out even faster then, and I really needed help and no one was around!"

"Lucky you were able to get the valve in. I know that's a tough job," Dad said.

"And you were alone when Valentine stood on your foot?" Mom asked rhetorically.

"Yes. After I got her off my foot, Maggie and Jimmy *finally* came home."

Joey's emphasis on the word *finally* resonated with Jimmy. *I guess I can't blame him for trying to work up some sympathy for himself. Wonder what Mags will say. She's mad at me anyway. Will she use this moment as a chance to get back at me?* He didn't have to wait long to find out.

"Going to search for Mary was Jimmy's idea," Maggie said. "I was okay with it when he first suggested it, but the more I thought about it, the more I was sure it was the wrong thing to do."

"Then why did you and Robert go along?" Mom asked.

"Mainly, to stop Jimmy from doing anything stupid. He seemed to have this idea he was going to be some kind of hero and save Mary from being lonely. Good thing we were with him, too. He did plenty of stupid things."

Jimmy scooped the last of the water out and then leaned against the wall as Maggie spilled the details of the day: the bull, the girls, the flat tires, the DQ, the Webers, the bales, the ditch, the blue pickup, and Robert telling her he was moving. *The only thing she held back was that I met Mary. For Mary's sake, of course, not mine. She elaborated way too much on my anger and my reckless driving. Didn't mention that if I hadn't taken the ditch, we would all be dead. Thanks a lot, sister.*

"Do you have anything to add, Jimmy?" Mom asked. "Want to tell your side of it?"

"As I told Dad earlier, it's all my fault. I'm the oldest, and I should know better. The long trip, the late return, the cover-up, the lies—it's all on me. They were just going along with it."

"Well, Jimmy," Dad said, "no more driving the car for you until we tell you otherwise. Same with the driver's license test: postponed until further notice. And tell Billy you can't train with him anymore. You're lucky I let you exercise on the rope at all."

"And for you, Maggie," Mom said, "call Robert from Droesers' phone and tell him he can't come over. You won't be dating anyone. Neither of you will be going anywhere for a long time."

"Joey," Dad said, "you will be helping with all morning chores until Christmas, and don't expect to have any friends over to play ball. And now, the three of you can go get the cows. We have chores to do. Get to it!"

As they walked toward the pasture, Maggie complained, "My punishment is worse than yours, Jimmy. I have to tell Robert he can't visit."

"That's punishment for me too! Robert is my best friend. But, hey, let's not compete for who got the worst punishment, okay? Dad threatened to not let me use the rope to exercise. Jeez, who ever heard of taking away rope privileges?"

"No more playing ball with the neighbors for me," Joey complained. "And I have to get up to help milk every morning until Christmas. And what exactly did I even do wrong? I milked the cows while my brother and sister were out goofing around and Mom and Dad were out visiting someone! Jeez, anyway!"

"It's more about the lying than anything," Maggie said. "And not telling them you milked alone was your idea, Joey, and that was our first lie."

"Sure, blame it on your little brother," Joey whined. "I'm just a kid."

"Oh, so now you want to be 'just a kid'!" Mags exclaimed. "Whatever happened to wanting to be treated like a grown-up?"

"Let's not get into blaming each other," Jimmy said. "We each jumped on the lying bandwagon with both feet, but you nailed me pretty good in your story of the day, Mags."

"You deserved it!"

"But you left out one part—the part about Mary."

"That's between us. And until you tell me what happened, I'll be your worst enemy."

CHAPTER 23

OPEN WOUNDS

Late morning, Thursday, July 19, 1956

Four days later, Jimmy enjoyed the relative solitude of driving the tractor as it pulled the grain binder through the field of golden-brown oat stalks, their heads heavy with kernels swaying in the summer breeze. A soft brown jacket of husk held each kernel securely as the grain binder cut its swath through the standing grain. Jimmy imagined each stalk as a terrified individual, overwhelmed with the fear of losing its grain as the deadly clicking sickle approached and mercilessly cut down the stalks several inches from the ground. Thus stricken, they fell onto a moving platform canvas that whisked them away, feeding them to the upper and lower elevator canvases, which sandwiched the stalks between them like lunchmeat and raised them to be gathered into a bundle, bound with twine, tied, and then kicked to the ground, helpless to do anything but endure their fate. *Just like the rest of us. Helpless.*

Jimmy glanced back at his father perched on the seat mounted up high near the back of the rig, where he could observe the functioning of the grain binder and quickly make adjustments as the height of the grain varied. One lever adjusted the height of the reel, another moved the reel forward or back, another adjusted the butt of the bundle to ensure the bundle was tied in the center, and another moved the entire front of the binder up or down to adjust the height of cut. Jimmy watched his father's grim face for signs of the joy he usually brought to farmwork, but he found none. Dad's usual joking manner had been replaced with gruff, abrupt comments that seemed to lack any feeling of love for the land or his family.

I guess this is part of our punishment for lying about what happened during search day. And Mom and Dad are still mad at each other, too, which makes them angry and grumpy all the time. And Mags is mad at me, which makes her grumpy all the time. How long will this last? Instead of joking about the heat like he usually did, his father had said, "Gotta have heat for the crops to ripen and dry out." When a heavy dew had delayed their starting time, he simply grunted, "Can't bind up grain when it's soaked with dew." *No joking around. This year, harvesting grain is not going to be fun like it used to be.*

Although a wide-brimmed hat kept the sun off Jimmy's face, the heat of the tractor's engine added to the scorching heat of the sun, and the tractor's light-gray hood burned skin if touched. Sweat had saturated the back of his shirt after less than half an hour in the field, but he could not let that affect his concentration. As the driver of the rig, Jimmy had plenty things to watch. He kept the tractor's speed at three-quarters throttle, a slower pace than he would travel if he were not driving over standing grain to cut the swath next to the pasture fence. He took pride in being able to maneuver the tractor so the end wheel of the binder was in the sweet spot, where the wheel at the far end of the eight-foot platform missed the fence posts but the sickle bar reached all the stalks of grain. *Don't want the wheel to hit a fence post or the sickle to miss any standing oats. Dad will get mad as hell if I do.*

The new Model 860 Ford pulled the binder easily compared to the 8N Ford he used last year. The 860 was much bigger and had nearly twenty more horsepower, for one thing, and the newer binder pulled easier because it was not ground-driven by a drive wheel but instead was powered by a power-take-off shaft, or PTO, extending from the rear end of the tractor. Emil Rosincek had sold Dad the binder at a good price because he had bought a new swather to cut his grain for combining.

Jimmy glanced back to see Joey hurrying to move the row of bundles that the binder had just kicked to the ground onto the standing grain. He had to pick them up and set them near the fence so the tractor and binder could fit in the open cut area and begin to cut the next swath going the opposite direction, the direction that would be followed until the field had been totally cut and bundled. One of the disadvantages of taking the back cut first, as the method was called, was that someone had to move the bundles before a second swath could be made. But even if you took the back cut last, someone had to remove bundles before you cut the outside swath. To cut a field of grain with a grain binder, you had to begin by running down some standing grain regardless of the method you chose.

Jimmy smiled to see Joey trying in vain to keep up with the binder. Suddenly, he caught his father's hand signal—a raised arm and extended index finger moving in a swift circle from the wrist joint. *He wants me to go faster? Jeez, Dad, I'm going as fast as I dare next to the fence.* Shaking his head back and forth to indicate he refused, Jimmy yelled, "This is fast enough!"

Using a wider circle and more vigorous movement, his father repeated the hand signal and yelled back, "More gas! More gas! We don't have all day!" Jimmy complied, increasing to a speed that satisfied his father. *This isn't like Dad. He usually respects my choice of speed.* After twenty yards or so, Jimmy got used to the faster speed, but he swerved away from the fence for a moment to avoid a wide post and, unable to get back to the sweet spot in time, left a few stalks of grain standing.

He heard his father yell, "Whoa!" as he gave the signal to stop, a closed fist held high in the air. Jimmy engaged the clutch on the tractor and disengaged the PTO before he shut the engine off, bringing silence to the grainfield for a moment before his father's outburst.

"What the hell, Jimmy?" Dad yelled from his seat on the grain binder. "The rig too big for you to handle?"

"I don't like going that fast, Dad. I got too close to the fence and then swerved away too fast and missed some oats."

Dad's voice got louder. "I'll say you missed some oats! Hey, we only got a little more than fifteen acres. We can't afford to leave any standing. Do I need to get Maggie up here to drive?"

Jimmy remained silent. It was not like his dad to yell at him for so little reason or to use sarcasm.

"Well, what do you have to say for yourself?"

"Come on, Dad. You know I'm a good driver. Better than Mags."

"Maybe! But maybe I should send you home to get your mom or drive over to get Billy. They couldn't do any worse than you're doing!"

Feeling slighted, Jimmy yelled back, "Maybe not, but if they did screw up once, I'll bet you wouldn't yell at them like you're yelling at me now! What's wrong with you?" *Jeez, did I really say that?*

Dismounting the binder seat, his father yelled, "Get off the tractor, boy!" As Jimmy dismounted, his father stormed through the standing grain toward him. Dad had never struck Jimmy, and Jimmy was sure he would never strike his father, but something between them had changed. As his fuming father approached him, Jimmy kept his arms at his sides and stood still, fearing what might happen and unable to do anything but wait. Joey was watching them from about ten yards behind the binder. *He looks shocked. Does Dad realize he's watching?*

Martin moved up within a foot of Jimmy, who stood his ground but kept his arms at his sides. He smelled his father's familiar odors, the odors of a working man—Copenhagen and sweat. Large drops of sweat hung on his father's face. Jimmy saw the fire in his eyes and the tension in his jaw. After a moment, Jimmy looked down at the heads of the crotch-high standing grain, the spaces between the stalks crowded with dull green grasses. Then he heard his father say, "Get back on the tractor, son."

Confused and shaken, Jimmy mounted the tractor, started the engine, engaged the PTO, and awaited his father's signal. When Martin raised his hand in the air and pointed his fingers forward, Jimmy let out the tractor's clutch slowly, moving the rig forward. After he adjusted the speed to where his father had previously suggested, his father signaled to slow down, the palm of his hand facing downward as he waved it down and then up several times. Jimmy slowed down and gave his father a friendly wave.

He's really a good guy. All this crap can't last forever.

After they completed the outside round, Jimmy turned the rig around to prepare to take the next swath in the other direction and then waited for Joey to move the last bundle out of the path. As he tossed the last bundle, Joey looked up in triumph, yelling, "Done!"

Jimmy looked back to see his father smile and then holler, "Nice job, Joe!" And as Joey wiped the sweat from his face with his red handkerchief, Dad raised his hand and pointed his index finger forward. Jimmy slowly let out the clutch and the cutting began. He would drive around and around the field until the standing grain was cut and bundled. The work might appear tedious to an observer, but as the driver, Jimmy had too many things to watch to get bored. Everything moved so fast. As he pushed the throttle faster, he watched for his father's hand signal. When he saw none, he searched his face and thought he found a hint of a smile.

As Mom and Maggie made sandwiches of buttered homemade bread and thick slices of minced ham, mother and daughter exchanged no words of friendly chatter. Maggie missed her mother's bright optimism, which usually spilled over to the entire family, making farmwork or household chores almost fun. *How long will this crabby mood last? We said we were sorry and meant it. I will not lie to them again.* She was glad to have the strained silence interrupted by Joey, who barged into the kitchen to announce what both she and Mom already knew.

"Boy, is it hot!"

Mom asked, "How did it go?"

"I stopped at the milk house to run some cool water on my head. Yeah, it went okay."

"Did you move the row of bundles?"

"Yeah, I even kept up pretty good for a while, but then I got behind."

"Well, no one can keep up to the tractor and binder."

"But when they stopped, I caught up to them again."

"Why did they stop?" Mom asked. "Breakdown?"

Joey hesitated and let his mouth fall open before he spoke. "Don't know."

"Don't get in the habit of lying to me. Did you learn nothing from last Saturday? What do I have to do to get you to tell the truth?"

"Okay, okay, but I just don't want to make things worse."

"What things?"

"I can't explain it," Joey muttered.

"Well, I can," Maggie offered. "Everyone is mad all the time! Sure, we screwed up, but can't we just get our punishment and have things go back to how they were?"

Mom glared at her and said, "We'll talk later. Right now, you stay out of this. It's me and Joey."

Maggie busied herself making sandwiches.

"Let's hear it all, son."

"Okay, okay. I think Jimmy missed some grain along the fence, and Dad yelled and Jimmy yelled back at him, and then Dad ordered him off the tractor and Dad got off the binder too. I thought they were going to fight or something. It scared me, Mom."

"He didn't hit him, did he?" Mom asked in a flash.

The question left Maggie wondering, *Is she worried Dad hit Jimmy or Jimmy hit Dad?*

"No, they just got close and stared at each other. I kept away from them. I was scared, Mom. I don't know what I would've done if they'd started slugging each other, but they kept their arms down at their sides."

"Thank God," Mom muttered. "Then what happened?"

"I couldn't hear them talk. After a while, Jimmy left and got back on the tractor. He waited for Dad's signal, and then away they went again."

Mom heaved a sigh of relief. "See, telling the truth isn't so hard now, is it?"

"No," Joey said quickly. "I don't know what got into me last Saturday, Mom. Honestly, it really was my idea to lie about the milking after Maggie told me how mad you got when they tried milking alone once."

"And one lie led to another," Maggie inserted quickly.

Mom glared at her. "As it always does."

Maggie said nothing more. She wanted to defend Joey, but she knew further explanation was useless. Mom was in no mood for it. *She's like a different person who doesn't even like us anymore.*

"Okay, kids, here's what I want you to do. Make sandwiches for yourselves and eat your fill before we leave. Then, finish packing the dinner sandwiches and cupcakes in the big roaster pan with the cover, and we'll take it out to them with the 8N tractor and hay wagon. They'll be cutting grain straight through until this evening and won't be coming home at noon for dinner, so all of this lunch is for them. Oh, and fill a five-gallon can of gas from the tank and load it on the hay wagon. I'll take these three half-gallon jars to the milk house and fill them with water, wrap towels around them, and put them in a milk pail. When I bring them back to get some ice from the freezer, you two should be ready to go. We'll be shocking grain the rest of the day, so wear long sleeves and a hat and gloves. We'll have plenty water, but we won't be back to the house to eat anything for a couple of hours. Then we'll take another lunch out to the men. They don't like to take the time to come to the house to eat." She grabbed the jars and, as she walked out the door, added, "Get at it, kids."

Maggie and Joey glanced at each other. Maggie said, "Well, we'd better eat some sandwiches."

Joey looked down at his hands and then up at his sister. "Why is Mom so crabby? When we did this last year, she made it sound like we were going on a picnic."

"I know. But you'd better start eating something fast so we can get ready to go. Here, I'll get a jar of milk out and make some sandwiches for you."

They sat at the table, drinking milk and eating sandwiches and cupcakes. Maggie wanted to say something to her little brother to cheer him up, but her mother's constant crabby mood had dampened her spirits too. *I can see how Mom can stay mad at me and Jimmy, but Joey is such a sweet kid. How can she not see how much this hurts him?* She looked at him fondly as he swallowed some food and opened his mouth.

"You know what, Maggie?"

"What?"

"There's something bothering Mom."

"Yeah, Sherlock," Maggie said, regretting the smart-ass comment as soon as it was out if her mouth. Softening her tone, she added, "She's mad at us for lying. It's mostly me and Jimmy's fault. She knows that. She's not so mad at you."

"I know."

"She seems mad at everything."

"Yeah," Joey said. "I mean, the way she talks to us now is so different from the way she used to be. She's even mad at the cows! She used to talk nice to the cows all the time, remember? She'd milk Valentine and talk to her or even sing. That's how I learned to talk to the cows. Mom did it, so I did it."

"You're right," Maggie said. "During evening milking yesterday, she was crabby to the cows. And when she milked Valentine, she didn't sing at all. I watched her, and she didn't smile either like she usually does when she milks her. She didn't talk to her the whole time."

"Yeah," Joey remarked seriously, "and, you know, the cows didn't lie about things like we did."

Maggie smiled at her little brother.

"And you know what else?" Joey asked. "She treats Dad even worse than us. And he didn't lie, either."

"Right again," Maggie said as she stood up. "I hate it when they fight. But we'd better get a move on. She'll be back soon." *How stupid am I? Think-*

ing it was all about me! I need to try to talk to Mom. That won't be easy. Maybe Jimmy can help? No, I'm still mad at him. Things are so messed up! And I don't know what to do about it.

CHAPTER 24

TALKING TO COWS

Thursday afternoon, July 19, 1956

By the time Mom drove the 8N and hay wagon onto the field, the men were nearly done cutting. She parked the rig where they would pass by when they drove to the next field, and as the kids dismounted, she instructed, "Joey, wait here and ride over with them to toss out the first row of bundles when they start cutting the next field. Maggie, we can get started shocking."

"Aren't you going to wait until they get here to visit while they eat lunch?" *Jeez, they always talk over the farmwork.* As Mom turned to stare at her, Maggie added quickly, "Or maybe unpack the lunch for them?" More staring. "Like you usually do?"

"I can see how things went. The grain is cut, isn't it? And they can find their own darn lunch. Now, let's you and me get to work."

Maggie followed her mother to where the binder had begun cutting and listened to her instructions: "We don't use a bundle carrier on our little fields, and the grain is thick so the bundles lay nearly end to end anyway. If I take three rows when I shock, they lie just perfect for making six in a shock and one for a cap. I'll take these outside three rows of bundles, which are actually four rows because the one row has the bundle Joey threw on it. You take the next three rows so I can check up on you."

"I remember how to shock grain," Maggie declared, feeling a little slighted.

"Do you, really? You used to just bring bundles to add to my shocks. This year, I want you to shock on your own so you don't slow me down. Now watch as I demonstrate and explain."

Picking up a bundle under each arm, Mom set them down hard with the butts a little over a foot apart. "Make sure that when you set them on the stubble, the stubble stays upright as much as possible and goes into the butt of the bundle, especially if the stubble is long. If the stubble is bent by the bundle, it will try to straighten up and put pressure to topple the shock. This may not seem like much, but if there is a strong wind, every little bit helps to keep the shock standing, and six bundles with stubble helping them stand versus six bundles with stubble trying to push them over can make a big difference."

Leaning the heads of the bundles against each other, Mom said, "Make sure the two bundles stand on their own before you leave to get more bundles. Then pick up two more bundles, set them down on one side, and lean them against each other and the first two. Do the same on the other side, and you should have a sturdy shock that will let air in underneath the pairs of bundles." Mom pushed on the shock with her foot to demonstrate the sturdiness. "Now, get a seventh bundle and twist the butt and the head to fit on the top like a cap to protect the heads of the other bundles from rain." Mom stood back to look at the shock and then looked at Maggie. "Now, you try it on your three rows."

Maggie built her shock carefully, setting the six bundles in place as fast as she could. But as she moved to get a bundle for a cap, Mom softly kicked the shock, which collapsed to the ground. Maggie exclaimed, "Why did you do that!?"

"Either do this right or go home! Look, you can't be a wimp and set those bundles down like they were on eggshells. Use some force! Look at the stubble. The wind is both our enemy and our friend. She will work for us to dry the grain and the grass in it, but she will work against us to blow down the shocks. Making a good shock is important!"

"You couldn't have just told me? No, you had to embarrass me!"

"Embarrass you? Who the hell is watching? And I did tell you, and I showed you too. Get your head into the work! Now try again."

Maggie grabbed the bundles aggressively and used force when she set them. After she finished, she kicked the shock and it stood. Mom nodded and said, "Okay, let's get to work."

Fifteen minutes later, Maggie looked back to see the fine row of shocks she had created. They looked as good as Mom's row, though her mother's shocks were closer together because one of her rows was double. Also, despite that fact, Mom was several yards ahead of her. *She sure is fast, but I'm going as fast as I can.*

After nearly an hour had passed, Mom said, "I'll walk back to the wagon and get a jar of water. Maybe you'll catch up to me by then, and we'll cross the fence to the pasture by that tree, drink some water, and rest in the shade."

When Mom returned with the water, Maggie felt proud that she had brought her row up to being even with Mom's. "It's really hot. I'll be glad to drink some water." *Maybe Mom has eased up a bit. Maybe I'll talk to her about Dad.*

Seated on the grass with their backs against an American elm tree, the two women silently passed the jar of water back and forth, each taking small drinks and savoring the cool liquid before swallowing. Maggie searched for a way to begin.

"You know, Mom, Robert will be leaving before the end of July so the family can get settled in before school starts."

"I suppose."

"I was hoping you'd let him come over so Jimmy and I could say good-bye. He's been a really good friend."

"Your father and I agreed that part of your punishment was you couldn't see him."

"Maybe you could talk with Dad about it."

"I don't want to have to talk to your father about it."

"Why not?"

"That's between us."

"You're really madder at him than at us, aren't you, Mom?"

"I said, that's between us. Now drop it!"

Maggie forced herself to push on. "No, it's affecting the whole family."

"Your lies are what affected you. It has nothing to do with your father and me."

"Not true!" Maggie spoke louder than she had intended. She lowered her volume and said again, "Not true. You seemed angry about something when you came home on search day, and now you're angry at everyone all the time."

"Well, there is no one in the family that deserves anything but anger. Every one of you has betrayed me!"

"How?"

"You kids have all lied to me."

"That's no reason to be angry at everyone all the time! We said we were sorry. And you don't even talk to the cows anymore! Even Joey noticed. Nothing is fun anymore!"

"Maybe life isn't meant to be fun."

"The anger between you and Dad affects us all. You guys only think of yourselves!"

Mom got up and headed back to the field. "Let's get to work. Your father and I have no problems, other than dealing with you kids."

Maggie hollered after her, "Then why are you sleeping on the couch?"

Mom stopped and turned to face her. "That, dear girl, is none of your business. I'm stuck with three kids who lie and a man who sides against me. I've got no one who is loyal to me. Now, I don't want another word out of you. Follow me back to the field and we'll get to work."

They began shocking again. Mom had brought the jar of water along and moved it every ten yards so they could drink as needed, but they took no more sit-down breaks.

After two hours of silent shocking, Mom said, "After we finish this field, we'll take the 8N and the hay wagon to the other field and feed the men lunch. I'm sure there are enough sandwiches left in the roaster. They'll probably cut until the evening dampness sets in. I'll start shocking, but I want you and Joey to do chicken chores. When you are done, I need you to peel those boiled potatoes that are in the refrigerator. We'll have potato salad and wieners for supper. Make sure we have enough boiled eggs. Take the buns out of the freezer. I think we still have plenty cupcakes for dessert."

Maggie nodded and continued shocking. *And that's Mom. She feels we have all turned against her, and yet she continues to take care of us. And of the farm. What's wrong with me? I accused her of only thinking of herself. I'm such a selfish jerk.* "Are Joey and I going to help you milk the cows while Dad and Jimmy continue to cut grain?"

"No, just Joey and I will milk. When I come back from the field, you can take the 8N back to the field with some fresh water and a few cupcakes and then shock until the men come home. This afternoon you showed me you're pretty good at shocking grain."

Maggie thought she detected a small smile on her mother's lips. *Not sure if this is a reward or a punishment, but I'll take it as a positive sign.*

Jimmy was glad to see the 8N coming over the hill. *I could use a couple of sandwiches and some fresh water.* As the rig approached the end of the field, he saw Mom get off the tractor to start shocking while Maggie put the roaster and the pail of water jars on the ground by a bundle. Then she and Joey left with the 8N. Jimmy completed the swath before Dad signaled for him to stop. When he looked at the jar in the pail, he was disappointed the water was warm, but he was pleased when he took the top off the roaster to discover that he and Dad had two sandwiches and two cupcakes each. A feast for hungry men.

From about twenty yards away, Mom yelled, "Maggie will be back in an hour or so with fresh water and some cupcakes. Then she'll stay and shock while I go back to milk the cows with Joey. I'll make a late supper after milking when you get back from the field."

Jimmy and Dad ate in silence. After about ten minutes, Dad said, "Well, we got maybe two hours before the evening air gets damp. When we finish cutting, we will shock as long as the evening air will allow. If we can cut it all today and the weather is clear tomorrow, we can easily finish shocking tomorrow and have it all shocked before we get a rain on it. Might as well get to it."

Later, in the barn, Joey hustled to carry up milk, change belts on the cows, and release each cow after she was milked, making sure to chase her off the cow porch. Mary handled the three buckets and let Joey know when pails were full. "Don't wait until I fill the pail before you carry it up to the milkhouse. Never be too lazy to make two trips." *Same advice I gave to Maggie. And to Jimmy too. But no one ever listens. Might as well hold my peace. Yeah, like I have any peace. I feel alone, but not at peace. What does my family think of me? I even wonder what Joey is thinking about me. And he's such a sweet boy.*

As she placed a bucket on the last cow, she watched Joey remove a belt from the cow across the aisle. *He looks happy. I hate to picture him milking the cows all alone. What the kids did on the search day shocks me still. And then to lie about it! Did I ever know them? And then Martin—defending Rose like he did. Going against me and John! How could he? Here I am, working my ass off for this family, and no one cares about me. No one sticks up for me! Maggie wants to know why I sleep on the couch. All she cares about is if Robert can come over.*

She removed a bucket from another cow and dumped the milk. "You can take this milk up, Joey. And then take the belt off Valentine. I'll milk her by hand while you feed the calves."

"Okay, Mom."

After she removed the milkers from the final two cows, she grabbed a milk pail and stool and tapped Valentine on the thigh. "Move over, old girl. It's just you and me, now. Just you and me." And for a moment, she stopped moving as she recognized her own voice. "I guess maybe I haven't talked to you in a while, Valentine. Maybe Maggie was right."

Listen to me, thinking the teenager had a point. She blames it all on me. They all do. I'm starting to understand why Rose ran away from the farm and her family.

Really? I need to think about that.

She watched Joey as he returned and began pouring milk into pails to feed the calves. *Such a good boy.* "We trained him well, didn't we, Valentine? That's right. We all trained him really. We used to be quite a team. This family used to be quite a team. What happened? Now nobody can trust anybody anymore. And I feel so alone."

Suddenly she smelled the milk on her hands as she found herself wiping away tears from her blurry eyes. "Sorry, old girl. You shouldn't have to put up with my blubbering like some whining wimp. But who can I talk to but you? Martin? Not anymore. He's not a loyal husband."

Suddenly, she noticed Joey standing nearby. *How much did he hear?*

"Mom," Joey said slowly, "why are you crying?"

"Well, I'm sad, Joey."

"You're usually happy when you milk Valentine. Doesn't milking cows make you happy anymore, Mom?"

"It's more like I'm not sure if I make anyone happy anymore."

"You make me happy."

The simple declaration opened her heart, for it seems the heart can hear what the mind cannot. But the boy was not finished. Before she could speak, he added, "You won't leave us like Aunt Rose left Uncle John, will you?"

Mary cleared her throat and replied, "Never, dear boy. Don't you ever worry about it. Not ever. Now, I'll finish milking Valentine here, and you can rinse the empty buckets before you shut off the vacuum pump. I'll be done with Valentine soon, and we'll carry everything up to the milk house and wash the equipment."

CHAPTER 25

FIRST STEPS

Suppertime, Thursday, July 19, 1956

Maggie drove into the yard with the 8N just as Mom and Joey finished up in the milk house and reported, "They've finished cutting, but Dad said it was getting too damp to shock, so he sent me home. They removed the binder canvases and put them on the hayrack. Dad said he'll carry them to the hayloft when he gets to the yard. They're parking the grain binder in its usual spot by the old hog barn."

"Go get us some towels from the house, Maggie. You and I will clean ourselves up in the milk house. Then we'll go to make supper while the boys wash up here too. Joey, just wait for the guys."

While Maggie sliced bread and set the table with tableware, cheese, and the standard condiments, Mary made potato salad, cooked the wieners, and heated up beans. By the time the men were cleaned up, the women had supper on the table. No one had to tell anyone to sit down and eat. Everyone was hungry, and eating, not talking, was the first priority.

With Joey's concerns about her leaving on her mind, Mary tried to smile. *I need to look happy. I should be happy anyway.* Then Martin surprised her with a comment.

"We all worked hard today," he said. "And we got a lot done. You kids all did good. And your mom did her usual magic: She spent the day working in the fields, milking the cows, making lunches, managing the rest of you, and then, magically, she had supper ready by the time the rest of us got cleaned up. How does she do it? I say it's magic."

She did not have to force a smile in response to the compliment. "Well, Maggie helped, and Joey too." After a moment, she said, "Thanks, Dad. And you're right. Everyone worked hard today. We got a lot done."

Mary ate slowly, trying to watch her family but without staring at their faces. *Such beautiful faces. Where has my mind been? I have no right to be crabby.* Dinner started to move in slow motion, as if she were somewhere else, listening and watching her family act out a moment in their lives.

Jimmy: "*I love potato salad and these spicy wieners.*"

Maggie: "*Especially on Mom's homemade bread. No boughten hot dog buns for us!*"

Joey, sweet Joey: "*But Maggie sliced up the last of the bread and we're almost out of cupcakes.*"

The present snapped in as Mary realized her family's eyes were on her. "Well," she began slowly, trying to put her thoughts together, "I know getting the grain bundles off the ground and into shocks is a priority, but if it's okay with your father, after chores tomorrow morning, Maggie and I can bake while he and Jimmy go shocking. Joey can stay back and do the chicken chores and help us with the barn cleaning."

"I'd say bread and cupcakes should be the priority!" Martin exclaimed.

As the children clapped their agreement and hollered for more of Mom's bread and cupcakes, Mary covered her smile with more instructions. "Kids, clear the table and start the dishes. I'll put the food away and finish up as you all get ready for bed. We have a big day tomorrow, and you've earned your sleep. And Jimmy, I don't expect you're going to get up early to train tomorrow morning."

"Heck, no."

"Then, don't set your alarm. I'll wake you when we get up."

After Martin was in the bedroom and the kids were upstairs, Mary made her bed on the couch and fell asleep instantly, only to awake after an hour's deep slumber. *Okay, I wanted to say more after Martin's kind words, but why didn't I? Everyone worked so hard today, and no one complained. Amazing kids! And watching them eat after a day's hard work is the joy of love for any mom. I put this alone feeling on myself. And sleeping on the couch! What a dumbass idea that was. Yet Martin reached out to me at supper. He has reached out every day in his own way, but at supper, well, that was pretty great. I've got to do something.*

She dozed off for a few minutes, but her problem-solving mind pulled her awake. *I couldn't say much at supper. I wasn't ready. I want to tell Maggie that I'm back talking to the cows and that we need to have Robert come over. And I want to tell Jimmy that he is the greatest kid anyone could wish for despite his mistakes. And I want to tell Joey how proud I am that he milked the cows alone. I could've told them those things the evening we came home from the parsonage, but I let the thing with Rose and John get in the way of what I always knew to be true—that I am the luckiest woman alive! And I want to make sure the children know that Dad and I are solid again and always will be. But first, I have to make sure it's true.*

Still aching from the day's work, Mary forced herself off the couch and turned on a dim light in the living room before she walked to the bedroom and lay down near her sleeping husband, who, wearing only his underwear, lay uncovered in the heat of the night.

"Martin," she said as she gently shook his hairy forearm. "Martin." His eyes blinked and he turned to look at her.

"What is it?"

"Sorry to wake you up, but I have to talk to you. It can't wait until morning."

Martin rubbed the sleep from his eyes. "Go on, then."

"Well, I've been thinking. Maybe Rose was right to leave John and . . ."

"You're not leaving me!" Martin interrupted her with a gasp. "Please don't." He sat up, put his back against the headboard, and leaned in earnestly toward his wife. "We're not like John and Rose! This family needs you. This farm needs you. Most of all, I need you. Not just as a worker—God know you're the best—but as a wife and a companion."

When he took a breath, Mary said, "No, no, that's not what I was going to say. Let me finish, although I'm kind of glad you interrupted me." She smiled a little as she took a moment to reflect on his words. "I was going to say that I understand why Rose felt she had to leave and could not return to the farm and to a life with John."

"You do?"

"I don't just *understand*. I feel it firsthand. Though I was wrong to feel it. I mean, I got angry at you for sticking up for Rose, but now I see you were right to stick up for her. I see it now because I found myself feeling like she must have felt—useless, unnecessary, all alone, and with everyone against her."

"But that was never true for you!"

"I made it seem true. I made your comments for Rose into a declaration of disloyalty to me instead of what they were: honest statements that were meant to jar John into a realistic approach to the separation. And when I got angry at you, that made the kids' lies worse somehow and that made me angrier than I should've been, and then in self-defense, I distanced myself from everyone. Sleeping on the couch was a stupid move, and it really upset Maggie. She even noticed I quit talking to the cows. I even cut off communicating with the cows! How could I be so stupid?"

"If you were stupid, so was I."

"Maybe, but you see, by cutting myself off from everyone, I feel what Rose must feel, and I understand why she had to leave!"

"Jeez, Mary. Slap me or something so I know I'm not dreaming."

Mary stroked his whiskered cheek. "There will be no slapping, and this is no dream. Your wife has come to her senses."

"Mary, I've been struggling all week to break out of this cloud we're all in. The kids are mad at us and each other."

"But nothing will heal until the rift between us is mended. We have to start, and that's why I had to wake you tonight. I want to move back to the bed tonight. Can we consider the argument over? Do you forgive me?"

"Of course. Do you forgive me? I am sorry for sounding like Rose was my priority."

"Forgiven. But now we have to deal with the damage done to our family and to John."

"You sound like you have a plan."

"I do. Well, I have the start of one, but we'll talk about it tomorrow morning. Jimmy said he isn't going to train before milking, so if I don't wake him, he'll sleep late and we can go over our plans tomorrow during milking. For now, I want to get some sleep as I snuggle up to my husband."

"I need sleep too. And I'll sleep better now that I know I'll have you beside me when I wake up."

CHAPTER 26

MEETINGS IN THE HAYLOFT

Friday morning, July 20, 1956

Jimmy awoke in a daze. After rubbing his face with his hands, he exclaimed, "Darn it! I overslept. I never do that! I don't remember hearing Mom call me." He scrambled out of bed, grabbed his clothes, and rushed downstairs. Within minutes, he was on his way to the barn. He met Mom carrying up a pail of milk.

"Sorry I overslept, Mom. I'll get right down there now."

"Wait for me while I empty this pail."

Jimmy followed her back to the milk house as she explained, "I didn't call you because your father and I thought you could use some more sleep."

"Oh, thanks." *Now this is a different tone. And she said "your father and I," so they must be talking.* "I'm ready to get to work now, though."

"Dad and I want to tell you our plans for today."

"You said last night we'd be shocking grain until we finished."

"True, but we have some other ideas too."

Jimmy followed his mother down the stairs and onto the aisle. They stopped where his dad was removing a milker from a cow. "This is the last one, Jim. You can use her milk for the calves."

While Jimmy split the milk up into several pails for the calves and mixed in some cold water from the hose, Dad rinsed the buckets and shut off the switch to the vacuum pump.

"I'll carry up a couple buckets and come back down, Martin," Mom said. "You and I can talk to Jimmy as he feeds calves."

A little nervous about the forthcoming conversation, Jimmy scanned his memory. *Did Mags elaborate on the story of my reckless behavior with the bull? Or my driving? She might be mad enough at me to do that. Or did she make up something she thinks I said to Mary? Why would she do that?*

The calves finished their portions just as his parents came over to talk.

"Jimmy," Dad said in an even tone, "we decided a week of punishment was enough for your deeds on search day. Sunday at church you can tell Billy to come over in the afternoon to train with you again. And next week we'll make an appointment with the driver's license place for you to take your behind-the-wheel test. We want you to get a license as soon as possible."

After a speechless moment, Jimmy found his voice. "Thanks. Thanks a lot. What about Mags and Joey?"

"Their punishment is over too."

"Can I call Robert?"

"We'll stop at Berris's tomorrow and call him from there."

"That's it, then?"

"That's it," Mom said. "We'll tell Mags and Joey at breakfast. Or I may as well tell them as soon as they come downstairs before breakfast. We were going to tell all of you at breakfast, but since you showed up this morning, we figured we might as well tell you first. Now, I'll go clean up the milk house."

As Mom left, Dad said, "Let's make short work of cleaning the barn before we clean up to eat, okay?"

Jimmy was elated, not just because the punishment was lifted, but because the worse punishment had been his parents' sour demeanor, and that seemed to have vanished. They were back to their usual good-natured selves. In fact, they seemed more relaxed than ever. *Whatever happened, I'll take it! Now I have to make sure I pass the driver's test. I hope that's the end of it.*

But as they ascended the stairs to the barn entryway, Dad said, "Step into the hayloft for a minute. I want to talk to you about something."

Jimmy eyed his dad's face carefully, searching for any hint of his mood. He seemed serious but not angry. As Jimmy entered the hayloft, the strong, sweet odor of hay filled his nostrils.

"We put up some good hay early in the week," Dad said as he sat on a bale, "and we got all the grain cut and we'll finish shocking it today. We've been lucky with the weather."

"Yeah, we have been lucky." *What is he up to? This isn't a birds and bees talk, is it? I mean, we've talked about that ever since I was little.*

"I think you already know," Dad began slowly, "that Mom and I have been struggling all week being angry at each other. Well, she was mad at me for some things. She thought I was sticking up for Rose instead of her. Now, normally, I wouldn't drag you in to any fight between Mom and me, and I'm not doing that now either because our fight is over. But, you see, the reason for our fight still exists. John and Rose are getting divorced, and unless John can be convinced that she deserves a good settlement, things can really fall apart."

"What things?"

"Our friendship with John. Our friendship with Billy. Even your training relationship with Billy. And then, there's the fact that Rose is my sister and your godmother. No matter what she is guilty of, she is still my sister. And Mom says she is her friend too."

"What are you going to do?"

"We could just stay out of it because it isn't our business, but it's too late for that. We talked with John about it when he bought us supper the day we came back from going to get Rose. I'm afraid he thinks he knows where we stand, but he is mistaken, so we want to talk to him again. But before we do, I'd like to know how Billy sees it. I don't want you to ask him, but if he says anything about the divorce, listen carefully. He and his mother were pretty much on the outs when she left, but I know he doesn't wish anything bad for her. Just let us know what he says. I'm sure he won't mind, but he might open up to you while you two are training, and we don't really have much of an opportunity to talk to him, other than at church."

Jimmy had never been consciously involved in his folks' relationships with other adults. He decided to be helpful. "Yeah, I'll let you know if he says anything."

"Thanks. Now let's go eat breakfast."

As they walked back to the house, Maggie came rushing out the door.

"Where are you going in such a hurry?" Jimmy asked.

"Mom told us punishment is over. I'm going over to Droesers' to call Robert. Mom said he could come over on Sunday afternoon."

As she dashed down the driveway, Dad said, "Wonder why she didn't ask me to take her over there with the car."

Jimmy laughed. "She doesn't want any of us around when Frank teases her about her boyfriend."

Two days later, on Sunday afternoon, Robert and Maggie sat on a bale near the peak of the hayloft watching Jimmy and Billy go through their exercise routines. Joey sat on the floor closer to the action.

"What I can't get over is how fast they both are," Robert said.

"Yeah," Maggie said. She wanted to tell Robert about the trouble they'd gotten into when they got home on search day, but she wanted to be sure Jimmy and Billy were out of hearing range. She whispered, "I need to tell you that it has been a terrible week here until this morning."

"What happened?"

"We got into big trouble for being so late and for letting Joey milk alone, and then we got onto bigger trouble because we tried to lie our way out if it."

"Ooo, lying to your parents. That doesn't sound like you guys. Say, you didn't pick that up from me, did you?"

Maggie smiled and gently hit Robert's arm before she continued. "I was supposed to call you to tell you not to come over. That was to be part of my punishment—and Jimmy's too—but I kept putting it off, and then Friday morning, Mom told me the punishment was over. So don't tell anyone I never called the first time."

"More lies," he teased.

She hit him in the arm again. "Just don't mention it."

"Your secret is safe with me."

"Did you get into trouble for getting home so late?"

"No, my parents got home an hour after I did. Lucky for me, they'd gone to visit one of Mom's teacher friends and stayed for supper. They played cards until late."

"Lucky you."

"Yeah, so your punishment is over and all is well at the farm. Glad to hear it."

"I'm still mad at Jimmy, though. He won't tell me what he said to Mary."

"Give the guy a break."

"He doesn't deserve a break until he tells the whole truth. End of discussion."

Robert said nothing.

"When I told Mom you and your folks were moving this coming Wednesday, she said I could go for a drive with you if you asked."

"Will you go for a drive with me today?"

"Sure."

"How about a movie? We have time to get to the matinee if we leave now."

"I should change."

"No time. You look great."

"But I'm in jeans, and it's our first real date. I'll change when I go in to tell Mom. I'll be back in a sec. Tell Jimmy we're leaving. I talk to him as little as possible." Maggie jumped off the bales and scrambled out of the hayloft, eager to let her mom know about the date.

Hoping to be left alone with Billy, Jimmy stopped his workout to ask, "Where's she going, Robert?"

"I'm taking your sister to a movie." Robert got up off the bale to leave. "I'll have her back for chores."

"Good!" Jimmy shouted after his friend. "You and I can talk later."

"Hey, Robert," Joey shouted. "Tell her I'll do the chicken chores."

"Why don't you tell her yourself, Joey?" Jimmy said. "You can catch her before they leave. I'm sure she'd like to hear it from you in person." He watched his little brother run after her.

Good. Mags and Joey are gone. Now what can I say to encourage Billy to talk? Dad said just let him talk, but Mom said to ask about Uncle Roman. Then let him talk.

"Is Uncle Roman still working out for you and your dad?"

"Dad likes him. I do too. He doesn't cook as good as Mom did." Billy laughed a little before he added, "Dad says he's easier to get along with, though. And as strange as that sounds, it's true."

Billy sat on a bale to take a break. Disappointed when Billy didn't continue on the topic, Jimmy said, "You mean they don't even disagree on when to cut hay or when to bale it or anything like that?" *Maybe if I move closer, he'll keep talking.*

"No, they hardly ever disagree about farm stuff."

"Strange." Jimmy watched Billy look up at the rafters and then down at his hands. *Seems he wants to say more.* Billy leaned forward to rest his elbows on his knees. Finally, he opened up.

"Dad drinks a lot more now that Roman is with us. We often play three-handed euchre after chores, and sometimes it gets pretty late. Last Wednesday, after they had drunk quite bit of beer, they got into a big argument."

"What did they argue about?"

"Well, it's a funny thing, you know. I think most of us figure that Roman is an old bachelor who wouldn't have a good word to say about marriage or women, but when they were pie-eyed and Dad started blabbing about how Mom wanted half the farm to get a divorce and how she didn't deserve it because she never did any farmwork, Roman stood up, threw his cards on the table, and said, 'Boss, my mind I gotta speak.' And he did. I don't remember all of what he said, but he went on about how 'some women ain't meant to do farmwork just like some men ain't either,' but 'Rose cooked and cleaned up after you for twenty-four years. Made you a good home. Gave you two great boys.' He said, 'Without her you'd a been just a lonely old man like me. Only you'd be too quiet to have as much fun as I do.'

"Dad started to protest, but Roman just yelled louder. 'I see it in nearly every farm I stay at. How the man would be lost without his wife. Even a guy like Martin. Hell of a great guy and good to his family. A good farmer, making a living on that crap farm of his. Hell, he'd be the first to tell you that without my sister Mary, he'd never've amounted to crap as a farmer. He told me that once himself. We were drunk but talking the truth. Like now.'"

"Wow!" Jimmy couldn't help but say. "Did your dad say anything?"

"Not much. He mostly got beet red. I think he was especially embarrassed because I was there. But there's more. Roman said 'Any man knows you can't put a value on a good woman. On any person. That's not how it works. But this I tell you now. I'd work my ass off any time to have a farm and a woman for twenty-four years. You didn't deserve it. No man does. You were a lucky SOB. You got the farm for nothing. Sure, you worked on it as a kid, but lots of kids do and don't end up with a nice farm out of the deal. If you don't think Rose earned half the farm, think again! Maybe you didn't deserve a whole farm either.' After that, Roman stormed out of the house."

"Did you say anything?"

"Well, Dad said nothing for a while after that, and then he asked me what I thought. Well, he knew how difficult Mom made it for me and Anna, and I think he expected me to agree that Mom shouldn't get half the farm, but I told Dad I agreed with Roman. Then he went to bed."

"Where did Roman go that night?"

"I think he slept in the barn. The next morning the three of us did chores and not a word was said about it. At breakfast, I remember Roman asked Dad, 'How you want your eggs, Boss?' No mention has been made since about their argument."

"You know," Jimmy ventured, "my mom and dad argued with your dad about that too—whether or not your mom deserves half the farm."

"Yeah, Dad said that they did. He said that your mom agreed with him and your dad didn't. I was surprised to hear they disagreed on it. Usually they agree on stuff, don't they?"

"They usually do. But the argument between them made our place hell for the past week. They're over it now, though. I think Mom and Dad both side with your mom, although they don't want to say much to your dad about it."

"That will be hard to avoid. Dad told me to invite your family over next Sunday afternoon."

CHAPTER 27

DIVIDING AGAIN

Sunday afternoon, July 29, 1956

"Knock, knock," Mary called as she pounded lightly on John's kitchen door before swinging it open to let her family in. As Martin set a case of beer down on the floor, he commented, "Would have been here earlier, but you know how Berris is—he won't do off-sale in the morning. He's strict with the Sunday rules. So, we waited till noon before we picked up a case."

"And Billy's home too!" Mary exclaimed as she set a package down on the table and moved in for a hug. "I brought you a freshly baked cake. I baked bread and cakes instead of going to church this morning. And Maggie helped me make this red hot dish to bring along too, but I see you've already eaten dinner. Maggie, put the hot dish in the refrigerator for later. We'll leave the cake here too."

John stood up to shake hands with Martin. "Glad you all came to visit your lonely old brother-in-law." Then he added, "And uncle," as he shook hands with the kids.

Roman exclaimed in Czech, "Jak se máš?"

"Dobře," Mary answered, while the kids each said, "Fine."

As Billy started to clear the table of eating utensils, Maggie got a dish-cloth to wipe it clean.

"So, you already know my new hired man," John joked as he nodded at Roman.

"More than I care to," Mary kidded. "What's the deal? You haven't agreed to hire him, have you?"

"Smart thing for him he did!" Roman crowed.

John explained the arrangement as Martin opened beers for the adults.

"None for me," Mary said. "The beer is cold now, but I'll stick about twelve of the bottles in the refrigerator in case you're slow drinkers today."

Roman took a big drink, set the bottle down hard on the table, and proclaimed, "Being a slow drinker. Never been accused of that before!"

They all laughed as they toasted to the day.

"I'll get the cards," John said. "I think we have enough for eight-handed euchre! Joey can play, right? I'll throw jacks for partners."

"Yeah, Joey's a good euchre player. We brought him along because if we're home late, we're afraid he'll milk the cows without us," Martin joked. "What do you think of that, Roman? When we got home late from our trip to see Rose, our eleven-year-old son had milked the cows all by himself."

Roman gave him a startled look. "What?"

Mary had hoped to have an hour or two of friendly conversation before discussing search day. *Darn it, Martin!* She hurried to steer the conversation. "Yeah, Joey had the chores all done by the time Maggie and Jimmy got home."

"Christ!" Roman exclaimed. "Was things okay?"

Mary said, "All was okay, but when I think about the danger of it—well, I still shudder. A little kid with all those big cows. I wanted to cuss him out, but I was so proud of him."

"He's quite the boy," John said.

Roman stood up to add some important words. "I've never been married, and I have no kids raised. So, I know nothing. But I've learned kids are all different. This I know. I think sometimes that parents are the worst judge of kids. They think all kids are the same but their kid is great. Worse, some think all kids are great but their kid isn't good enough. I see kids from the outside. Not comparing them to mine because I'm kidless. Your boy Joey was a man from the start. He was about five when I came over one time and kneeled down to say 'Jak se máš' and explain to him that it meant 'How are you?' He said, 'You don't have to kneel down to talk to me, Uncle Roman. I can just look up at you. I'm not just a kid, you know.'"

"I remember that," Martin said. "We were in the hayloft."

"Ya, ya, I tell you, that boy was a man when he was born."

Pleased that the subject was Joey and not Rose, Mary said, "Go ahead and throw jacks, John. I'm looking forward to playing euchre."

The afternoon passed swiftly. Billy made some buttered popcorn. Roman said it went great with the beer but complained it made the cards sticky. Mary stayed ready to steer the conversation to John's opinion on a divorce settlement but was reluctant to break the party atmosphere. *Too many people. John won't want to talk about it on front of everyone. Though they're on the second case of beer, and John seems to be drinking more than usual. He's keeping up with Roman! They get along so well. So funny how they rib each other about nearly everything.*

"So, that Chevy made it back from the preacher's place," Roman asked. "No stalls?"

"It's a good car," John asserted with pride.

"I like the 'forty-nine Ford better. Billy let me drive it."

"Good, because I'm not letting you drive the Chevy."

"Don't want to. It's an ugly color."

Roman seemed to bring out another personality in John, a little like Emma's husband, Joe, did. Both men played music, and John seemed to like that. But Billy was right—John drank a lot with Roman there. Mary tried to relax and enjoy the friendly bickering between the men, but she feared the tension between them was becoming real.

"Ya, ya," Roman said. "I thought you guys would be bringing the missus home and I'd be out of a job. Lucky for me it didn't go that way."

Shocked into the sad truth of the statement, Mary glanced at John, whose expression turned angry as he shouted, "Lucky for me too, damn it! Lucky to be rid of her. Never did anything on the farm. She always thought she was too good for me!"

"That's because she was!" Roman exclaimed without regard for any rules of delicacy. "Ha, ha, Boss. That's because she was!"

Mary understood that for her brother this was all just drunken fun, but she also knew John hurt from the inside out and that this brought the pain to the surface again. *I've got to say something. But what can I say that will not sound like I'm piling on Rose, which could reopen the rift between Martin and me?*

"Hey, John," Martin said evenly as he stared at Roman. "She wasn't then, and isn't now, any better than you. But if it makes anyone feel any better, Rose thought she was better than me too. In fact, she thought she was better than our folks and too good for the whole farm. I was glad she married you, John, because you are a good man, but I was surprised she married a farmer."

Torn between wishing the men had kept quiet and relief that they had brought up the topic, Mary decided to try to use the moment to sway John toward the divorce settlement. But John spoke first.

"And now," John exploded, "I'm supposed to give her half the farm. I'll bet she won't think she's too good for the money! But she doesn't deserve a penny!"

"Hell," Roman interjected, "when it comes to money, no one is too good to take money."

"But," Martin said, "the law says she does deserve something. And fighting it will cost you money, and you will lose in the end. And there will be more bad feelings."

"The bad feelings can't get much worse," John said.

Billy rose from his chair. "I think they can, Dad. Maybe Mom and I have had lots of arguments, but I think she deserves a decent settlement. And others here do too."

"And why is it anyone's business but mine and Rose's? Why do Martin and Mary give a rip about Rose, even while they claim to be my friends?"

"You and Rose and Billy are part of our family too," Mary said.

"Not when it comes to my farm! That belongs to me and someday to Billy, if he wants it."

"Of course, I want it, Dad, but I think Mom deserves half of its worth now, and I'd be happy to inherit the other half with the mortgage on it just so you could pay off Mom now."

"Billy, you've been spending too much time over at Carlsons' place listening to their opinions. The question is, Why are you two, Martin and Mary, so set on Rose getting a big settlement? Why? What's in it for you?"

"Nothing. We are concerned about Rose and you, John," Mary said. "It's not my business what the settlement is, but I just want you to get it done and move on. Maybe if you tried to call Rose to find out exactly what she wants before it all gets out of hand." *John has tuned me out totally. He's not listening. This is going downhill fast.*

"Wait a minute!" John exclaimed. "Just wait a damn minute. I know now. You two are looking for a cut! Rose will have no descendants other than Billy, who will be taken care of. Just maybe she'll leave her money to her dear younger brother. Or, yeah, I remember now. Jimmy is her godson. Maybe she'll leave some to Jimmy."

Mary saw Martin bristle. "Leave the kids out of it," he said evenly.

"Too late for that, Martin!" John exclaimed as he stood up. "My kid is already in it, and you guys probably dragged him into it."

"Not true!" Billy exclaimed.

Mary held her breath as her husband stood up too. *He never backs away from an argument, especially if it gets physical. He wouldn't throw the first punch at John, but John is drunk and angry. Would he swing first?*

"John," Martin said calmly. "You've accused me and my family of conniving to get money out of your divorce. Just listen to yourself. I don't want to hear any more of it. We've said our bit. I think we need to leave. Jimmy, bring the empty case to the car. I'll be waiting for you all there." And, to Mary's relief, he walked out the door.

Five minutes later, the family returned to the car and discovered Martin in the front passenger seat.

"You're driving, Jimmy," he said. "I've had quite a few beers. I could drive, but I'm mad as hell and I'd sooner not drive. Besides, Maggie told us that you are quite the driver."

Mary saw Jimmy give his sister an angry look. "Relax, Jimmy," Mary said. "She just explained how you took the ditch when a car came at you in your lane. Now, get behind the wheel before your old man changes his mind!"

As Jimmy drove out of the yard, Dad said, "I had to get out of there. John was getting as nuts as Rose."

"And in front of the kids, too," Mom said. "I'm glad you walked out, Martin. I'm proud of you. Things could have gone from bad to worse in a hurry. Are you kids okay?"

"I'm just sad," Maggie volunteered. "Sad that Rose left and sad that Uncle John is so angry. I don't blame him for being mad, though."

"I don't get it," Joey said. "Why can't they still own the farm together?"

"They never did own it together," Mom said. "It's John's farm, but when you marry someone, what you have is theirs too."

"It's so strange, though," Maggie said. "Things I think are forever are suddenly gone forever. I grew up saying 'We're going over to see John and Rose' as if they were one. Going over to Thorsons' place meant seeing Rose and John and Billy. Now there is no Rose. There's only Billy and John there now. Will we be saying 'Going to John's place'?"

"Probably," Mom said, "if he ever lets us on the place again."

"Oh, he will," Jimmy said. "Billy told me as I was leaving that he'd work on his dad. He said his dad was hurt pretty bad when Rose left him. He said Roman knew it too and was trying to get him to admit it. Billy said he thought he'd get him to agree to a fair settlement with Rose."

"Even after that blowup?" Mom asked. "He's pretty optimistic."

"Billy is an optimistic guy," Maggie said thoughtfully.

"He told me he'd be over to train next Sunday," Jimmy said.

No one said any more, and Mom was content to ride in silence. *Glad we don't have far to go.* As Jimmy drove the car into their farm's driveway, she recited her favorite coming-home line, "Home again, home again, jiggety-jig."

CHAPTER 28

WINNOWING

Sunday, August 5, 1956

On Sunday afternoon a week later, Billy stood by as Jimmy climbed the rope to the peak in his usual fashion, lifting himself up hand over hand while extending his legs straight forward on either side of the rope. Then he pushed away from the rope and did two flips before landing on his feet.

"That's pretty good, son," Dad said as he entered the hayloft and sat on a bale of hay. "I'll bet there aren't a lot of guys who can do that. If we put much more hay in here, you won't have far to climb."

"I know, Dad, but Billy and I have lots of other routines we can do. The hay will be fed out soon enough. I won't get rusty." Jimmy joined Billy to sit on a bale of hay facing his father.

Dad asked Billy, "Is your dad still mad at us?"

"Well, you know Dad. He's not one to say much, but he did say before I left that I should be sure to tell you that he'd send me over with the Farmall H tractor and a rack to help you thresh."

"That's what I was going to ask you next. Thanks."

"So, I don't think there are hard feelings from his end. He did mention he wondered how you felt after he accused you of . . . things. He asked me to tell him about what he said. I don't think he remembered everything. When he tries to keep up to Roman's drinking, Dad gets pretty drunk. That's the only bad part about having Roman live with us, but Roman isn't forcing the beer down him. It's Dad's choice."

"Don't you think losing Rose is harder on him than he admits?"

"A lot harder. He says it's like taking on a partner when you already own a business, and after twenty-four years the partner says he wants out and deserves half of the business."

"When you look at it that way," Martin admitted, "it doesn't sound fair."

"Well, when Roman heard him say that, he lit into Dad about the value of a woman, claiming all the time, of course, that as a bachelor he had no knowledge of the experience himself."

"I'm surprised your dad puts up with Roman."

"It's strange, I know, but Roman can say things to Dad that neither Mom or me ever would dare say, and Dad listens. He actually listens!"

"I wonder why."

"I've thought a lot about it, and I even asked Roman. You know, Roman is a pretty wise man."

"True. He comes on as the loudmouth smart-ass, but he can get pretty serious. Why did he think your dad listens to him?"

"When Dad was sleeping it off on Monday morning after your visit, we had quite a talk. He said as a farmhand he's been in and out of many jobs and witnessed the workings and failings of many marriages. A farmer usually hires him because he needs help on the farm, but sometimes out of sympathy too. To give him a home, you know. He thought Dad had both those reasons. But when Mom left, Roman told Dad that if she hadn't married him, Dad would have been no different than he was, a lonely, ornery old man who no one wanted around. You heard him say things like that when you were over that Sunday."

"Yeah, I was surprised Roman was so blunt."

"Well, Roman has a way of saying serious things that seem almost funny. 'You may have had a farm,' Roman told Dad, 'but that wouldn't have made you less lonely.' Roman told me then, in his comical way of putting it, 'Leave to me your dad's convincing. Rose will get her share.' Roman says he was only there a short time before Rose left, but he could see what she had given to the place and he'd get Dad to see it too."

"Wonder why he seems to take it on as his goal?"

"I don't know, but Mom was pretty good to him, even though he wasn't the cleanest guy when he came to our place, and she liked it when he played music. Roman never forgot that."

"Do you see any signs of Roman's progress with your dad?"

"I do. He talked a little to me about when Betty introduced her to him and how quickly they decided to marry. He didn't sound regretful about it. Oh, and he said that without Rose, he would've been a lonely old man like Roman. He repeated Roman's words almost exactly."

"Well, Billy," Dad said, "we know where he got that idea." Jimmy and the two men laughed as they nodded. "Come up to the house and tell Mary."

"Sorry, but I really got to go. I've got to grind feed before evening milking or the cows will be mad at me for a week." With that he laughed and said, "See you, Jimmy. And Uncle Martin, let me know the day before you're going to thresh."

"Can you make it this Thursday?" Dad asked. "This weather has dried the grain and all the grass in the straw, so there's no use waiting."

"I'll be here with my rig by midmorning. See you then." And he left the hayloft for home.

"That's a load off my mind," Dad said. "We'll need Billy's help as well as his rig. We'll get the threshing machine ready and check all the belts so we can get started on Thursday and finish on Friday."

Five days later, on Friday morning, Dad complained to Jimmy as they drove the 860 out to the threshing machine, "Heavy dew caused us a late start yesterday and will again today." From his perch on the fender, Jimmy watched the profile of his dad's whiskered, sunburned face. "A heavy dew soaks into those bundles worse than a small shower of rain. We can't even spread the shocks out to dry until the dew is off the ground. Can't put a wet bundle on the wet ground and expect it to dry off. Yeah, two days in a row now the heavy dew has made us start late," he repeated. "If we'd had an early start yesterday, we could've finished if we'd had a dry evening too."

Dad stopped the tractor near the threshing machine in the field south of the barn, where it was parked on top of a hill with the feeder on the south end of the rig. Jimmy waited for his father to dismount before he climbed down. Noticing his father's grimace, Jimmy verbalized the cause: "The wind is from the north, Dad. We're going to have to reset the threshing machine, right?"

"Yep, yesterday's wind blew from the south, so we had to blow the straw north, but today's wind is straight from the north, so we'll have to turn it around to blow it south. There was no predicting the wind direction to try to angle the machine to accommodate a switch. Well, we have plenty of time to do it since we have to wait for the dew to be off before we spread the bundles out to dry. Once they dry, loading won't take long. Billy will be here early, no doubt."

After they folded up the feeder, Jimmy prepared to put in the hitch pin as his father backed up the tractor. Once the tractor and machine were hitched, Dad said, "We may as well make a new straw pile. The ground isn't level enough to park the machine on the north side of this one, so we'll just turn it around and park it in the same area and start a new pile south of it. We'll have to dig new holes to level the machine, but I forgot the shovel. Can you run back to the barn to get it?"

"Sure, Dad." And Jimmy was off. He found running the two-hundred-yard distance in the cool morning air pleasant, and he found the shovel just as Billy drove his rig into the yard. After they exchanged greetings, Jimmy put the shovel on the wagon, mounted the 8N, and, with Billy riding on the wagon, drove the rig out to the threshing site.

"Hi, Uncle Martin," Billy said. "I hope we can finish early today. Looks like it's clouding up in the far northwest."

"Hi, Billy," Dad said. "The breeze has picked up, and the grain is drying out fast. While Jimmy and I set and belt the machine, you can take the 8N out to the field and spread bundles in the last field and then load. Stop at the house to get Mary and the kids. Better yet, you drive out your rig and let Mary drive the 8N. That way both rigs will be ready to load. The big question is if we can finish before it clouds up and rains."

"We only have the one field left, but it's the biggest one," Jimmy explained. "Hey, I'll bet you don't miss spreading bundles and threshing at home!"

"No, I don't. Combining the grain is easier, but it has its own headaches. You're on the machine all day and it's dusty as heck. There is no one to talk to. I miss all the people that came to help thresh. But it was a slow process compared to combining. When we combine, we can get it all done so much faster and with only a couple people."

"But then your dad makes you help us. So, you end up doing the hard labor anyway."

"Oh, I like helping you guys. I really do. And with Roman working at our place, Dad has plenty help so he doesn't miss me too much for a day or two."

"I wish I'd borrowed Droesers' double box when I got their elevator," Dad said, "but he was using it. With only one wagon for the oats, when this double box gets full, we'll have to quit threshing while we unload it. Shutting down when the rain is coming isn't smart. Well, we'll just unload as fast as we can. I'll have to use the 8N on the elevator, so we won't be able to use it to get another load until I finish."

"Okay—I'll be on our way to spread the shocks, Uncle Martin."

"Wait," Dad said as Billy mounted the tractor. "Gusts of wind are rising and will dry the bundles fast. Maybe you don't have to spread the whole field—you can load the bundles from the shocks. We've had a lot of sunshine and wind this morning. Bring in one load and leave the others out there to load the other rig."

"Right," Billy said. "I'll check it out."

Later, when Dad tossed the last bundle of a load into the feeder, a gust of wind nearly stole his cap as he said to Jimmy, "Loading and threshing the loads went fast, but the oats are running a high yield and the double box is full. We have to shut down to unload."

"I can see Billy, Mom, and Maggie coming to the yard with their load now," Jimmy said. "Looks like they're stopping by the house to pick up lunch."

"Everyone might as well grab a sandwich while you and I unload the oats. Have Billy pull up to the thresher and unhook. Then he can hitch up to our empty wagon and get another load instead of waiting for the 8N. But now, after I shut down the machine, you ride with me to the granary and help me shovel off the grain into the elevator as fast as we can." Dad faced into the northeast wind. "Damn! I hate to waste time unloading. Wish we had a shed to just pull the double box in and hook up to another double box and keep threshing."

As Jimmy looked northwest at the dark clouds in the near distance, he spotted a good sign. "Wait a minute!" he exclaimed. "Here comes Uncle John's new grain truck!"

Dad turned to look and smiled. "Looks like Roman is driving! I hope he didn't steal it," he joked.

Roman waved as he drove past them to park the truck under the grain spout on the side of the threshing machine. Jimmy heard the door open and then slam shut, and a moment later, he spotted Roman carrying a case of beer as he walked past the 860 tractor at the far end of the drive belt.

"Start her up again, Martin," he hollered as he set the beer down. "You stay here with the thresher and pitch off the load. Me and Jimmy, we'll shovel off oats. Better yet, throw a tarp over the double box, and me and Jimmy will go out and load up bundles. No use tying up a tractor on the elevator when we got bundles to load before a storm. The new grain box on John's truck will hold all the grain for today, and we can just roll the tarp over the top when we're done. Billy told us last night that your granary would be full before the end of the day anyway. He said you're running around ninety bushels an acre!"

"You're a sight for sore eyes, Roman," Dad exclaimed. "Billy will be here in a minute with another load and some sandwiches. Grab one when you can. We won't be stopping for lunch."

Jimmy said, "I'll pull the double box to the yard, park it, and cover it with a tarp. Joey and Mom are in the yard with a load, and they can help while Billy drives the load in. Then I'll be back to get the rack and we'll all go out to get another load."

Minutes later, as they finished tying twine to secure the tarp on the double box, Jimmy heard the sound of another tractor. "I can't believe it, Mom. It's Uncle John and his Farmall M pulling a wagon and rack."

John throttled back, braked the M to a stop, and shut off the engine. "I got to thinking," he said from the tractor's seat, "maybe you guys could use another rig. So, I pulled my other rack out of the weeds—haven't used it since we got the combine two years ago—and came over ready to pitch some bundles."

Mary and Jimmy both laughed before Mary said, "Out to get some exercise, are you?"

"I figure a little hard work will do me good. Riding that combine all day is filthy hard work, but it doesn't do much for the muscles. What do you two say? Can we send Joey back to the thresher with the 8N while the three of us go get a load? You can drive, Mary. Jimmy and I'll pitch."

Jimmy sensed John had more planned than just getting exercise, and he suspected Mom knew it too. *Coming over here with a rig to help thresh, plus having his son help and Roman drive a grain truck over—all pretty good signs he's sorry for the other night. But he must still feel he needs to say something. Apologies aren't easy for anyone, especially Uncle John.*

"Hop on. I'll drive to the field," John said as he started the tractor.

Jimmy sat on the rack next to Mom, and they both dangled their legs over the side as they bounced along on the path to the field.

"I've not driven that tractor before," Mom said. "Maybe you should drive and I can pitch."

"If that's what you want, Mom, but what if he wants to talk to you? If you pitch from one side and he pitches from the other, he won't get much talking done."

"Probably just as well," Mom said as she gave Jimmy a weak smile.

When John stopped the tractor, Jimmy jumped off the rack and said, "Mom's never driven the M, so she wants to pitch and have me drive."

"That's okay with me, but, Mary, you have to promise to let me keep up with you."

"It's a promise," she said as she took her fork.

The remaining shocks had not been spread, so they pitched bundles from the rows of shocks on either side of the rack. Jimmy drove forward and stopped according to their needs, and the two pitchers kept an even pace most of time. When the load was made, Jimmy let John drive while he and Mom stood on the drawbar and held onto the back of the seat, which put their heads a little above John's shoulders.

Once everyone was settled, John started the tractor and said, "What a pleasure it would have been to do fieldwork like that with my Rose—although I hate to bring it up again."

Jimmy decided to say nothing unless spoken to. *I wonder if Mom will say anything.*

Keeping his eyes on the path ahead, John continued, "I know she told me before we were married that she wouldn't do fieldwork, but even if she'd just driven the tractor, we would have had a better time on the farm." *He didn't turn to look at Mom even once. Maybe he finds it easier to talk about the hard things if he doesn't make eye contact. I know I did when I drove home on search day. And like then, we have a long, slow ride home. What else will he say?*

And then, John said it outright, answering the question that Jimmy knew was on his mother's mind.

"But Mary, that's all in the past now. I signed the divorce papers and mailed them this morning with a cashier's check for the settlement."

Jimmy watched the surprised look on his mother's face as John went on, "I realized you guys were right. And after you guys left that Sunday, Roman and Billy kept after me, harping about how it would be best to make a complete break. A clean break. I finally agreed. I think a big part of me just didn't want to admit Rose was gone for good. We had a lot of good years together, you know, before things started falling apart."

Mom put her hand on his shoulder. "You did the right thing."

"Yeah, I think so. I called Pastor Mark, and he said he'd help Rose get an account at the local bank. I didn't know that most banks won't let a woman open an account on her own."

"Does Billy know that you've settled?"

"Only that I was ready to sign it. No one knew I was going to go to the bank today, sign off on the loan, and have a notary stamp as I signed off on the document. Then, all I had to do was get a cashier's check at the post office and mail it."

"I'll bet you're relieved it's done."

"I am. But now I got a mortgage. Never had a mortgage. I inherited the farm free and clear. I was pretty lucky, I guess. Before now, I only took out loans for operating expenses."

"Welcome to the mortgage club," Mary joked. "Must be popular. Everyone is joining."

As Jimmy dreamed how great it would be to own a farm without a mortgage, John said, "I want to say one more thing to you both." Eyes still focused straight ahead, John increased his volume. "Billy will end up with the farm, but if he were to die or something, I can't think of any people I'd sooner have running the place than you guys."

They rode the remaining distance in silence, each with their own thoughts.

Once at the threshing site, things moved fast. Jimmy checked on Joey, who was tending the grain spout in the truck box. "Here," he said handing him a jar of water, "keep this so you can get a drink when you need it. Put your handkerchief over your face if it gets too dusty."

"Thanks," Joey said. "Dad said I'm supposed to load it full so we don't have to waste time unloading any grain today."

"Give a wave if you need me. Dad said he wanted me to pitch into the thresher with him. The grain is really dry, and we can push the rig harder. He's worried about the rain coming. Now that we have three rigs hauling, we can leave pitchers in the field and the drivers can bring in the loads. It's going to go a lot faster than yesterday."

By late afternoon the truck box was filling up. Roman parked the last load of bundles by the feeder and pitched the bundles with Jimmy, placing them on the apron in single file so the heads entered the thresher first, leaving a small space between the butt of one and the head of the next. The big thresher roared as it ground through some weeds, and Roman backed off, saying, "We don't want to plug her up."

When a sharp gust of wind brought oversized raindrops that smacked Jimmy and Roman in their faces, Roman said, "You pitch the last few bundles off, Jimmy. I see John and Martin are starting to roll out the tarp over the grain truck. As soon as the thresher is empty, they'll tie the tarp down, and they'll want me to drive the truck out before the field gets wet."

A few minutes later, Jimmy threw in the last bundle. He saw Dad crawl atop the thresher, ready to manually trip the hopper so the last of the oats would run out the auger into the grain box. A few big raindrops fell, but the wind was growing more desperate to control everything. Jimmy jumped off the rack and waited by the 860 for Dad to signal him to cut the power and leave the pulley to run free. *There, he tripped the hopper.* More raindrops fell. *There's the signal from Dad.* Jimmy disengaged the PTO, released the brake, and backed slowly up until the belt slowed itself down by just brushing the ground. After the belt stopped, he rolled it up and thew it into the large enclosed area of the thresher while Dad and John hurriedly removed the many smaller belts that ran the rig, rolled them up, and stored them inside the thresher. Just as they finished, a wall of rain arrived. Jimmy could barely see Roman drive away in the truck full of grain.

"I've already rolled back the blower and set it in its place," Dad said to Jimmy. "Help me fold back the feeder. The machine will have to sit here in the storm. John, you may as well take off with your M. See you at the house. Jimmy and I will take the 860 to the yard. With no more bundles in the fields to load, the others were smart and parked their rigs in the yard and went to the house. I'll bet they didn't get wet either." He laughed as he turned away in the soaking rain.

Facing the sky so the rain hit his face and fell into his open mouth, Jimmy roared with laughter. "The rain feels good! The drops hit me hard, but I love it!" He climbed onto the 860 Ford and clung to the fender, standing comfortably on its rear end. As his father drove swiftly away, Jimmy felt the cold sting of the large drops of rain battering his face, reminding him again of search day and getting another crop in the barn before the crew got soaked in the rain. *So much has happened since that day. It started out so good and ended up with everybody mad at everybody. It's over for everybody but Mags. She's still mad at me.*

And in his heart, he knew that for him it wasn't over. *Jeez, Uncle John lost a wife and half a farm. And I can't stop thinking about a kiss from a girl who told me to forget her as she ran away the night before our first date.*

CHAPTER 29

THE BUS

First Day of School, Tuesday, September 4, 1956

"Well, I don't know about you guys," Jimmy groaned to Maggie and Joey as they waited for the school bus on the roadside across from their driveway, "but I'm not ready for another nine and a half months of torturous BS." Brakes screeched, and he watched the bright orange vehicle slowly come to a stop in front of the four Shaurel girls, who were lined up to board at the end of their driveway. "And it looks like it's the same old bus, number seven, which only has sixteen seats, and if we have the same route, it'll be standing room only again for the kids we pick up on the home stretch to Rock River."

"And with our country school closed, there will be even more kids from each family riding the bus," Maggie said. "But don't be so grumpy. You promised to be positive and to try to be more social, remember?"

"Yeah, I guess so, but look who's blaming me for being grumpy—Miss Grumpy herself. You're setting a bad example for our little brother here. Joey is still young and enthusiastic. It's his first time on the bus."

Joey complained, "You know I hate it when you talk to each other like I'm not here."

"That's why he does it," Maggie explained. "He likes to irritate people. By the way, big brother, figured out which one of your girlfriends you're going to sit with?"

"Oh, I've been worried about that all night," Jimmy said sarcastically. "But you still haven't told me the details of your date with Robert. Must have been a bust. He left three days later."

"You've already heard all the details you're going to, buster. But tell me what you said to Mary to get her so mad, and maybe I'll tell you about my date with Robert."

"You just don't want to get past that," Jimmy said. "But I'm more curious if Joey is going to sit with Caroline Shaurel. Thought about that, Joey?"

Joey flippantly said, "Maybe the bus route will change, Maggie, and we'll pick up the Schoen kids. Then you can sit with Ralph."

"Way to change the subject," Maggie said. "See the crap he's learned from his older brother?"

"I do what I can to pass on my talent."

"The Shaurels are loaded," Maggie said. "We're next. My first day of my sophomore year."

The driver closed the door, and the bus groaned louder as it labored up the hill toward them. "Good," Jimmy observed. "Looks like Albert is driving again this year."

"Yeah, he's a good guy," Maggie replied. "It's good to have some things stay the same. There are too many other changes already at school."

"Like what?" Jimmy demanded.

"No Robert or Mary Schroedler at school this year. That's a big deal, don't you think?"

"Yeah, I'll miss them both big-time, but maybe we're friendlier with the neighborhood kids after the dance last summer."

"And the ball game," Joey added. "That was a pretty great day."

"Jeez!" Maggie exclaimed. "Suddenly my brothers are optimistic and I'm the pessimist. Never thought I'd see the day."

The bus slowed down to stop in front of them, and before the door opened, Jimmy said with a big smile, "Okay, brother and sister, remember that we are a happy family. Smile as if we like each other."

"Won't be easy," Maggie remarked with some venom.

Letting Joey and Mags board first gave Jimmy a few extra seconds to decide where to sit. He said hello to Albert as he surveyed the seating. Mary Ryan and her cousin, first grader Joan O'Keran, sat in the front seat behind the driver. *Probably saving a seat for her best friend, Liz Brummer.* The signals from those already seated were clear: Those who sat on the inside edge of the seat and looked down were saving the seat, those who sat by the window and nonchalantly stared outside didn't care if you sat with them or not, and those who sat on the outside or the inside and made eye contact and yelled your name wanted you to sit with them. Caroline Shaurel sat near the front and looked straight ahead. Joey took an empty seat behind her. *Joey said he didn't want me or Mags to sit anywhere near him. Wants to be on his own. He said we're too crabby to each other.* Katherine O'Keran beckoned Mags to join her in the second seat from the back. Mags scooted in to take the window seat. *That's an adventuresome choice, dear sister. Sitting with Katherine. Why would you put yourself through that?* Across from Mags and Katherine, Peggy Ryan and Ann Shaurel sat together. Both smiled and said hello, making Jimmy's choice easy. He took the back seat right behind them.

"So, how does it feel to be a senior, Ann? You'll be out in the world next year while Peggy and I will have a whole year left." Jimmy saw them both grin.

"Feels good. I promise not to rub it in, but since you brought it up . . .'"

"Jimmy and his big mouth," Peggy interrupted her.

"Wow! I'm here less than a minute and you're on my case already. Some things never change." Surprised to be enjoying the playful banter, he decided to risk a bit more. "My regret is that next year I'll be sitting behind only one good-looking neighbor instead of two."

"Clever little compliment, Jimmy," Peggy said. "Very clever, but I've already thought about that, and I have a plan."

"Yeah," Ann remarked. "She'll sit with you. Good luck, Jimmy."

The two girls snickered and turned to face forward.

"I've a whole year to figure how to foil that plan," Jimmy countered. He expected a quick retort to follow, but when both girls remained silent, he figured the chat was over. He leaned back and slid his torso down so he could put his knees up on the back of their seat. He put his red folder on the seat, retrieved his comb from his back pocket, and ran it through his hair. Just as he put it away, the bus turned north and slowed to stop at Bummers' driveway, where Liz waited.

"Looks like it'll be the same bus route as last year," Jimmy said loudly enough for all the kids to hear. "I'll bet bus number eight will have the same route as last year too. It'll pick up the Newburg town kids and then the Schoens before it turns south to go by Rosinceks' farm and then Schroedlers' place. No kids at either place this year, though."

"Are you sure about that?" Katherine asked. She seemed poised to say more, but Liz boarded the bus and announced brightly, "Hello, everyone!

Hope you are all looking forward to school this year. I sure am." Then she plopped down in the front with Mary Ryan and Joan O'Keran.

Peggy explained, "Mary and Liz planned it over on the phone yesterday and decided they would take care of Joan on the bus. Nice of them to do it. Liz's idea, I'm sure."

"And I was glad to hear it," Katherine remarked. "Otherwise, Mom would've made me take care of her."

"Gotta like Liz," Ann said. "She's so positive."

"Gets a little tiresome for my taste," Peggy whispered. "But what I like about her is that her cheer rubs off some on my little sister. Otherwise, Mary is so grim."

"Wonder where she gets that?" Jimmy said sarcastically, but after Peggy glared at him, he added, "Hey, just kidding."

"Say," Peggy asked, "where's your lunch? You always bring a lunch. Hey, Maggie doesn't have one either."

"Yeah, all three of the Carlsons are going to buy their lunches this year. Gives us a little extra time in the morning."

"You'd have a lot more time if you weren't still getting up early to train. Or don't you still do that?"

"I do, but how do you know about that?"

"Everybody knows about that. We know that's how you were able to beat Jack Drude and break his wrist," Ann said with certainty.

"That was mostly dumb luck, and the second time I wasn't so lucky."

Katherine O'Keran turned toward Jimmy and put her feet in the aisle before asking, "Are you training for a third fight with Jack?"

Is that anticipation in her face? Jimmy wondered. *Her mouth has a smirk? Her eyes seem to glow?* He took a breath and tried to appear nonchalant. "No, I just like to be physically fit."

"Tom says you are," Peggy offered.

"And your brother would know," Ann said. "He's quite the athlete."

"You know what?" Jimmy said without knowing where he was going. *Where is my talent for changing the subject when I need it?* The bus slowed down, and he stood up to glance out Ann's road-side window. "I think we have a new family on the route. Kryser must've fixed up the extra house on the farm and rented it out."

"Look, they all have the same yellow hair," Peggy said. "Two young boys and two older girls. Damn, more competition, Ann, and those boys are just too young for us."

"I heard that school-bus romances never last anyway," Jimmy joked.

"So that's what you've heard." Peggy smiled. "I've heard otherwise."

The new kids boarded the bus. The two girls sat together near the front, and the two boys sat behind them.

Suddenly Maggie stood up. "Look, I'm going to go up and sit in the seat ahead of the girls and say hello. It's gotta be hard getting on a bus with all strangers."

"Sure, abandon me for some new kids," Katherine griped.

"I'll be back before we get too close to Rock River."

Proud of his sister for reaching out to the new kids, Jimmy considered following her lead and talking to the boys. *What would I say? "Hi, I'm Jimmy Carlson." I could ask what grades they are in. Pretty lame. I'll ask Mags what she said and how it worked out.*

"I hate to say it," Peggy said, "but those girls have hair like Mary Schroedler and they are almost as pretty. Don't you think, Jimmy?"

Jimmy got into BS mode. "I think, yes. But I've made no decision as to the degree of prettiness of the two new girls."

"But now that we're talking about Mary," Katherine said, "have you received a letter from her yet? Or do you at least know where she is?"

Jimmy was surprised at how much the question irritated him. Disappointed him, too. Trying not to show his feelings, he took a deep breath before he answered, "No and no, Katherine, but if the answer was yes, I'd have to lie to you and say no anyway because I wouldn't want to endanger her. Get it?"

"Gee, I just asked."

"And I just answered."

"Well, what am I supposed to think about an answer like that?"

"My advice is to not think about it at all. Mary is gone. But my sister is back! What news, Mags?"

Jimmy felt Maggie's glare, communicating that she was not ready to be nice to him in public. She sat with Katherine and leaned her head toward the group. "They seem like sweet girls. Alice is the one on the left and she is in Ann's grade, and Gloria is the one on the right, and she is in my grade. The boys are in second and first grades. Donald and Lewis. Last name is Gustafs-son. Swedish, I think. Cute boys. Donald is the older one, and he doesn't talk much because he stutters, poor kid. Lewis loves to talk, but he won't smile because his baby teeth came out brown and decayed. Doesn't keep him from talking, though. He's not shy, that's for sure."

"Gotta be tough for them, going to a new school and all," Peggy said.

"Peggy Ryan with a heart," Jimmy kidded. "I like that."

"I wouldn't get too used to it, Carlson," Peggy shot back.

"You should try it sometime, Jimmy," Maggie added.

"Ooo-ooo!" Peggy exclaimed. "Little sister criticizing big brother. I like it."

Jimmy smiled and slumped down with his knees up on the back of the seat again. After the bus turned west, it picked up four young Westlund children plus the family's hired man, Jeff Otterly, who spotted Jimmy and waved. He was a senior and about Jimmy's height. He had a heavy build, but no one called him fat unless they wanted to get punched in the nose. Everyone liked Jeff, but he had a reputation for retaining barn odor after he did morning milking. Jimmy didn't mind, and he waved for the kid to come back to sit with him.

"Hi, Jeff," Jimmy said as he slid over to give Jeff the aisle side of the seat. "Did you work at Westlunds' farm all summer?"

"Yeah, I pretty well live there. Nothing to do at home anyway. Dad still works at the river docks."

The bus stopped to pick up four young Anderson kids before it turned south onto the highway to Rock River. The next stop picked up eight Mur-phy kids, which filled all the seats with two or more, and the next five miles would keep adding children until every seat had three riders and the aisle was filled with those standing for the last mile to town.

Once in town, the bus stopped at the Catholic school and let off most of the Catholic kids in grades one through six. They scrambled to get past those standing in the aisle even as those standing in the aisle pushed to get seats. After the chaos was over, the bus proceeded another four blocks to the public school, where the rest of the children, each of them eager and apprehensive, got off and rushed to their assigned buildings for their first day of the school year.

Searching for the bus after school, Jimmy passed by Albert, who was shooting the breeze with another bus driver. "We're the next bus, Jimmy. The door is open."

"Thanks, Al," Jimmy said. He was in a good mood as he boarded the bus, happy that the day had gone well. He really wasn't in a hurry. He didn't care where he sat on the bus. He envisioned himself in the back seat, sharing stories of the day with the other kids, but after he stepped onto the bus and into the aisle, a shocking scene played out before him. Joe Murphy, one of Maggie's classmates, held little Lewis Gustafsson by the arm with his left hand while, with the thumb of his right hand, he peeled the boy's upper lip back to show his brown teeth. Lewis's face flushed with anger as he tried to twist free from Joe's grasp. Donald stood behind Joe, his little body pushing and pulling at the big boy as he stuttered, "S-s-stop!"

Jimmy's first instinct was to slap Joe across the face and yell at him, but he restrained himself when he saw the faces of the young neighborhood kids watching in awe. *Jeez, the kids from the Catholic school and the public elementary have boarded already. Too risky. More kids are coming on the bus now.* Then he saw Maggie board the bus with Gloria, the new girl. *I hate having an audience.*

Joe turned to say to Jimmy, "Donald Duck and his nephew Louie, get it? Huey, Dewey, and Louie."

He was repeating the words again when Jimmy roughly pulled his arm away from the boy. "What the heck, Murphy? Leave the boy alone."

"Jeez, Carlson, look at his teeth."

"So, is it your big accomplishment that your teeth are halfway good? Or is it just luck?"

"But ain't it funny about them named Donald and Louie?"

"Yeah, I've read these classic pieces of literature too, but I fail to see the big joke. This is their first day here. Now leave them alone."

Joe's face was defiant, and Jimmy resisted the urge to slap him. Instead, he glared at Joe and said, "Hey, you guys, Donald and Lewis. Why not come back and sit with me? I want to know all about your first day at Rock River."

"I was gonna save the two back seats for my brother Richard and me," Joe said.

"Too late. I'm claiming them both."

"We'll see what Rich says when he gets here. He's a senior, you know."

"Yeah, I know Rich. Nice guy—not a bully like you. Interesting to see what he'll think of your business with the little boys." *I barely know Rich, but he seems nice. Uncle John hired him to haul bales one time when I was there. Can't believe he'd be like Joe and treat those kids so mean.* Jimmy scooted the new boys to the back seats, settled them down in one, and stretched out in the other. "I'll move over to sit with you guys as soon as some of my friends come to sit back here."

Suddenly nervous about making small talk with the boys, Jimmy smiled at them as they stared back. Maggie and Gloria sat down in the seat ahead of him, and Ann and Peggy came down the aisle, so Jimmy moved over to sit with the boys and said, "Here, take this seat. I'm going to sit with my new friends."

"Well," Peggy said in a kind of sing-song voice, "Jimmy Carlson, I thought you were smarter than to make friends with boys who were better looking than you are."

Jimmy thought the joke would go over the new kids' heads, but Donald grinned. Jimmy laughed when Peggy added, "Of course, I did the same mistake hanging round Ann here."

"Peggy Ryan making fun of herself. What happened to you?"

"Jimmy Carlson befriending little kids. What happened to you?"

"Yeah," Maggie said curtly, "he's just trying to be the hero again."

Ann replied, "Actually, Maggie, that's the kindness I've come to expect from Jimmy, but I think your talking with the two girls this morning gave him the idea."

Eyes turned to Donald, who stuttered before getting out, "Boy was hurting Lewis." He looked down at his hands.

"The guy up there," Lewis pointed. "Joe."

By this this time, others had boarded the bus. Peggy turned to Maggie and said, "I think your brother has a story to tell us."

Jimmy made brief work of the story, trying to down play any heroic references, but Lewis, emboldened by the older kids' attention, piped up more than once. "Joe was hurting me. Jimmy made him stop."

"We saw part of it," Gloria said. "Thanks for sticking up for my little brother."

As the bus started its bumpy trek home, Jimmy slumped down and put his knees up on the back of the seat ahead of him. The confrontation had pumped him up. Just as he was beginning to relax, he felt Lewis's eyes on him and turned to smile at the boy. *Is he worried about what Joe might do tomorrow? Is he trying to thank me again?*

Suddenly, Lewis said, "You got nice teeth."

Jimmy laughed without wanting to and then slowly said, "You know, I've been working on growing my teeth for sixteen years. How long have you been growing yours?"

Lewis looked puzzled until his brother answered for him. "F-f-f five," Donald said. "S-s-s-six in October."

Lewis smiled before he pursed his lips in a tight grin. Setting his lunch pail on his lap, he looped his arms around Jimmy's wrist. Moved by the gesture, Jimmy felt obligated to say something. "Hey, the kid that bothered you. His name is Joe Murphy. He gets off the bus before you do, and he gets on after you every day. So, I'll always be around. Don't worry about him. Okay?"

Neither boy said anything, but Donald smiled. Jimmy glanced over at their small thin bodies. With their backs against the seat back and their legs outstretched, their worn brown high-top shoes barely reached the edge of the cushion. *How can anyone want to hurt these little guys? And Murphy didn't seem to feel any guilt about it either! But is Mags right? Am I just trying to be the hero again? I'm just trying to protect those little guys! And, jeez, there are five of those Murphy boys. Way to make enemies, Jimmy. I'm hoping Joe is the only asshole of the bunch. But what are the chances of that?*

"Goodbye, Lewis and Donald," Jimmy said to his two new friends as the bus slowed to a stop at Carlsons' driveway. He stood up and waited for Maggie to move to the aisle ahead of him while she said goodbye to Gloria. Joey led the procession to the front to disembark while their schoolmates shouted, "Goodbye!" and "See ya tomorrow."

While Albert waited for them to cross the road in front of the bus, Jimmy waved to him. The bus driver smiled and waved back. Feeling good about how the day had gone, Jimmy commented to his siblings, "Not too bad of a day for me. How did it go for you two?"

Mags ignored the question and increased her pace, but Joey slowed up and said, "It was okay, I guess. Dragging all my stuff from class to class after the bell rings wasn't as bad as I thought it would be. And three minutes between classes is plenty time to get where I need to go. The bus ride was kind of fun. I met some new kids."

Maggie suddenly stopped. "I wasn't going to say anything more about this, but it's bugging me," she said, her voice expressing anger and impatience. "How can you charm everybody on the bus like you did today and yet manage to say and do something that made our best friend hate us?"

Jimmy looked away. "Here we go again."

"You were so smooth with the neighbor girls on the bus! And you acted like Jeff was your lifelong buddy. You came to the rescue of those two little boys like some kind hero! I saw it."

"You're mad at me for being nice?"

"I'm mad at you for not using that charm when you talked to Mary!"

Jimmy waited. *What can I say? Mags is convinced I said something wrong, and maybe I did. I don't know anymore.* Halfway up the driveway, he faced his sister. Jimmy heard the anger in her voice, but more than that, he saw the pain in her face. *I have to earn back her trust.*

"I've thought a lot about this, Mags. In fact, I've thought about it way too much ever since that day I went out to the trees and found Mary under the tarp. I've come to believe her reaction was more about her than it was about anything else."

"Sure, blame it on her."

"Not what I mean. Maybe what she's been through with her brothers and her dad and Jack, maybe that's more than she can handle. I mean, could you be the same Maggie Carlson if you had been through all that? What we did—going to search for her—was crazy enough, but her actions were totally nuts! She hides from us. She spies on us. She follows us as if to meet up, but then she hides again. Then she explodes in anger when I try to talk to her."

"You'd be more convincing if you told me what you did."

Jimmy took a deep breath. "Well, she put her hand on the edge of the pickup's bed when she crawled out from under the tarp. I was glad to see her, and I put my hand on hers. Her reaction was wild. Her eyes got big as if she was remembering something. It was like she was somewhere else and I wasn't even there. I tried to talk to her—"

"What exactly did you say? Tell me!"

Jimmy looked down for a moment. *I have to tell her.* He stepped forward, looked Mags in the eye, and swallowed hard before he spoke softly. "I told her I loved her." He swallowed again and shouted, "I told her I loved her and that I thought she loved me too!" He paused and looked away. "I'll be careful before I ever say that to someone again. If I ever do."

Maggie said nothing at first. "And then she yelled at you?"

"She said that we had been just foolish kids with foolish crushes. Then she screamed, 'Grow up, for God's sake!' The look on her face scared me."

"What did you say then?"

"Not much. She looked like a wild animal that was cornered and ready to attack anything. I just said I was sorry and promised to never bother her again. Then I left and saw you and Robert standing there."

Jimmy had turned to leave when Maggie shouted, "Wait a minute."

He stopped and turned to see his sister looking down at the gravel driveway. He waited for her to look up at him.

"I'm sorry, Jimmy. I had no idea that . . . that you told her . . . well, I thought you said something mean to her. I should've known better."

Jimmy looked away. "It's okay, Mags. It's okay."

CHAPTER 30

THE SOLDIER AND THE FLEDGLING

Saturday morning, September 8, 1956

Shortly before noon on a cool Saturday morning in early September, Mary Schroedler enjoyed the peaceful freedom of her garden, on a mission to find a ripe watermelon. Wearing bib overalls, high-top work shoes, and a blue work shirt, she flitted from one watermelon to the next, looking for dried stems before turning a melon over to tap on its rind. With most of her blond hair tucked under a striped engineer's cap, she looked like a little kid, and with her mind free of past troubles for the moment, she felt like one too.

After tapping on a particularly large melon, she exclaimed, "Ah, yes. This one will do!" She snapped the green-brown vine and hoisted the melon onto her shoulder.

Suddenly a man's cheerful voice shattered her tranquility.

"So, you found one you liked."

Mary's mouth dropped open as she turned to stare at the stranger, who wore the Army summer uniform of khaki trousers, short-sleeved shirt, and garrison cap.

Almost dropping the watermelon, she asked, "Who are you?"

"I'm Jerry Weber. You must know my family. They just live a hundred yards or so away. Dory helps them out all the time."

Shocked, Mary said nothing. She noticed his smile. His good looks. His kind, strong voice. She felt embarrassed by her attire, although she had been exceedingly comfortable in it before he had arrived.

He covered the distance to her in a few long steps. "Here, let me carry that for you."

"Sure," she said as she handed it to him. *I can carry my own melon, but . . .* She recited the story she and Dory had rehearsed for such a surprise occasion. "I'm Mary, Dory's niece. I'm staying with her for a while."

"Well, Mary, I got home late yesterday on a three-day pass from Fort Leonard Wood, and I just walked over to fetch Dory to join us or for a dinner with the family at noon. You'd better join us. I've not been gone long, but I've missed my family. Haven't you met them yet? If Dory intended to hide a beautiful young woman from me, I'll never forgive her."

His words were a tease, and she found herself drawn to him even as she worried. *Jeez, I've met Rusty but not the others, and Dory and I told her to keep it secret. How is this going to work if we come busting into Webers' house to visit now?* She was relieved to hear Dory's voice.

"Jerry, you're back!" Dory moved in to hug him as he shifted the watermelon. "So good to see you. Let me introduce you to my niece, Mary. And, Mary, this is Jerry Weber from the next farm south. Mary's staying with me for a while. She hasn't met your family yet, Jerry, but now would be a good time. Let's walk over there and take the melon with us."

"I should change clothes if we're going to their home," Mary hedged.

"No, you're perfect as you are," Jerry offered.

"I'm in my work clothes too," Dory added.

"And so is my whole family!" Jerry exclaimed. "Come on. Time's a-wasting."

They ambled across the yard, down the driveway a few yards, and then southeast on a worn path leading another fifty yards through the small group of trees before arriving at the back of Webers' house, where they followed a path around to the south-facing front porch.

"I have to leave early this afternoon to pick up my buddy in Iowa and get back to Fort Leonard Wood by midnight Sunday," Jerry said.

"Did you get to see Diane?"

"I got all dressed up in uniform hoping to impress her, you know, but when I phoned, she told me not to come over."

"So sorry, Jerry."

"Don't be. I figured as much. It's over."

Mary hoped her eavesdropping wasn't too obvious. *Diane, huh? It's over. I like to hear that.*

"Here we are," Jerry announced. And as they walked through the front door, he insisted, "Let me do the introductions, Dory."

The family was seated in the kitchen, but when the guests entered, Rusty ran up to hug Dory while Jerry began the introductions. "Mary, these are my parents, Tom and Katy, and my sister, Jean—we call her Rusty—and my brother, John. Everyone, this is Dory's niece, Mary."

Mary was happy to see that the family was dressed in everyday clothes, just as Jerry had said. Tom wore a clean bib overall and a blue work shirt, and Katy wore a flowered sleeveless housedress and a full apron with the words *Kitchen Boss* embroidered across the front. John wore jeans and a striped short-sleeved shirt that was clearly becoming too small for a growing boy. To Mary's delight, Rusty was dressed much like she was, in a bib overall and a blue work shirt. Glad to match faces to the names that Dory had included in stories over the past seven months, Mary smiled and said, "I'm really pleased to meet you." Both she and Rusty smiled as if they were meeting for the first time.

Jerry added hastily, "And the latest addition is our little brother, James, who is sleeping in the bedroom. He was born the day I left for the Army after my two-week leave after basic training. He was named after a fella I met at the Dairy Queen. I asked this guy to go to the farm and help Dory and the kids put up hay before a storm, and he and his friend and his sister actually did. Great kids!"

Mary was relieved when Dory changed the direction of the conversation. "Fine-looking cake, Katy. Can't wait to try it."

And with that, the two visitors sat down with the family to a celebration meal of meat loaf, potatoes, gravy, and a macaroni salad with peas. The next half hour was full of spirited joking as the Weber family enjoyed having their soldier home on leave. Mary sensed Dory was part of this happy family, and at the moment, she felt as if she belonged too. Recalling moments of joy at the Carlsons' and the Rosinceks' kitchen tables, Mary smiled as her thoughts brought her images of Maggie and Jimmy. But as Katy placed the melon to the table and began cutting slices for everyone, her mind jumped quickly to the warmth of the present moment.

As Jerry stood up to pass out slices of melon to each person, he said, "Okay, now follow me outside so we can see who can spit the seeds the farthest. If I remember right, I usually win."

"That's because you have the most wind!" Rusty exclaimed.

After Jerry won the seed-spitting competition, he reminded everyone that he had to leave. Dory and Mary said their goodbyes and left the family to their private farewells.

Once the two of them had walked most of the way home from Webers' house, Dory said, "Jerry surprising you in the garden isn't the way I wanted you to meet the neighbors, but I think it worked out okay. You seemed to enjoy yourself."

"Yeah, I haven't laughed that much in years. Maybe never. I liked being with Rusty without having to hide. But I'm glad you handled all the questions about me."

"What did you think of Jerry?"

"He's nice." Her heart wanted to say more, but what exactly did she want to say? *Should I tell Dory how I struggled to not stare at him? How I strained to hear his voice even when he was clearly out of hearing range? How much he reminded me of Jimmy when he looked at me and made me feel special?*

"You say, 'He's nice,' but I saw how you looked at him."

"Was it that obvious?"

"It was to me."

"Was it to him? Then I'm embarrassed."

"Don't be embarrassed, but do be careful," she said as she opened the door to the house. "Sit down at the table and we'll talk a bit, okay?"

Dory sat on the end, and Mary sat next to her on the side of the table.

"Don't know if you noticed, but Jerry tried to talk to me privately when we were outside eating watermelon. He wanted to know everything about you, but I just told him your parents are dead. I gave him no details."

Mary winced at the thought of him knowing details.

"He wants to write to you. He asked my permission."

"What did you say?"

"I told him he could write, but it was up to you if you wanted to write back."

Mary looked down at her hands, which were folded on her lap. "Do you think I should?" *Please say yes.*

"Look, dear, Jerry is a great guy. I've known him all my life, but he just broke up with his girlfriend of a couple years. Diane broke it off on the day James was born, the day Jerry went back after his two-week leave. She said two years was too long to wait, and she didn't answer any of his letters. He was pretty heartbroken. He tried to get back with her, but she refused to see him."

"That's sad," Mary said before she looked up and met her aunt's eyes. "How much did you really tell him about me?"

"Like I said, just that your folks are dead. Your story isn't mine to tell, and you should be careful how much you tell anyone. Your story may not do you harm to a good man like Jerry, but I can't promise he won't judge you poorly."

"What should I do?"

"You're so young, dear. I was glad when you and your friends broke contact. You need to get away from the past. You need a new life, but I hate to see you get mixed up with a guy again so soon."

"So, you don't want me to write back?"

"I see no harm in a few letters, but how are you going to answer his questions? What if he wants to take you for a ride on his next leave home? How will you explain that you can't let yourself be seen anywhere?"

"And now all of the Webers know that I'm your niece, but they don't know I need to stay hidden. Rusty won't say anything at school, but John doesn't know about me. I'm a little scared, Dory."

"Me too. Maybe, I need to have a talk with the Webers and—"

Rap! Rap! Rap! Three sharp knocks on the door startled them both.

"Hey, Dory. It's me, Jerry. Can I come in and talk?"

Dory moved fast to open the door. "Sure, Jerry, come on in. Mary and I were just talking about . . . your family and how much fun she had today. Sit down at the table."

Jerry took the seat across from Mary and said, "I don't know how to begin, but I know I can't just say nothing and pretend I know nothing."

Mary's body stiffened. *What could he know?*

"I wasn't sure at first, but your answers seemed so vague, Dory. If I'm wrong, please don't be mad at me. Either of you."

Mary made quick eye contact with Dory before she looked down. *Say it! Say it!* She braced herself for the worst.

"When I met those kids at the DQ last summer, the kids that helped Dad haul bales, I asked them why they were in town, and they looked at each other kind of cautiously, you know, and then the boy, Jimmy, said they were searching for a girl who ran away. Then the sister—her name was Maggie, I think—showed me a picture of the girl when she was in the eighth grade. They told me she was a couple years older now. I thought right away when I saw you today, Mary, that you sure looked like the girl in the picture." He turned to look at Dory. "Is it true? Is Mary the runaway?"

Mary turned away. Tears pooled in her eyes. *He must think I'm terrible. He won't want to write to me now. But should I even try to explain?*

"Jimmy said you were a close friend and ran away because a boy had threatened you and your friends. He said you ran away to keep them all safe. He made you sound like a hero."

"She's a brave girl," Dory said.

Mary wiped her eyes with her hanky and turned back to face her visitor.

"Well, Maggie was right about one thing," Jerry said, flashing his wide smile at her.

Mary met his eyes.

"When she showed me the picture, she said, 'She's even prettier now.' I'd have to agree with that."

Mary smiled and then blushed before she looked away.

Jerry stood up abruptly. "I hate to leave, but I've got to get on the road. If it's okay, I want to write to you, Mary."

Mary nodded. "I'd like that," she said softly.

"But," Dory said, "while your whole family knows Mary is here, they don't know that she has to stay hidden. I know they won't do harm on purpose, but they don't know how dangerous it can be if the word gets out that Mary is here. What if the post office hangs up a poster of her as a runaway?"

Jerry stood behind the back of his chair for a moment. "What if I had a talk with my family? I'll do it right now before I leave. I just tell them that Mary ran away to keep her friends safe, and that they must not say anything to anyone. Okay?"

"I think that would be best," Dory said. "What do you think, Mary?"

Mary nodded. "Sorry I'm so much trouble, but I need to stay hidden for now."

"Okay, I'm off. I'll write soon, Mary, and I'll address the letters to Dory so no one will know you're here. On my next leave, maybe you'll let me take you for a ride. I promise we won't go anywhere that will put you in danger. You'll be hearing from me soon." He smiled at her before he closed the door behind himself.

Mary looked up at her aunt.

"Don't look so sad," Dory whispered. "It could have turned out worse. Now you and Rusty don't have to sneak around. You've gained a whole family."

"But there is so much he doesn't know about me. How much do I tell him when he asks?"

"When you write back, just avoid answering any questions you don't want to. Don't lie, but don't talk about things you don't want to talk about."

"Easy to do in a letter, but how about if we go for a drive?"

"Hold on, dear, I didn't say you could date him. You're so young yet."

"You wouldn't let me go?"

"I won't forbid it, but I'll encourage you not to date yet. I'm kind of torn on the subject. I want you to move on from your old friends and childhood sweetheart—they're part of a difficult past you want to bury. But you have to be really careful."

"What do you mean?"

Dory took two glasses from the cupboard, filled them with water, and gave one to Mary before she sat down at the end of the table. "After you had your miscarriage, I told you of mine. I've not told anyone else about my little Violet."

Mary said, "Yes, you told me that before. But why did you place the gravestones where we see them every day? Seeing them causes me pain and guilt."

"For me too, dear. But you and I are all they have. Our duty is to remember them. The pain and guilt will be with us anyway. We can't run from them. The stones just remind us of the humans connected to our pain. They deserve that much."

Mary looked down. "I think your memory of your baby is more positive than mine. I hated my baby's father."

"I know. I loved my baby's father, but he broke my heart, which is a story for another time. I have some fond memories, though, so I like to think about them. Maybe for you it's better to forget the past. Try to start all over again up here. You have new friends and a new family."

"So, what are you saying? What should I do?"

"Well, Jerry is a fine man and a single man. Follow your heart, Mary, and you will be okay. Even if your heart ends up broken, it's better than denying it what it needs."

"You can say that even after a guy broke your heart?"

"Just go slow and be careful. And ask yourself if you are ready for dating."

Tears pooled in Mary's eyes, but they did not escape to her cheeks. "I like him. I don't want to turn him away, but I don't know if I can . . ."—Mary searched for the right phrase—"be social with a man." Briefly, her mind flashed to moment Jimmy had touched her hand in the pickup and the horrible images that had flooded her mind. *If I couldn't be close to Jimmy, who I've known for years, how can I ever be close to anyone?* Mary wiped her tears with her handkerchief and then clasped it in her folded hands.

"You'll have time to decide before he gets leave again. And the letters will help. You can learn a lot about people through their letters. One good thing is that after today, you won't have to hide from the neighbors, though I still will not take you to town with me. The other limitations still exist." She continued, "I know it's early and neither one of us is very hungry, but I'll make us a light supper, okay? And now that our neighbors know about you, we can eat together in the kitchen."

After supper, she and Dory played cards until Mary retreated to her bedroom and then to her rooftop perch to enjoy the quiet of the evening. Noting that the barn swallows' nest was empty, she murmured, "I wonder if the fledglings will come back or if they leave for good. It's too late for the momma to start another batch."

Thinking on today's events, she wondered aloud, "Can I have a normal kind of life? Will *I* ever be ready to fly one day?"

With that thought, she climbed back through the attic window and changed into her pajamas. Tired, but not sleepy, she reached for the journal and pen on her dresser. Sitting cross-legged on her bed, she began writing.

About 8 o'clock, Saturday evening

September 8, 1956

Today I met Jerry Weber. He surprised me in the garden as I was picking a watermelon. Then Dory came and we went over to Webers' for dinner. Now they know about me. They don't know everything, but I am worried a little that my whereabouts might be discovered by the wrong people.

But I am glad I met Jerry. He makes me feel good all over. Kinda like Jimmy used to. I still think of Jimmy sometimes, but I know we will never be together, and for the first time I think I can really accept that fact. I swear I felt electricity when Jerry's eyes met mine.

I think Dory mentioned her own heartbreak so that I learn about consequences of love. It's all deep and scary to me. Jimmy and I were just kids, but Jerry is an adult. I don't know how I'll handle it or if I can date at all. Well, he hasn't asked me yet for sure, but if all goes well, I might be writing a lot of letters!

CHAPTER 31

FAMILY TIME

Sunday, September 9, 1956

"Just this once," Maggie said, pleading with her parents in the kitchen. "We'd only have to start milking an hour early to finish in time to watch the *Ed Sullivan Show*. Please."

Mom countered, "You don't need to help with evening milking, Maggie. You can watch the program."

"I know. I know, but Jimmy wants to watch it too, and I think you and Dad would like it. I want you to see him sing his songs."

"Do you want to watch the program, Jimmy?" Mom asked.

"Very much," Jimmy said firmly. "That he's on television is a big deal."

Dad looked up from working on his cash-flow budget. "We can't rearrange our farm schedule to fit television shows every time there's something you want to watch. The television does not pay the bills. Milking at the same time every day is important."

Maggie saw the muscles in her brother's jaw strain. *He's probably grinding his teeth to keep from mentioning the times we milked late because the folks stayed in town too long. Bringing up our folks' exceptions to their own rules will get us nowhere.* But she had an idea.

"Sometimes we milk early so we have more time after milking to work in the fields when it's cooler, and the cows don't suffer then."

"Maybe not," Mom said as she brushed glaze on top of the buns she had just removed from the oven. "But we're not going to argue about it."

Maybe an honest compliment might help. "The buns smell great, Mom. They're so good with butter when they're warm. Can I eat one now?"

"Don't think I don't know what you're doing. Sure, you can have one, but wait till they cool a little."

Maggie glanced at Jimmy and nodded until he asked, "Can I have one too?"

"Of course."

"But I imagine you'll be starting supper soon," Maggie said. *If we can get Mom to start supper early, early milking will follow.* She waited just a moment before she added, "Maybe I should wait for supper."

"Oh, aren't you a clever girl. 'Starting supper soon,' you say. If I start supper now, we'll be done eating by five and done milking by the time your show begins."

"Gee," Maggie said feigning surprise as she left for the living room, "I never thought of that."

"Me either," Jimmy said with a grin. "But I'm sure you'd enjoy the show."

The rich baritone voice of Elvis Presley singing "Blue Moon" wafted into the kitchen from the living room, where Maggie had dropped the phonograph needle onto Mom's favorite Elvis song.

Maggie strutted into the kitchen to remark casually, "He might sing this song tonight, Mom. Along with many others. The show starts at seven. We've been playing his records ever since we got them as gifts at our birthday party. You and Dad have heard them too. Of course, I get to watch the show anyway because I'm not milking cows, but I know it would mean a lot to Jimmy if he could see Elvis on television."

Mom quit working for a moment. "I'm not sure I like it when you two gang up on me, but it's not often I hear my daughter so sympathetic to the wants of her brother, especially lately. And that, I kind of like. Okay, Dad, what do you think?"

Maggie and Jimmy braced for the answer as Dad looked up from his papers. Finally, he smiled and said, "It's up to you, Mary."

"Thanks, Dad," Jimmy said. "I promise I won't make a habit of it." He turned to smile at Maggie as he whispered, "Good work, Mags."

"I'll help you start supper," Maggie said to Mom.

After chores were done, Maggie helped Mom rush to make popcorn and chocolate milk before the family sat down to watch the *Ed Sullivan Show*. When Sullivan introduced his famous guest, Elvis Presley, screams from the audience nearly drowned out his words.

Maggie watched the faces of her folks and her siblings as he performed. Jimmy was an Elvis fan, of course, and Joey seemed to like his music too, now that he'd softened his attitude about not liking songs about love.

Maggie laughed as Dad commented, "He's like your uncle Roman—he sings and jigs at the same time."

"That's why the camera only shows him from the waist up," Maggie explained. "Some of the network people thought there would be a fuss if they showed how he wiggles."

"You can tell he's moving around a lot just by watching him from the waist up," Jimmy said. "I don't see what could be so bad about showing his whole body."

"Just as long as he has pants on," Dad joked. "Heck, your uncle Roman moves more than that when he plays his button accordion."

"But this man is younger and better looking," Mom said. "Some of his music would take some getting used to, all right, but he sure can sing. We've heard some of these songs on your records, Maggie."

At that moment Elvis introduced his song "Love Me Tender" and explained that he would be in a movie with the same name.

"We have to see that movie, Jimmy!" Maggie exclaimed.

As Elvis began singing, Mom remarked, "Now that is nice."

"Good voice," Dad agreed.

After his appearance, the entire family listened with some reverence as Ed Sullivan praised Elvis's performances and his character.

"Not heard him say that about anyone before," Dad said.

Pleased, Maggie explained, "And now we have a local station that plays his music. A year ago, we couldn't find it on any radio stations in Minnesota."

"Things change, that's for sure," Dad said.

"What did they call the music?" Mom asked.

"Rock 'n' roll," Jimmy answered. "But all rock 'n' roll doesn't sound the same, either. Just like all country music doesn't. Depends on the singer."

"I prefer Johnny Cash," Dad said.

"I like them both," Jimmy said.

"And they even know each other," Maggie added, "because they perform at the same shows sometimes."

After the program, Jimmy headed upstairs, saying, "I got a little school-work to finish up."

Joey followed him to the room they shared, and Maggie decided to work on some geometry problems in her own room. After she had finished a couple more problems than the assignment required, her thoughts took her elsewhere. *Why did Robert have to move? I liked him. Not true love or anything, but a nice fellow who was fun. We were comfortable just being ourselves. Perfect kind of boyfriend for high school.*

Then she thought about the Weber family and Dory and the dancing girls and the mean boys in the blue pickup. *We did all that in one day last summer. Search day. Then I go back to school and they treat us all like kids and are suspicious of everything we do.*

She changed into her pajamas, pulled the chain on the lightbulb, and crawled into bed. *I like school, but Jimmy was right when he complained about the stupid rules. Jimmy gets his hair pulled and Jane Swanson gets ridiculed for wearing tight sweaters. She has big boobs. Of course her sweaters are going to look tight. Jeez, if she got a sweater that fit her boobs, it would be too big for the rest of her. This is a problem I should have!* Maggie giggled and sat up in bed. Bored with her own thoughts, she decided to see if her brothers were still up.

Joey was reclining on his bed, reading a book, and Jimmy was on the floor with pages of his old journal notes scattered in order around him.

"What you got there, Bandit?" Maggie teased.

"Someone's been thinking of Robert."

"I have been. So what?"

"Nothing. I've been thinking of him too. I miss him. Haven't made a new friend yet, unless you count Donald and Lewis Gustafsson."

"I'm pretty sure you'll be their hero for life. Maybe their older sisters' hero too."

"Hadn't thought of that," Jimmy said, grinning at his sister.

"Yeah, I'll bet."

"But now I could have five Murphy brothers on my butt. Add that to the Jack Drude threat, and what boy in his right mind would want to befriend a marked man like me?"

"Your smart-ass skepticism hasn't exactly attracted anyone yet, huh?"

"I'm patient. There are some kids I could like. I like my teachers. Some more than others. Glad I don't have phy ed."

"Have you talked to Anne Busch at all?"

"No, but you know I talk to Peggy Ryan and Ann Shaurel on the bus. The bus is kind of a neutral place. I'm not hanging around with girls in the hall at school, though. You know I'm not dating while in high school."

"Just talk to them. You don't have to date them."

"That's usually not how it goes. If I talk to a girl more than a couple times, the words *homecoming dance* or *sock hop* are bound to come up. First thing you know, I'll be taking off my shoes to dance on the gym floor."

"Would that be so bad?"

"I like to keep my shoes on when I dance."

"You know that's not what I meant. I mean, would it be so bad to go to a school dance?"

"It would. So rinky-dink."

"Go to a movie, then."

"Might just do that. Might try to be more social."

"Robert told me he thought you should go out for track."

"I've thought about it."

"Really?"

"Yes. I've got Mr. Shaebler for English this year. I like him and he's the track coach. He hasn't made any stupid comments about my hair yet, and if that lasts till spring, I may cut it all off and go out for track. I can train all year by myself to increase my stamina, and I won't have to cut my hair till spring."

"Would it be so bad to cut your hair before that?"

"No, not really. I'd cut my hair sooner, but I kind of enjoy how some teachers get their shorts all knotted up about it, even though the principal doesn't seem to mind."

Maggie turned to Joey. "I'm glad you're not as ornery as your big brother." Joey did not look up from his book, so Maggie asked, "What are you reading?"

"*The Call of the Wild.* One thing I like about being bused to the big school is the library. So many books! And the encyclopedia has all these great colored pictures of birds. I could spend the whole day there."

"That's one thing we have in common, little buddy," Jimmy said. "I always loved the library. How about phy ed? How's that going?"

"Oh, it's okay. We never get to play softball, though. I like it when we play soccer because we all get to play all the time. Football is so much standing around, and just the town kids call the plays. The rest of us don't know what to do. One day it rained and we played soccer in the gym. That was even more fun than playing soccer outside. Then one of the kids got hit in the face with the ball and we had to quit. I think he was okay, though."

"Yeah, I always liked playing soccer too. Probably because we could do a lot of running. There were other things I liked about high school when I first started at Rock River in the ninth grade—the different teachers, the challenging subjects, and as I said before, the big library. Now, though, they've added some stupid rules that are supposed to prevent bad behavior before it happens, I guess."

"Like what?" Maggie asked.

"We can't wear jeans. Somehow, wearing dress slacks is supposed to make us behave better. I didn't see that happening with Joe Murphy on the bus when he was teasing Lewis."

"Or with the jackasses in Sunday school," Maggie added. "Seems the better-dressed kids behaved the worst!"

"Yeah," Jimmy agreed. "Like their nice clothes gives them some kind of license to be cruel. We need to wear dress shoes and shirts with a collar, and we can't carry a pocketknife. I admit that I have no use for a pocketknife in school, but I've carried one all my life and feel a little lost without it. Also, keeping myself in dress pants will cost more money. A lot more money than just buying new jeans. And when the jeans got worn, I could use them for everyday. Dress pants aren't worth a darn for everyday wearing, and it's hard to find them with a watch pocket. I'm starting to understand Huck Finn's resistance to becoming civilized."

"I can't feel too sorry for the guys," Maggie said. "Girls have been stuck with restrictions forever."

"Yeah, but the way to make it better would be to free it up for the girls, not to make it worse for the guys."

No one spoke for a whole minute, as if the critique of school was over. Jimmy rearranged his papers on the floor, and Mags shifted to a more comfortable position. Joey went back to reading.

"This is strange," Maggie commented. "Our folks aren't even in bed yet. We don't have to whisper. If this were last year, we'd be looking out the window to watch for the White Dancer."

"Not for a couple hours yet, and you thought it was a ghost, remember, Mags?"

"Don't gloat," Maggie scolded lightly. "For months, none of us knew what it was. I'm just glad Jack Drude is still locked up. I don't think I could handle the idea of him prowling the neighborhood. Scary."

"Scary for me too," Jimmy admitted as he rearranged his papers again. "I hope he stays locked up for a long time. No telling what he'll try to do when he gets out. I'm pretty sure he will try for some kind of revenge."

Maggie eyed her brother closely before she carefully asked, "Are you scared? I mean, it's okay to be scared. I'm scared of him."

Jimmy shrugged his shoulders and considered his papers.

Maggie sat down next to him and asked, "What are you doing with those old lists of events?"

"Don't know, really. I was going to toss them out, but I started reading and remembering things. Things I kind of forgot about. And then I got into reading about Mary and . . ." He gave her a weak smile.

"All the things that happened to her made her life one tragedy after another," Maggie filled in.

Jimmy's smile faded. He turned to face her, pointed to his papers, and asked, "What's a guy supposed to do with his past? Does he just throw it away?"

Stunned by the depth of the question and the honesty with which he had asked, Maggie thought, *Vulnerable. That's the word. I've never seen my big brother so vulnerable. Is this the same guy who ripped off his shirt to challenge three boys to fight?*

Finally, she mustered up an answer. "You can't discard your past. It's part of you whether you like it or not. Before she left, Mary and I talked about this. She wanted to forget her past because it haunted her in dreams and memories. She said she was just going to try to make better memories and take control of her life. She said she wasn't going to let her past control her. I don't know if that will work for everybody. Or even if it will work for her."

"I agree. Forgetting your past is a tough thing to do. I suppose we're part of Mary's past. That's why we need to leave her alone. Maybe she needs to forget her past, but I don't think we can all do that."

"No, I have too many good memories."

Maggie saw Jimmy's face sag as he looked down to avoid her eyes before he said, "I can still see the terror on her face when I tried to hold her hand."

"I'm sure she was just shocked and embarrassed. I'm sure she was glad to see you." *Is giving him hope the right thing to do?*

"I don't think so." Jimmy gave her a shaky smile before he rolled up the papers and put them in a dresser drawer. "I'm not ready to toss them. Many of my memories are good ones. I can't change the past anyway. And I like my present. It's my future I need to work on."

Maggie said, "Now you're sounding like the guidance counselor."

Jimmy smiled and asserted with almost no irony, "That's what I want to be when I grow up. A guidance counselor."

"I suppose you're just kidding."

"Yeah, I'm really tired of guys in suits reading a few of my test scores and thinking they know all about me. That they know what career I fit into."

Joey put his book down. "Hey, you guys, I love this book but I've read the same page over six times because I was listening to your blabbering."

"Not that long ago," Jimmy reminded him, "you wanted to listen and take part. Are you too good for us now that you're so grown up?"

"No," Joey said. "I got something to say about my past. I like most of it. And even the parts I don't like—when the kids called me names or my Valentine's Day experience—I kind of see how that was good too, although I hated it at the time."

"I think you should become the guidance counselor in the family," Jimmy teased.

"Maybe I will, but now, I think I'm going to go to bed."

"I'm going to go to my room and write to Robert," Maggie announced, and she left the room.

"Tell him I say hello and I miss him," Jimmy said. "I think I'm going to write to Annette."

Meanwhile, Mary had waited until Martin went to bed before she sat at the kitchen table to write to Rose. Nearly two months had passed since those angry words had passed between them at Betty and Pastor Mark's home. *Sure, she deserved them, but angry words are almost always better off left unsaid.* She had wanted to write sooner but had trouble getting started. One time she had half a page written but realized everything she'd written was about her own kids. Thinking that raving about her kids was too insensitive a subject for Rose, Mary had torn it up. Tonight, though, she had some ideas.

September 9, 1956

Dear Rose,

I hope you and Betty and Pastor Mark are all doing well. My family is fine, and John seems to be doing okay too. Hiring my brother Roman as a permanent hand on the farm seems to be working out fine.

I apologize for not writing sooner, but the summer was so busy and just flew by like it usually does. The summer has been good to us. Enough rain fell and yet we were able to harvest crops during short dry spells. Our kids are back in school, which changes our routine at home some, and I was wondering if the start of school changes your meetings with students. Are you teaching piano and involved with the choir? Do you tutor students for other subjects? Martin said you were always good at every subject in school.

I have no big news to announce, but I just wanted you to know we're all thinking of you and continue to wish you well. Please write when you have a chance. We would all like to hear from you. Martin and the children all say "Hello."

Your friend,

Mary

Relieved that she had finally accomplished this simple task, she reread the letter several times to ensure she was striking the right tone. *I didn't bring up our discussion at the parsonage. I didn't talk about my kids too much. I didn't explain how well John seems to be getting along without her. I didn't mention Billy, but maybe I should have. I will in the next letter. I didn't admonish her for past deeds, nor did I bring up mine. But I did rave just a little about her talents in a subtle way. Just maybe that will encourage her to write and open up a bit. I didn't mention the settlement with the divorce. And I didn't lie about anything!* She folded the letter neatly, stuffed it into an envelope that she had addressed a month ago, and licked a three-cent stamp to place in the corner.

Exhausted, she went to bed, but her mind wouldn't let her sleep immediately. The story of Rose's and John's separation and divorce continued to bother her. Just as she was about to fall asleep, she recalled the secret she hadn't told Rose. *She has a grandchild due in October, although Anna says it's due in December. They will never know the baby was Billy's. How would they feel if they learned they were grandparents? Will they ever learn the truth? Not from me. Not my secret to tell.*

She wondered, *How did John and Rose grow apart? Could Martin and I grow apart like that too? I almost let it happen! John and Rose were always so different from each other. Martin and I are alike. We're farmers. Opposites may attract, but they usually have some trouble living with each other.* She lifted herself up on one elbow so she could see her husband sleeping. She liked watching him sleep. He looked peaceful and vulnerable. *I love him so much. We have kids, so it's hard to imagine our lives without them, but I'm sure, Martin, I would love you no less.*

She lay back down and adjusted her head on the pillow until she was comfortable. *Three children in high school. Such good kids. We did a good job so far, but there is so far to go for them. So many things can happen. So many choices for them to make—so many dark paths to follow. And so many things out of our control, and out of their control too!*

We've been lucky so far. I have so many blessings. My marriage, my kids, the farm. My life is not easy and we work hard, but I am so lucky. Mary said a silent prayer of thanks, listing blessings she hadn't thought about lately—her family's health, having loving parents, and the privilege of being born poor but able. She asked that her children be guided to choose the right paths in life. *There are so many bad choices to make. So many dark paths to take.*

As she snuggled under the sheet, she put her hand on her belly. *I may just be late. I'll tell Martin when I'm absolutely sure.* And then sleep took her away until morning.

The End

ACKNOWLEDGMENTS

I thank the entire workforce at Beaver's Pond Press, St. Paul, Minnesota, who have supported Nancy and me through the publishing of twenty books. We especially thank my managing editor, Alicia Ester, who kept the process moving along; my editor, Kellie M. Hultgren, who offered many valuable insights to make my novel a better story; my proofreader, Abbie Phelps, who put a final set of sharp eyes on the text; and my designer, Dan Pitts, who gave the book the right look.

I thank my friends who graciously answered questions about the era, especially my two dear sisters, Joyce Tornio and Judy Malz; my aunt, Elaine Moss; and my cousin, Janet Mueller.

I thank my sister Judy for creating the cover artwork for *The Search*. Working with her once again to create the scene brings joy and memories to me.

Beyond all other measures of gratitude, I thank my dear wife, Nancy A. Fredrickson, who tirelessly and enthusiastically read many drafts and revisions and provided me with the kind of loving encouragement each artist needs.

Gordon W. Fredrickson, at age twelve, in 1958, returning to the barn with an empty pail after dumping the milk into the strainer, which rested on a portal of the bulk tank. Family photo collection. The cows were milked in the lower level of the barn, and milk had to be carried up a stairway to the milk house, a separate building that housed the bulk tank. The upper-left corner of photo shows the back part of the milk house. The four-gallon shotgun pail in the photo had straight sides and a cover for the top.

ABOUT THE AUTHOR

Gordon W. Fredrickson was raised on a small dairy farm in Minnesota, served three years in the United States Army after high school, graduated with a teaching degree from the University of Minnesota, taught English to grades nine through twelve, directed high school plays and musicals, and has written nineteen books for adults and children with the aim to enlighten and entertain. His wife, Nancy, contributed to several of the books as photographer and photo editor. For nearly two decades, Gordon performed programs about his books for more than 52,000 children and adults at more than 1,000 elementary schools, middle schools, high schools, historical societies, museums, and banquets of all kinds.

Gordon and Nancy have downsized from their hobby farm and now reside in a townhome less than twenty miles from where they grew up. Visit their website www.GordonFredrickson.com for details and sample pages of their books.

OTHER BOOKS BY GORDON AND NANCY FREDRICKSON

The Search is the twentieth book Gordon and his wife, Nancy, have published with Beaver's Pond Press of St. Paul, Minnesota. Their books include memoir, fiction, nonfiction, children's books, poetry, and fantasy stories. Visit www.GordonFredrickson.com for details and excerpts.

The first three novels of the Discovery series, *Discovery*, *The Dance,* and *The Search*, are available now on Fredricksons' website, on Amazon, and in many bookstores. The fourth novel in the series, *Dark Path to Destiny*, will be available in 2027. Two more novels, tentatively called *Mags* and *Going Forth*, will complete the *Discovery* series, following the lives of the characters from 1955 to the late 1980s.

WANT TO READ MORE ABOUT THE CHARACTERS IN THE SEARCH?

Join them in *Dark Path to Destiny*, which follows the characters through over a decade of conflicts, changes, and challenges. Loyalty, love, and courage are tested, alliances shift dramatically, and choices and fate lead people down paths both dark and bright.

Follow Jimmy as he strives to overcome his skepticism about humanity while being betrayed by friends, doubted by family members, and abandoned by love. After he hits bottom, can he leave the dark paths and claim his destiny?

Like Fredrickson's other novels, *Dark Path to Destiny* links fictional events and characters to historic events that affected farm country and the world in an era of unprecedented change. Visit www.GordonFredrickson.com for the latest book news.

www.ingramcontent.com/pod-product-compliance
Lightning Source LLC
Chambersburg PA
CBHW020607110726
47899CB00002B/410